The Revolving Heart

Chuck Augello

Black Rose Writing | Texas

Second printing

ISBN: 978-1-68433-477-3
PUBLISHED BY BLACK ROSE WRITING
www.blackrosewriting.com

Printed in the United States of America
Suggested Retail Price (SRP) $18.95

The Revolving Heart is printed in Calluna

As a planet-friendly publisher, Black Rose Writing does its best to eliminate unnecessary waste to reduce paper usage and energy costs, while never compromising the reading experience. As a result, the final word count vs. page count may not meet common expectations.

For Sheri: Secret handshake!

The Revolving Heart

Voices from the Town: Mario C., Holman Beach Diner, April 20XX

"What happened to that little girl was a damn shame. I remember her coming into the diner with that Marcino kid and his girlfriend two or three times a week. They always bought her a vanilla sundae with a maraschino cherry on top. Such a cute little kid. You couldn't help but want to tussle that curly blonde hair. Like Shirley Temple ...the good ship lollipop and all that. What were we talking about again? Yeah, Sarah Carpenter ...such a goddamn shame."

-I-

I was still in bed, half-asleep, wrapped in a tangle of blankets and sheets when the ring tone smacked me awake. It was that old Nirvana song "Lithium" with its cool opening bass line and depressed stoner lyrics about finding your friends inside your head. After the first five notes I knew that it was Amy, but I let the song play out anyway, at least the first few lines. Talking with Amy was always easier after a few bars of "Lithium."

I rolled over and grabbed the phone, careful not to wake Kelly.

"Hey, Donatello, it's me," Amy said. "I'm surprised you're awake. Isn't it like three days earlier out there?"

For almost ten years I'd been living in California, a perennial sore point with Amy, who'd never left Holman Beach, the little shore town in New Jersey where we'd both grown up. For some reason she blamed me for this, as if there'd been a single ticket out of town and I'd snatched it from her fingers. Not true. She'd had her chances but hadn't taken them. Our last contact, two months earlier, had ended with an e-mail about some new guy she was seeing titled "Thirty-Seven Reasons Why Mark is Better than You." I disagreed with reasons nine and fourteen, but otherwise her logic was sound.

"What's up, Amy?" I whispered. It was Saturday morning. Kelly had spent the night and was sleeping beside me.

"I was just thinking how great it would be to get away from here," Amy said in her hangover voice, deep and scratchy. "My head is killing me. It's like the Army is testing new explosives in that little space between my eyes."

I peeked over my shoulder to see if Kelly had stirred and realized that she was gone, the sheets pushed down from her side of the bed, her pillow jammed between the mattress and the headboard. For a second I panicked, abandonment being a *thing* with me, but her keys and her phone were still on the nightstand, her dress folded neatly over a chair by the dresser, and I heard the water running in the shower. This was a good thing. I had just assigned her a new ring tone, The Cure's "Just like Heaven," which meant I was hooked and hoping to hang on.

"I'm sorry about your head," I said. "Excedrin and Dr. Pepper; it works every time. Listen, I'll call you later, okay? I'm kind of busy..."

"What's her name?" Amy asked.

"It's not a woman." I ransacked my brain for an excuse. "I'm late for my run. I'm training for a 10K."

There was silence, and then a sigh of immense disappointment, as if I'd been letting her down since birth.

"Please don't lie to your oldest friend. A 5K, maybe, but a 10K? No way. You'd quit somewhere between the seventh and eighth K. Christ, my head is killing me. What's her name?"

"Kelly."

"Blonde or brunette?" she asked.

"Strawberry blonde."

"Great—she's not one of those carbon copies of me. Congratulations: all that therapy must work," Amy said. "I think I approve. I wish you love and happiness and at least six weeks of decent sex. I'll bet she's a wonderful person, isn't she, our little strawberry blonde California Kelly?"

"Yes, she *is*." It needed to be said—for both of us. Amy had a habit of dismissing my relationships as weak substitutes for her, but Kelly was different.

"Kelly, Kelly, Kelly," Amy sang, like Woody on *Cheers*, and I couldn't tell if she was baiting me. I was out of practice in the art of Amy, a genre in which I'd once been the world's foremost expert. It sounded like play, but my instincts sensed trouble.

"That Kelly is *such* a sweetheart," Amy said. "I'm sure she'll understand when you tell her you're flying back home this afternoon. I'll bet she even drives you to the airport. You're a lucky man."

When we were kids, Amy would throw rocks at my bedroom window and expect me to jump out whenever she wanted to play. She'd walk into the pizzeria where I worked and ask for a ride to the mall while my hands were still sticky from kneading dough. Saying "no" was never an option.

"And why exactly am I flying back home? The last time I checked I already *was* home here in San Diego. Go Padres! I've got a lot going on, you know..."

"Yes, I know...California girls are *like* so much fun. *Totally.* But there's been some trouble...I need you, Duck."

And there it was—Duck: a teenage nickname that only Amy and one other person had ever used. A simple word, really, one syllable, a small white bird floating in a pond, but for Amy and me it carried its own definition. Duck—a quick and dirty way to drag me back into the past.

"Let's see," Amy said. "It might have been an accident but...okay, well...I swallowed some pills and some wine and some more pills and...well, they had to pump my stomach last night, which is *really* gross. They're calling it attempted suicide...maybe they're right."

The pipes in the bathroom grew quiet as the shower switched off and Kelly cracked open the door, steam floating out in puffs and dissolving in the cool bedroom air. I squinted toward the television—CNN with the sound muted. Kelly must have turned it on before jumping in the shower. On the screen three guys in hazmat suits loitered outside a Wal-Mart parking lot.

"Where are you?" I asked.

"In the hospital—the psych ward, the cuckoo's nest. They take your shoelaces, but you can keep your cell phone at the front desk and borrow it three times a day. They haven't shaved my head yet or scheduled the lobotomy, but I have no idea when I'm going home."

"What happened?"

"I had a bad day," she said. "I'm always on edge. With the world we live in, how could I *not* be?"

I read the crawl across the bottom of the TV, something about a virus in Texas and reports of an earthquake in Chile. Everything was falling apart.

"Twenty years; it's hard to believe, isn't it, Duck?" Amy said. "Don't tell me you haven't thought about it."

It: that most promiscuous of pronouns, willing to replace everything from a spoon to a Lamborghini. But I knew what she meant.

"I still keep our promise," Amy said. "*You* haven't been around for years, but I still do it: I walk down to the beach with a vanilla ice cream cone with rainbow sprinkles and a maraschino cherry—every fucking year."

"You have a good heart."

I couldn't remember a time when Amy hadn't been part of my life. I hoped she was exaggerating, that by psych ward she meant the pharmacy counter at CVS, by suicide she meant reading Sylvia Plath in the bathtub and writing gloomy free verse in her journal.

"You weren't *really* trying to kill yourself, were you?"

"I don't know. I kept the gun in the drawer, so there's that..."

"You still have that goddamn gun?"

"Hey, it's my Second Amendment right!"

"My shoulder disagrees."

Once, when she and I briefly shared an apartment, I came home late one night and Amy, assuming I was an intruder, shot me in the left shoulder. The bullet had only grazed me, but it was hard to forget.

"Isn't there a statute of limitations on your bringing that up?"

"It still hurts whenever it rains."

"I thought it never rains in San Diego," she said. "And for the six hundred and forty-seventh time, I'm sorry. When you get here tonight, I'll kiss it and make it feel better, okay?"

"I'm three thousand miles away, Amy. I can't be there tonight."

"Look, I need you. I'm alone here."

"What about that guy who's thirty-seven times better than me?"

"Mark isn't around anymore. We broke up last month."

"Which shoulder did you shoot?" Immediately I felt like an asshole. "I'm sorry. I didn't mean that."

"Yes, you did, but so what?" She took a breath. "Look, I didn't want to say anything because I know you won't believe me, but ...I think he's back. It's a big reason I've been so shaky."

I kicked off the blankets and swung my legs over the side of the bed, checking the bathroom door to make sure Kelly couldn't hear me.

"Amy, please...not again."

"I'm serious, Duck. Someone's been following me, creeping around the backyard, staring up at the window."

"Amy..."

"Don't '*Amy*' me—I know what I saw. It was him."

"It's been twenty years. How would you even know what he looks like anymore?"

"I'd know," she said, in her best shut-up-and-listen tone. "Just a few days, Duck, until Sarah's birthday. Until I know for sure that it's not *him*."

After twenty years, it still came back to the two of them, him and her, Mr. Ronan and Sarah Carpenter.

"Things have been falling apart for a while, Duck," Amy said. "I know I shouldn't drink but...I've been freaking out about Ronan. Maybe I'm imagining it, but what if I'm not? And Sarah's birthday ...she would have been twenty-four. *Twenty-four*, Duck!" Her voice skipped, as if holding back tears. "It's just...everything is shit. I didn't want to face the beach alone this year, so I drank a bottle of wine, swallowed some Skittles and however the fuck many Ambien were left in the bottle, and crawled into bed. There was some vodka left so I drank that, too. When Jill came home, I was passed out, so she called the First Aid Squad."

Jill was Amy's sixteen-year-old daughter from her first marriage.

"The next thing I know I'm in an ambulance with a tube down my throat. So here I am...Room Number Nine on the loony bin floor." She did that weird voice from The Beatles' *White Album*. "Number nine, number nine..."

On CNN the weather map had storm clouds and lightning strikes all across the heartland, an angry red 110° hovering over Phoenix. There were floods in Kansas City and in Tulsa, Oklahoma. Back home in New Jersey— my *old* home—it was sunny and 75°, perfect weather.

"You don't have to *stay*," Amy said. "Come out for a few days until I'm discharged. Be here for Sarah. That's all I'm asking."

The bathroom door swung open and Kelly padded into the room wrapped in a plush green towel, beads of water dotting her legs and shoulders as she drew a comb through her long blonde hair. "Hey, you're awake!" she said, and then saw me on the phone. "Oh—sorry!"

"No, it's okay," I told her. How could it not be when the towel clung so perfectly to her hips? On her left shoulder was a tattoo of a double clef note, its tip touching the folded rim of the towel as if coaxing me to throw the phone out the window, slowly unwrap that soft green fabric, and spend the rest of the morning worshipping that double clef.

I covered the phone, whispering "just a minute," Kelly slipping back into the bathroom as if following stage directions to exit the scene. Years back I'd been a playwright, and sometimes I still thought that way.

"Look, I'll even reimburse you for the ticket ...I've got sixty-two bucks worth of pennies in a shoebox in the closet," Amy said. "Come on, you haven't been home in years. Your uncle would love to see you. Just for a few days ...you promised, remember? You said..."

"...if you ever need me, I'll be there—always," I said, repeating the promise as if I were still seventeen, still radio pop-song in love with her, expecting our lives to be some long-playing lesson to all those timid hearts who knew nothing about the purity and passion of Amy and Duck. "That was centuries ago. We were kids."

"When do promises come with an expiration date?"

There was nothing I could say because she was right. Twenty years earlier something terrible had happened and I'd promised to always be there for her. My life hadn't turned out exactly as I'd hoped, but on this I'd never slipped: whenever Amy had needed me, I'd been there for her. I had kept my promise.

Suddenly I started yawning.

"Before I, you know, did what I did, I thought about calling you. I already checked the airlines," Amy said. "There's a Southwest flight out of Newark..."

I tried to listen, but I yawned again, and felt my body slipping away, my eyelids growing heavy as my head began to pound. *Here we go again*, I thought. It rarely happened in the morning, but sometimes, when my nerves were rattled, my condition struck hard and quick. The tips of my fingers began to tingle, as if my nails had turned into bees, and I knew what was coming, the warning signs reliable town criers. My legs became bags of wet sand; I fell back into the bed, my arms merging with the mattress.

I was falling asleep—but still had a few seconds left to fight it. *Get out of bed and do some jumping jacks*, I thought, which often bought some time before I shut down, but my body was a marionette without strings, a crumble of muscle and flesh.

"...if you catch the two o'clock, you can be here by sundown."

The urge to sleep grew overwhelming, my blurred eyes catching glimpses on CNN of uniformed cops whacking protesters with heavy sticks, the protesters collapsing to the pavement.

I heard Amy's voice through the phone, her frustration palpable and historic.

"Are you still there? Come on, Donatello, not *now*..."

The light drained from the room, and I must have dropped the phone because Amy's voice drifted away, and the last thing I heard before everything disappeared was her voice, tiny and frightened.

"...goddamn it, not again, not *now*, Duck, I need you..."

And then the world, like a movie, faded to black.

.　　.　　.　　.　　.

Imaginary Interview: NPR Morning Edition (Sometime in September, 20XX)

Q: How old were you when you were first diagnosed?

A: Fifteen. I kept falling asleep at the strangest times. Most people thought I was drunk or a stoner but I was pretty straight edge, even back then. Finally, Uncle Dan brought me to the hospital for some tests. Narcolepsy—I had never even heard of the word before I found out that I had it.

Q: How did the narcolepsy influence your experience as a playwright?

A: Opening night we got a standing ovation, but I slept through it. Story of my life. Whenever anything *big* happens, I'm fast asleep.

.　　.　　.　　.　　.

"Welcome back," Kelly said.

I'd wound up on the floor, face down, my lower legs under the bed, my head resting on an old slipper. This often happened after one of my narcoleptic funks. I'd wake up in weird positions, as if while sleeping God had rearranged my body as a practical joke.

I blinked against the light as my eyes focused on the television, still on CNN, where a freeze-dried blonde interviewed a fat guy in a black suit as commodity prices crawled across the screen like a trail of army ants.

"Hey," I mumbled, the dust falling from my synapses.

Kelly sat on the floor beside me stroking my hair, the way a mother might, although this was speculation—I had no recollections of a maternal touch; my mother had skipped out when I was two months old. I flipped over so I could see Kelly's face, which was warm and pretty and organically kind, unlike all those sculpted California faces, those actress-model-anchorwomen types with their perfect, professional looks, undeniably beautiful but a desperate kind of beauty, as if Satan were waiting around the corner with an invoice. But that wasn't Kelly—her face reminded me of a wildflower that had popped up in the garden, more colorful and vibrant than all those designer flowers cross-bred so carefully to please.

"Are you okay?" she asked.

"I'm almost back."

This was true, for part of me at least. I had a major erection, the bulge in my pajamas a frequent occurrence during the post-narcoleptic re-awakening.

"How long was I out?"

"The usual—about twenty minutes. You were on the phone when you fell asleep. I told your friend you would call her back. She seemed worried."

My heart jumped. "You talked to her?"

"Briefly—she sounded nice." Kelly flexed her bare feet, her stubby toes wiggling as her thigh muscles tensed. "Is she a childhood friend?"

Before she could finish, the room seemed to shrink to the approximate size of a thimble, the core rule of my existence in sudden violation—*my history with Amy must always remain secret.* Even my ex-wife Kristen had no clue.

I rolled over and popped to my feet, stumbling toward the door and heading for the kitchen, Kelly following a few strides behind as I crashed against the baker's rack and wobbled toward the sink, the blood rush rabbit-punching between my eyes, my body shaky and dizzy—except for my erection, still on alert.

"Are you okay?" Kelly asked, unnerved but not panicked since after a blackout I did weird crap like this all the time.

I drank cold water straight from the faucet, the heavy stream sluicing my lips.

"It's nothing," I said, pulling away from the sink. "Just, you know...dry mouth from being asleep."

Kelly folded her arms and stood by the stove, watching as I dotted my face with a paper towel. The kitchen was a wreck from last night's meal prep; I'd made stuffed shells with an arugula and gorgonzola salad, her favorite, and we hadn't bothered to clean up before heading to bed. I started filling the dishwasher as Kelly watched, her feet crossed as she tugged the hem of the white T-shirt she wore over yoga pants. I handled each knife and fork as if it were fragile, and if I could have crawled into the dishwasher to escape, I would have gladly surrendered to a wash and rinse, even the heated dry. I had never been unfaithful in any relationship, or perhaps it was the opposite; my long-standing whatever-the-hell-it-was with Amy had made fidelity to any other woman moot, crushed by the weight of my first love and its resilient habit of popping up at the worst of times.

"I'm not having an affair," I said. "She lives in New Jersey."

"Who said anything about an affair? Is she an old girlfriend or something?"

"Something; in high school—sort of. It was nothing."

A lie—it was *everything.*

"She said you were flying out to visit her tonight."

"I haven't decided yet," I said, though part of me was already checking luggage, buckling my seatbelt as the flight attendants stalked the aisles. Amy was my caffeine, my double-shot of espresso with a Red Bull chaser. Whenever I thought of her, everything accelerated.

"Well, of course you'll go," Kelly said. "She needs your help—you *have* to go." She walked over and pecked my lips, side-stepping my wilting erection. "I think it's sweet...you're a good guy, helping out an old friend. It's one of the reasons we love you."

She often said it that way—*we* love you, as if there were a committee involved, perhaps four cats and several dead relatives. Kelly believed in ghosts.

"We love you, too," I said, my "we" restricted to the personal council of me, myself, and I. I felt like a jerk, then reassured myself that it was possible to love Kelly and still love Amy, too; there were different strata of love, Kelly at the surface, bright and in bloom, Amy a more structural love, woven deep into the primordial ooze.

"Hey, maybe I'll come with you," Kelly said, setting the kettle on the front burner as she switched on the stove. "It's not like I'm *doing* anything these days."

Budget cuts had killed her job as a music teacher. She'd been out of work since we'd met, scraping by on unemployment and the few private piano lessons she gave on the side.

"You don't want to..."

"Yes, I do. I'd love a change of scenery. We could go into Manhattan, visit Central Park. I could meet your Uncle Dan. I've got a bazillion miles on my credit card—I'm sure I could get a free flight. Your Uncle...he'd let us stay with him, right?"

"Probably, but...it's a small house...outdated...the carpeting will scare you. Won't it be awkward?"

"Not if we don't want it to be," she said. "This has nothing to do with your visiting an old girlfriend. I'm just coming along to check out New Jersey. You know I love *The Sopranos.*"

She sprinkled some loose tea into the infuser and poured the hot water, the steam rising from the mug in twisted wisps. "You have a past. So what? Who doesn't?"

True, but most pasts didn't include an armed and unstable ex-girlfriend with a nervous trigger finger.

Most pasts didn't include a dead four-year-old girl.

"I'll check with Steffi to make sure she can watch the cats," Kelly said. "It's been such a crappy year—I deserve a trip. Unless you don't want me to come ..."

"Of course I want you with me," I said, surprised by how gut-level true it felt, how much our lives had become intertwined.

"I'm glad." She smiled. "We've got a good feeling about you."

She grabbed her tea and padded off to the bedroom, leaving me flattered but a minor wreck, certain that whatever council of spirits had signed off on her good feelings would turn on me the second she learned the truth—I'd be cast out of our little Garden of Eden, no snake or God required, just the sad ugly facts of what I'd let happen. Avoiding this seemed possible in California, but in Holman Beach three-quarters of the town would see my face and think *dead little girl.*

I bit into an apple and struggled for ideas. Nothing came, except the urgency of a ringing phone; "Lithium" again, as if Amy, in the hospital three thousand miles away, had sensed my feelings for Kelly and was reeling me back home like only Amy could.

There was no hello, no greeting, only Amy's voice, soft and ethereal.

"Do you ever dream about her?" she asked.

There was only one *her.* Sarah Carpenter.

"Sometimes."

"I do—constantly," she said. "A few nights back I dreamt I found her body underneath the boardwalk. She was all bloated, and her skin was grey, like ash. There were all these little bite marks along her legs, and there was a hole in her stomach, like in *Alien*, and this doll's head was peeking out ..."

"Amy, don't do this to yourself ...just stop thinking about it."

"I can't *not* think about it, Duck. All these years—how could they never find her body? Sometimes I think about Sarah more than I think about my own daughter. I *miss* her. I'm a *horrible* person."

"Amy ..."

"Are you a horrible person, too? Are we both horrible? Let's walk into the ocean and drown ourselves. Will you do that with me, Duck?"

"You need to talk to a doctor. You're in the hospital...let them help you."

"Help, shmelp..." she said. "All they care about is the insurance and the co-pay. Yes, Big Nurse, I'll take my pill. That was her name in the book...did you ever read it, Duck? The movie is so much better...*I want to watch the damn World Series!* God, I hate baseball. Mark called me a crazy bitch before he left. I'm not a bitch, am I?"

"You're wonderful," I said—instinctively—and from that moment on, I knew I was going home.

Voices from the Town: Jean K., Holman Beach Mini-Golf, April 20XX

"You know how teenagers always travel in packs? They were never like that. It was just the two of them, like they were some old married couple at age 13. Everyone knew him from the pizzeria and that weird thing he did with falling asleep all the time, and she had this smart mouth on her …but they were good kids, you know? They looked after that Sarah Carpenter like she was their own. I still get choked up thinking about it. No wonder he moved to California. Would you stick around if you were responsible for a little girl's death?"

-2-

"Well, it's complicated," I said. "I'm not sure where to begin. Amy and I have known each other since we were five."

"Was she the first girl you ever kissed?"

"Yes."

"The first boy I ever kissed is in prison now," Kelly said. "Securities fraud. See? You're not the only one with a colorful past."

She smiled, as if her admission had been scandalous, and I wanted to kiss her pretty knuckles and say, *Sweetie, that's not even close.*

We were on a plane, thirty thousand miles off the ground, where only God and radar could see us, as good a place as any for a man to unravel.

"If you're not ready…" Kelly said.

Yes, exactly! I'm not ready! I thought—but I was trying to be better than that. It was time to man up, a phrase I hated, mostly because I rarely did it.

"Amy and I used to babysit for this girl named Sarah Carpenter," I said. "She was four years old, really smart…absolutely adorable. Her mother was a single parent who had some issues. That's a *kind* description: Laura Carpenter was a fuck-up. Not a *bad* fuck-up; just overwhelmed. She was twenty-five, not much older than us really, and had to work three jobs just to make rent. The father, whoever he was, was long gone; it's possible Laura didn't even know who he was—monogamy wasn't her thing. She was supposed to pay Amy three bucks an hour to look after Sarah but most weeks she was too broke to settle up, and after a while Amy watched Sarah for free.

Since Amy and I were always together back then, we became a team. What were we going to do? Leave a four-year-old on her own?"

All true, of course, but not quite true enough. What was missing was the love. Amy and I weren't just "babysitters." In the months before Sarah's disappearance, we were practically raising her, buying her clothes, fixing her dinner, taking her to doctor appointments. I earned decent money working at my Uncle's pizzeria, and whenever Laura fell short, which was nearly every month, I'd make up the difference, whether it was buying groceries, paying the cable bill, or making the co-pay for one of those doctor visits. People wondered if maybe *I* was Sarah's father. Why else would a seventeen-year-old spend his money on a little kid? It might have *seemed* strange, but I was trying to be a good person, and I knew that Sarah's childhood could easily have been my own.

Like Sarah, I had no idea who my birth father was.

· · · · ·

All I knew was that my mother had dropped out of high school her senior year and moved to New York to become famous. According to Uncle Dan, letters home would arrive sporadically with brief, sometimes cryptic notes about her life. One such letter included a clipping from the Sunday circular for Sears, my seventeen-year-old mother posed in her underwear along with three other girls in a half-page spread, the other half featuring blow-out deals on lawn mowers and barbecue grills.

Eventually the letters stopped coming, her final one nothing but the hand-written lyrics to Elton John's "Goodbye Yellow Brick Road" scrawled on the back on a strip club napkin. The most Uncle Dan ever told me about her childhood—*his* childhood, too—was that they'd grown up in an "unhappy" home. My grandparents died when I was three and I had no recollection of them, only a single photograph of the three of us taken beside an artificial Christmas tree, the string of lights dim, a star perched crookedly on the top branch. In the photo, I'm lodged in my grandfather's hairy arms, my grandmother looking away from the camera, a bulky black pocketbook resting on her lap, her arms folded as if she were waiting for a bus. Everyone appears pissed, even me, my clenched baby-face fighting back tears.

Maybe Mom had a good reason for running away.

Eventually she wound up in the punk world in New York City when the scene was at its peak. My birth father could have been any number of punks or speed freaks who had hung out at CBGB or Max's Kansas City. Lucky for me my mother was clean when she got knocked up and managed to stay that way until I was born. For two months, she tried to raise me in a squatter's loft deep in the Bowery, but when some drummer invited her to join him on his band's Midwest tour, my mother packed whatever things she had for me and hitched a ride to her older brother's place in New Jersey. Uncle Dan wasn't home, so Mom, anxious to get back to her drummer, left me on the front stoop. Before taking off she grabbed a pizza box from the trash can next door and placed me on top of it, the cardboard, I suppose, meant to shield me from the damp cement. This was the apex of her maternal instinct.

When Uncle Dan came home, he found me crying atop a crushed pizza box from Donatello's Pasta and Pie. That was how I got my name. My birth name, until Uncle Dan had it legally changed two months before I started kindergarten, was Razor Trip.

I've seen the birth certificate. Razor Trip Marcino. Father unknown. That was me.

What did a single man, a Vietnam vet trying to escape his demons by opening a pizza joint in a fading town on the Jersey Shore, need with a two-month-old colicky baby boy? Not a damn thing. All these years later it was still hard to believe my uncle hadn't shipped me off to Social Services with a *Free to a Good Home* sign pinned to my blanket. But he didn't. I was lucky, and I wanted to make sure that Sarah Carpenter was lucky, too.

. . . . .

The flight attendant squeezed down the aisle, handing out peanuts and little plastic cups of water or ginger ale, the cart bumping against my shoulder as it stopped at our row, the bearded guy across the aisle waving his credit card and ordering a Bloody Mary as I snatched our peanuts and handed Kelly her warm ginger ale.

The plane hit some turbulence, and we leaned back in our seats.

"I never realized you like children," Kelly said. "Was Sarah's mother, Laura...was she at least appreciative?"

"Sometimes, but she took us for granted. Who knows? If we were five years older, she might have given us custody. But she wasn't a *bad* mother. She loved Sarah, too. If I'm giving the opposite impression, that's wrong. She loved her. We all did. It was impossible *not* to love Sarah."

I drank my water and shared some "cute Sarah" stories, how she had called me Duck and liked to decorate my face with the sprinkles from her ice cream cone, how she loved the merry-go-round but would only go on it if I rode with her, the two of us straddling a painted pony spinning up and down, Sarah raising her arms and screaming with each revolution, my hands wrapped around her belly so she wouldn't slip. These were good memories, the best ones that I had, provided the memory remained in a two-shot of Sarah and me and excluded Amy, who was sometimes drunk or stoned out of her mind, sprawled out on the floor while I put on puppet shows, Sarah giggling her way toward sleep while Amy stared at the ceiling, humming Tori Amos songs and waiting for the room to stop spinning.

When I told Kelly that Amy and I were Sarah's babysitters it wasn't a lie, but it hid the reason *why* I'd become so involved. Between her junior and senior years Amy had become unreliable, and I didn't trust her to watch Sarah by herself. I never used words like alcoholic or addict, but back then Amy started her mornings with Cheerios and a joint, and she was never without her silver flask, a hand-me-down from her grandfather, a classic out-of-the-closet drunk who died from a broken liver when Amy was thirteen. The flask, usually filled with her favorites, Peach Schnapps, lived in her backpack, stashed behind an old sweater and the sketch pad she carried around to capture her bursts of artistic inspiration, Amy a master at sneaking sips, able to empty half the flask without my noticing, except when we kissed, her lips creamy-sweet, her breath warm and boozy.

During sophomore year, she was suspended for a week when three joints were found in her locker, and though she promised she'd never mess up like that again—fortunately the principal hadn't called the police—I knew her promises were shaky, reinforcing my suspicions that I needed to be around to keep them both safe.

· · · · ·

From my tenth birthday until I left for college, I worked nights at Jaybird Pizza, my Uncle Dan's pizzeria a block from the ocean. In the off-season, it was just me, Uncle Dan, and a woman named Bonnie, who sometimes showed up with a black eye until Uncle Dan visited her boyfriend one night, letting him know that he had killed seventeen men in 'Nam and one more wouldn't mean a damn thing to his wretched soul. I suspected the body count was an exaggeration, but Uncle Dan didn't talk much about his Army days other than to say that if the draft ever came back, he was shipping me to Canada, no questions asked.

For the summer rush Uncle Dan always hired extra help, but for most of the year it was just the three of us, two of us, really; the minute her shift ended, Bonnie disappeared. At the Jaybird, there were two small cots in the back room where we stored the extra flour and cans of tomatoes, and some nights, when I was still too young to look after myself, we'd sleep in the pizzeria, Uncle Dan preferring it to our small ranch house three blocks away. In the morning, we'd hustle home for a shower and a change of clothes, and then it was back to The Jaybird for another session of garlic knots, calzones, and large cheese pizzas, usually half pepperoni.

"When you find a good foxhole, don't leave it," Uncle Dan said, explaining why he never closed, why he never took a vacation even though he had enough savings to shut down for a week and get the hell out of Holman Beach, to relax and see the world.

During the off-season, whenever it was slow, Uncle Dan would send me home early, and I'd meet up with Amy, who was usually with Sarah at Laura's house watching videos or playing *Candyland* on the living room floor. One time I came over around 9:00 PM on a Thursday night, figuring Sarah would be asleep and Amy curled on the couch watching *Seinfeld*. Instead, when I pulled my bike into the driveway, I saw a spiral of black smoke billowing from the kitchen window.

I banged on the side door, then banged on the front, calling Amy's name, but there was no answer. The heavy smoke should have triggered the detectors, but I didn't hear them, Laura, no doubt, having forgotten to change the batteries—if she'd ever bothered to install them at all. Through the front window, I saw the glow of the television, clouded and hazy. I should have run to the neighbor's house and called the fire department— this was before cell phones, or at least before *everyone* had one—but all I could think was that I needed to get inside the house.

I ran to the side, grabbed a metal garbage can, and smashed it against the front picture window, the glass shattering, and I pulled myself through the opening, my palms bloody and nicked, shards of glass in my hair as I hoisted my legs through the window and dropped to the living room floor.

Passed out on the couch, Amy snored roughly but didn't stir, her head propped up by a giant throw pillow, her glasses pushed down around her nose, the silver flask wedged between her legs. I shouted her name, but she only kept snoring, her glasses fogged from the smoke. (Only later would I learn that Amy, expecting my arrival, had left the front door unlocked. Too busy knocking and banging, I'd never tried the knob.) When I ran into the kitchen, I found a frying pan on the stove, a blackened hamburger patty doing its best firewood impression, the flames having jumped from the pan to a dishtowel to the curtains above the sink in a jagged dance and crackle, the orange tendrils snaking toward the ceiling as I grabbed the fire extinguisher—Laura actually had one!—and shot a fat blast of thick white foam straight at the blaze, my hands shaking as I pointed the nozzle every damn place I could see, the fire quickly yielding to the chemical spray, the smoke turning dense and putrid as it smoldered under the foam.

I held my breath until the extinguisher hit empty and the fire finally ceased, then opened the windows and ran to Sarah's bedroom. Snuggled under her Snoopy sheets, Sarah slept peacefully, her face undisturbed.

Amy was sleeping, too. I shook her awake, her eyes finally opening as she looked at me and smiled. "Oh hey, you're here," she said, glancing at the television. "Great! *Friends* is on!"

I pulled her to her feet, but she was too smashed to stand. She flopped back on the couch and adjusted her glasses. "Shit! What happened to the window?"

"You almost burned the house down."

"No. I was making a hamburger..." Her voice trailed off as her mind cleared, her eyes tearing from the smoke. "Oh, shit."

"You could have killed yourself. And Sarah!"

"No, I don't think so," she said. "I was making a hamburger .... damn it, meat is murder...we should be vegetarians, Duck."

She reached for the flask and brought it to her lips, the last few drops of Schnapps dripping onto her tongue.

"Is Sarah okay?"

"I checked. She's still sleeping."

"Good," she said. "Hey, you're bleeding."

In the frenzy of the moment I hadn't realized it. I ran my hand over my cheek, fresh blood smearing my fingertips.

"I'll kiss it and make it better," Amy said, rising from the couch, but her knees buckled, and she lurched forward, grabbing her stomach and moaning before she threw up all over my shoes.

A minute later Laura Carpenter walked through the front door with some guy she'd picked up at a bar that night, a tall dude with a mustache and a tattoo of a cobra coiled around his bicep. Laura was heavily inked, the creepiest one being the black crow with an arrow through its heart drawn on the back of her neck.

She surveyed the damage and lit up a cigarette, looking straight at me.

"You're paying to fix this, right?" she said.

.   .   .   .   .

Kelly sipped her ginger ale and looked out the window, the broad squares of the Midwest landscape visible through the glare like a checkerboard no one ever bothered to play.

"This story doesn't end well, does it?" Kelly said. "If something happens to the little girl...to Sarah...I don't want to hear it."

"Okay."

I picked up a magazine and started reading. Maybe five seconds passed before she grabbed my arm.

"What happened?"

All those years back, when the police had asked the same question, I had answered simply, "I don't know." This was after Amy had talked, after she made her accusations and turned our lives bat-shit crazy. The cops, of course, were skeptical of my ignorance. I was there at the beach, only a few yards away.

How could I possibly *not* know what had happened?

.   .   .   .   .

From *The Pizza Elegies*, Draft seven, an unproduced screenplay by Donatello Marcino:

EXT.A NEW JERSEY BEACH – MORNING
FADE IN from DONNIE'S POV: eyes squinting against the sun as he slowly awakens. We see the waves crashing against the shore, stronger now.

DONNIE sits up, shakes his head, and grabs a bottle of water and drinks. He sees AMY standing at the shore, staring toward the ocean. SARAH is not there.

He rises slowly, still sleepy, and walks toward AMY. He joins her by the water.

DONNIE
I hate sleeping on the beach. You should have woken me.

AMY
(a lethargic whisper)
I tried. You were out. You should take those pills.

DONNIE
I do, sometimes.

He looks around for SARAH.

DONNIE
Where's Sarah?

AMY doesn't respond. DONNIE sees a single child's flip-flop bobbing in the water twenty feet from the shore.

DONNIE
(concerned)
Where's Sarah?

AMY cries, hugging herself as she sobs.

AMY
She's gone. It took her away. She's gone....

DONNIE runs along the shoreline shouting SARAH's name as AMY drops to the sand, curling into a fetal position, shaking, sobbing as the tide crashes against her body.

In the ocean, the single flip-flop floats back and forth on the waves.

FADE OUT

•   •   •   •   •

Voices from the Town: Kathleen R., Davenport Street, April 20XX
"The whole thing seems sketchy to me. A four-year-old drowns and they never find the body? Don't tell me it wouldn't have washed up on the shore somewhere! That Sarah was a little sweetheart, but her mother was a real slut—sorry, I know we're not supposed to judge people anymore—but that's

what she was. And that Marcino kid was always falling asleep, and that Amy was a drunk. Who knows what really happened to that poor little girl?"

．　　．　　．　　．　　．

The selectivity of what I'd shared with Kelly dampened any potential relief, the truth chopped up into bite-sized portions, easily swallowed. Yes, I'd fallen asleep, and when I woke up Sarah was gone. Every rational path concluded that she'd drowned. Amy hadn't been watching, and Sarah had waded into the water just a little deeper than she should have. A wave knocked her down, or maybe she stepped on a jellyfish and slipped; *something* had happened, and the ocean had carried her away. It made perfect, tragic sense, but Amy, the only eyewitness, told a different story.

All these years later, I remembered her exact words: *it took her away.* I'd thought she meant the ocean, the waves, even a shark, but when she repeated it a few seconds later, her words garbled with sobs, I heard instead: *he* took her away, a pronoun switch that changed everything.

He took her away...he took her away. *He* took her away.

It had been hard to hear, the waves hissing and popping over the sand, the gulls singing their hungry songs as they swooped around us, a sea plane buzzing in circles with a *Kenny's Cove-$5 Drinks All Night* banner flapping behind its wings, but as Amy looked at me with those sad, hypnotic eyes, I heard those four words more clearly than I'd ever heard any words spoken before or since.

He took her away.

I dropped to the sand next to Amy. "He? What are you talking about? Where's Sarah?"

We were close enough to the shore that the tide washed over our feet, the water pooling around our ankles, Sarah's lonely flip-flop drifting in the surf, the surge carrying it back to us as the waves broke against the sand.

I picked up the flip-flop and stared at the ocean.

"He took her away," Amy said. "Mr. Ronan."

．　　．　　．　　．　　．

From Asbury Park Press, May 19, 199X:

LOCAL DRAMA TEACHER QUESTIONED IN DISAPPEARANCE OF 4-YEAR-OLD

By David Daley
Staff Reporter

A local high school drama teacher has been questioned by the Ocean County Sheriff's Office in connection to the recent disappearance of four-year-old Sarah Carpenter of Holman Beach. According to Sergeant Alan Pangborn, the lead investigator in Carpenter's disappearance, an eyewitness has accused Michael Ronan, 32, of Aberdeen, of abducting Carpenter from the beach in the early morning hours of May 17. The witness, whose name is being withheld due to her age, has been identified only as "the babysitter" who was caring for Carpenter at the time of the alleged abduction. A second potential witness, also a minor, slept through the event and could not corroborate the first witness's testimony.

Ronan, a popular drama teacher at Ocean County Regional High School, is a long-time member of the faculty and director of a popular summer stock theater in Spring Lake. No comment has been made by any of the parties to date. When questioned, High School Principal Bernadette Harvey said, "Mr. Ronan is respected by his colleagues and adored by his students. While these allegations must be taken seriously, he has the school community's full support, and we hope this tragic event is resolved shortly." Ronan's drama class had just completed four performances of its Spring play, a comedy written by senior Donatella Marcino of Holman Beach, the first time the school had staged a play written by a member of the student body.

Sergeant Pangborn stated that the U.S. Coast Guard will continue to search the waters around Holman Beach for evidence of a drowning. Laura Carpenter, Sarah's mother, was released from the hospital yesterday, where she'd been treated for shock. She has yet to comment.

Anyone with information regarding Sarah Carpenter's disappearance should contact the Ocean County Sheriff's Office at 1-800-654-9823.

. . . . .

Eventually the police believed me. What choice did they have, as three doctors confirmed my narcolepsy, and half the town had seen me, at some point, curled on the floor of the supermarket or slumped face-down behind the counter at the Jaybird. But that didn't make it easier to accept. During the most critical twenty minutes of my life—maybe the only twenty minutes that ever mattered—I'd been fast asleep, dead to the world, and in that time Sarah Carpenter had drowned.

But Amy said differently. In twenty years, never once had she strayed from those words: *He took her.* And never once did she relent on the identity of the "he." It was always Mr. Ronan, our high school drama teacher, a man I respected, admired, maybe even loved; the same man Amy accused of kidnapping and murdering a four-year-old girl, the same man whose life, in those dreadful moments after Sarah disappeared, Amy set out to destroy. Even after she recanted, telling the police that "maybe" what she'd seen had been part of a dream, she never changed her story with me. Not even an airtight alibi could shake her belief—Mr. Ronan had been at the dentist when Sarah had disappeared, his mouth stuffed with X-ray film, a hygienist in the room the whole time.

He took her. And nothing else was ever said.

·   ·   ·   ·   ·

"I'm sorry," Kelly said, smart enough to sense that anything else would be ping-ponged back to her, that I didn't want empathy or understanding—I wanted tar and feathers and pitchforks; I wanted the Captain's voice on the intercom telling everyone they were free to move around the cabin and beat the hell out of the guy in 14-D. I'd been through years of unsuccessful therapy and attended enough overpriced Buddhist retreats to know that what happened to Sarah *wasn't my fault.* But of course it was. I felt grateful for Kelly's silence, her eschewing the word "closure" and all its smug assumptions.

The plane swiveled and dipped, the descent underway.

"Hang on," Kelly said, our fingers clasped as the tarmac loomed, the plane headed straight toward that most complicated word in my vocabulary: *home.*

-3-

The moment we landed, I headed for the restroom, eager to check on Amy but determined to seem cool for Kelly's sake. While Kelly waited for our bags, I grabbed an empty stall and pulled up Amy's number. No answer, so I texted twice—no response. Immediately I imagined the worst—she'd mouthed off one too many times and been prescribed a bout of electro-shock. My ruminations were junk—I'd seen too many B-movies over the years—but with Amy I always felt responsible, an instinct both noble and limiting, a kind of extended adolescence certain to muck things up with Kelly. As I waited in vain for Amy to return my text, I couldn't ignore the obvious: using a bathroom stall for anything but its intended purpose is a good sign you should do something else.

I hurried back toward Baggage Claim, where Kelly leaned against her suitcase, reading, my battered bag M.I.A. as the carousel grinded along its methodical circuit.

"Shouldn't our bags have come out at the same time?" I said, then froze, the world coming to a sudden stop when I saw what she was reading.

. . . . .

Imaginary Interview: *City Beat, PBS* (Sometime in September, 20XX)

Q: When you began writing *The Revolving Heart* you hadn't written anything for almost five years. What made you start again?

A: I don't know. I was sort of like a cat. When a cat is upset, sometimes he'll start grooming himself to self-soothe. My ex-wife had just left me, and I was miserable and didn't know what else to do. So I started writing a play, sort of like a cat licking himself.

. . . . .

"Um, where did you find that?" I asked.

Kelly folded the page top, marking her place before closing the manuscript. "In the freezer where you put it, I assume."

"You shouldn't have taken it," I said.

"I asked. I was in the kitchen and you said, 'Help yourself, take anything.' I wasn't snooping around. I was looking for the frozen strawberries. How was I supposed to know you keep manuscripts in the freezer? Most people use a desk." She tucked the pages under her arm and smiled, ready to play. "Why didn't you share that you'd started writing again?"

Kelly was big on *sharing*.

"It's nothing—just something I worked on before we met. It's crap."

"I see. Do you always store crap with your frozen food?"

It was a good quip—something Amy might have said. Kelly unzipped the side pocket of her suitcase and slipped the manuscript inside. "Come on, if you really thought it was crap you would have done something rash like shred every page and burn the scraps."

She knew me well. "It's just a draft. No one's supposed to read it. It's rough ...can I have it back, please?"

"The title page says Draft Seven. It can't be *that* rough. Honestly, I wasn't going to read it, Donnie—I do respect your privacy—but the title sucked me in. *The Revolving Heart.* I was curious. Does your friend Amy know about it?"

"No one knows ..."

"Except me," she smiled. "Actually, this is my second time through. I've had it for a week. You need to check your freezer more often."

She was having fun. My intestines felt like piano wire, ready to snap. "You've *read* it?"

"Yes, and I loved it. You're *very* talented, Donnie...."

"No, I'm a washed-up hack. It's crap..."

"The sensitive *artiste* cannot accept a compliment," she said. "Fine...tell yourself I'm some unemployed music teacher who doesn't know a damn thing about '*the theater*.' But I thought it was great. Funny, moving...you should send it to your agent."

"I don't have an agent anymore. George wouldn't even remember my name."

"No one forgets a name like Donatello Marcino," she said, but on that point, she was wrong. I'd had my chance, and like so many other things, I'd blown it.

· · · · ·

From "Family Farce Brings Buoyant *Chair* to Life" by Frank Rich, *New York Times*, (4/9/XX)

Donatello Marcino shows great promise, exhibiting a sharp ear for lively dialogue and an instinct for impeccable timing. The playwright grounds the show in a tense family drama while interweaving absurdist flights of fancy through each of the three acts. For Mr. Marcino, the future is vast.

.　　.　　.　　.　　.

During my junior year in college, I wrote a play that was produced off-Broadway and for a while I was special. *Confessions of the Midnight Chair* by Donatello Marcino debuted at the New World Theater and ran for nearly a year. *The New York Times* and *The Village Voice* gave it glowing reviews and the weekend performances always sold out. I was nominated for an Obie for Best Playwriting, and though I lost to Eve Ensler and *The Vagina Monologues*, it seemed clear I was about to emerge. Yet I didn't. After *Midnight Chair* I wrote five other plays but only one was produced, if a staged reading by semi-professional actors in a church basement even qualified as "produced." I wasn't sure what had happened except that everything I wrote was never quite good enough. I kept working, thinking that the next one might hit, but it never did.

Eventually I moved to Los Angeles and tried screenplays for a while, then worked on a few quickly cancelled sitcoms. I even collaborated on a remake of *Citizen Kane* being developed for a twelve-year-old pop star who thought the film should open and close with scenes of extreme sledding. The money was good, but I hated Los Angeles and hated the industry. I felt pathetic chasing after deals and pretending that *The Adventures of Superhero Man* was exciting work because it had grossed ninety million its opening weekend. When I turned down a rewrite assignment on a low-budget comedy called *Diapers 4*, I knew that I was done.

For a while life was bleak. I thought about heading home to New Jersey, but Amy had just kicked off marriage number two and I wasn't sure I could handle seeing her happy with some other guy; dealing with failure seemed easier three thousand miles away from the promise of my youth. In the anonymity of Southern California, I could embrace my failure, make it my friend, pour it a drink and let it spend the night. I had some money saved, but only enough for a few months and no real experience except in the theater, yet there was one thing at which I excelled.

I might have flopped as a playwright, but I was a master pizza chef, a virtuoso at turning dough, mozzarella, and spicy marinara into delicious works of art. My Uncle Dan had trained me well. We used only the best ingredients, everything fresh, *always*, including the homemade sauce that Uncle Dan would jar and sell to his favorite customers. I'd grown up in the kitchen, my after-school hours and summer vacations spent dishing dollar-slices to the hungry denizens of Holman Beach. Sometimes I'd get into a zone where the dough and I became one; I'd close my eyes and surrender to my other senses, the scent of cayenne and basil guiding my fingers, the fleshy push and pull of homemade dough driving me to late-night bursts of pizza mania. I could hit the perfect blend of sauce and cheese without even looking, and I could feel with my skin the exact moment when to slide the pie from the oven to keep the crust tender beneath its sheath of golden brown. Eve Ensler's *Vagina* might have beaten my *Midnight Chair,* but had the judges tasted a slice of my Sicilian, the Obie would have been mine.

So when I finally quit writing, my life turned back to pizza. I lacked the cash to open my own place but found a struggling shop near the zoo in San Diego run by a pair of Vietnamese brothers who seemed to be avenging our bombing the shit out of their native country by serving pizza that tasted like Wonder Bread topped with ketchup and melted Velveeta cheese. I was only in town for the weekend visiting a friend, but my instincts told me I should get the hell out of L.A. and make a change. I emptied my bank account and bought 25% of the business, the brothers gladly turning over control of the kitchen. As a rule, you can't get good pizza anywhere except New Jersey. There are some Brooklyn guys who will argue this to the death, sometimes literally, but the true pizza gourmand will always go Garden State, and this was my great advantage. Within three months, we were the hottest place in the city.

While most of the profits went to the brothers, I earned enough to get by and tried to lose whatever ambitions I'd had for a life in the theater. In a weird way making pizza was healing. I didn't have to worry about plot, pacing, or character anymore; in the kitchen, I became Zen-like and precise. It was like being home again, almost—and then one day my future ex-wife Kristin stopped in to pick up twenty pies for an office wedding shower. Six months later we were married, the serious business of Starting Over ready to launch.

This is how life works, I thought. You have a dream; you fall short and then compromise, and if you're lucky you scratch out a marginally comfortable existence with enough distractions to keep you from hating yourself. Wasn't that how *most* people lived? All those high-five American dreams of loving your job and creating your Oprah-life were bullshit; everyone knew that. At least I enjoyed making pizza, and I was good at it, satisfied, mostly; yet I still snuck off to local theaters to watch dreadful productions of *The Glass Menagerie* and *The Odd Couple*, hiding in the dark like a priest at a strip club, praying for strength.

Yet overall things were *okay*, they were almost *good*, and then... they weren't.

One day I came home early from work to catch a nap before the evening rush and found Kristin naked on the couch, perched on all fours while some pony-tailed plumber fucked her from behind, his tool belt *and* his pants pooled around his ankles, his cock deep inside my (soon-to-be-ex) wife. On the coffee table sat a pizza from Sal's Famous, our top rival. (Sal was from Nevada. Really—why did he even try?) A pie from Sal's Pizza seemed a worse betrayal than the dick in her ass. I suppose I knew the marriage was over even *before* I started flinging Sal's crappy slices at the plumber's hairy white butt, and for the next year and a half, until the lucky break of meeting Kelly, I spent most of my days alone—making pizza, staring into space, and writing a new play.

· · · · ·

"Seriously, Donnie, I loved it."

"That's because you love *me.*"

"We don't love you *that* much," she said. "I'm not some teenager who thinks her boyfriend walks on water. If your play sucked, I might not tell you, but I wouldn't say that it was great."

"I'm happy you liked it," I said, "but ...it's sub-par, trite..."

"Okay, whatever. I'm not Richard Frank from *The New York Times.*"

"Frank Rich."

"I know who he is. And I find it interesting that you corrected me so quickly, that you're so possessive of your rave review. But whatever, your new play is crap..."

"It's not *crap*..."

"No, it's not," she said, this time in her teacher voice, her line-up-at-the-door-and-get-ready- for-next-period tone telling me to drop it. I could, and *would*, continue to dismiss her praise, but in that private corner everyone keeps in the back of one's head, Kelly's words were already in lights, flashing across the face of a Broadway marquee. As much as I tried to hold back, as many times as I told myself *you gave up that life you make pizza now, pizza, pizza, pizza*, part of me was already in New York for Opening Night, as if all the years in between had just been me, asleep as usual, loitering in the lobby of a mediocre dream.

"Hey, isn't that your bag?" Kelly said.

On the luggage carousel, a black suitcase looped toward us, its side slashed open at the zipper, the top and bottom bound precariously by an inch of tattered thread. Somewhere on the long chute from the plane to the terminal my bag must have collided with a sharp edge. My clothes spilled out as I grabbed the bag and yanked it from the conveyer, shirts, socks, and underwear littering the carousel as I struggled for control of the bag. Kelly reached out to help, but all she could salvage was a single T-shirt before the rest of my clothes began another sad loop.

And so we waited, side by side in the Newark Airport Baggage Claim, while my socks and underpants rode the carousel a second time, my suitcase beside me like a stabbing victim found dumped at the side of the Turnpike.

I kissed Kelly's cheek. "Welcome to New Jersey."

-4-

Three years had passed since I'd last been home, unforgiveable really, considering that Uncle Dan was the only family I had. When my screenwriting career tanked, I'd thought about heading back to New Jersey, even more so when Kristin and I had split. *Maybe it's time to go home*, I'd think each time I drove near the beach, disappointed and a little pissed off that the ocean was on the wrong side, the Pacific refusing to be where the ocean belonged, to the East, off the coast of Holman Beach, a quarter-mile from Jaybird Pizza and everything I'd known for the first twenty years of my life. I felt pride for what I'd built in California, but even when Kristin and I had bought a house in San Diego, talked about kids and school systems and rising property values, it had still felt temporary, as if it were only a question of time before I'd return to my native habitat.

At least I was good about staying in touch. Uncle Dan and I talked every Sunday, more for the familiar music of each other's voices than anything else, but lately the conversation was all about the Jaybird. Rare was the call in which he didn't offer me the business, his beloved pizzeria mine for the taking.

"Say the word and I'll retire and get the hell out of your way. It'll all be yours when I die anyway, right?" He'd always pause, waiting for me to say "yes." "Right? Remember, if you shut down and sell the ovens, I will haunt your ass until the end of time. And you'd better not sell out to some Pakistani who doesn't know a goddamn thing about pizza. This is where you belong, right here, with me."

I didn't believe him about being ready to retire. The Jaybird was all he knew, and he'd probably hang on for as long as his hands could knead a fresh roll of dough. Yet I knew he wanted me home. He never said it outright, but it hurt him that I chose to make pizza in San Diego rather than back home, at The Jaybird, with him. When I moved to New York for the theater, and later to L.A. to write scripts, it made sense to him—you couldn't be a screenwriter in Holman Beach. But pizza? You could do that anywhere, and where better than at the pizzeria he'd built and carried on his shoulders for almost forty years, the place where I'd learned my trade, the one place on Earth where I was loved the best? Over the last few months he'd been especially persistent, letting me know that he was eager for my help.

"There's an old man living in my bathroom mirror," he said, "and I think he's me."

"You know I miss The Jaybird," I said, another way of saying that I missed *him*. "But it's not that easy."

"You give that woman too much power over you."

And there she was again: Amy, the elephant in every room.

"You don't understand," I said, but of course he did—he understood perfectly. I changed the subject. "Why don't you come out to San Diego for a while?"

"The last time I was in California, they shipped me off to Vietnam. No thanks."

"The war is over, Uncle Dan. I think it's safe to visit."

"The war's never over," he said, his way of ending any conversation he wanted to avoid. Uncle Dan never talked specifics about his war experiences except to say that part of him was still there deep in the jungle waiting to be shot. That was it—you didn't ask him anything more. Even the name of the pizzeria—The Jaybird, an odd name for a New Jersey pizza joint—was strictly off-limits. Since I was five, I'd been badgering him about it—why The Jaybird? Why not Dan's Pizza? Marcino's Pizza? But the closest he ever came to telling was a brief reference to an Army buddy from New England who'd loved pizza.

"Hey, it's safe for *you* to fly here, too," he said.

"I'll think about it. Maybe in a few weeks…"

"Here's an idea. I'll sell The Jaybird to Amy for a buck and let *her* run the place. You'd be back before the first Sicilian made it out of the oven."

·　·　·　·　·

And now I *was* back, with three suitcases, a pretty California girl, and the manuscript of a new play along for the ride in a rented Honda Civic. I'd called and texted Amy multiple times since we left the airport, but still no response. Since visiting hours were almost up, I wouldn't see her until the next day. *No big deal; she's safe, in a hospital,* I thought, but my nervous system didn't buy it.

The depressing concrete real estate around Newark Airport shrunk into the rear-view mirror as we merged onto Route 78, the potholes rattling the Civic as I weaved between the lanes.

"When do we start singing Bruce Springsteen songs?" Kelly asked. "Isn't that mandatory around here?"

It was still hard to fathom that Kelly had made the trip, that soon we'd be in Holman Beach, together. That stock phrase, *worlds collide*, banged around in my head like a pinball.

"Maybe we can visit one of the local bars and I can sit in with the band," she said.

During high school and college, she'd played in a few groups, some surf pop and a brief Riot Grrrl phase, but mostly she'd stopped once she landed the job in the school system. It was hard to keep up your chops, she'd explained, while spending your days teaching second and third graders to play "Hot Crossed Buns" on piano and flute. Now that she was unemployed, the music department budget unlikely to be restored, she'd joked about reuniting her old band.

"I think they all have kids now except me. How is it possible that I'm thirty-one?"

"Time is a hungry beast."

"Who said that?"

"I don't know. I think I did."

"I don't like it," she said. She turned on the radio and found the classic rock station. Sure enough—it was Springsteen and "Rosalita."

"Did you plan that?"

"No, but this station only plays three songs. I was hoping for 'Comfortably Numb'."

"This is hard for you, isn't it? Coming back home, seeing ...old friends."

The pause said it all—Kelly was no dummy; she knew that Amy had been more than a friend.

"I'll be okay," I told her. "It's all in my head, really. Nothing's going to *happen*. I'm more worried about you."

"I'm a big girl."

"There might be a lot you don't like on this trip," I said. "Full disclosure: things could get weird."

"You're planning to dump me on the boardwalk and run off with the Jersey girl?"

She said it jokingly, but the concern was hard to miss.

"Of course not," I said. "It's nothing, really. My uncle can be a bit prickly, and some of the townies are downright strange."

"I grew up on military bases, remember? I think I can handle some beach town in New Jersey."

The sign for the Parkway loomed over the right lane, and I signaled for the exit.

"I'm sure you can. I'm just saying...things might get weird."

. . . . .

Voices from the Town: Mrs. Arlene F., Proprietor, Arlene's House of Hair, April 20XX

"That drowning story was pure bull-crap cooked up by the government to keep us in the dark. They paid that Marcino kid a million bucks to keep quiet; Sarah's mother—she was in on it. Bill Clinton and Oprah, too. There's a spot beneath the boardwalk where they gather at night and play pinochle and whoever wins gets to steal another girl. Watch the skies. They signal each other through the contrails."

. . . . .

When we passed Mr. Ronan's old house, I said nothing, because what *could* I say?

"Um, Kelly," I imagined saying, the desperate words spinning in my head. "See that house on the corner? My high school drama teacher once lived there. Mr. Ronan. He was great to me, encouraged my writing, encouraged *me*; he showed me how theater was more than just "Climb Every Mountain" and *Hello, Dolly.* Freshman year he gave me a copy of *Waiting for Godot* and it kind of changed my life. And that house over there...that's where he lived.

"Only it's not the same house. *That* house burned down the week after Sarah Carpenter disappeared. They ruled it an accident, but I knew that it wasn't. Three nights before it happened, Amy asked me to help start the fire. I wouldn't do it—I *couldn't* do it—and so I'm certain she asked this asshole named Alex Clyde (also known as Amy's first husband), who of course said yes. She never admitted it, but she never denied it, either, and I'm positive she and Clyde burned the place down. A week later, Mr. Ronan left town for good.

"So there it is: my 'old friend' once tried to kill a man by burning down his house. But don't worry, Kelly, *you'll* be fine."

Nope—not a conversation I was ready to have.

-5-

The key, as expected, was under the mat, Uncle Dan having left it so we could unpack and recharge before meeting him at the Jaybird.

The exterior of the house, surprisingly, had been updated. The previous year an ass-kick of a hurricane had ripped through the state, damaging the roof and much of the siding; had Uncle Dan used the insurance money to buy new ovens for the pizzeria it wouldn't have surprised me, but instead he put the cash back into the house—a new roof, new siding, a large bay window facing the front yard. I wondered what had changed to make him care about the house, which was small but had been plenty big enough for just him and me. The last time I'd been home my room hadn't changed since I'd left, my twin bed still angled against the wall, my desk, where I'd worked on my first plays, parked to the left of the window, old playbills tacked to the walls—Ionesco's *Rhinoceros*, Dario Fo's *Accidental Death of an Anarchist*, *Krapp's Last Tape* by Beckett—the absurdist classics that first drew me toward the theater. (Uncle Dan, on seeing the poster for the Beckett play, had asked, "Who the hell is Krapp? Why doesn't he just buy another tape?") Would the posters still be there, the edges curled and coated with dust?

Kelly seemed to enjoy it, watching my face go time machine as we walked the brick path toward the front door. A half-mile from the ocean, our street ("our" street—as if I still lived there!) stayed quiet most of the time, and though the houses lined up along the block on tight quarter-acre lots, the neighbors kept to themselves. It was early afternoon, the sun peeking through the haze. I reached under the mat, grabbed the key, and opened the front door.

"Uncle Dan will be hurt if we don't stay at least one night, but tomorrow we can find a hotel."

"You told him I was coming, right?"

"He knows I'm not alone."

"Wow. Did you give him my name or am I just 'plus one'?"

I carried our luggage through the door, bracing for a massive déjà vu. While the furniture appeared new, everything, as expected, was still in its place, the couch against the wall, the TV (now a forty-inch flat screen) on a stand in the corner, the bookcase with the photos of Uncle Dan and his old Army buddies wedged beside the window. After the war Uncle Dan had embraced a radical critique, his bookcase stacked with tomes by Noam Chomsky and Howard Zinn, plus *two* copies of David Halberstam's *The Making of a Quagmire,* both ragged from decades of re-reading, the pages covered with angry margin notes and blocks of yellow highlighter. On the top shelf, the place of honor, sat a paperback copy of *Confessions of the Midnight Chair,* my only published play. Next to it, in a silver-rimmed frame, was the clipping of *The New York Times* review by Frank Rich, the highlight of my dead career, along with various ribbons and certificates I'd won from the Young Playwright's Foundation.

For a moment, I was a kid again, coming home from school to an empty house, silent and still, but as I looked toward the kitchen (hey—a new fridge!) expecting a snack to be waiting on the counter alongside a *Do your Homework* sticky note from Uncle Dan, I noticed something moving—some*one* moving, and realized we weren't alone.

An obese woman in a bright floral housecoat gaped at us from the hallway, a chocolate chip cookie in one hand, and nothing in the other—because there *was* no other hand. She was missing her left arm, an empty sleeve hanging from her shoulder like a deflated balloon.

"Who—who are you?" she said, and bit into her cookie. Her grey hair was short like a man's and her age was hard to tell, maybe around sixty. Cookie crumbs dropped to the floor as she stepped toward us, the hardwood planks creaking under her heavy foot.

"I live here," I told her.

She shook her head, looking around as if trying to remember where she was.

"If you live here, how come I ain't seen you before?"

"This is my Uncle's house. I *used* to live here. He left me the key." I held it up, dangling the rubber band Uncle Dan had tied around the tip. "We brought luggage. See?" Our suitcases stood by the door. "Who are you?"

The fat woman's eyes drifted around the room, avoiding eye contact as she finished the cookie and brushed her hand, her *only* hand, against the side of her hip. The housecoat reached just above her knees, her mottled calves grey and veiny, ankles squat like pumpkins; she was barefoot, her toenails jagged and grey.

"Danny said someone was coming. I thought he meant that County woman." She nodded toward Kelly. "You her replacement?"

"I'm a friend of Donnie's," Kelly said. She leaned forward to shake hands but then reconsidered, stepping back and settling for a friendly wave. "I'm Kelly Price. What's your name?"

The woman watched us curiously. "Nancy."

"Hi, Nancy," Kelly said.

"How do you know my uncle?" I asked.

"I live here," she said. "He didn't mention *two* people coming."

Nancy waddled toward the kitchen, her eyes keeping sight of us as she opened the fridge and grabbed a bottle of Mountain Dew, tucking it under her arm like a football so she could unscrew the cap with her one good hand.

Had an antelope or a kangaroo been living in my uncle's house I would have been less surprised. Kelly nudged me and whispered, "Is that your Uncle's girlfriend?"

Nancy put down the Mountain Dew, farted, and asked if we wanted anything to eat.

"Thank you, I'm good," Kelly said.

"Suit yourself. Gotta watch the show now."

She put the soda back in the fridge without capping it and headed down the hall.

"So that's the famous Donnie all growed up," she said—to herself, to whatever voices lurked in her giant head. She slipped into the bedroom—*my* bedroom—and slammed the door. The TV volume filled the house, a commercial for feminine hygiene products blaring through the hallway.

I walked into the kitchen and capped the Mountain Dew. "We're not staying here."

"Do you think—?"

"She's *not* his girlfriend," I said, sharper than I should have.

"Don't be like that. Just because she's heavy and missing an arm, it doesn't mean she can't be in a relationship."

The thought that this Nancy person might be my uncle's girlfriend made me want to slam my head against the wall. Uncle Dan had *never* had a girlfriend. As a teen, I'd speculated that he and Bonnie from the Jaybird were fooling around on the sly, but he never acknowledged it, and eventually Bonnie married some realtor. The closest Uncle Dan ever came to talking about relationships were the occasional cryptic references to someone he'd "cared for a lot" back in Vietnam. This, of course, was raw meat for a young storytelling beast like the teenage me. One of my first plays, written during freshman year, was about a GI from New Jersey who falls in love with a Vietnamese girl who may, or may not, be Vietcong. The play ended with the girl, Linh, killed by American bombs, the Uncle Dan character finding her charred body just as he was about to propose. When I showed the play to Uncle Dan, he praised it, like he did with all my work, but didn't comment on any real-life connections.

Growing up, in my solipsistic way, I assumed Uncle Dan had no interest in a relationship, that the Jaybird and I were enough to make him happy, and why would things ever change? But maybe they had. *Uncle Dan is living with a woman.* I auditioned the thought, played around with it—rejected it. Had Nancy been some sleek, foxy senior lady, I might have accepted it, but the woman now occupying my bedroom, even minus a hundred pounds, was all wrong for him. You could see it in her eyes, the essential *ain't quite right* hovering around her like a stench.

Kelly pulled our suitcases away from the door and sat on the couch.

"I'm hungry," she said. "Let's go meet your uncle. I'm all stoked for one of these legendary Jersey slices."

"I want that woman out of my room."

"Maybe it's *her* room now. You haven't lived here in twenty years."

"*Sixteen* years. During college, this was my legal residence."

"Fine. Sixteen years. But Donnie, it's not your house. It's not your room."

"Who is she, anyway? She farted in the kitchen!"

"It happens."

"It shouldn't."

"Let's hope we never live together," Kelly said. "You get another five minutes to be an ass about this before I get annoyed. Why are you so bothered by her? It's not that big a deal."

I joined her on the couch and put my feet on the coffee table, exhaustion working through me like a spasm. I could understand why Uncle Dan might be quiet about it, but why hadn't Amy warned me that my uncle was living with someone? Her house was only three blocks away. She couldn't have missed it. Holman Beach was a small town—weird one-armed fat women couldn't just *move in* without people noticing.

I yawned, my muscles slackening.

"I know that look," Kelly said, shaking my shoulder. "Don't fall asleep on me, please. Come on, let's get out of here."

"Okay," I said, my fingertips going pins and needles as I yawned again, my eyelids ready to drop.

"Donnie!"

Over the years several doctors had suggested that my narcolepsy was psychological instead of neurological, that physically there was nothing wrong with me, my falling asleep an obvious avoidance tactic, an extreme reaction to stress. I didn't buy it—I'd had plenty of narcoleptic events during stress-free times, but I couldn't deny that falling asleep was often a godsend. I pictured my old room, invaded and occupied by the troubling Nancy—my playbills replaced by grainy pages ripped from *The National Enquirer*, my closet stuffed with tacky housecoats and dingy slippers, perhaps even leftover fried chicken—and I pulled my legs onto the couch and reached for a pillow.

"You need to start taking those pills," Kelly said, her voice fading, as if she—or I—had been sucked into a tunnel. "If you get up and start walking..."

"Okay," I said. "But really, I'm not going to..."

.   .   .   .   .

I woke up to her hand caressing my hair, a gentle, comforting touch as my eyes drew focus near the bookcase, where Kelly, her back facing me, browsed the different titles on the shelf. I felt her fingers brushing the side of my ear, but if Kelly was by the bookshelf...?

I jumped, lurching away from Nancy's meaty paw. She looked startled, as if a cat had bolted from her lap without warning, and she leaned back into the couch cushions, resting her one hand on the slight impression where my head, moments before, had lay sleeping.

"Good, you're awake," Kelly said, turning from the bookcase.

I stumbled back, crashed into the coffee table, and grabbed for the wall, steadying myself against a floor lamp. With a deep, phlegmy breath Nancy heaved her bulk from the couch and turned toward the hall. "Commercials almost over," she said, bounding toward the bedroom—*my* bedroom—her housecoat bunched around her hips, her gigantic pink underpants sagging over the back of her thighs.

I waited until the door shut. Kelly flipped through a book, trying not to laugh.

"You let her touch me?"

"Don't worry. She kept it above the waist."

"It's not funny."

"You seemed to enjoy it. You were sleeping like a baby."

"If that happens again, drag me outside and let me sleep in the driveway. Do *not* let her touch me."

"Donnie, it was nothing. She seemed genuinely caring..."

"So did Frankenstein's monster until he killed that little girl."

"Okay," she said, clearly done with me. "Let's go meet your Uncle, and then I'm heading for the beach. I think some time apart is a good idea."

The TV bellowed from the other end of the house, one laugh-tracked inanity after another, and I imagined Nancy crushing my old twin bed with her sloppy girth. I fished the car keys from my pocket, fuming.

Near the front door, a small mirror hung on the wall. Kelly checked her face, but even though my sleep-hair was in corkscrews and knots, screaming for a comb, I lowered my head and dodged the mirror, certain my reflection would show a fat thumbprint smack in the middle of my forehead.

·   ·   ·   ·   ·

After the introductions, all those *nice-to-finally-meet-you* and *I've-heard-so-much-about-you* handshakes and hugs, Kelly sat down with a Caesar salad and a slice of white mushroom while Uncle Dan and I headed for the storage room for a few private words.

Three years had passed since I'd last seen him, and his thinner, older face was a shock. Uncle Dan was sixty-five now, a *senior citizen*, for God's sake, and while he was still in great shape, his chest still taut beneath his T-shirt and apron, his arms rock-solid from cutting all those slices and hauling those forty-pound bags of flour, he seemed smaller somehow, as if he'd shed a layer of himself and buried it somewhere behind the Jaybird. His shoulders, always a bit hunched from the years kneading dough, had a downward sloop, like a wire hanger trying to hold up a heavy winter coat. Time had played its tricks on me, too, no doubt; my hairline had crept back a few inches, and I caught Uncle Dan eyeing with dismay the scattered greys that had set up camp along my scalp.

But at least the storage room hadn't changed. Uncle Dan still used the same brand of flour, the shelves lined with familiar labels, vibrant red tomato vines and smiling cartoon chefs, everything in its place, the jars of minced garlic beside the paprika and cayenne pepper, the boxes of penne and angel hair pasta stacked on the top shelf. Even the Army cots were still there, folded up and standing by the fridge like soldiers waiting for duty.

"I like her," he said, meaning Kelly. "She reminds me of that actress, the one on TV."

"Yep. They look exactly alike."

"Wiseass," he said. "I meant her voice, not her looks, and I *know* you have no idea who I'm talking about. Who cares, anyway? I like her—keep her."

"I'm trying."

He grabbed a loaf of bread and sliced it down the middle, working the knife from end to end. "Remember that when you visit your little girlfriend." Meaning Amy—he'd been calling her that since we were twelve.

I handed him the olive oil, which he drizzled over the bread before sprinkling the garlic.

"I stopped by the house," I told him. "The bay window looks great."

"Insurance money," he said, then put down the garlic, rubbing his neck. "Look, I should have warned you about Nancy. I'm sorry about that."

"It's okay," I said. On the ride over, Kelly had coached me on what *not* to say, my responses limited to creative varieties of *best wishes* and *I'm-so-happy-for-you-both*. "It was a bit of a surprise."

"I wanted to tell you, explain how it happened, but it seemed wrong to do it over the phone. It's not something I planned...it just happened, and I couldn't say no."

"Hey, it's fine. It's your house; you're entitled to a life, Uncle Dan. I'm happy for you."

"Happy?"

"It's hard being alone. I'm glad you finally found someone."

He shifted his feet, his forehead crinkling. "What are you talking about?"

"You and Nancy, living together. It's great!"

"We're not 'living together'," he said.

"You don't have to lie, Uncle Dan. I'm not a kid. If she makes you happy..."

"Wait a minute. You think she's my girlfriend?"

"You were always very private when I was a kid, but really, you don't have to hide things anymore...we all have needs."

"Oh, shit," he said. "She didn't tell you, did she?"

"We didn't stay long. I fell asleep, and then Kelly was hungry..."

"Shit," Uncle Dan said. "She was supposed to tell you..."

"...you make a lovely couple."

"Stop talking," he said, and walked to the far shelf. He pushed aside a five-gallon jar of pickles and grabbed a bottle of red wine, an already-opened merlot, Uncle Dan yanking the cork and swigging from the bottle like a pro.

My uncle rarely drank. Was it worse than I thought? Were they already *married?*

"She showed up at the Jaybird last winter with nowhere else to go," he said. "I couldn't say no. She has problems...and she's family."

He offered me the wine, but I waved him off.

"She's family," he repeated. "You get it, right?"

As far as I knew we didn't have any family, just a few distant cousins.

"Christ, what are you smoking out there in California?" he said. "She's family...she's my sister...I couldn't turn her away. *My* sister; *your* mother."

"My mother's name is Kathy," I said. "I've seen the birth certificate. Kathleen Ann Marcino."

"I know her name, Donnie. Nancy is her 'stage' name. She's...not all there. She was homeless for a while...I should have told you; I'm sorry about that, but it's not bullshit. She's your mother."

I waited for him to start laughing, but Uncle Dan had never been one for jokes.

"I think she might be conning you...she looks nothing like my mother."

Didn't he remember that Sears ad, my seventeen-year-old mother and her two arms smiling in her summer clearance underwear, her hair cascading over her bare shoulders in waves of dark curls, her body tan and slender, her smile warm and inviting, Sunday-circular approved.

Uncle Dan put the wine back on the shelf. "Trust me, it's her. Nancy. She showed up at my door with literally nothing except some clothes and a prescription bottle of Risperdal. That's an anti-psychotic."

"I know what it is."

My head spun. As a kid, I'd always daydreamed about my mother coming home. I'd even written about in *Confessions of the Midnight Chair*. Act Two, Scene One: the hero's mother returns as a disembodied head projected over the stage. (It sounds dumb, but it worked—even Frank Rich thought so!) I never expected it could happen for real.

"How did she even find you?"

Uncle Dan shifted his feet, eager to get back to the counter. "How could she not find me? I haven't left town since 1975. We've been in touch over the years. I never told you...maybe that was a mistake."

"In touch?"

"Letters, phone calls, I'd send her money every now and then...you haven't been around for a *long* time, you know. Things *happen* that have nothing to do with you.... I'm sorry. She's my sister...I couldn't toss her out on the street."

"No, of course not," I said, my legs suddenly weak. I searched for a bucket in case I threw up.

"It's something we deal with," Uncle Dan said. "We might not like it, but we deal with it. Story of my life."

Somewhere in that story, of course, was *me,* two months old and crying on the doorstep, and Uncle Dan had dealt with it. I thought about waking up on the couch, Nancy (my *mother?)* stroking my hair, comforting me. Was it possible that I was starting to cry?

"Risperdal...that's pretty strong, isn't it?" I asked, getting a grip. "What's wrong with her?"

"Schizophrenia," Uncle Dan said. "There's a social worker from the County who comes and checks on her twice a month. She sees an MD for her prescriptions."

"What happened to her arm?"

"She doesn't know," he said.

"She doesn't *know?*"

"She doesn't remember. From what she's said, it happened a while ago."

"How do you lose an arm and not know what happened?"

"How the hell do I know?" he said. "She said something once about it being in a locker at Penn Station, but she doesn't always make sense. I'm working on getting her a prosthetic, but it takes time, and I'm not sure she wants one."

"This is insane," I said.

"No, it's not. It's just life. She's better now than when she first arrived. It's not so bad, really. I'm not home that much. She watches TV and drinks Mountain Dew. She started a little garden in the back: tomatoes, basil, cucumbers." He stepped back, looking away. "We had a rough childhood, Donnie. You have no idea, and you never will. I made it out okay, but she didn't. I can't tell you what to do, but it might be a good thing for you to spend some time with her."

He rubbed his temples and squinted, his headache face.

"Look, you can fly back to San Diego tonight and never come home again, pretend she doesn't exist...but why would you do that? Maybe Amy isn't the only one who needs you to stick around for a while."

He turned to the shelf and grabbed a five-pound bag of onions and a jar of minced garlic, tossing the onions straight at me, just like the old days, when I followed his lead without question.

"That's enough of this. I need to get an order ready, twenty large cheese and five orders of knots."

And there it was, our escape hatch: when in doubt, make pizza. My strongest memories of Uncle Dan, the ones that *stuck,* were always at the

Jaybird, the two of us side by side at the prep table, rolling dough and spreading cheese. Some kids remember their fathers tossing a football or holding onto the seat the first time they rode without training wheels. Me? I'd never learned to ride a bike and, outside of gym class, a football had never touched my hands. Instead we had pizza and garlic bread and small garden salads arranged in aluminum tins.

"Do you need any help?"

Uncle Dan smirked. "A California boy in my kitchen? What do you guys do, put sprouts or kale on everything? *Vegan* cheese?"

"Pineapples," I said. "Avocados and kumquats."

"Don't use that kind of language around here. This is a *family* joint."

He walked to the closet in back, edging it open with his foot, and pulled an apron from the hook, not just any apron, *my* apron, from my high school days at the Jaybird, *Donnie Pizza – Apprentice Chef* stitched in red across the chest, Donnie Pizza an old, forgotten nickname. All these years he'd kept the apron hanging in the closet like a retired jersey, like I was due back the next day for the lunchtime shift, and sure enough, when I slipped it over my neck and tied the strings in back, the apron still fit, a little snug around the waist perhaps, but still the right size, and even though I'd made thousands of pizzas back in San Diego, this felt different, like the real thing.

It felt like home.

.　.　.　.　.

That night, while Kelly slept, I snuck out and drove to the hospital.

We'd checked into a motel, spending the night at Uncle Dan's house out of the question now that it was Nancy's house, too. Nancy—my *mother*. The whole idea loitered in my stomach like an undigested burrito—the enzymes unable to break it down and shoot it into my bloodstream. Worrying about Amy—a more familiar, comfortable crisis—made it easier to pretend that a mentally ill one-armed fat woman didn't exist in relation to *me*. For the moment, I could avoid it. Amy needed me.

I waited for Kelly to nod off before grabbing my shoes and keys, tiptoeing in the dark like a second-story man. (*Did I feel like a jerk for doing this? Yes, of course, he said.*) Fifteen minutes later I was in the parking lot looking up at the third-floor windows of the Ocean County Medical Center, my heart beating hard against my chest as if I'd ran the whole way, my skin sweaty and electric.

I walked across the parking lot, hoping I'd see Amy's reflection in a window. It would be impossible to tell, but I felt that if I saw her, even in silhouette, my body would sense it. It was dark, and the moonlight threw ribbons of light across the hoods of the parked cars as I strode zombie-like toward the entrance, and for a moment I thought I saw her standing by the door—but it was only a potted plant and my fermenting imagination. It was past midnight—she'd be asleep for sure, curled under stiff hospital sheets, an anti-depressant cocktail surging through her veins, but that didn't stop me from calling out to her, from throwing my head up toward the black sky and shouting her name as if I could magically bridge twenty years and make her happy, as if I could conjure both Amy and Sarah and, somehow, find a way to keep them safe.

INTERLUDE

I'm seventeen, and I wake up with a head like a closet stuffed with costumes and props and wild soliloquies waiting for their cue; seventeen and every moment is improvisation, say "yes" and build the scene, say yes and yes and yes. I jump out of bed and already I'm someone else, spouting nonsense to the empty house in a bad British accent as I peel a banana, holding it aloft like Hamlet contemplating Yorick's skull, alas, poor Chiquita, I knew him; and then I'm showered and dressed and out the door, in the car, blasting Dramarama and the Pixies as I glide my four-door, double-dented Saturn left, left, right, left, right, and three Dutch gable roofed American Dreams later I'm parked by the curb of chez Willingham, Amy's father, a business casual coffee cup of a man, his white shirt pulled tight around a gut stuffed with bagels and undigested dreams, her father waving from the driveway as he slides into his Taurus. I am grateful to his sperm and his tolerance of my constant jones for his only daughter, who bounds out of the house like some bohemian dropout from the Grunge School of Angels, Class of '96. Tight faded denim and slashed knees, baggy red t-shirt and a matching scrunchy for her purple-streaked black hair, a loose plaid Salvation Army flannel, the sleeves scissored off at the shoulders, in her hands nothing but a key. She blows her dad a kiss and hops into the passenger seat, rolls down the window, and declares a new holiday, National Whatever Day; as for school, well, it's not like they're going to *shoot* us for seeking our knowledge elsewhere, our neuroplasticity ready to play-doh new experiences out in the world of the great unwashed. Three right turns will aim us for classrooms-lockers-pencils-up pencils-down, but no—she drapes her arm over my shoulder and whispers, "go left, young man."

I am the lock, she is the key; foot meets gas pedal and we are a Springsteen song on the open road; we're Kurt Cobain howling in pain and Patti Smith reminding us that Jesus, well, he died for somebody's sins but sure as hell not ours, and the next stop will be whatever we decide; I've got two hundred and thirty-seven dollars of pizza delivery tips rolled inside a sock in the glove compartment; our friends and enemies can wither the day with gerunds and geometry and lunch room blather, we're chasing the higher angels now, whoever and wherever they may be, and yes, I'm actually saying this, words form in my throat and fill the car like soap bubbles, Amy beat-tapping the dashboard shouting, "Well said, sire! Well said!" after each lunatic burst, and eventually we'll tire but still enthralled with the blank open spaces of National Whatever Day we clasp hands... and accelerate.

. . . . .

We swing by Sarah Carpenter's house so Amy can brush Sarah's curls before day care, one hundred strokes with a pink comb and brush, a ritual Amy never misses. Sarah's mother Laura is a dirty blonde nicotine patch, a boardwalk-stand gold crucifix dangling over fake breasts, a tattoo of a black crow with an arrow through its heart on the back of her neck, but she is always grateful for the time-out we give her from all that Mommy stuff, nobody ever told poor Laura it was be so non-stop. While Sarah and Amy curl up on the couch, I grab a stuffed monkey and put on a puppet show until Laura grabs her daughter and chases us out, already late, goddamn it, and why won't those day care bastards ever give her a break? She clerks part-time in the same real estate office where Amy's mother hangs her license; eventually her constant bitching prompts Mrs. Willingham to volunteer her teenage daughter for babysitting duties, despite Amy's avowed disinterest in children or formal work of any kind. Yet from Day One, Amy is smitten. As Laura dumps Sarah into her car seat and tightens the straps, Amy stands on the sidewalk waving and blowing kisses as if *we* are the parents, Laura merely an intrusion into our happy little troika. From the back seat, Sarah waves goodbye as the beat-up Dodge Charger scrapes the driveway and disappears down the block.

From there we are off. We stop at a diner off Exit 130 and order French fries and toast and a large carafe of black coffee. I hate the stuff, but Amy needs her morning transfusion; insisting that I drink some too, no room for narcolepsy on *this* train, not today; she pours me half a mug and watches until my face screws bitter and swallows it down. She flips over the paper placemat and starts drawing my caricature, a giant-head baby man with mud slide eyes.

"Where should we go, what should we do, Scooby-Do?" she says, scratching lines across the cheap paper placemat, looking up at my face every few seconds, studying the angles and slopes, the curly overgrown garden of my hair.

"I'm feeling a bit Kerouac today. Let's go to the village and hang with the *mad* ones," she says. "We'll make out in a pew at the back of St. Mark's Church and turn thrift-shop rags into diamonds. I'm sick of the ocean and the sand and all those little birds pecking along the shore. I want concrete and trash and fat angry pigeons waiting to mug you in an alley and steal that hot salty pretzel right from your lips. Are you with me in Rockland, Carl Solomon?"

Are you with me in Rockland?

Amy's way of testing my limits. For we are both burgeoning artists, and while the theater is my world, Amy gravitates toward Art, poetry and the Beats, Kerouac and *Dharma Bums*, Ginsberg and his "Howl;" she can recite chunks of it breathless verbatim, watch her storm down the halls of West Ocean Regional shouting "Moloch the Incomprehensible Prison, Moloch the cross-bone soulless jailhouse!" Watch her shouting in the principal's office, "I'm with you in Rockland, Carl Solomon! I'm with you in Rockland!" Principal Seavers befuddled and scrunched, wondering if Carl Solomon is a freshman or a sophomore and what exactly do you *do* with a student who cuts class to draw wild rainbow murals on the bathroom wall but still makes honor role? Already she is selling her paintings on the boardwalk each summer, winning ribbons in local exhibitions, and if perhaps I'm ahead of her with my one Young Playwrights Award and the second on its way, it seems that our nascent genius is equal, complementary, and thank God we found each other in that Jersey backwater of a Rockland, Holman Beach. *No one understands us*, except *us*, and if perhaps we are bubbled from our peers, outside the circle, the clique, the high school homecoming hierarchy of beer pong house parties, beach bonfires, and most-likely-to-be-everything yearbook smiles, we've created a private universe, a subculture of two, immune to everything but our imaginations and their complicated muses.

Of course I am with her in Rockland. Move over, Carl Solomon, we've got fries to finish, toast to butter and chomp. Next stop: south of Houston

Street, which sounds just so fucking cool we clink our mugs together in the back booth of a crappy little Parkway diner and feel like we're making history.

In the car, back on the road, we listen to The Breeders and The Lemonheads and Matthew Sweet, the exit signs waving *arrivederci* as we motor toward the city. We've known each other since kindergarten—there I am, standing on the playground, alone, terrified, unprepared for twenty other kids screaming tag, swings, monkey bars, you're it—I'm the boy who lives in the back of the pizza shop, and while yes, I can already chop garlic and grate mozzarella, I'm the boy raised by a Vietnam vet who knows nothing about play dates and pre-school and the social and developmental needs of ages two through five; my only friends are Ernie and Bert, Felix and Oscar, Richie and the Fonz; they're on TV or inside my head or names and faces that pop in and out of The Jaybird, but they're not like me, they're *adults*, local characters, and I never *played* with another kid my age until I started school, and on that first day playground time I'm in my head haven't said a word, my invisible friend Butchie beside me *can we just go back inside teacher, **please?***

And then I see her on the swing, pink jeans and Keds, a white T-shirt with a big yellow smiley face emblazoned across the front, her dark curls flying crazy as she swings back and forth with the biggest smile I've ever seen and Butchie that good old invisible pal says, "you should be friends with *her*," and maybe Butchie says something to her because when the bell rings and we all line up quiet by the door she stands behind me and pokes me in the back and says, "My dad and I really like your pizza. Do you live there or something?"

I am too shy to speak, but the next day on the playground she grabs my hand and says, "Wanna swing? It's fun! I'll show you how," and in that moment maybe my future is written, and does she already know that someday we'll be in love? For the first time that day I speak, "okay," only two syllables but for me the equivalent of the Gettysburg Address and the next day I am beside her on the swings, and away we go, a long unbroken trail into the rest of our lives.

·　·　·　·　·

In Central Park we buy big salty pretzels from a Chinese guy in sunglasses and a turban; his dog, a red Pomeranian chained to the cart, paces in circles, yipping at our heels as we bite into the thick, warm sweaty dough. When

Amy tries to pet the dog he lunges at her fingertips, and the Chinese guy pulls out a gun, a little snub-nosed .38, the handle spray-painted orange. Aiming the gun at the dog, the Chinese guy starts yelling, "I fucking warn you ... I fucking warn you" until the dog backs off, lifts it leg, and pees on the wheel of the cart. We don't stick around after that, and the pretzels, their Board of Health seal of approval suddenly in doubt, wind up in a garbage can swarming with flies.

"He'd better not shoot that dog," Amy says. "That gun wasn't loaded, right? If he shoots that dog, it's my fault. I shouldn't have tried to pet him."

I double back to make sure the dog is okay, and find the Chinese guy sitting on the sidewalk, the Pomeranian curled in his lap licking the pretzel salt from the guy's outstretched thumb.

We settle on a park bench holding hands, watching the young mothers in their Lycra shorts and baseball caps stroller-jog their babies, their legs throwing shadows like angry snakes marching along the asphalt path.

"Too bad we didn't bring Sarah," Amy says. "We should do that someday, definitely. Isn't there a zoo somewhere in this park? We'll bring Sarah and visit the zoo and the planetarium and find the best fucking ice cream cones in the Big Apple. Maybe next year when she turns four; four seems perfect for New York. We'll do it, right?"

"Of course," I say, although in less than a year, Sarah will be gone. The clock is ticking but we don't hear it; at seventeen we don't even know clocks exist.

Amy leans back and studies the penthouses looming over the tree line of Central Park West. "Someday..." she says, squeezing my hand, her foot tapping my shin. As if to prove that our destiny lies elsewhere, that already the world has embraced us and set us on our golden path, we hop the subway to the theater district and climb the concrete steps out into the Great White Way. We walk beneath the marquees and touch the playbills, pretending that my name is in lights, my name on every poster beneath of a string of starred reviews. I fall into the spell of Amy's imagination, her absolutely-no-fucking-doubt-about-it vision that this is my destiny, as if I'm not some average-looking kid from a no-name town who falls asleep all the time, who spends most afternoons with pizza dough and specks of garlic and oregano lodged beneath his fingernails. If Amy is the sun around which my life revolves, her belief in me is the gravitational pull that keeps me on my axis. *Amy believes.* It's my fuel, my protein, the amino acids that build my DNA. Without her I am nothing.

On 45th Street, in front of The Booth Theater, I pull her toward me and we kiss, the hustling hordes of New York streaming past us, the steam rising through a sewer grate ten yards ahead, angry cab horns screaming every time a car touches its brakes, and while the world doesn't quite stop to circle us like a camera in a cheesy film, from the top of a double-decker tourist bus a bearded old man shouts, "That's amore!"

For me the kiss is enough, but Amy spies two stagehands hanging by the side door smoking down Marlboros and somehow persuades them to let us inside. The evening performance is still hours away and you can see the 'what the hell, why not?" gears spinning in their minds as they lead us backstage. Playing at the Booth that night is *Broken Glass* by the great Arthur Miller, one of his later plays, one I'm not then familiar with, but that name—Arthur Miller—is like an eight-ounce bottle of vodka chugged in three frantic gulps. My head spins as I walk out on the stage. The set is minimalist; heavy black drapes along the back wall, a wooden bed, a nightstand. Amy hangs back, watching me; the stagehands ignore us. It is my first time on a New York stage, and as I look out into the dark theater, the empty orchestra seats, the red carpets leading down the aisles, the balcony looming in the shadows, my head begins to the fill in the blanks. I see actors on stage, props, a different set—instead of a drab 1940s apartment I see a make-believe arcade, something like Dizzy's Game World, the boardwalk arcade back home in Holman Beach. I see an old man polishing a pinball machine, a beautiful young girl sweeping the floor, and a pizza delivery boy holding a brown shopping bag and a liter of diet Coke.

I don't know it yet but it's the opening scene of *Anything but That*, a play I will write that summer that will eventually win my second Young Playwrights Award and earn me a summer fellowship at Yale before I start college at NYU. All that is still to come, but I can feel something growing, the people and the words moving around my head, chunks of dialogue taking shape, the rising action, the climax, and then this happens, and then this....and somehow I know that Amy is the key, the inspiration, the muse... and thank you very much, Arthur Miller, for the use of your stage.

As we exit the back door, squinting into the daylight, Amy tells the two stagehands that soon they'll be working on one of *my* productions, Donatello Marcino, remember that name, and one stagehand shrugs and lights another cigarette while the other waves and says, "Good luck, kid! We'll see you around!"

· · · · ·

A final moment: Amy, Sarah, and I on the beach, a blanket spread beneath us on the sand. The full moon glistens; waves roll over the shoreline, back and forth, like a heartbeat. Sarah holds her cone with both hands, the maraschino cherry lodged atop a swirl of vanilla as she licks the rainbow sprinkles one by one, the wafer cone steady in her tiny hands. I kiss Amy and taste the fading tang of Peach Schnapps; her eyes are tired and dreamy; she hugs her knees and gazes toward the ocean, its dark horizon vast and eternal.

"Do you see it, Duck?" Sarah asks, pointing at the water.

There are rabbits on the pockets of her jeans, funky yellow stars across the front of her T-shirt. Curly bangs droop over her forehead.

"Yes, I do," I tell her, because this is our game. "It's a unicorn, right?"

"Right!" she says, delighted, although had I said a puppy or an elephant or a certified public accountant, her answer would have been the same, because this is our game. "A purple unicorn, with green hair!"

"And a pink horn!"

"And glasses!" she squeals.

"And a necklace made of seashells."

"And a baseball hat."

"And he's riding a surfboard," I say.

Sarah giggles, almost dropping her cone, and I cup her hands as she licks the melting vanilla trickling down the back of her fingers.

"His name is Elmo," she says. "He's a good surfer."

"He's the best; but look at those big waves behind him. Watch out, Elmo!"

"Watch out, Elmo!" Sarah cries.

Does Elmo make it? Of course he does; Sarah and I go back and forth, building Elmo's story until Amy breaks in with "Elmo has a headache. Elmo went *home!*" But not even that stops us. He has a *purple* headache, and he needs new *shoes* before he can walk home, *orange* shoes, and on and on until Sarah finishes her cone, the treasured maraschino cherry the last thing she eats, her thumb and forefinger scooping it from the cone's pointed bottom and popping it into her little mouth, her eyes looking up at me with the world's most satisfied smile.

"I love ice cream, and sprinkles, and cherries, and you," Sarah says, and within minutes she is sleeping, her face resting on Amy's lap, her perfect little feet burrowed in the sand.

-6-

Back home in California, in my bottom desk drawer, was a picture of Amy on her sixteenth birthday, an actual photograph instead of pixels on a phone, the edges curled yet the image Kodachrome sharp: Amy standing by the counter at the Jaybird holding a slice of pizza, her brown eyes flirting with the lens, her mouth posed in this everything-is-possible smile, her lips a glossy pink, a funky gold hoop dangling from her left ear. Her jeans, frayed at the knees, hugged her hips like a second skin, her Nirvana T-shirt cut off at the sleeves, arms in full-summer golden, her purple-streaked hair draped in waves across her shoulders. She looked happy, sober, untroubled; perhaps even innocent. Sweet, beautiful Amy—at the Jaybird *then* ...and *now*, standing by the reception desk at the Ocean County Medical Center, head down, checking her phone, her jeans still painted onto those sexy hips, her dark hair cascading to her shoulders, a black t-shirt stretched tight across her chest, purple toenails poking through her flip-flops, her face still glowing sweet-sixteen, her lips a glossy pink.

How was it possible that she hadn't changed? Would a quick glance in the mirror show that *I* was sixteen again too, tossed back in time for a monumental do-over?

If only. The resemblance, while real, was only that, a resemblance. For it wasn't my erstwhile *amour fou* leaning against the Reception Desk with a bored expression and iPhone-glazed eyes, nor was it a daydream or some nerve-triggered memory loop. Because suddenly, from an unseen corner of the haunted house, or more accurately, from the long corridor marked Behavioral Health Unit, came the much-loathed figure of Alex Clyde, Amy's first husband, now a cop, all-dressed-up in his spiffy, hard-ass blue uniform, service revolver included, and the young female at the desk, object of my almost Lolita-like daydream, looked up as Clyde approached and muttered the word, "Dad."

It was Amy's daughter Jill, now sixteen, a virtual doppelganger of her mother as I remembered her best; it was *Jill* who had pulled me into this momentary time warp, who looked so much like her mother that I wanted to shout, "Hey! That's not fair!" to the God I didn't quite believe in.

I looked for an escape hatch, eager to avoid a potential encounter with Clyde, but the only option was turning and hustling toward the exit. While good portions of my life had been spent in retreat, I'd run away from Alex Clyde enough times that I didn't need to do it again. That Amy had married and had a child with the bastard gnawed at me like few things did. After the nightmare of Sarah's disappearance and all that had followed, Uncle Dan had urged me to break things off, but instead Amy and I grew closer and, of course, more dysfunctional, our love and friendship stronger than ever but tainted with deep currents of anger. While Amy smothered hers with Peppermint Schnapps and Bailey's Irish Crème, I channeled mine into an absurd surrealist play, the anger so hidden that even Frank Rich missed it. Still, the idea that I could ever *not* be with Amy remained unfathomable. We'd been paired since kindergarten, since *forever.* Yet after the success of my play, she started seeing other guys, never quite ending things, but never committing, either.

During high school, she'd hated Clyde, too, and yet she had married the bastard and stayed with him for almost four years. Watching Clyde standing there with the daughter that, in an alternative, *better* narrative would have been mine, made me burn.

Clyde's radar must have been up. He spotted me immediately, breaking out his best shit-eating grin as he barked, "Holy shit—blast from the past," swaggering down the hall with his hand outstretched, Amy's daughter peeking up with a mortified grimace at the sound of her father's bullhorn voice.

"How the hell are you, man?" Clyde said, his handshake all tight and testosterone. My knuckles cringed. "I thought you lived in California."

"I do. There are these things called airplanes. They're great."

"Wiseass. You still writing for the movies? I keep expecting to see your name on the screen but never do."

"I've got a project in development," I said, although "in the trunk of a rental car" would have been more accurate.

Clyde looked me over, gauging who had held up better over the years. It wasn't me. He tapped his holster, reminding himself he could shoot me should the need arise.

"I'm not surprised she called you. You always were her favorite lap dog. If I were you, man, I'd turn around and keep walking. She's over the edge this time, keeps saying how she saw Ronan at the supermarket, Ronan outside her bedroom window, Ronan on the fucking moon. She knows that's impossible."

"Improbable, maybe."

"Try im-fucking-possible." He scratched his nose and grinned. "I guess you didn't hear."

When I failed to respond, he seemed to grow taller, as if his spine had developed a hard-on.

"He's dead. Your old drama teacher hanged himself six years ago."

He paused for a reaction, Officer Tough Guy waiting for the suspect to crack, but all I gave him was deadpan Buster Keaton from an old silent film reel; I'd taken my share of acting classes and had a few chops.

"He lived outside Chicago," Clyde said. "He never taught again; I think he sold real estate. Now he's in the ground somewhere, snack food for maggots."

"Does Amy know?"

"She doesn't believe me, thinks I'm lying just to shut her up, the crazy bitch."

"You shouldn't call her that. She's the mother of your daughter."

"My daughter's a crazy bitch, too, ever since she hit puberty. The apple doesn't fall far from the bush."

Jill looked up from her phone, rolling her eyes.

"Apples grow on trees, not bushes," I said.

"For those two, bush is more appropriate." He chuckled and turned toward his daughter. "Jill, get over here."

She slipped her phone into her back pocket and trudged toward us, her eyes looking everywhere except at Officer Daddy. Up close the differences between the girl and her mother sharpened; Jill's nose was slightly bigger, her hair a shade lighter, her legs longer, her shoulders more pronounced than Amy's, yet she still qualified for that weird phrase "spitting image," and suddenly I felt like a kid again, shy and uneasy.

"This is your mother's old boyfriend," Clyde said. "In high school they were like Siamese twins."

Her eyes brightened. "You're Donatello Marcino?"

"It's nice to meet you, Jill," I said, "although we met once before, when you were three. You wouldn't remember."

"Your play ...was amazing. I loved it," she said.

It'd been a *long* time since I'd heard anyone say that. "You've seen it?"

"Twice! Last year Mom and I drove up to Vermont to this theater in Rutland. We stayed two nights ...we saw the evening show *and* the matine

"Your Mom never mentioned that."

"You know that speech Andrea makes right before the chair reappears?" Andrea was the character inspired by her mother. "I memorized it. Do you want to hear it? I'm an actress."

"No, we *don't* want to hear it," Clyde said. "And forget this actress crap. Get a nursing license, and you'll always have a job. The world will never run out of old bastards who need catheters and drips."

"That's disgusting," Jill said.

"So?" Clyde said, and I could sense Jill reigning in her restless middle finger, an inheritance from her mother, who'd flip off anyone who suggested that being an artist was crazy, artists *starve*.

"I'm glad you enjoyed it," I told her. "It's rarely produced these days."

"It should be. I wrote a paper about it for my theater class. It would have been an "A" if I hadn't screwed up the footnotes. Would you read it sometime?"

She gave me a half-shrug and a smile, her mother's signature, irresistible move; over the years that half-shrug and smile had launched a thousand yes's.

"Of course,' I said, and waited for her next request: a ride to the mall, help with her chores, a "loan" of twenty bucks.

"Maybe when Mom...gets out...we could go see a play, something off-Broadway, something *cool*," Jill said.

Clyde almost sneered. "Not on my dime."

"Mom has her own money."

"She's got better things to spend it on than the theater." He looked around the corridor, maybe searching for a locker to throw me up against. "So much like her goddamn mother."

All I could think in response was "Fuck you,"—admittedly poor dialogue—so I said nothing.

"I need to talk to Mr. Marcino," Clyde told Jill. "Go wait in the car."

"*Go wait in the car,*" Jill mimicked, capturing the Cro-Magnon in Clyde's delivery. She looked at me, bowed twice, and said, "Someday *I'll* be on Broadway, too."

Midnight Chair had been off-Broadway, but I didn't correct her. She ᵈ her phone and hurried down the corridor, as if late for a costume ᵠuired for the next scene.

ᵉs me crazy," Clyde said.

ᶜharming."

"Big surprise *you'd* think so," he said. "Just do me a favor, okay? Don't encourage her with this acting crap and don't believe a word Amy says. She's gonna tell you she's being stalked by Ronan ...Ronan at the supermarket, Ronan in the panty aisle. Whatever she says, don't buy into it. No one's stalking her."

"How can you be so certain? Even if it's not Ronan ..."

"It's not. Don't empower her delusions."

"Look at you, Clyde, using a word like 'empower.' Did someone leave a copy of *Psychology Today* in the police station john?"

He smiled. "That's the best you've got? I guess that's why your name's never in the credits. Just don't make things worse, okay? You've been gone for years, hanging out in California banging actresses while people like me do the real work."

"What makes you think I 'bang' actresses?"

"Actors?" He raised his eyebrows, enjoying the smirk.

"I'm just here because Amy needs me."

"She needs a lot of things," Clyde said, "and I'm the one who has to deal with her. I'm serious—if you tell her that maybe she *did* see Ronan, it'll be a straight ride to shit-creek for all of us. No one's stalking her. I'm the goddamn police in this town. If there was a problem, I'd know about it. Ronan's dead—that's all you need to say."

His words—*Ronan's dead*—were like a punch to the gut. I nodded, turned my face blank, let his words bounce around unmoored as I waited for him to leave.

"I'll see you around," he said, hitching up his belt like Andy Griffith on TV. "Remember, Pizza Boy—dead, dead, dead!"

He strode down the hall like a pro wrestler leaving the ring. *Asshole,* I thought, but it could have been worse. At least he didn't stay.

At the reception desk a grey-haired volunteer checked me in, confirming my name on the visitor list and handing me a pass. I peeled off the little guest badge and stuck it to my chest, then headed toward the elevators and the third-floor Behavioral Health Unit, where Amy waited behind locked doors.

· · · · ·

But first I stopped at the restroom, found an empty stall, and fell apart, thinking of Mr. Ronan, alone in some dingy apartment, a rope hanging from the base of a ceiling fan, the dark blades twirling shadows across the f beneath his pointed, dangling feet, his eyes still open even after the neck-snap ends his troubled life.

Had I known, had there been a funeral, I would have gone. I would have paid my respects and let the world know how much this man had helped me, how much his life had *mattered.* Instead I stood sobbing in a hospital bathroom stall, pleading.

I'm sorry, I'm sorry, I'm sorry.

.   .   .   .   .

Voices from the Town: Adam R., Principal (retired), West Ocean High School, April 20XX

It's a cliché of the profession but true: a teacher can change a student's life. Donatello Marcino was bright enough, but too quiet, too passive and socially awkward, too reliant on his friendship with Amy Willingham to engage with the rest of the school. Yet somehow Mr. Ronan got through to him, encouraged him to join the Drama Club and write plays. Something sparked—the transformation was stunning. We were all so proud when Donny won the New Jersey Young Playwright's Award—twice! He owed so much to Mr. Ronan, who was a passionate, dedicated teacher. I considered him a friend. What happened that last year was a tragedy. Amy's accusations were completely ungrounded. Unforgiveable, really.

-7-

Though I knew better, I still expected something straight out of *Cuckoo's Nest*, Big Nurse and teams of "colored" men in starched white uniforms, maybe even a young Danny DeVito bouncing around in his feral glory. Amy, of course, would be the Jack Nicholson character, riling up the league of mental defectives, if not to watch the World Series, then perhaps for a chardonnay and a pedicure, utterly adorable in that black ski cap Nicholson wore for half the film. And me? Maybe I was the Chief, the sly observer, the quiet rebel, the key to her escape—or perhaps something worse, like one of those dumb party girls who showed up at the end of the film, had a little fun, and left poor Billy Bibbit bleeding to death in the corner of his room.

Yet the Visitors Lounge for the Behavioral Health Unit looked nothing like *Cuckoo's Nest*. It felt more like the member's club for some low-budget airline minus the salty snacks—couches and easy chairs set up in haphazard circles, a long folding table by the back wall, a big TV propped on a stand in front of the couch, the walls lined with unmatched bookcases stacked with year-old magazines and ancient board games like Parcheesi and Risk.

In the center of the room Amy sat on the couch facing the television, her head tilted against her shoulder as if sleeping. The room was empty except for a cranky-looking nurse on a chair by the door and an old man in slippers and a blue plaid robe, who sat on the far side of the couch admiring his feet. The TV was muted, tuned to the Food Network, a bald guy in cooking whites chopping carrots on the screen.

Although I'd seen plenty of recent photos on Instagram, I hadn't seen Amy in person in over three years. (Between boyfriends, she'd invited me to meet her in Vegas for the Fourth of July weekend, and I, unable to avoid a bad idea, had spent three wonderful days with her at the Paris Casino Hotel.) As I approached, I braced myself for the worst. They'd pumped her stomach and shot her up with meds; how could she not look ragged and pale, glassy-eyed and weak? Yet the moment I spotted her, it didn't matter that she wor no make-up, or that her hair was flat, or that she'd added a few extra pour around her hips. Anyone else might have found her a mess, but to me, ⟨

she looked like Amy, and that was enough. Butterflies danced in my gut, a familiar two-step.

"Hi, Amy."

She turned her head, her face slack, her eyes droopy as she roused herself from a half-sleep, reminiscent of me coming out of a narcoleptic funk. She wore big purple socks, sweatpants, and an extra-large T-shirt with Property of Jaybird Pizza stitched across the chest. On her left arm was a paper wristlet with her name and room number; her other wrist had a thin plastic band, no doubt some kind of GPS gizmo monitoring her whereabouts and vitals. I waved, stupidly, and the old man in the blue plaid robe turned to me and smiled, as if I'd waved to *him*, his pink wrinkled mouth showing a single yellow tooth.

"Well, well, there you are, my hero," Amy said, in a sleepy drawl. "I've always relied on the kindness of strangers."

I wasn't sure what to say. On the phone two days earlier she'd been her usual self, the sharp bantering Jersey girl ready to play, but maybe the pills had kicked in and dragged her to fog-land. Her voice was weak, breathy; her hair, tied in a ponytail, hung limply over her right shoulder.

"In what dimension do I qualify as a stranger?"

"In here everyone's a stranger except for me and my buddy Glenn," she said. "Isn't that right, Glenn?"

The old man, Glenn, turned his head and mumbled into his chest. Amy yawned.

"Sorry. I'm a little beat. Probably the Xanax, plus we're not allowed any caffeine. And my pain-in-the-ass ex-husband just left..."

"I saw him in the hallway. I saw your daughter, too."

"Want to adopt her? She's mad at me and hates her father—smart girl." She yawned again, but I could sense her coming back, her voice picking up strength and speed. "She wants to run away to California and be a star."

She held out her hand and I helped her off the couch, her legs unsteady. She looked at the old man and pointed toward the wall.

"I'm going to stand over there for a while, okay, Glenn?"

"Don't go far," he said, his eyes peeking up hesitantly as he cracked a knuckle.

worry, I've got your back," she told him, and we walked over to

g with him?" I asked.

he weather."

thunderstorms?"

"No, all weather, all the time. Seventy-two and sunny can send him into a panic attack."

"That's a problem."

"I think they're working on a pill for it. Until then he masturbates a lot. It seems to help."

As if having heard, he twisted his right hand, cracked another knuckle, then dropped his palm for a quick feel.

We looked out the window, with its dull view of the parking lot, the cars squeezed between slanted orange lines, the open dumpsters standing along the back, the pigeons circling and swooping for snacks. In the window we could see our faint reflections, his and her ghosts in grimy, finger-stained glass.

"You can hug me, if you want," she said. "It's allowed. You can even kiss me but wait until the nurse looks away before you add any tongue." She put her palm against my chest. "Oh yeah, that's not allowed, is it? California Kelly might find out."

She fell into my arms, and of course she fit perfectly, as if our bodies, in the early larval stage, had evolved as interlocking puzzle pieces. It had always been that way, from the time we were eight years old and paired up for square dancing in afternoon gym class.

"Please tell me this isn't real," I said. "You needed a break and wanted the insurance company to pick up the tab, right? You didn't actually try to kill yourself?"

Her shoulders stiffened. "People never take me seriously," she said. "Even you, Duck."

"I take you seriously. I just…"

"No, you don't. I know the crack about the insurance company was just your signature bullshit one-liner, but really, Duck…" She gestured around the room. "Does this look like a 'break'? Do you know how many sick days I get a year? Three! And four of them are already gone. My next paycheck will be twenty-eight cents."

"I'm sorry."

"You always are."

Her hands mimed opening an imaginary wine bottle, poured an invisible glass, and pretended to throw it back in one gulp.

"Nope, not the same," she said, tossing the not-there glass over h. shoulder. "I'm not faking it. Hook me up to a lie detector and I'll prove i She held out her hands, as if waiting for someone to slip electrodes over fingertips. "Every night I dream about a dead little girl. And the bastard who stole her won't stop following me."

If Clyde knew about Ronan's death, then Amy knew, too.

"Clyde told me about what happened to Mr. Ronan," I said.

"Ronan didn't hang himself. Clyde just says that to shut me up."

"You think he's lying?"

"When is he *not* lying? Google it—you won't find a damn thing. He says it's in some secret police database, but he's full of crap. I know what's true and what isn't—I always have, even if no one believes me, not even you."

"It can't be …"

"Look, I don't want to talk about it now. They tell me I'm supposed to focus on *happy* thoughts." She leaned against the window, pressing her palm against the dim hospital glass. "I should thank you for coming. You're a good friend. You're my *only* friend, really."

"I'm sure that's not true."

"It's mostly true." She leaned forward and kissed my cheek. "I need a favor, Duck. The doctor will sign my release tomorrow morning if I can show that there's a stable environment waiting for me at home."

"What does that mean?"

"They don't want me living alone, you know…without supervision. Otherwise I'll have to stay here for at least two weeks. I could petition the court, but if I'm ruled a danger to myself, or someone else, they could ship me out to a state hospital, where they send the violent schizophrenics and the angry bi-polar chicks who beat the crap out of their kids. No thanks." She flipped her ponytail over her left shoulder. "I *think* the court would release me, but I don't want to risk it. And I don't want to be here for two weeks. I can't *afford* to stay here that long. So … I need someone to sign as a responsible party."

"You want *me* to sign?"

"Exactly," she said.

"That's it? I just need to sign a form and they let you go?"

"Yes," she said, "and well, you'll need to stay around for a while, a week ¬st. You'll stay at the house…"

¬ich house?"

¬use," Amy said. "There's plenty of room. It'll be easy. It's not like ¬ange my bedpan or anything. Just drive me to the outpatient ¬u know, stick around."

¬ *joke*. What the hell is wrong with you, Duck?"

At the table the cranky nurse looked up from her phone, her eyes zeroing in as Amy's voice turned loud and sharp. "Everything okay?" the nurse asked. "Amy?"

"I'm fine," Amy barked, before her voice softened. "Sorry. I'm fine."

"How about another five minutes with your visitor and then some quiet time back in your room?" the nurse said. "We don't want another meltdown like in Art Therapy."

Clearly it wasn't a question. Amy turned her back and flipped off the nurse.

"What happened in Art Therapy?" I asked.

"Nothing. An appearance by Captain Sick…"

The name struck me. During high school Amy had invented a character, Captain Sick, a harbinger of doom whose presence meant something *bad* was lurking. His name became shorthand for our nervousness and apprehension. Captain Sick could show up anywhere from third period Geometry to her Aunt Becky's hospital room the day before she died. Sometimes Amy would draw his figure, a dark hooded man with a bowtie and no face. On hangover days she'd draw pages of him chasing her across the backyard with a whip. Though he was Amy's invention, I'd embraced him, too. When my play opened, I kept waiting for him to appear backstage with a smoke bomb and a bad review.

We never spoke it, but we knew he'd been there the day Sarah Carpenter had disappeared.

"Captain Sick …it's that bad?"

"Forget about Captain Sick," she said, her voice soft but frantic. "I need your help, Donnie. Clyde won't do it, and I don't want him to, either. I'd ask my parents but they're away on a cruise, and my mother would probably suggest they keep me here *forever*. Jill is still a minor, so she doesn't count." She pulled over a chair and sat down. "There really is no one else I can ask."

"You can't stay here?"

"You'd prefer I rot in a mental hospital than take care of me for a few days?"

"No…"

"Am I really *such* an inconvenience?" She looked at me with her big brown eyes, her sad-puppy-please-adopt-me-from-this-kill-shelter brown eyes, her hand touching my arm. "You always said if I ever needed you…"

"I know what I said," I told her. "But I'm not sure I can get away for long."

"You're already here. Just don't go back. What could be easier?"

"I have a business to run..."

"California can survive a few days without your goddamn pizza, Duck. If you lose money, I'll pay you back... eventually."

Two Spanish-speaking women came into the lounge, an older pair, one of them carrying a jar of salsa, the other a baguette. They sat at a table and broke the bread into pieces, their voices hyper and high-pitched. From the couch, Glenn looked over his shoulder and glared.

"It's not the money," I said. "The thing is...I'm not alone."

Amy closed her eyes, and for a moment her face seemed to melt, the muscles in her jaw quivering as she inhaled, clenching her lips. Across the room the Hispanic women started dipping the bread into the salsa and setting it out on paper plates, as if preparing for a church social. I put my hand on Amy's shoulder, but she pushed it away, and I felt like a bastard and a colossal dick. Had I really flown three thousand miles *not* to help her? And didn't the idea of living with her for a week excite me in ways too obvious to ignore? She dropped her head and I waited for the tears, but thankfully she held it together, the Xanax and whatever else she was taking working overtime, and when she opened her eyes, she wore the best fake smile I'd ever seen.

"I get it. The California Girl," she said. "I knew she'd drive you to the airport; I didn't think she'd get on the plane, too."

"She lost her job a while back. She needed a vacation."

"And this is it? You're a crappy travel agent, Duck."

"She's never been to New Jersey."

"And I've never been to the psych ward. It's a week of firsts for the women in your life. Where is she?"

"At the beach. I need to pick her up soon, look for a better hotel," I said, my jerkiness complete.

By now one of the patients had joined the two women: a third woman, in pajamas and white paper slippers, sat between them and joined the ̓ipping party, the three women taking turns dunking the bread into the ˑ. Amy walked over to them and said something in Spanish. Whatever it ̓e was spot-on; they handed her some bread and slid the salsa across Amy conversed a bit more, and then walked over to the couch, ̓ sat with his feet on the cushions, hugging his drawn-in knees, old withered gargoyle squatting on a ledge. Amy plopped ̓ed the TV remote, and started channel-surfing, jumping ̓n, never landing on a specific show.

I joined her on the couch, but she ignored me, turning toward Glenn as if they were old buddies.

"If you ever need me, I'll be there for you—always. That's what he said, Glenn," Amy said. "That's pretty special, right? Did anyone ever make a promise like that to you?"

Glenn held his stomach, as if ready to hurl.

"Of course promises are cheap if you never plan to honor them. What do you think, Glenn? It's been twenty years. Am I being unreasonable? Does a promise become null and void when the first party replaces the second party with a younger model? Is there some kind of exclusionary clause that releases the first party when said party becomes involved with a bigger set of tits and a smaller, tighter ass?"

"Jesus, Amy!"

"Bigger tits," Glenn mumbled, and stared at Amy's chest.

"I believe there's legal precedent in the Second Court of Appeals decision in Vulnerable Single Mother versus Lying Bastard of a Friend..."

"You've made your point," I told her.

"Tighter ass," Glenn said.

"Don't worry about it, Duck," Amy said. "If I stay here long enough the electro-shock is fifty percent off. I've got a Groupon. Plus, we get little cartons of orange juice for breakfast. And muffins." She aimed the remote and hit the Off button. The screen turned black. "I hope the California Girl enjoys her vacation."

The nurse stormed over, snatched the remote from Amy's hand, and turned the television back on, the Food Network reappearing as the nurse tucked the remote in her side pocket.

"That was rude!" Nurse said. "You have another two minutes, Ms. Willingham, and then it's back to your room. Say goodbye to your guest."

She stood by the couch, hands on hips, waiting for Amy to say something, but Amy, keeping her cool, only nodded with a blank expression. Glenn grabbed a pillow and covered his chest, as if waiting for a body shot. The nurse, giving her best *don't fuck with me* glare, stomped back to her seat.

"Yep, it's a real break, Duck," Amy said. "Maybe later I'll hang out by the pool and catch some rays. If I stay long enough, I'll get a free T-shirt and VIP card for ten percent off on my next stay. Maybe they'll throw in a scr for some medical marijuana. Did you bring any Phish CDs? And Che man—gots to have some Cheetos."

I started laughing, and soon Amy was giggling too. Glenn looked over as if we were both crazy, and it reminded me of sitting on the couch in Amy's old living room, she and I cracking up over some private joke, the kind of thing only thirteen-year-old kids would ever find funny, her father glaring from his recliner, telling us to pipe down so he could hear the goddamn television, *MacGyver* or *Hunter* or *Magnum, P.I.* Sometimes we'd wind up rolling on the floor, clutching our stomachs, laughing so hard we'd be gasping for breath, not even sure anymore about what had been so funny, just laughing at ourselves for laughing—until her father would peg us with the *TV Guide*, or an orange peel, or whatever else he could grab without rising from his chair. At some point we would catch each other's eyes and suddenly we'd be as close as two people could be, and yes, it was different now—we were older and had been apart for years. The living room couch was long gone. We were behind locked doors in the psych ward because Amy *had tried to kill herself*, yet in that moment of spontaneous laughter we landed in the warm pools of each other's eyes, and it really didn't matter *where* we were. Everything felt *right*, like it always had.

"What do I do? Sign a few forms?" I asked her. "I just check you out like a library book?"

"Yes, that's it—exactly!" Amy said, and we kept laughing, even after Glenn cracked his knuckles and fled the couch; we laughed as the three women cried "loco" and started laughing, too. We laughed until the nurse stormed over, her face twisted like an angry hawk as she grabbed Amy's arm and pulled her away from the couch.

"That's enough out of you," the nurse said, and Amy, like the diva exiting the stage after another bravura performance, blew me a kiss as the nurse led her down the hallway, back to her room behind locked doors for one final night.

-8-

For now the boardwalk was quiet, but soon the invasion would begin, the pilgrims from upstate hauling their pale winter asses down the Shore for the summer's first saturnalia, six-packs of Coronas and six-packed frat boys in search of an easy lay, the boardwalk teeming with bodies young and old; the amusement stands ready to suck up the quarters and wrinkled dollar bills for a chance to win a dime's worth of made in China crap. Holman Beach in its summer skin, the natives girded for three and a half months of swearing at traffic and complaining about all those errant beer cans littering the beach, the only upside being all that cash, and if you were lucky you sold enough slices of pizza to bank your way through the rest of the year. Ready or not, summer was barreling down the Parkway, on the Exit ramp, and picking up speed.

Yet we still had a week, eight days until Memorial Day weekend, and so Kelly and I had the boardwalk pretty much to ourselves, except for a few locals walking their dogs or just squeezing in a peaceful stroll before the madness kicked in. Some faces seemed familiar, and I spotted a few people checking me out.

Hey, didn't he write a play or something? Whatever happened to him? Remember that poor little girl ...?

The day had been long, and I was beat, but Kelly seemed high octane in her sneakers and shorts, her pace quick enough to raise my heartbeat. Though most of the boardwalk stands remained closed for the season, a few shops had opened early, and from the avenue we could hear the music drifting from the double-doors of Bar X, where bands played nightly, and where, during the Nineties, Springsteen showed up every few months and jammed with a local band.

We walked toward the pier, watching the fishermen dangling their lines, waiting for fluke. On the morning that Sarah Carpenter disappeared, a single fisherman had manned the pier; eyes glued to the tension of his rod, he hadn't seen a thing. He was an old guy, hard of hearing, oblivious to everything except the jerk of his line. The following summer he died, a heart attack on a charter boat while fishing for bass, which, I was told, was a fisherman's ideal death.

"So...are we all going to sleep in the same bed?" Kelly asked. "I hope she doesn't snore or kick, even if it *is* her bed."

"I'm sure we'll have our own room," I told her. "It's her grandmother's old house. Grammy moved to a retirement village in Carolina and sold it to her cheap. It's better than staying with my uncle, and that woman."

"Better for whom?" Kelly said. "And all you have to do is sign her out? What kind of hospital is this? Back home it took a week before they approved me to adopt Mr. Biggles, but here I guess you can just pick out a mental patient and bring her home the next day."

"It's the insurance companies," I said, though it sounded dubious to me, too.

"It reminds me of one of those late-night movies on Cinemax that ends in a threesome...and *a murder.*"

"There won't be any threesomes ...Amy can't afford Cinemax."

"Hey, maybe I'm into it," Kelly said. "Not the murder ... but if she's half as hot as your devotion implies..." She leaned over to tie her shoelaces as a bird swooped down and snatched a peanut from between the boardwalk slats. "What's that expression? What happens in Jersey stays in Jersey?"

She smiled, enjoying my discomfort.

"I think you mean Vegas," I said, and suddenly I was gone.

．　．　．　．　．

Imaginary Interview: *Backstage with Brody* (Podcast Episode 9 - September, 20XX)

Q: And then you went to Vegas for a weekend with Amy. What was that like?
A: Unexpected and wonderful and, like everything else with Amy, confusing as hell.

．　．　．　．　．

I'm fist-deep in dough with a killer headache and the post-divorce blues when I hear "Lithium" calling from the pocket of my apron. It's the afternoon rush and I've got nine pies to make in the next twenty minutes— listening to Amy bitch about her job or her mother or her latest bum boyfriend is the *last* thing I want, but of course I answer.

"Hey, it's me. I won a weekend in Vegas; can you believe it? I never win anything. Two nights at the Paris, meals, airfare ... I'll have to listen to some time-share crap for ninety minutes, but that's it. It's all free. Jill's with Clyde next weekend, so ...you're in, right?"

"What about ...what's his name?"

"I'm offering you a free trip. Well, *my* part is free. I won't charge you for the room. We'll have fun."

"Amy, I can't just leave work and fly to Vegas on a week's notice..."

"Why not?" she says, as if she alone can grant me a permission slip, and she must be right because a week later I'm on the plane with nothing but a carry-on and my week's split of the receipts stuffed into my pocket, sauce-stained tens and twenties screaming for some action.

The flight is quick, and the cab drops me off at the Paris, where three guys dressed like Bogart in *Casablanca* stand by the entrance while a busload of seniors from Kansas clog the revolving doors with their suitcases and walkers, an Asian guy with a huge camera darting around taking photos of *everything*. When I step inside, I feel like I've been dropped in the middle of a pinball machine, the bleeps and snaps of the slots like post-new wave electronica; I steady myself and take a breath. At a nearby slot, a hunched old guy in suspenders and a straw hat pumps his fist at a jackpot payout. Ten dollars, ten thousand? Does it matter? He's a winner, and maybe it'll be contagious. It's been *forever* since I've been on anything but a losing streak. I pull out my phone and call Amy, who tells me she'll be down in five minutes.

A cocktail waitress offers me a Jack and coke, smiling at me like I'm the best-looking guy in the place, and though I know the smile and the cleavage is a tip-gimmick offered to one and all, it still works. I start feeling like a guy who almost won an Obie instead of a divorced nervous pizza-maker out of his element; I drink the Jack and coke and slip the waitress twenty bucks. "Thanks, sweetie," she says, "find me if you want more." More! Yes, I am here to get *more*, and finally I feel ready to dazzle Amy with my *oh shit here it comes ...*

Twenty minutes later I wake up next to a *Dukes of Hazzard* slot machine, two security guards shining flashlights in my face while Amy insists that I'm not drunk or on opioids it's *medical, dammit,* "narcolepsy—just give him a break, okay?"

The guards look pissed but move on anyway, and Amy motor-mouths through a story about some obnoxious guy on her flight until I'm back on my feet. After thirty seconds of *good to see you,* blah-blah-blah, Amy says,

"Okay, now that you're awake and we've got that Christmas card crap out of the way, are we ready to have fun?"

It's past midnight and I'm beat, but who goes to bed in Vegas? Amy hands me a Red Bull and a shot glass of vodka, not the best idea in the world but I drink it anyway, and then we're out on the Strip, Amy electric and beautiful in her black skirt and red tank, wobbling on high heels I know she never wears, pointing up at the phony castle, the looming billboards with Carrot Top and Donnie and Marie and all those faces you wouldn't pay a dime for back home but in Vegas it's standing room only.

"I was thinking," Amy says, which in the blur of street noise sounds like *I was drinking* or even *I was sinking* but no, that's me, *I'm* the one who's sinking, my career dead and buried, my marriage gone, my life measured out in pizza spoons, "...what if we pretended that we're someone else, two people meeting in Vegas for the first time, I'll be Rhonda or Lady Penelope and you can be Rick or Henry or the Duke of Cumberbatch ...whatever. Just not Duck and Amy, okay?"

No, I think; *I don't want Rhonda or Lady Penelope; I want Amy Willingham of Holman Beach, New Jersey,* but I learn to play along as we saunter down the Strip. A grey-haired woman in a sombrero hands me a baseball card with a topless stripper on it, a dude with a blank CD asks for ten bucks *come on, man, support the arts!* as the bachelorette party girls with their tiaras and feather-boas rush toward the open doors of a silver Town Car, Lady Penelope blowing them kisses and wishing them luck. She grabs my hand and pulls me through the air-conditioned rush of a casino entrance, past the shops filled with diamond necklaces and thousand-dollar handbags; we drink espresso, eat crepes, and converse in bad French accents, *oui, mademoiselle, tu etes tres jolie,* laughing at everything like kids again, and when was the last time I had this much fun *any fun at all?* We pay a hundred bucks for a gondola ride, take mime lessons from a street artist, and dance to a string quartet on the pedestrian bridge crossing the Strip. Inside every hotel there's a wedding chapel, Amy pointing out the signs, saying "You and me—I wonder what *that* would be like." I'm clueless on whether she means it.

We wind up at a Magic Shop, *hey, there's a show in five minutes, come on in,* the clerk says, so we step behind the curtain for The Amazing Kid Charlemagne and find two empty seats in the front row. It's a tiny theater, converted storage space a better description, but in Vegas everyone's an aspiring performer, and Kid Charlemagne is *good,* card tricks and levitating bowling balls and how exactly did the sexy woman with the torn black stockings disappear inside the laundry bag?

"Volunteers, please," the Kid says, and Amy pulls me toward the stage, a six-inch platform at the head of the room. "Let me guess ...childhood sweethearts on a second honeymoon. Am I right?" the Kid asks, but how can you define Amy and me in a Yes or No? We are an essay question all the way, supporting paragraphs and footnotes required, though Amy says, "You got it, Kid! Childhood sweethearts," which makes my knees weak, though maybe that's just the stage lights and the crepes and the long hours of no sleep.

After a brief explanation and some cheesy patter, the Kid pulls a set of handcuffs from inside his black jacket and snaps one cuff around Amy's wrist, the other cuff around mine. "These aren't trick cuffs," he says, "try to get out." Amy and I play along and make of show of it, tugging and pulling, trying to break free. The handcuffs don't yield.

"The only way out is to say the magic word," he says, "but you don't know what that word is, do you?"

"Abra-ca-dabra?" I say.

"Sha-zaam?" Amy offers.

"Not even close." The Kid winks toward the audience. "Now remember everyone, these handcuffs have no key, and the only way out is to say the magic word ...and *they* don't know what it is. Should I tell them?"

There's a smattering of restless applause as the Kid hams it up, Amy's hair glistening under the lights, our wrists bound by metal cuffs and the foot-long chain between them. The Kid leans over, a hand on each of our shoulders and says, "Okay, childhood sweethearts, if you want to escape, all you need to say is ..."

He says the word, but we can't hear him, no one can over the sound of a giant gong—the house lights rise and music plays, an old-time carnival rag, as the Kid bows and says, "Sorry folks, time's up, thanks for coming!" He bounds off-stage to laughter and applause, leaving us hand-cuffed and abandoned as the audience exits, ha-ha, *good luck, sweethearts* some guy from Texas says as he and his wife head back toward the slots, and it takes maybe five minutes before the Kid returns with the handcuff key, five strange and stressful and wildly romantic minutes during which Amy and I stand three feet apart in the empty theater, circled by the overhead light, our bodies warm and magnetic. We rattle the handcuffs like Marley's Ghost, make dumb jokes and flirt like we did in 8th grade, our free hands finding excuses to touch each other, a piece of lint on her shoulder strap, a loose button on my shirt, and as the time passes and we wait for the Kid, the handcuffs tight around our wrists, I wonder if she thinks the same as I do, that it feels sort of right.

Back outside we lose eighty bucks at roulette and then it's onward and upward, which means the elevator and the 14th floor, her arm draped over my shoulder as she struggles with the room key. *You're my best friend,* she whispers, then sings, "oh, you make me live," from that Queen song I've heard at every wedding I've ever attended, even my own, when my *real* best friend was back in New Jersey while Kristin and I made legal our mistake. Inside the room I sit on the bed and reassemble my head while Amy disappears into the bathroom, the room dark but the curtains pulled back, the lights of Vegas reflected in the solid glass, the room bathed in neon as fireworks appear in the sky, streaks of red and gold, green bursts and plumes of smoke and Amy steps out into the room wearing nothing but her skin.

We stand by the window, Amy wrapped in a blanket as we watch the fountains across the street begin their synchronized dance to the feint sounds of Rachmaninov. I undress and join her in the blanket, our hands finding the places we've always longed for as we meet in a deep kiss. *I love you,* she whispers, and I feel like I'm glowing. I could light the city with my skin. *I love you, too, always have,* I say, touching her beautiful face, my hand caressing her lovely hair, and I think *this is it.*

But five minutes later we are side by side in bed, staring at the ceiling, thoroughly chaste, and why does this surprise me after all these years? Everyone always assumed...but my virginity held strong until the ridiculous age of 25, another playwright, Jessica Thatcher, is my shocked and disappointed first, and growing up Amy always said *someday* but what does that mean when you're in your thirties lying in bed in a Vegas hotel? This is our thing: we're the lovers who've never made love, and in the darkened room on the 14th floor of a fake Eiffel Tower, while I think of all the different ways I want to touch her, Amy turns her back and whispers *goodnight,* and for once it's not me who's falling asleep.

·　·　·　·　·

"That's a new one," Kelly said. "You've never slept with your eyes open before."

"What? Oh ..." I said, snapping out of it. "Sorry."

"That's okay. Imagining a threesome can be distracting."

"Will you stop that, please? I know this trip was a bad idea, but once we're back home, I'll make it up to you. I promise."

"I'm a big girl. You don't owe me anything. We'll see what happens, right? If we're meant to be together, we'll get through it and this will be one of those trips we argue over and then laugh about when we're old. And if we're meant to fall apart it would have happened anyway, right?"

"I don't want it to fall apart."

"The better answer is, you don't know what you want," Kelly said, then kissed my cheek and started running down the boardwalk, spinning around and jogging backward, waving me to catch her.

Fifty yards ahead she stopped outside a brightened door, the entrance to Toby's Rock Lobster, a music shop that sold CDs and vintage vinyl, instruments, too, guitars mostly, though once there'd been a tuba in the front window for seven years before someone finally bought it. Over the door hung a cartoon lobster with the name Toby printed across its body, a drumstick clutched in each of its cartoon claws. Kelly stood by the long window, peeking through the glass until I reached her, out of breath and spent.

"I was thinking ..." she said. "Since I'm being *so* open-minded about this whole weird arrangement, it would be nice if you bought me a present." She pointed toward a guitar hanging in the window, an acoustic model with a mahogany neck. "I'd buy it myself but being out of work and all...I'll pay you back if I ever get a job."

She gave me a cute smile, and that was enough.

Inside the shop, an old Black Sabbath song groaned through the speakers as Father Toby, the owner, stood by the register studying a chessboard set up on the counter. I'd known Toby since childhood. He was in his mid-sixties, a chubby guy with a shaved head and a neat Van Dyke, John Lennon glasses and a black T-shirt. Around his neck was a minister's white collar, allegedly the real thing. In the 80s he'd been a Catholic priest, but as Toby told it, one night he saw U2 on their *Rattle and Hum* tour and during "Bullet the Blue Sky" had experienced a second calling—by the end of the month he'd left the church and started his own band, a power trio called Easter Egg Salad. People who remembered them said they were pretty good, a decent cover band with some catchy originals, but after a few years on the bar band circuit Toby shut it down and set up shop on the Boardwalk. Supposedly he was still an ordained priest, never having been officially ex-communicated, and rumor had it that the Church had donated the cash to open the store, hush money for some dirty secrets Toby had on the

Archbishop. When all those scandals popped up about priests and young boys, I immediately thought of Father Toby, wondering what he knew.

Years back Amy and I would stop in after school looking for the new Soup Dragons or Matthew Sweet CD. Although no one bought albums anymore, the store remained in business. Maybe the Catholics still had Toby on the payroll. On the counter the chessboard was populated with guitar picks instead of chess pieces, the picks arranged on opposite sides in strategic patterns, Father Toby engaged in a match against himself. There seemed to be a theme, the Fender picks again the Martins, but it was hard to tell. Adjusting his glasses, he looked up, his eyes squinting as he tried to place me. Then it hit.

"Good Lord, it's the prince of the Jaybird," he said, "Dan Marcino's loyal squire has returned at last."

He and Uncle Dan were good friends, two small businessmen with similar interests and a shared aversion to change. Father Toby moved from the counter and shook my hand, then turned to Kelly, touching her arm as a big grin broke over his face. "You, my dear, are a musician. About this I'm never wrong. What do you play?"

Kelly brightened. "Piano, flute, clarinet, violin...a little guitar," she said. "I teach music...well, I did before my job became a budget cut."

"Philistines!" Toby said.

"We were wondering about that guitar in the window," I said.

"The Martin? It's a beauty, isn't it?' He lifted it from the display and cradled it against his stomach. "The fingerboard is Indian rosewood; the strings ...it's like they're made from the hair of baby angels." Stepping back, he strummed a few chords, then played the opening of the Beatles song "Blackbird." I tried to catch the price, but the tag wasn't visible.

"You play wonderfully," Kelly said.

"I dabble. I'm a lonely man, and these are my friends." He gestured at the guitars hanging from the walls. "These days everyone just listens to their phone. Abysmal sound quality, but they don't care, do they? I look out at the boardwalk sometimes and everyone's taking pictures of themselves! There's the stunning grace of God's creation, the beautiful Atlantic, so close in view, but all they want is their own grinning faces. The United States of Narcissism." He winked at Kelly. "Yes, I'm a bit of a crank, but my years of service leave me entitled. People see the collar and they rather expect it."

"How much for the guitar?" I asked.

"This guy here," Toby said, pointing to me. "A good customer. He and his friend would come in and actually buy something. They'd bring that darling little girl. What a shame!"

It always shook me when someone mentioned Sarah, as if what had happened belonged only to Amy and me. Toby played a few bars of a song I recognized but couldn't quite place, the music filling the shop with its deep somber beauty.

"Your friend still comes in, you know. She bought the new Morrissey a few weeks back. It doesn't sound the same if you download it. That's true, you know, but they'll never let anyone prove it."

"Would you mind?" Kelly asked.

"It's my pleasure. Every guitar yearns to be played by a beautiful woman."

Kelly took the guitar, Toby handing it over like it was his first-born, Kelly balancing her grip as she checked the frets and started strumming the opening melody of "You've Got a Friend," the James Taylor song, written by Carole King, I think, the sweet harmonic lines rising and falling. Amazingly, I'd never heard Kelly play guitar before, and suddenly I felt ashamed of how something so important to her could get lost in the rabbit hole of me. Even awake, I was so often sleeping.

I watched her fingers slide around the frets, her hands so deft and confident, her face at peace, lost inside the notes as her head nodded rhythmically with the changing chords, Father Toby's foot keeping gentle time against the floor. Had I ever seen Kelly happier?

"How much?" I asked.

"Nine hundred," he said.

Immediately she stopped playing and offered the guitar back to Toby, but I grabbed its neck and guided it back to her, my credit card reluctant but ready for the hit.

"We'll take it," I said.

-9-

"It's a gradual process," Uncle Dan said, "but eventually you get used to her."

We stood in the kitchen watching Nancy devour her breakfast like some cheap carnival act, the Amazing One-Armed Fat Woman, brought to you by Cocoa Puffs. It was all set out in front of her: a bowl of cereal; ten slices of microwave bacon; an onion bagel smothered in cream cheese; and one-half of an Entenmann's crumb cake, all chased down with a tall glass of chocolate milk. Watch closely enough and a pattern emerged: after three spoonfuls of cereal, she'd drop the spoon, gobble two slices of bacon, then chomp on the bagel, the crumb cake the final stop before the whole routine repeated with three more hits of Cocoa Puffs.

"Shouldn't you be feeding her something healthier?"

"I don't *feed* her...she's not a cat." Uncle Dan sipped his coffee and checked the clock. "She's lost ten pounds since she's been here. If you'd like to start planning her diet, she's all yours, doctor."

She reached the last slice of bacon, and instead of eating it, crumbled it in her fist and brought her hand over the cereal, bacon bits raining from her palm into the Cocoa Puffs. She must have known we were watching but didn't seem to care, and I felt guilty for my smug self-righteousness.

'Couldn't you find any group housing or...someplace to put her?"

Uncle Dan glared. "I didn't hear what you said, and I hope you're smart enough not to repeat it."

"Sorry," I told him. "It's just...*hard.*"

"Being in a firefight in Da Nang—*that* was hard. This is just something we deal with."

Earlier Kelly had suggested how lucky I was having this chance to get to know my mother. It didn't matter that Nancy wasn't what I'd envisioned, or even what I wanted. She was here, in this moment of my life, and whether or not I welcomed it, I had a mother who needed care. She quoted some old Buddhist saying: *There is the path of fear and the path of love. Which will you follow?* I loved Kelly for saying it but I hated *path*s, so I had pretended to be asleep.

Uncle Dan refilled his mug and poured a second cup, which he handed to me, even though I loathed coffee. I looked at Nancy, studying her face, wondering if, beneath the age and the flab and the medicated haze, I'd find traces of me. Here was my gene pool; swim at your own risk. Growing up, I'd sometimes stare at that one image of her I had, the underwear ad from the Sears circular, searching her face for a connection, a resemblance in her eyes or in the color of her hair, even in the slope of her chin, but nothing ever clicked.

Over the years, I'd sometimes spot strangers in various public spaces who, in some vague, hard-to-pin-down way, reminded me of myself, and I'd wonder if it might be her, the long-lost mother who'd abandoned me, but the encounters were always fleeting or, after a better look, nowhere near a match. Only once did I really believe it was her: opening night off-Broadway for *Confessions of the Midnight Chair,* a sharply dressed woman in her early to mid-forties in the fifth-row center aisle, three seats in, whose face seemed eerily similar to my own. I considered approaching, but she disappeared before the final curtain, and when I asked Amy about her, she said she was pretty sure that the woman in question had been a guy in drag.

I watched Nancy's face as she finished off the crumb cake. *This is my mother,* I thought, but the phrase sounded foreign, theoretical. I was the boy *without* a mother. How could that change? And why had Uncle Dan kept it a secret? On the phone he rambled through every picayune detail about the pizzeria, from the price of garlic powder to how many rolls of toilet paper The Jaybird went through each month, but about my mother reappearing, after *thirty-eight years,* not a word.

Nancy smeared another glob of cream cheese over the bagel, her eyes peering above the cereal box, sneaking a glance in my direction. His coffee finished, Uncle Dan placed his mug in the dishwasher and gave me a nod.

"I'll be at the Jaybird," he said, handing me a pair of prescription bottles, the caps undone. "Make sure she takes two of each before you leave."

I checked the labels: Lipitor and Thorazine.

"See you later, Nance," Uncle Dan said, leaning over and pecking her forehead. Despite the mouthful of Cocoa Puffs, she managed a smile, nearly beaming at the attention, and Uncle Dan patted her shoulder before hustling out the door.

My God, they like each other! I thought, and I wondered what was wrong with me that the possibility of affection between them felt so distasteful.

I shook the pills from the prescription bottles, two of each, and filled a glass with tap water.

In the driveway Uncle Dan's pick-up choked itself awake, the chassis scraping the pavement as he backed into the street. From the bedroom I could hear the fake chatter of a morning show, some dumb celebrity interview and waves of forced, awkward laughter. Nancy put down the crumb cake and scanned the room. It was just the two of us. Kelly had gone jogging on the beach and wasn't due back for another thirty minutes.

I set the pills on the table, next to the crumb cake. "Uncle Dan said you should take these."

She popped the pills into her mouth, swallowed, then followed with a long gulp of chocolate milk. "Thank you," she said, staring at me, perhaps her turn to search for resemblances, her baby boy ten feet away in the guise of a middle-aged man.

She spoke slowly, as if each word required assembly in her mouth before she could speak it.

"You look... normal," she said. "Are you?"

"Mostly."

"Good. I was... normal, too. Then I got... sick. Then I got fat." She shrugged, as if it were all some random accident, which maybe it was. "I like living here with Danny."

"He's a good man," I said.

"That woman...is she your wife?"

"No."

"I was... married, twice. Not a very nice... man. He stabbed me. See?"

She pushed back the chair and stood, lifting her nightgown, the rolls of fat spilling out, pale and blotchy, a melting Jell-O cup of skin. She wasn't wearing underwear, but her gut hung down far enough to cover her privates, thank God, and she held the nightgown just below her breasts. On her left side, above her navel, faded by time and nearly swallowed by fat cells, was a six-inch scar, the ghost of a jagged incision crawling across her stomach. Her legs were a map of varicose veins poking through cellulite. I looked away, repulsed.

"See?"

"Yes, I do," I said, staring at my feet. She lowered the nightgown and finished off the chocolate milk.

"It still hurts. I... was thinner back then."

"I'm sorry," I mumbled.

She grabbed the cereal bowl and the two empty milk glasses, somehow holding all three with her one good hand and wobbled toward the kitchen. She trudged toward the dishwasher and I stepped aside, flattening myself against the counter to avoid her girth. She smelled of morning breath and sour sweat, and I baby-stepped away from her. The dishwasher snapped shut, and she turned to me, inches away.

"You were a good... baby," she said, "...except that one night...you cried and cried. Sid wanted to smother you... with that pillow and put you... in a garbage bag, but I wouldn't let him." She tilted her head, gazing up, as if watching the memory play out across the ceiling. "I wouldn't let him."

She looked at me, smiling, expecting a medal perhaps, or at least a "good job!" or "Atta girl!" Maybe this was her bright shining moment of maternal care, keeping her baby boy from the inside of a Hefty bag.

"I appreciate it."

She squinted, eyeing me up and down, and I counted the seconds until she backed away.

"Time to watch Ryan and Kelly," she said, turning from the kitchen and bounding toward the hall. "They're in my... room, if you wanna... watch, too."

It's not your room, I thought, *it's mine!*

But no—that was a lifetime ago. It *was* her room now.

'I wouldn't let him," she repeated, to no one, to herself, and she ambled toward the bedroom, the hardwood floor creaking beneath her feet as she disappeared into the hallway, the same hallway I had walked, alone, so many times as a little boy. For a moment I had an urge to follow, to enter my room—*her* room now—but I snuffed it out, grabbing the coffee Uncle Dan had left on the counter, staring at the dark, steaming mug.

I stood in the kitchen and drank it all down, the coffee hot and black, without a drop of sugar, exactly as I hated it.

. . . . .

On the way to the hospital we stopped at the grocery store to pick up flowers and a card for Amy, the flowers being Kelly's idea, her good-hearted instincts overcoming her reservations about staying at Amy's house.

"Thank you for making this easy," I said.

"Easy? When did you become an optimist?" She lowered her sunglasses and rubbed a smudge from the lens. "This isn't easy, but your friend tried to kill herself, and that's really sad, so we need to be supportive. Well, *you* need to be supportive, and since it was my idea to come along, I need to do the same. We're a team, right?"

I nodded, uncertain of what we were, but confident I wanted her near.

"I did a lot of thinking last night, about us, about other things. There's a reason we're here, as a couple. It's a great test of our relationship, don't you think?"

"Can you make it a quiz instead?"

"Relax—I'm grading on a curve."

"That could be trouble. I'm sure you hang with the smart kids."

"The last guy I dated cheated on me with his sister-in-law. I think you've got this aced, Donnie."

She waited in the car while I ran into the store to grab the flowers, but when I came back with a bouquet of lavender-colored roses and a package of Tic-Tacs she looked like I'd just stomped on the tail of her favorite cat.

"You bought roses?"

"You told me to get flowers. These were on sale—$8.99."

"I said *flowers*, not roses. Did you pick up an engagement ring, too?"

"It was your idea. They're not *red* roses..."

"Lavender means love at first sight." She googled it on her phone and waved it in my face. "See?" She read from the screen. "Those who have been enraptured by feelings of love and adoration have used lavender roses to express their romantic feelings."

"How was I supposed to know that?"

"Your subconscious did."

I tossed the roses out the window and started the car. "Is there a problem with the Tic-Tacs? They're green."

"Minty fresh. Just how you want it when she gives you that big thank you smooch."

"I thought we were a team."

She took a breath, counted to three, and unhooked her seatbelt. "You're right—the flowers *were* my idea."

"If you don't like roses, I can pull some dead weeds from the side of the road."

She adjusted her glasses, then opened the door, stepping out to retrieve the roses, fluffing them up and rearranging the baby's breath before handing them back through the window.

"$8.99...that *is* a good price," she said. "Forget it. Let's go."

She pecked my cheek and off we drove, neither of us saying much the rest of the way. I found a spot at the back of the hospital lot, the flowers wilting in the sun as we walked toward the entrance. No wonder they were only $8.99.

Amy's daughter Jill waited by the Reception Desk as we entered, her feet fidgeting as she scanned her phone. Seeing us approach, she slipped the phone into her back pocket and hurried over, shaking my hand and thanking me for coming before introducing herself to Kelly in a cheerful but formal voice. Her resemblance to the teenaged Amy still freaked me out, and I wondered how much she knew about Sarah Carpenter, or if the name Mr. Ronan meant anything to her, or even how much Amy had told her about *me*.

"Such beautiful roses!" Jill said. "*Very* romantic!"

Kelly smirked, and we followed Jill down the hall toward Behavioral Health.

"Don't worry about, like, trying to protect me," Jill said. "I know my mom's a nutcase, and she drinks too much wine, and we're always down at Wal-Mart refilling her prescriptions. And she has really bad instincts about men." She looked at me and smiled. "Not you, of course. I mean, she's never said anything bad about you. But other guys...even my Dad... I love her, but Mom's a mess. I've been raised by Blanche DuBois; you know—the character from *Streetcar Named Desire?*"

"I've seen it once or twice."

She stepped back, turning her head momentarily before launching into a Southern drawl.

"I don't want realism. I want magic! Yes, yes, magic!" she said, her voice rising as she turned herself into a sixteen-year-old Jersey Shore Blanche. An orderly in green scrubs, an inked-up guy around my age, passed us in the hall pushing a mop. Jill jumped in front of him, clutching her chest in high drama.

"How about taking a swim, a moonlight swim in the old rock quarry?" she said, still fully Blanche, though the accent started to crack as she spouted lines from the play. "Is anyone sober enough to drive a car? Ha-ha! Best way in the world to stop your head buzzing."

"Head's not buzzing," the orderly said, and hustled away, the mop dragging behind.

Kelly applauded, and Jill bowed, taking the roses from my hand as if she'd just received opening night raves.

"I have it memorized, almost. I can do Stella, too, and even some Stanley."

"It was quite vivid," I told her.

"Thank you, thank you," she said, bowing again, spinning around and landing in a curtsy, blowing us each a kiss before handing back the roses. "I'm an actress—all the time. I'm always in character. There is no real me. That's good, right?"

"Well, you want to be yourself *sometimes*," I said.

"Why? It's better being someone else." Her phone buzzed, and she grabbed it from her pocket, glancing at the screen before texting back. "That's Mom. She's ready for us. Come on, it's this way..."

We followed her down the hall, Jill walking backwards, like a tour guide leading us through a museum. "I don't understand anything about you," she said, "But I don't understand clouds, either, and that doesn't stop me from enjoying their shapes in the sky, or from getting wet whenever it rains."

"Is that from *Streetcar*, too?" Kelly asked.

"No, it's from one of the lesser playwrights," I said.

The lines, of course, were from *my* play, *Confessions of the Midnight Chair*, part of a brief monologue delivered by the protagonist to the character inspired by Amy. It had been almost fifteen years since I'd heard anyone speak those lines. Jill winked at me, scrunching her shoulders and peering left and right, each step hesitant, her face tense, lips in a *Nightmare on Elm Street* grimace. "I think he's...watching us!" she said, her voice hushed as she tip-toed ahead and slipped into the elevator.

"A bit histrionic, don't you think?" Kelly whispered. "I hope her school has a good counselor."

"Aspiring actresses are like that. She's just having fun."

"Hm."

We signed in at the entry desk and waited five minutes before a woman arrived and introduced herself as Lorraine Sandifer, the social worker assigned to Amy's file. She led us into her musty office and we each grabbed a seat, waiting quietly as she skimmed through some papers in a manila folder. In her fifties, she looked exhausted, little black flecks of mascara dotting her cheeks, decaf breath wafting over her desk. She grabbed a pen and peered over her glasses, eyeing the roses as if I'd brought a toaster or a boa constrictor, something totally inappropriate for the moment at hand.

"And you are...?" she asked.

"Donatello Marcino."

"The playwright!" Jill said, as if I were a name someone might recognize.

"Just a family friend. I've known Amy since we were five," I said. "And this is..."

"Kelly Price. I'm here on vacation." She put her hand on my shoulder and squeezed. 'I've known him since he was thirty-seven. We're not sure what we are, but we like each other, at least so far."

Ms. Sandifer flashed us a fake smile and made some notes in the folder.

"Due to HIPPA laws, I'm unable to share information without Ms. Willingham's permission, but her doctor did recommend that she stay another forty-eight hours. She declined to follow our suggestion."

"She needs to get back to work. The Regional Manager's been calling three times a day," Jill said. "Her store is the fourth busiest *Victoria's Secret* in New Jersey. On an average weekend, they sell four hundred panties!"

Ms. Sandifer gave her a look, and Jill sunk back into her chair.

"We understand," I said. "Where do I sign?"

"Excuse me?"

"Amy said I had to sign for her. I need to stay with her for ten days as a condition of her release."

Ms. Sandifer put down her pen, the lines above her eyes curving into troubled arches.

"You must have misunderstood; otherwise she lied to you. Many of our patients can be quite manipulative." She grabbed a plastic water bottle and took three sips. "There are no 'conditional' discharges. We provide a structured out-patient program but it's the patient's responsibility to follow it. You don't need to sign anything, Mr. Marcino. I assumed you were here to drive her home."

Kelly poked my leg and mouthed "I knew it!"

Jill leaned forward, her hands on the desk. "You're still going to release my Mom today, right?"

"We can't hold her here without a court order, and we're not going to pursue that. Except for an incident in Art Therapy yesterday, your mother has done well here."

I remembered the nurse's comment from the other day. "What happened in Art Therapy?"

"She drew some disturbing images, but I really can't discuss it with you."

I wasn't surprised—most likely she'd been drawing Captain Sick again. Growing up, Amy often drew wild images as a release valve. When she got busted for having pot in her locker, she filled three notebooks with vicious caricatures of the principal, the chief of police, and the black-hooded Captain Sick, each of them bearing down on her like vultures eyeing a field mouse.

Jill turned, her voice anxious. "You'll still stay with us, right? We won't be any trouble." She put her hand on my arm, lightly, and flashed those big brown Amy eyes. "Please! Just a few days until Mom feels better..."

"Of course," Kelly said, poking my leg again and mouthing "you're welcome." Jill eased back into her chair.

"I'll go get Ms. Willingham," Ms. Sandifer said, bored with our act. As soon as she left, Jill grabbed my hand.

"I know Mom lied to you, but she was afraid to tell you the real reason. It's that guy who keeps stalking her—your old teacher."

So Jill knew about Mr. Ronan.

"She's being stalked?" Kelly said.

"Yes!"

"Amy is mistaken. Mr. Ronan is *not* stalking her. It's impossible."

"Have you called the police?" Kelly asked.

"My Dad is the police. He doesn't believe her."

"He's right."

"He's an asshole," Jill said.

I couldn't argue Clyde's essential assholery, but if Mr. Ronan had hung himself, he wasn't stalking Amy; that much was certain.

"I've seen him outside our house. He always runs away, but Mom's not lying. I promise," Jill said. "Stay a few days and you'll see."

Through the open door, Ms. Sandifer returned, Amy trailing behind. I braced for a bad reaction to Kelly's presence, but all Amy said, to both of us, was "Thank you for coming," as if we were neighbors who had just stopped by to drop off some mail. In black sweats and the same Property of Jaybird Pizza t-shirt from the day before, she looked exhausted, a folder stuffed with drawing paper sticking out of her bag.

Kelly offered her hand. "It's nice to meet you," she said, sounding like she meant it. Amy nodded but let Kelly's hand dangle. I held the roses stupidly while the women in my life pretended that they weren't checking each other out.

Suddenly my legs felt like sand, and I started yawning, the roses falling from my grip.

"No!" Amy and Kelly yelled, simultaneously, both attuned to the warning signs of my narcolepsy. Kelly grabbed my shoulders and shook them roughly, which sometimes worked, while Amy jabbed me in the stomach with her fist, which never worked but which she enjoyed anyway.

Ms. Sandifer watched closely, considering a court order for all three of us.

"I have narcolepsy," I told her. "They're trying to keep me awake."

I yawned again, but my legs felt fresh, my mind sharp. Whatever it was, it had passed.

"Can we go now?" Jill asked.

"Ms. Willingham, you need to sign the discharge forms."

Sandifer slid some papers across the desk along with a pen. Though her grip seemed unsteady, Amy scratched her signature across the bottom of the form, and three days after her suicide attempt, she was back in the world.

· · · · ·

It was Amy's idea to stop at the beach. On the drive from the hospital she had said little; we relied on the radio to mask the awkward silence, the rental car suddenly too cramped for such a strange quartet. In the rear-view mirror, I saw glimpses of Amy and her daughter whispering like schoolgirls while Kelly, riding shotgun, fidgeted with her sunglasses and stared out the window, awkwardly commenting on the scenery, as if the billboard for Larry's Lobster House were some famous Jersey landmark. Finally, we escaped the car, and Kelly, bless her heart, started chatting with Jill about her Drama Club, the two of them hanging back, Kelly's way of saying, *go ahead, do what you need to do*. With the Memorial Day holiday still a week away, the beach was empty. Overhead a red sea plane buzzed along the coast, pulling a long banner touting thirty-dollar lube jobs at Sam's Automotive. The sun was at its peak and I felt the heat spreading across my shoulders, the crook of my neck already slick, the beginning of an early season burn. I checked on Kelly, who had settled down by the dunes with Jill; she gave me her little "I'm okay" wave, so Amy and I continued toward the ocean, our feet leaving soft trails in the warm, damp sand.

"She stays away from the water," Amy said, glancing back at Jill. "I never taught her to swim.'

The Atlantic stretched forever in front of us, beautiful and deadly. I wondered, as I always did whenever near water: what would a drowned body look like after twenty years? I had googled it once and immediately wished that I hadn't; sea lice can enter the body quickly, causing internal lacerations and the pooling of blood; discoloration of skin; bloating. In saltwater the lips and eyelids are consumed within hours. Maybe it was a blessing that Sarah's body was never found.

We came to a spot ten feet from the shoreline, and Amy sat cross-legged in the sand.

"Are you okay?"

"My brain is soup. They doubled the medication, but it'll level off soon. I'm fine ...I think."

Her halting cadence reminded me of Nancy. I had to ask. "How come you never told me about Uncle Dan's houseguest?"

"What? Oh...that woman. Is that what you mean?"

"Her name is Nancy."

"Weird, huh? But your uncle has always been...I don't know...off-beat."

"You've met her?"

"Once or twice, at the Jaybird."

"Did he mention his relationship with her?"

"He's in a *relationship* with her?"

"Yes. He's not *dating* her, but...there's a relationship."

"I never gave it much thought," she said, yawning, stretching her legs and flexing her toes, and for a flash all other thoughts disappeared except this one: I wanted to kiss those pretty toes.

"So you don't know who she is?" I asked.

"Should I? Is she a *famous* one-armed fat woman?"

I wanted to tell her but felt like a jerk bringing up *my* crap when less than an hour ago she'd been in the hospital. Whatever we were doing, or were about to do, was about Amy's need to heal. There'd be plenty of time later to make it all about me.

"It's nothing," I said. "I was just surprised he was living with someone."

She read my face as only Amy could. "There's something more, isn't there?"

"No—"

"Yes," she said, "but whatever. You'll tell me when you're ready. I'm not exactly losing sleep wondering who your uncle is living with."

We watched the gulls swoop over the shoreline, buzzing the water for snacks.

"I'm sorry I lied," Amy said. "About needing you to sign me out of the hospital. You don't have to stay at the house if you don't want. But maybe you will anyway, at least until...you know ..."

I did—the anniversary of Sarah's disappearance was fast approaching.

"What about Kelly? I can't stay without her."

Amy looked over her shoulder, where Jill and Kelly sat cross-legged by the dunes, deep in conversation.

"Good old California Kelly," Amy said. "She's inconvenient, but I'll try not to be *too* giant a bitch."

I spotted a seashell poking out of the sand and dug it out, holding it up to my ear; sometimes you could hear the ocean echoing through the curves of the shell, but this one had nothing to say. I tossed it back in the sand.

"Jill said there's been a strange man popping up around the house."

"Before you say it's not him..."

"It's not him."

"Say what you want about *my* mental state, but my daughter is not delusional."

"I didn't say that. Maybe there *is* a man stalking your house. It's just not...."

"Okay, Scooby-Do, then who is it?"

"Maybe it's some horny high school kid chasing after your daughter."

"No," she said. "Stay a few days. You'll see. If it's not him..."

"It won't be."

"Fine. If I'm wrong...I'll marry you."

"That's the medication talking."

"No, it's not...when I was in the ER getting my stomach pumped, I realized that I should have married you the first time you asked. I could have saved myself a lot of trouble."

She brushed back her hair, pushing the bangs away from her forehead, her feet pressing into the sand as her hand touched my shoulder for balance. I didn't believe her—it was just chatter—but my mind cherished it anyway: I pictured Amy on a gurney with a tube shoved down her throat fighting back nausea and thinking of *me.*

"Maybe we shouldn't be talking about this," I said.

"Right—the California girl awaits. So what *should* we talk about, Duckster? Here we are at the beach, Amy and Donatello returning to the scene of the crime." Her voice dropped as she gazed toward the water. "Should we talk about dead four-year-girls instead?"

I almost said, "Yes." But I needed to be careful.

Amy's body suddenly tensed, and she jumped to her feet.

"What *is* that?" she said, and started walking toward the ocean, pointing toward something dark bobbing in the water fifty yards from the shoreline.

I squinted but couldn't see much, just a small dark patch on the surface which, from a distance, could have been anything. When we were kids half the state's beaches had closed one year because of medical waste washing up on the shore, but nothing like that had happened in decades. Amy's dark spot, from a distance, looked more like some trick of shadow and sun than anything *real.*

"It's nothing," I said. "It's a shadow, or a jellyfish. It's nothing."

"You're blind. It's not a jellyfish. You never see anything," she said, and she took three steps into the surf.

"Amy, it's nothing."

She waded further, to her ankles, to her knees, her pants getting soaked as the water pooled around her. I followed her up to the shoreline and started calling her back. Amy had never been a strong swimmer; neither was I. The dark spot was at least twenty-five yards deeper than you were legally allowed.

"It's not what you think," I yelled, but she kept moving, her arms slapping the water as she pushed further out. A sudden wave lifted her, propelling her back, her hair drenched as the spray splashed over her face.

A second wave broke, and suddenly her head bobbed underwater.

At that moment I should have gone after her, but instead I just watched, as if, even wide awake, I was still sleeping. The wave subsided and Amy reappeared, her t-shirt soaked, her arms held high as she jumped back toward the surf, the next wave already upon her. Again she went under, emerging seconds later, hell-bent on forward progress, plunging into the surf in weak, struggling breast strokes.

A sick feeling surged in my gut.

She's going to drown herself in front of me, I thought, her ultimate penance for Sarah's death; this was retribution; this was a test, and I stood watching from the beach, immobile as a totem pole, knowing I was failing as another wave, and another, crashed up and over her slight frame.

Suddenly Kelly ran past me, diving into the ocean and swimming toward Amy. Jill hurried beside me, grabbing my arm.

"What's happening? She *never* goes in the water," Jill said.

Kelly, that strong California swimmer, quickly caught up and reached out for Amy, whose arms flailed and slapped at the water as she bobbed against the angry waves. I feared she might resist, might prefer drowning to being rescued by my new girlfriend, or even worse, try to take Kelly down with her, a murder-suicide, but Kelly, raised by a military father who made sure his daughter would always survive, handled Amy with ease, hooking her arm around Amy's shoulder and leaning back, the water balancing their weight as they floated on the steady up and down of the tide.

The waves subsided, and Kelly slowly paddled the two of them back to the shoreline.

Jill rushed to greet them, and I stood transfixed as Kelly guided Amy back to the beach, their feet finally reaching sand, their street clothes soaked, me standing ghost-like as the two women I loved walked out of the sea.

-10-

According to Kelly, who'd worked as a lifeguard two summers during high school, pulling Amy out of the ocean had been no big deal, but I could tell the episode had shaken her—not the rescue part, but the plunge itself. Why had Amy, loaded on meds, rushed into the water when she wasn't a good swimmer?

"It doesn't make sense," Kelly said. "I think she wanted your attention, and your sympathy, in case her 'suicide attempt' wasn't enough."

"That's pretty cynical."

"She's manipulating you. All this drama ...she's playing you."

"I'm not stupid," I said, although when it came to Amy I probably was.

"We'll see," Kelly said. "But whatever's going on, it's messed up."

While Amy slept and Kelly took Jill on a grocery run, I settled on the front porch to do some reading, barely finishing a page before Clyde arrived, the heavy tires of his cruiser scraping the curb as he pulled into the driveway. He killed the engine and opened the door, his big frame unfolding like a picnic umbrella reaching its full height. I watched him strut across the walkway, the local cop in full performance mode, shoulders pushed back, his hand cupping the knob of his nightstick, the dark sunglasses like a prop from some Seventies TV cop show, not the cool Seventies of *The Rockford Files* but the more fascist end like *S.W.A.T.* or *CHIPS*.

"Where's your girlfriend?" he asked.

"At the grocery store with your daughter. If you mean Amy, she's taking a nap."

"Two women...nice little set-up you have here."

He sat down in the other rocking chair and smirked.

"Is there a reason for this lovely visit?"

"My child support keeps the mortgage on this house paid," he said. "I'm entitled."

He grabbed the book from my hand, turned it upside down, and handed it back.

"Very clever," I said.

Two teenage girls in shorts and bikini tops rode their bikes past the house. Clyde's eyes took them in, spit them out. He pulled off his sunglasses and slid them into his pocket.

"I've been thinking...me and a buddy on the force, we've got this idea," he said. "A TV show about cops at the Jersey Shore. You know anything about getting a show on TV?"

After the minor success of *Midnight Chair* my agent warned me that everyone I knew, no exceptions, would pitch an idea for a movie, a play, or a TV show. He was mostly right.

"I never worked much in TV," I said. When I first moved to California, I'd had a staff job on a sitcom that lasted six episodes. That was it. "My connections are mostly in theater and a few in film. It's been a while."

Even that was an exaggeration. It had been *forever*. My current top connection was a cardboard guy who hooked me up with pizza boxes at a 20% markdown.

"My buddy, he wrote something up, like a pilot," Clyde said. "Maybe you could look at it and, you know, make sure the commas are in the right places."

"Absolutely; commas can make or break a script." I should have told him to fuck off, but I needed information. "Sure, Clyde, I'd be happy to read it."

"I'll drop it off later," he said, the absence of a "thank you" impossible to miss.

I put down the book. "Jill told us there's a guy stalking the house."

"No, she's just playing into her mother's delusions. There's no stalker. I told you: Ronan is dead."

"What if it's someone else?"

"It's bullshit. Look, I drive up and down this block every day. This is my town. If some asshole was stalking them, I'd know about it."

"You don't believe your own daughter?"

"She'll say whatever her mother wants to hear." A mosquito buzzed his face, and Clyde swatted it away. "You really are a gullible shit for brains. How the hell did you ever write a Broadway play?"

It was *off-*Broadway, but I didn't correct him.

"You're an arsonist," I said. Had we still been in high school he would have punched me clean, and for a moment I sensed him thinking about it. "You burned down Mr. Ronan's house. That's a felony, Mister Po-lice Man."

He leaned back in the chair and pulled out a cigarette, which he popped between his lips but didn't light.

"You're wrong, but let's say you're not," he said. "The statute of limitations is five years. Ancient history, bub."

The unlit cigarette dangled from his lips. The window of Amy's second-floor bedroom, open to catch the afternoon breeze, was ten feet above us. I kept my voice low.

"You knew Mr. Ronan had been cleared. Even back then you thought Amy was a nut. Why'd you do it?"

"I didn't," he said, "but I'll play along, for shits and giggles. Why did I do it? Simple: she gave me a blow job. Your precious Amy took my dick into her hot little mouth and it was quid pro quo. I was eighteen. I would have burned down St. Patrick's Cathedral for a blow job. Isn't that obvious, shit for brains?"

He wanted a reaction, but I held my best poker face.

"Burning it down—*that* was a mistake," Clyde said. "But playing along with your little fantasy, all we wanted was to scare the son of a bitch. The fire got out of control. There was no *intent* to endanger anyone. Ronan wasn't home. We *knew* that. And there were other reasons, too, beside the blow job—not that I'm admitting anything. But if I did set that fire, I had a good reason. I'm a cop's son—we're raised to *serve* and *protect*. Ronan got what he deserved."

"Sarah Carpenter drowned. He had nothing to do with it."

"Sarah Carpenter's disappearance is not the only bad thing that ever happened in this town," Clyde said. "You think you know everything, but you don't know jack, Donnie Boy. Even about your precious Amy. You think you're so close? I was *married* to her. We have a child together. Maybe she and I don't get along anymore, but we've shared things you can't even imagine."

The rental car arrived in front of the house, Kelly and Jill back from the store; Clyde bit down on the cigarette as he stood, reaching for his sunglasses like he was auditioning for the remake of *Cool Hand Luke*. Freed from his weight, the chair rocked gently back and forth.

"Ask her about Art Therapy," Clyde said. "Look, I was an asshole to you in high school. I get that—I was an asshole to everybody. So you don't like me, and that's okay since I don't like you much, either. But I'm not the bad guy here. I never was."

He took a deep breath and stepped off the porch.

"What happened in Art Therapy?" I said. "If you know something, and you obviously do, why not just tell me?"

"It's not for me to tell—it's her choice," he said. "I'm only here to serve and protect." He eyed his daughter in the rental car before turning back with his signature smirk. "I'll drop off that script later tonight. Maybe you can help spruce it up. My buddy, he's a talented guy. It'd be pretty damn funny if we all got rich together." He gave me the finger and headed for the cruiser. "Go ahead. Ask your precious Amy about her drawings."

Kelly walked up the driveway, arms wrapped around two groceries bags, while Jill stayed in the car, head down, ignoring her father's presence. Clyde nodded, giving Kelly the standard local cop "afternoon, ma'am" as he strutted past her, turning to gawk at her ass before climbing back into his cruiser.

I grabbed one of the grocery bags as Kelly glanced back at Clyde.

"Everything okay?"

"He's leaving, so now it is."

"Jill *really* doesn't like him. When she spotted his car, she wouldn't even look up."

"Smart girl."

"God knows what her mother says about the guy. But something's up with her. She spent half the time speaking with a French accent. It was weird."

"Actresses are like that."

"She performed a monologue at the deli counter. I think it was from *The Crucible.* She kept talking about dancing naked in the woods with the Devil. The poor guy at the meat slicer... while she's going on and on about Tituba and howling frogs, he kept asking what kind of turkey breast we wanted. I doubt that's how Meryl Streep got started."

In the kitchen we unpacked the groceries, but after Clyde's visit it was tough to stay focused. The bastard had accomplished his mission. All I could think was: *what had happened in Art Therapy?*

· · · · ·

That night we stopped at the Jaybird, the four of us squeezing into a booth by the window while Uncle Dan started us with some garlic knots and Diet Cokes loaded with ice. Amy had brought a bottle of wine from home, a cheap Chianti with a kangaroo on the label, and after Uncle Dan popped the cork, she half-filled our paper cups, even her daughter's, pouring slowly, her hand still weak from the meds and the not-quite-drowning earlier that morning.

"I know what you're thinking, Mr. Straight Edge," Amy said, re-corking the bottle. "But it's only one glass—a *half*-glass. It's good for the circulatory system. I'm teaching my daughter to drink responsibly."

"I don't really *like* wine," Jill said. "But that buzzed feeling can be kind of cool."

"It's only cool in *moderation*," Amy said. She raised her cup and said, "Salud, chindon!" before downing her Chianti in one long, steady sip. Jill hesitated, glancing at Kelly and me before raising her cup.

"Cheers!" Kelly said, joining them. Only my wine sat untouched, my old reflex to remain sober whenever Amy drank.

Behind the counter some guy named Cliff worked with Uncle Dan while another guy, Jorge, holed up in back; a college girl, Tina, watched the register and made the salads. It was odd watching strangers working at the Jaybird, and for the first time in days I thought about my own pizzeria back in California. We had a few good workers who backed me up, and things could run smoothly without me, but the sad truth was that I didn't give a damn either way. If I never stepped through the door of Nguyen Brothers Pizza again, I wouldn't miss it one beat. Other than my weekly cut of the receipts, I had no real connection to the place, unlike the Jaybird, which, despite the long absence, I still considered mine.

Make that *ours*—it was impossible to think of the place without thinking of Uncle Dan. As I watched him and his team hustling behind the counter in that synchronized, almost psychic way one moves around a kitchen, I felt something akin to jealousy, and if Kelly hadn't been blocking me, I might have slipped out of the booth, grabbed my old apron, and joined the dance.

"Why is this place called The Jaybird, anyway?" Kelly asked. "It's an odd name for a pizzeria."

"It's a secret," Amy said. "We've been asking him forever. He won't even tell Donnie."

"I've bugged him about it for years," I said. "It's got something to do with Vietnam, but other than that ..."

"No, it's a woman, I'll bet anything," Amy said. "Jay-Bird, as in J, the letter, and bird, the British term for a chick. Jennifer, Jane, Jessica, maybe Joanne...could be anything, but it's definitely a reference to a woman, the Pizza Man's grand, unrequited love."

"No, it's Vietnam ..."

"Come on, why else would he never date, or show any interest ...he's pining for a lost love. Your uncle is one of the great romantics of our time."

"We should set him up," Jill said. "He's cute for an old guy. We'll get his picture and put him on Silver Singles."

"Uncle Dan doesn't do apps," I said. "He still has the same flip phone he got free with his AARP renewal. And I think he's happy as is."

"That's because you're one of the great romantics, too," Amy said. She poured more wine and looked at Kelly. "Despite the numerous and obvious flaws, he's a keeper. You'd be wise to hang on to him."

"*You* never did," Jill said.

"And if you ever have kids, prepare for smart-ass comments during those oh-so lovely teen years."

Beneath the table, Kelly took my hand. "My Dad is a colonel in the Marines, and let's just say you don't mouth off to a colonel. He never touched us, but he had a way of making you feel you should give him fifty push-ups just for *thinking* something fresh."

"He would have court-martialed my ass before I hit thirteen," Amy said.

"He's a good Dad. My older brothers had it harder than me."

"A colonel's daughter. Good luck, Donnie," Amy said. "Let's hope she's looking for the opposite of dear old dad."

"She's trying to say I'm the draft dodger type," I said.

"I was thinking more of a 4-F. That's the term for physical rejects, right? If Donnie had been at D-Day, he would have fallen asleep on the beach."

"I like him just the way he is," Kelly said, draping her arm across my shoulder and kissing my cheek. I kissed her back, which felt weird in front of Amy, who drank her wine and looked toward the exit, her fingers tapping the table.

"Maybe you should sketch my uncle sometime," I said, and turned to Jill. "Your mom would sit here for hours doing these funny sketches of the different customers. It was a big part of who she was." I gave them a brief run-down, tried to capture how Amy, in a more private way, had been just as crazy about her art as I'd been about my plays. Though her eyes shot me the occasional *look*, she seemed pleased. "I hope you're still drawing."

"You know that I'm not. I'm an exhausted single mom who works at *Victoria's Secret*—bras, panties, and *seductively silky sleepwear.*" The last part came in that fake British accent from the commercials. "I'm not the little artiste you remember. I guess we both never realized our potential."

"You could always pick up a pencil again."

"True. I know a great place I could shove it."

"At the hospital, it looked like you had a bunch of drawings. Art therapy?"

"Something like that,' she said, looking away.

"I'll bet they're great. I'd love to see them."

"Be careful what you wish for," she said, her voice on edge, and Jill, sensing the change in her mother's mood, leaned across the table.

"Hey, guess what? A bunch of people are planning to occupy the beach next week, right before Memorial Day, as a protest. They're going to set up tents and live there for the summer. It's being organized by some activists in New York, people who were at Occupy Wall Street. Real life radicals!"

"What are they protesting?" Kelly asked.

"Everything: climate change, racism, patriarchy...how the whole country is basically shit."

"Watch your language," Amy said.

"A few of the kids from the drama club are thinking of joining. We'll put on plays and draw crowds and be part of a *community*. Ms. Vaughn said there's a tradition of activist theater. We read this play called *Awake and Sing* by Eugene O'Neill..."

"Clifford Odets," I said. "He wrote *Awake and Sing*, not O'Neill."

"Oh yeah—Cliff; Ms. Vaughn said most people think the theater means *The Lion King* and *Mamma Mia*, but there's a whole tradition of social commentary."

"I liked *The Lion King*," Amy said, almost like a dare. She knew I hated musicals.

"It's Ms. Vaughn's first year at the school. She's opening my eyes!"

"You're better off keeping them closed," Amy said, reaching for the wine.

"I've never seen *The Lion King*. I've heard it's fantastic," Kelly said. "Before we leave, Donnie, I hope you're taking me to a play."

"The other kids are ready to do it," Jill said. "It's *our* beach, not theirs. Ms. Vaughn said she would join us, but she doesn't have tenure yet and the principal has a *small mind*. She can't risk her job because her student loans are like Godzilla."

"She sounds like an inspiring teacher," Kelly said.

"She's the best."

Her enthusiasm made me think of Mr. Ronan, who had charged my high school brain the same way Ms. Vaughn inspired Jill.

"She mentioned *your* play," Jill told me. "She said that you were the first and only student at West Ocean to write a play staged by the Drama Club. Your name was an extra credit question on our first quiz. Donatello Marcino—I got three extra points!"

Kelly kicked my leg. "Wow—you're worth three points!"

"Back in September Ms. Vaughn challenged us to write a play, but no one did. We're actors and directors, I think. At least I am."

Amy grabbed a napkin from the dispenser and began shredding it, one of her old nervous habits. As kids we'd hang out at the Jaybird for hours, and at the end of the night the table would be littered with white napkin shards, like a bed of snow.

"This occupy the beach thing will never work. Your father will arrest them the minute they hit the sand. I don't want you anywhere near it."

"He can't keep us down forever!" Jill said. "The world is changing!"

"Maybe this is the summer you finally visit your grandparents in the Poconos."

"The Poconos? That's child abuse. As soon as I'm eighteen, I'm moving to New York." She turned to me for validation. "That's what you did, right?"

"Guess again. He's a college boy," Amy said. "He has a degree from NYU. Dean's list and everything." Her eyes gave me a nudge. "Tell her how important it is *not* to run away to New York."

"A good theater program can help you immensely."

"Maybe Jill can intern on your new play," Kelly said.

Jill bounced in her seat, beaming. "That would be...amazing. Thank you!" She reached over the table and grabbed my hand. "Do you think my friend Maddie could intern, too?

Uncle Dan came by and set down a large cheese pizza.

"You wrote a new play?" Amy said.

"What's that?" Uncle Dan said, the pepper grinder tucked under his arm. "There's a new play?" He reached over and patted my shoulder. "I knew you weren't finished. Sometimes the dough just needs extra time in the oven. I'm proud of you for not quitting."

"Has it been cast yet? Who's in it?" Jill said. "Are there any young female roles? I'll audition if you want, but really, I'm perfect for it!"

"There's no new play yet. Yes, I wrote a *draft* ..."

"I've read it," Kelly said. "It's wonderful."

"It's a work in progress ..."

"What's the title?" Jill asked.

"*The Revolving Heart*," Kelly said.

"Oh God, it's not about us, is it?" Amy asked.

"Maybe ..." Kelly said, turning toward me.

"No," I said, maybe too quickly. "It's fiction. I made it all up. Why do people always think works of art are about real people?"

"Wait 'till I tell Ms. Vaughn!" Jill said. "Mister DeMille, I'm ready for my close-up. That's a line from ..."

"He knows where it's from," Amy said. "He knows where every line's from."

It felt weird, (weird *good,* but weird nonetheless) to discuss *The Revolving Heart* as if I were still an active playwright. *Maybe I should send it out to a few old theater friends for feedback,* I thought.

Jill kept babbling about try-outs and auditions, but all the talk about the play left me anxious, so I asked Amy about her parents, a subject guaranteed to launch a rant, and as expected, she launched into a lengthy bill of grievances, particularly about her mother, who she had never forgiven for not believing her accusations about Mr. Ronan.

Kelly grabbed a second slice and smiled politely, but I could tell she had tuned out Amy's soliloquy. She was probably thinking about her cats back home, maybe wondering what the hell she was doing in a pizzeria in New Jersey, wondering what the hell she was doing with *me.*

At that moment I felt alone, a ridiculous feeling considering that the people I loved most in the world were all within twenty-five feet of me. I knew these thoughts would pass—I didn't *always* moon over relationships like a thirteen-year-old—but suddenly, as if reading my mind and hoping to reassure me, Kelly caressed the side of my leg with her foot, her bare toes sneaking from my ankle to my shin, squiggling beneath my pants leg, poking and tickling. The smooth skin of her instep stroked my calf, and it was mission accomplished: I didn't feel alone anymore.

But something was wrong.

Kelly had worn sneakers, and unless her foot could do a total 360°, no way could her toes be so close against my leg. So it had to be Amy.

Just like old times, Amy and I squeezed inside a booth at the Jaybird playing footsie under the table, gobbling down slices of Uncle Dan's finest. But when I peeked under the table I found otherwise—it wasn't Amy, it was *Jill* who was playing footsie with me, Amy's sixteen-year-old daughter smiling across the table sucking Diet Coke through a bent straw, her pink toes stroking my overheated skin.

I looked up, and Jill winked at me, her eyes—*Amy's* eyes—drawing me in, like they always had, and all I could think was, *this is bad.*

"What's going on down there?" Amy asked, looking at Kelly and me. "Are Mr. and Mrs. California getting frisky?"

"It's nothing," Jill said. "It's just me. I had an itch."

"I told you to use moisturizer," Amy said. "Why do I buy that twenty-dollar lotion if you never use it?"

She grabbed the wine and emptied the bottle as Kelly slid closer, her hip nudging my side while Jill slurped the rest of her soda, the bent straw encircled by her plush, puckered lips.

Yes, I thought, *this is bad.*

.   .   .   .   .

"Move over, Donnie. It's my turn now."

Kelly pulled back the curtain and stepped into the shower with her strong, slinky legs, the hot water pinging my skin as she joined me under the spray, her lips tracing a lingering trail from my shoulder to my ear.

I breathed in her scent, lavender and honey. "Maybe we shouldn't ..."

"Why? Because we might get caught?" She held her face in exaggerated horror, Janet Leigh in the *Psycho* shower. "Oh no, they're *naked!* They might have *sex!* What if Amy finds out? Will she spank us?"

She slapped my butt, then bit my shoulder before turning her face toward the water. Downstairs Amy and Jill were watching TV, but the house was small, a Cape Cod on a corner lot with thin, Home Depot walls.

"Did you lock the door?"

"No, I kept it open and scattered breadcrumbs so your girlfriend can find us."

"Stop calling her that, please."

"Really, Donnie? We're in the shower, naked, inches apart, and you want to discuss *terminology?*"

The water sluiced over our skin, her purple toenails sparkling over the tub's white surface. "As least *part* of you is glad I'm here," she said, grabbing my already-hard cock and stroking it roughly as she nibbled my chest. I kissed her neck but, sensing my hesitation, she butted my chest with her forehead and stepped on my foot.

"Hey, this is my *vacation,* remember? I'm unemployed and depressed, and my partner would rather worry about his ex-girlfriend than *be* with me."

"You're depressed?"

"Well, *yeah,*" she said. "If I wasn't, would I be here? I rarely cast myself as the third wheel."

"You don't act depressed."

"Military brats wear a brave face, no matter what."

She kissed my stomach, her teeth leaving little bite marks up and down my skin, her hand sliding between my legs, caressing my thigh.

"You're not a third wheel."

"Spare tire?" She squeezed the extra flesh around my sides. "Stop talking, please."

She opened her legs and pulled me toward her as my body tensed. All those years growing up, *not* having sex with Amy, had left me permanently doubtful about my sexual abilities, something, as a man, you never wanted to admit to anyone, especially yourself.

"I want you inside me," Kelly said, and I kissed her wet mouth, closing my eyes as I entered her, letting my body take over even as my thoughts, in some dumb corner office of my brain, calculated the odds of Amy knocking on the door, the house having only one bathroom, and to whom exactly was I being unfaithful?

We moved against each other in sweet friction; I slipped out, slipped back in, shower sex, as always, a mechanical *challenge*, everything so slippery and wet.

"Slow," Kelly whispered, her face on the cusp of letting go, and I pushed deeper, my hands braced against the shower wall, Kelly's hips rocking in a sweet back and forth, her breaths growing shorter while my own breaths held back, wanting to last forever even as every nerve cell turned hair trigger. I lost balance and slipped out, but Kelly pulled me back; she began to tremble, her thighs squeezing together as she made her sexy little Kelly noises, our hearts pounding, our hips locked in this up and down rhythm, everything perfect—until we heard Amy scream.

And scream again—this time louder and more frantic, the sound cutting through the ceiling, through the hiss of the shower—and then the crack of a single gunshot ripped through the house.

We pulled apart and my body let go, ejaculating onto Kelly's thighs in a hopeless spasm as I stumbled back, my ass crashing into the faucet.

Semen dribbled down her leg as we froze, waiting for another shot. I pictured all kinds of horror, Amy dead on the floor, a bullet through her head, a wild-eyed gunman heading up the stairs to murder us next.

Breathing hard, I leaned against the shower wall, Kelly nestled beside me.

"Call the police," she whispered. "My cell is on the bed. Don't go downstairs."

"Stay here." I pulled back the shower curtain and reached for my clothes, my eyes wet and blurry as Kelly grabbed her towel.

"Donnie, be careful."

"Just stay here until I'm back, okay?"

I was too shocked to be frightened, but I knew *scared shitless* would soon arrive; I threw on my clothes and ran downstairs, where Amy stood in the living room pointing a revolver, her legs spread in a firing range stance, arms raised to eye level, the picture window a giant hole where the glass used to be.

On the floor behind the couch Jill clutched a pillow, knees drawn to her chest, a weird smell hanging over the room—gunpowder, I assumed, though it might have been burnt popcorn for all I knew. My left shoulder twitched, still gun shy after all these years.

"It was him," Amy said. "He was sneaking around outside, trying to peek in..."

"Amy..."

"Don't fucking *Amy* me, Duck. It was him."

From the floor, Jill nodded. "There was somebody out there—*really!*"

"Put the gun down, Amy," I said. "Jesus Christ, you can't just shoot at people. Maybe it was a neighbor looking for a lost cat."

"Our neighbor doesn't have a cat."

"Just put the goddamn gun down."

Across the street, the house lights blazed, the neighbors already speed dialing the police, grabbing their clothes and combing their hair in case the local TV news showed up with cameras. Amy lowered her arms but held onto the gun.

"Wait here," I said, and rushed outside, hoping there wouldn't be a dead body flat against the lawn. The night air felt cold against my still wet skin, and I could see right away that no one was there, except for a neighbor across the street, a middle-aged blob who stood on his porch in nothing but boxer shorts, a baseball bat cocked in his arms, hoping to smash some intruder ass.

"Hey, it's okay. Sorry about the noise," I said, hoping he and his Louisville Slugger wouldn't rush over thinking *I* was the bad guy. I moved carefully, my bare feet scratching the rough pavement, but there was no sign of anyone. Suddenly my toe brushed something hot—as my foot jerked back, I saw a cigarette butt lodged in a serpentine crack in the asphalt. I picked it up, its tip still smoldering. No one in the house smoked; any of Clyde's discarded butts would have long cooled. So Amy hadn't imagined it. Someone *had* been outside the window.

I snubbed out the cigarette and set it on the porch. Maybe it was evidence, maybe not, the cops unlikely to run a DNA test for a broken window, but what did I know? I headed for the front door just as Clyde arrived with his partner, their cruiser screeching into the driveway like vintage Starsky and Hutch.

"What the hell?" Clyde said, climbing out of the passenger side, a Starbucks cup in hand. He wore jeans and an old T-shirt, a Boston Red Sox cap at half-tilt, unlike his partner, dressed for business in his policeman blues.

"We received a call on a disturbance at this address," the partner said. He was young, early twenties, his hair buzzed, his chest thick and intimidating. He looked as if he head-butted steel garbage cans for fun.

"I told you, I've got this," Clyde said. The partner hung back by the cruiser as Clyde walked up the driveway, sipping his coffee and checking out the shattered window.

"Jesus. You should have left her in the hospital, Donnie Boy." He held up his phone and grabbed a few pictures of the damage. "My partner recognized the address and called; otherwise she'd be in one big pile of shit right now. You can bet your ass that gun is unregistered. She has no idea how much she owes me." He circled the porch, running his hand along the window frame. "I'll have Mike write it up; he'll say some teenage scumbag threw a rock. The insurance company won't even come out to investigate; they'll just cut the check and be done with it." He finished the coffee and handed me the empty cup. "But I want that goddamn gun. I'm not leaving here without it."

For once I agreed with him.

"Did she say it was Ronan?"

"Yes."

"She's like a dog with a bone." His heavy finger poked my chest. "Stay here. I don't want you screwing things up." He waved for his partner. "Mike, this is Marcino, the guy I told you about."

Officer Mike reached into the cruiser and pulled out a big envelope as Clyde climbed the porch and entered the house. I thought about following, but maybe he was right. When it came to her gun, Amy had always ignored me. Maybe Clyde and his badge would have better luck.

I took a breath, the adrenaline finally subsiding as Officer Mike dropped his keys into his pocket and shook my hand. In his other hand was a manila envelope. "Sergeant Clyde said you might help with my pilot."

"Pilot?" Then I remembered—he and Clyde had a *project*.

"N.J.B.P." he said. "New Jersey Beach Patrol."

He handed me the envelope tentatively, like a student afraid to let go of a final exam in case the answers were wrong.

"I'll read it in the morning," I said. "But full disclosure: I'm not in the business anymore."

"I know; Sarge told me all about it. We ride patrol together...it can get kind of boring, all that down time. I've heard every story of his at least twice. But he said you were talented, the only good thing to ever come out of this town."

"He said that?"

"He keeps a copy of your play in the cruiser. When it's slow, sometimes he and I read it out loud, you know, like a rehearsal."

"You're putting me on, right?"

"No, sir," Mike said.

I imagined Clyde and his partner parked in a Duncan Donuts lot, sipping coffee, crunching jelly donuts, and trading lines from my one good play. It may have been the weirdest thought I'd ever had.

From the house, I heard Amy giving Clyde all kinds of hell, and I hoped Kelly had stayed upstairs, out of the mix. Jill's voice popped in and out, part of the fray; Officer Mike perked up as soon as he heard her.

"She's beautiful, isn't she?" he said. "I'm sure Jesus will forgive her."

"Jill? Forgive her for what?"

"We don't talk about it," he said. "But I pray for her."

Across the street, the boxer shorts guy put down his baseball bat but kept watching, probably hoping I'd get cuffed and slammed against the cruiser. I looked back at Amy's house, the front window a gaping hole, so much like the window I'd busted that time Amy had almost burned down the Carpenter house. Officer Mike turned toward the porch as Clyde emerged from the front door, Amy's pistol flipped upside down in his grip.

"Still dangerous, but at least not armed," Clyde said.

"I'm surprised she let you take it."

"You just need to handle women the right way, Donnie Boy." He slapped my back like we were old pals. "She'll be quiet for a while."

Clyde nodded toward his partner, and they headed back to the cruiser. "Patch up that window," he said, "and read that pilot script. We'll be back tomorrow night to pick it up."

They folded their big frames back into the car, rolled out of the driveway, and drove off. I walked toward the house, that troubling cigarette still where I'd left it. Back inside, Amy seemed to have calmed down. She stood by the window with a broom, sweeping up shards of glass while Jill waited in the corner with a hand vac.

"I'm glad you gave him the gun," I said. "Maybe something *is* going on, but a gun always makes it worse."

"Okay, Mister Hollywood liberal. Did your California girlfriend make you say that?"

"No, my left shoulder did."

"It wasn't worth fighting over," Amy said. "I've still got a .22 upstairs under the mattress. And maybe a few more trick or treats ..."

"Mom's not imagining things," Jill said, her voice unsteady.

"I believe you," I told her, though I kept mute about the cigarette. "It's not who you think it is, but even if it *was* Mr. Ronan, you can't just shoot him. What if it was the paperboy?"

"There hasn't been a paperboy on this block for five years," Amy said. 'It's not 1995. Nobody gets 'the paper' anymore."

"Maybe they should." Suddenly exhausted, I headed for the stairs, eager to check on Kelly. "We'll talk about this in the morning. I'm going to bed."

"What about the window?" Amy said. "Shouldn't we board it up or something?"

"Do I look like a handyman?"

"Put on a pair of overalls and yeah...that would be a good look for you, Duck." She stepped around a pile of shards, her bare feet tiptoeing away from the glass. "Anybody could come through this window. You've got two women and a teenage girl here. Do you know how many sexual predators are out there? Do you really want the lovely Kelly sleeping in an unsafe house?"

"There are five motels within a mile of here. We can always get a room..."

"But you won't," Amy said. "You're not going to leave my daughter alone after everything that happened. You promised: whenever you need me, I'll be there for you. Remember?"

"Read the contract. 'There' doesn't include basic carpentry."

Jill stepped between us.

"I'll do it. Jesus, Mom...he's an artist, not a contractor. If Tennessee Williams was sleeping over, would you assign him *chores?*"

"Maybe. Mr. Marcino *wants* to help us. It's the reason that he's here. It gives his sad little life meaning."

"*Jesus*, Mom!"

"It's fine," I said. "Whatever. I'll do it."

Amy smiled, just like all those years back whenever her mother would catch me doing her homework and Amy would feign innocence, as if I'd somehow gotten her drunk until she turned over her notebook and let me finish her social studies. Mrs. Willingham never bought it, and usually kicked me out, but I'd always finish the assignment anyway, handing it over the next morning at the bus stop.

"There should be some two by fours in the basement," Amy said. "And my Dad's old toolbox."

"Fine. But all I can promise is a shoddy job."

"I expect nothing less," she said. "And I'm sorry I interrupted your little shower sex."

I blushed. "We weren't..."

"No worries. I think it's beautiful. But please, can you spray things down with Mr. Clean before you go to bed?"

Jill threw up her arms. "Mom!"

"Don't *Mom* me. If I fucked some guy in the shower at *his* house, I'd do a thorough wipe down. I'd even pick the little hairs out of the drain."

"I am *so* sorry," Jill said. "She's under a lot of stress. If you cast me in your play, she'll never come to rehearsal, I promise."

"It's been a long day..." I said, and pecked Amy's cheek. "Tomorrow we need to talk."

"Uh-oh, Amy Willingham, report to the principal's office." She dropped her voice as if speaking through an intercom. "Amy Willingham, report to the principal's office."

She started gigging, and I wondered if she was still drunk or just riding the wave of her breakdown. Because she looked like the old Amy and mouthed off like the old Amy, it was easy to forget that she'd tried to kill herself. I watched her standing in the corner with her broom laughing into her hands, and though it was hard not to burn at all her digs, no one was looking after her, except me. I had made a promise.

"I'll get started in a minute."

Upstairs Kelly sat cross-legged on the bed, dressed in an old nightshirt, her iPad balanced on her lap. I gave her a quick rundown and assured her everything was fine; she nodded but didn't say a word, and when I finished, she handed me the iPad. On the screen was the website for the Beach House Inn, a bed-and-breakfast right on the ocean, the most expensive place in Holman Beach.

"They have one room available: the Presidential suite," she said. "I reserved it online. We can check in tomorrow at noon."

She grabbed the iPad and clicked on a photo of the suite: a four-poster bed, a balcony overlooking the ocean, vases filled with roses on both nightstands, a private bath with a Jacuzzi; tea and scones on the wraparound porch at 4:00 PM...only three-hundred and fifty bucks per night off-season.

"It's too late to go anywhere now, so I'll sleep here tonight, but that's it," she said. "I'm not staying someplace where there's a gun in the house. I have a bad feeling about this ...whatever this is."

"Clyde took the gun from her," I said. "I'm pretty sure we're safe."

"Pretty sure doesn't cut it."

What could I say without it meaning *I love Amy more than I love you?*

"If you want me to go home, I will," Kelly said. "I understand that you have...unfinished business here, with her."

"I don't want you to leave," I said. Equally true: I didn't want to leave Amy's house. No matter how much trouble she could be, the proximity felt right. *The revolving heart*, I thought. Even if the play itself was crap, I was onto something with the title.

I leaned over the bed and kissed Kelly's beautiful mouth. "I'm anticipating a happy ending."

"Good luck with that," she said, but still kissed me back.

I grabbed my sneakers, laced up, and headed downstairs, but as I passed Amy's bedroom, the door wide open, I spotted the manila folder from the hospital, the drawings from Art Therapy.

Clyde's words echoed in my head. *Ask her what happened in Art Therapy.* I assumed she had drawn something troubling, perhaps an image of Sarah Carpenter drowning or even worse, Sarah's corpse being mauled by Captain Sick. I needed to see what was in that folder—it felt important that I know—yet my body froze by the mouth of the door. I stood there as if already asleep, stepping neither back nor forward, my eyes on the folder but not yet ready to see, and I felt relieved, even saved, when Amy started calling from downstairs. ("Hurry up, Donnie! The bugs are getting in!") I could always sneak a look at those drawings in the morning, I assured myself, or even the day after that. *There's no hurry*, I thought, procrastination a useful character flaw against all those sticky things I hoped to avoid.

-II-

It was Amy's first day back at Victoria's Secret and I had agreed to drive her to the mall after we dropped Jill at school, Amy's medication chock full of heavy machinery warnings and Jill too much the diva to take the bus. As a peace offering, it had softened her annoyance over the news that Kelly and I were hotel bound. She was still pissed, but at least she had eased up on her sad-puppy pout and dialed back her middle finger.

We idled in the parking lot of my former high school, good old West Ocean Regional, while Amy and Jill checked their lipstick in their compact mirrors, all those last-minute female adjustments that always seemed so unnecessary, as if an errant quarter-inch of glossy red could detract from the lure of their lips. Amy capped her lipstick tube and dropped it in her purse, then punched me in the arm, a jab more than a knockout punch, but clear in its intent.

"Abandoning us within the first twenty-four hours," Amy said. "You can forget about getting your security deposit back."

"I'm not abandoning you."

"What about the stalker? You heard Jill—I'm not making it up."

"She's not making it up!" Jill said.

"You're just going to *leave* us unprotected, a defenseless single mother and her vulnerable teenage daughter?"

"Defenseless? Really? I thought you still had a .22. Trust me: it's better this way, more space for everyone."

"The fucking Beach House Inn. I knew you had money."

"I'm just borrowing it from the bloodsuckers at VISA."

"That's a sweet deal, being California Kelly. Is she spending the day at DePasquale, too?" she said, name-checking a high-end spa.

"No," I said, although Kelly *had* mentioned something about a pedicure. "Hey, she's entitled. She's a struggling civil servant, an *unemployed* teacher."

"...with a sugar daddy setting her up in a beach-front suite."

"Sugar daddy? At best I'm a single packet of Splenda."

"Wow, such blazing wit. It's hard to believe you never won a Tony."

Jill leaned in from the back. "He was nominated for an Obie."

"He lost to a bunch of vaginas," Amy said, capping her lipstick and zipping up her purse.

"How many awards have *you* been nominated for?" Jill snapped.

"Only one: for my continuing role of the mother to a smart-mouth pain in the ass."

"That's a *supporting* role," Jill said, all teenage snark as she finished combing her hair. "Everyone knows that the smart-mouth pain in the ass is the real star!"

She kissed the side of her mother's head and opened the back door. "Thanks for the ride, Mr. Donatello Marcino. Ms. Vaughn will flip when I tell her you drove me to school."

Amy and I watched through the windshield as Jill rushed off toward a pack of other girls, all of them furiously tapping their smart phones, the parking lot filled with teens slouching toward the school entrance, half of them animated and energetic, the other half zombies, just like when Amy and I had made that same walk each morning twenty years earlier. Jill looked back and waved, then dropped her arm over the shoulder of some chunky girl in black leggings and a short pink dress.

"She's quite precocious," I said. "Your genes must have beaten the hell out of Clyde's DNA."

"Assuming he's the father."

"He's not?"

"There are other possibilities," Amy said. "I wasn't exactly chaste that year."

Except with me, I thought, but didn't say it. "I always assumed you married him because you were pregnant."

"I *was* pregnant, and when I told him, he proposed and I said yes. He *could* be her father. He probably is. I know you hate him, but for all his hard-ass attitude, he's a good guy. Those first few years with Jill, I couldn't have done it alone."

"You could have done it with me," I said, the words slipping out before I could reel them back in.

"I couldn't have done that to you," she said. "You were destined for better things. Maybe if I'd known you were going to blow it and end up making pizza again... hey, I'm kidding. I couldn't have tied you down like that. I loved you too much."

"I would have..."

"Don't rewrite history, Duck. I was there, remember? You were like this crazy man with a dream, writing scenes on paper plates when you couldn't find a pad, spending half the day in your head. I was lucky—it was exhilarating to watch. What should I have done? Dragged you away from what you were *born* to do so you could take care of me and some other guy's child?"

"I could have done both," I said. "You...and a baby...that sense of obligation and responsibility might have been good for me."

"That's *really* sexy, Duck. Every woman wants to be an obligation. Check her out, man. Her responsibilities are *tight*."

Few things had hurt more than learning that Amy was pregnant and engaged to Clyde. After the success of *Midnight Chair,* I had several offers, and my next script, *Maybe Tomorrow,* was scooped up by a well-known producing team, with Edward Norton and Mary-Louise Parker signing on for the lead roles. The producers, Debra and Annie, loved the script but thought the second act needed work. With rehearsals scheduled for September, they gave me the keys to their house in East Hampton so I could write without distractions. A fine idea perhaps, but I would have been better off in my old bedroom at Uncle Dan's place.

The Hamptons house overlooked the ocean, and each morning I saw a family with a curly-haired little blonde girl that reminded me of Sarah Carpenter. When Amy called with the news that she was pregnant and going to marry Clyde, I went a little psycho. I started following the little blonde girl's family, convinced that she was going to drown. After a few days the father, an investment banker with one of the big Wall Street firms, threatened to cut off my nuts if I didn't stop staring at his daughter. Those were his exact words: "cut off your nuts," and each time I explained that I meant no harm, he shouted "nuts" a little louder. Suddenly I couldn't write for shit, and the rewrites on *Maybe Tomorrow* made the play worse. The dialogue was ponderous, the conflicts muddled, and soon my narcolepsy went hyper. When Annie and Debra came out to check on me, they found their playwright face down in the kitchen, my head wedged inside the folds of an empty pizza box. Heroin, they thought, but even after I explained my condition and proved that I was clean, I could sense the shift. They gave me another week to fix the second act, after which I mailed them my original manuscript and said it was the best that I could do. Rehearsals were postponed, and Edward Norton made *Fight Club* instead. Though the producers held onto their option for another two years, they never called back. The downward spiral had begun.

Had Amy *not* gotten pregnant that summer, I was certain I would have nailed the rewrites and secured my second hit. Maybe that was a fantasy, a convenient excuse to get my lackluster talent off the hook, but I still believed it. Uncle Dan was convinced that Amy's timing was intentional, that she'd wanted to sabotage my career.

We pulled out of the high school parking lot and headed toward the mall.

"I appreciate the ride," Amy said. "I'm pretty sure I could drive, but ..."

"It's no problem," I said. "It's like old times, me driving you around ..."

"Don't go there, okay?" She turned toward the window. "It's not like old times at all."

．　　．　　．　　．　　．

Part of me hoped that it was true, that Mr. Ronan *was* stalking Amy. It would mean he was still alive, that I could still make amends for what she'd done.

In the days after Sarah's disappearance, I had tried to see him, to apologize, to *explain*. My testimony had neither helped nor hurt him—having slept through it all, I was the ultimate bad witness—but I still felt culpable. I was an absolute wreck—every thought, every second of my life consumed by what had happened. *Sarah had died because of me.* I couldn't escape it and couldn't understand why Amy had accused Mr. Ronan. *I* was the one who had fallen asleep and let it happen. I needed to tell him that Amy was *confused*, that she didn't mean it, *she didn't know what she had seen*, it was me she wanted to blame, not him, but I never got the chance. After the accusations, I saw him only once—at the police station, Clyde's father, the chief of police, guiding him toward the interrogation room while Uncle Dan and I sat in the corner on metal folding chairs waiting for the hypno-therapist to interview me. Mr. Ronan was drained of color, his posture stooped, his eyes cast toward the floor like a man already convicted. *Get your hands off him*, I wanted to shout, *he's a great person.* Who else would have noticed that the painfully shy narcoleptic kid who smelled like pepperoni had an imagination, had *potential?* The first time I gave him a skit

I had written, he had me paged during homeroom the next day, and when I walked into the Drama Room, he burst into applause. Not even the cheers on opening night of *Midnight Chair* had ever sounded better. He had changed my life, unquestionably, and seeing him being hustled through the police station turned my blood to ice. I jumped from the chair, but Uncle Dan pulled me back, Clyde's father bolstering his grip, and the only contact between us was Mr. Ronan turning his head, seeing me and, for a second, smiling. Then he was gone.

Over the years I thought about tracking him down, apologizing, but wasn't it obvious he wanted nothing to do with me? After he was cleared, he left town within a week, and in Holman Beach, was never seen or heard from again. Never having a chance to say *I'm sorry* seemed a fate I deserved.

Still—I needed proof. Uncle Dan had given me the name of his lawyer, who, as a favor, agreed to see me on short notice. Gerry Cobb, Esquire— when I was a kid, he'd come into the Jaybird to talk business, a heavy, balding guy in a wrinkled suit who called me squirt and never left without a sausage calzone tucked beneath his arm in a take-out bag. I expected his office to be a similar mess, but it was oddly neat and cleanser-scented, not a speck of dust or an errant folder in sight. He looked like he hadn't aged a day; if anything, he looked younger, his hair fuller and darker than I remembered, his weight a good twenty pounds less, the circles around his eyes smoothed, his posture straight. How was that possible?

The diploma on the wall solved the riddle. Gerald Cobb Jr. I was dealing with the son.

"Are you sure you want to pay me for this?" he said. "Death certificates are a public record. Go online. It might take a few hours if you don't know how to search, but it's really easy."

"I'd prefer not to do it," I said.

"It's your money. I'll have Sharon get right on it."

I assumed Sharon was the paralegal in the outer office. Cobb leaned back in his chair. "Michael Ronan. There's a name I haven't heard in forever. I was up at Seton Hall in my second year when all that happened. My Dad called him, you know, thought he should sue that girl, what was her name ...?"

"I don't remember."

"...he thought he should sue her for defamation. Even if *she* had no money, he could've hit the parents' homeowner policy's liability limit. An easy hundred grand, but he didn't bite. You've got to respect that. It's amazing no lawsuits ever came out of that tragedy."

I nodded, keeping quiet about the letter I'd received from Laura Carpenter after the success of *Midnight Chair*. It was rabid, rambling, at times incoherent, the pain of a lost child hovering over every word. *I'm going to sew your rich stupid, sleeping ass*, she wrote. (People assumed I had earned more money than I had.) After five pages of invective, she said she'd drop it for $987.16. An odd figure—I assumed she was looking at a past due notice when she wrote the letter. I sent her a check for $1,000 and didn't hear from her again for eight years (except for the cashed check, returned from the bank with *Fuck You* scrawled in the memo line.) Over the years I'd sent her nearly five grand, chump change considering what I'd taken from her.

"When did he die?" Cobb asked.

"I'm not sure."

"Well, that might make the search a little longer, probably cost you another billable hour. You're sure you want us working on this?"

There it was, my out, if I wanted it, a tempting justification for maintaining my habit of avoidance: it was too expensive! But no—it needed to be done.

"Okay, we'll get right on it. I'm guessing $750 gets you a copy of the death certificate." He typed a few notes into his computer. "Sharon's the best—she'll knock this one out quick. We should have something for you by tomorrow afternoon."

Cobb stood and shook my hand.

"My Dad will get a kick when he hears about this one. Michael Ronan. Jesus!"

. . . . .

I planned to stop at the Jaybird before meeting Kelly at the Inn, but as I stepped out of the rental car and headed for the entrance, I saw Nancy at the end of the block walking toward me, her one and only arm swinging a big black pocketbook as she wobbled along the sidewalk. It was the first time I'd seen her in normal clothes, black pants and a neat floral blouse, her short grey hair fluffed up in a brave attempt at a style. She was far enough away that I couldn't be certain, but it sounded like she was singing the old Monkees song "Daydream Believer," loud and off-key. Uncle Dan had mentioned that sometimes she "helped out" at The Jaybird, and perhaps this was one of those days, the late afternoon rush still a few hours off as she trudged toward her job, ready to help her older brother with her one good hand.

A sea plane buzzed overhead, one I had never seen before, an all-white biplane with a "Summer Blowout!" banner trailing its fin. I couldn't tell if Nancy had seen me yet, and I almost waited for her—how could it hurt to say 'hi?'—but the closer she came, the more I felt the incipient burn of the sun against my neck, the more I sensed the hard concrete pushing against my feet, and though I should have walked over and greeted her, I should have said 'hello,' I crossed the street instead, and then I started running.

-12-

From "New Jersey Beach Patrol – Pilot Episode" by Michael Reiken and Alex Clyde.

EXT.A NEW JERSY BEACH – DAY

Two hot-bodied college girls in skimpy bikinis stand on the beach holding hands. They look out at the ocean, then face each other and start kissing.

CUT TO:

POV – BOOKER

Through a pair of binoculars, we see the two hotties making out. We PULL BACK and see OFFICER KYLE BOOKER, handsome, upright, morally clean, standing on the boardwalk holding the binoculars, watching the little sluts in their PDA.

His partner, OFFICER ALAN STYLES, experienced, wise, somewhat jaded, pokes his shoulder.

STYLES
Hey, let me see them.

Booker hands him the binoculars.

BOOKER
God forgive them.

Styles looks through the binoculars. POV-STYLES – through the binoculars he sees the girls still making out. One of them has her hand on the other's ass.

STYLES
They might be little sluts, but those are some really nice legs.

BOOKER
Come on Alan; don't forget municipal ordinance 22.405 against public displays of a sexual nature. What if the children see them?

STYLES
You're right, we must think of the children. You always keep me honest, Kyle.

BOOKER
No, God keeps us honest.

STYLES and BOOKER
(Simultaneously)
Serve and protect!

The two partners shake hands and run toward the beach.

THEME SONG PLAYS

EXT. THE BEACH-DAY

The girls are still making out as Booker and Styles arrive.

BOOKER
New Jersey Beach Patrol!

STYLES
Serve and protect!

The girls stop kissing and look indignant.

LESBIAN SLUT #1
Hey man, stop hassling us!

LESBIAN SLUT #2
Yeah! The liberal activist judges say we can do whatever we want.

STYLES
Not according to town ordnance 22.405.

BOOKER
And not according to God.

STYLES and BOOKER
(Simultaneously)
Serve and protect!

They shake hands and reach for their handcuffs. The girls start to run.

BOOKER
Freeze!

STYLES
We can't let them escape. Think of the children!

They draw their service revolvers, aim, and fire. They are great shots. Both girls fall to the ground, shot in the back of the leg.

Booker and Styles holster their guns, smile, and approach the two sluts, who are crying in pain.

BOOKER
On this beach, we respect the law.

STYLES
(to the sluts)
You have the right to remain silent.

They grab the girls and handcuff them together. The officers exchange high fives!

BOOKER and STYLES
Serve and Protect!

THEME SONG PLAYS

INT. POLICE STATION – DAY

Booker and Styles enter the station house. Their commanding officer, CAPTAIN FARRELL, calls them over to his office. The two cops

. . . . .

I woke up with a throbbing headache and a stiff neck, a ceiling fan whirring above me, the loose pages of "New Jersey Beach Patrol" scattered across the bed as my eyes tried to focus on something, anything, like the white candle burning on the nightstand, its tiny flame bouncing up and down like an EKG from a heart attack. God, I hated waking up. I took a deep breath and started coughing.

"Welcome back," Kelly said.

She sat beside me lotus-style, her guitar propped in her lap as she strummed a three-chord progression I couldn't place, something mid-1990's and familiar, a gloomy old favorite. I noticed her white t-shirt, a Property of Jaybird Pizza special; it was all she was wearing, except for her fuzzy pink socks. She smiled, but kept her eyes on the frets, her fingers switching between the D, G and E chords, ... D, G, and E.

"How long have I been out?"

"Three hours, three days, three years...something like that."

She leaned over and kissed my forehead, the body of the guitar poking my abdomen, yet she didn't miss a beat. I still couldn't place the chords, but I could remember the video, silhouettes of wheels over blacktop, people stuck in traffic in their workaday lives. "I went downstairs to make some tea and when I came back you were *dead.*"

I checked my phone: two texts from Amy wondering where the hell I was.

"Don't worry. I picked her up at the Mall and drove her home. Everything's cool."

"You drove Amy home?"

"That's right."

She kept plucking the same strings, D-G-E, and the song finally came to me: "Everybody Hurts." R.E.M. Not a good sign.

"What did you talk about?" I asked.

"Nothing. The usual stuff."

I looked across the room, toward the balcony and its high-priced view, the double-doors pulled open to catch the breeze; we were close enough to hear the waves, the steady heartbeat of the ocean, and from the downstairs kitchen came the scent of freshly-baked scones, the remnants of the afternoon tea I had missed.

Kelly put down the guitar, leaning it against the nightstand as she turned to face me, her head settling against the pillow, her bare legs stretching out across the bed, her toes resting on my shins. The blood vessels in my temples twisted and screamed.

"My poor little narcolepsy boy."

The T-shirt rode high on her hip; I reached over and touched her treble clef note tattoo.

"What did you and Amy talk about?" I asked, again, the idea of the two of them alone in a car, a twenty-minute commute with nothing to discuss except *me* being somewhat equivalent to a rectal exam.

"Don't worry, she had nothing but rave reviews."

She petted my head, stroking my hair like I was one of her cats.

"We're going to her house for dinner tonight. I stopped at the pizzeria, too. Aren't you proud of me? Whipping around town like a Jersey girl? I invited your uncle to join us, but he said he had to work. Does he ever take a night off?"

"He did, once, in 1998. I don't think he liked it."

"He gave me this t-shirt and a garlic knot; he said he'd name a pizza after me if I convinced you to stay. He asked if you were upset about seeing your mother after all these years. I wasn't sure what to say, so I told him you were doing your best."

I pulled myself up and reached for the Excedrin, gobbling down two in a single dry gulp, still too dazed to freak out properly about Kelly and Amy talking. The last few hours, even the awake part, had been a blur. After my meeting with Cobb, Kelly and I had checked into the Beach House, my Visa groaning as the owner swiped the card and handed us the room key. While Kelly unpacked, I'd sat down with Clyde's crappy script, and then...sleep, the narcolepsy like a lightning strike. I must have been out longer than usual. I remembered the first few dreadful pages, but nothing else.

"I called home to check on the cats," Kelly said. "They're okay, although Mr. Biggles had an accident on my tapestry chair. I spoke to Katie, and she said…"

I smiled and nodded and did all those things one does to show the other person you're listening, but my brain was sludge, half-asleep, half-chasing anxious thoughts about Amy alone with Kelly.

"…I mean, I don't really want it, but what if nothing better comes along? Sometimes I think I should just go somewhere and *start over,* the hell with everything—except the cats, of course."

Kelly's big eyes dug into me as if, despite her better judgement, she still hoped I might offer something tangible, if not words of wisdom, then at least some guidance or a few helpful hints. Having read my play, she should have known better: I wasn't that kind of writer. As my head buzzed and my left eye twitched, I rolled across the bed and held her, which was the best I could do, hoping it was enough.

"I miss you," she said.

"I'm right here."

"I miss the 'you' from last week, before that stupid phone rang, and I found out about this whole other life of yours. I listened to Amy talking about you, all the years that she's known you, and I felt like a footnote at the end of a massive book. Back home you were always a little strange, but after growing up with all that military structure, I like *strange*, and you were *my* strangeness. Now it's like I'm in this weird time-share, and the Colonel always said, 'Time-shares are a rip-off. They're never fully yours'."

"You're not a time-share. We'll be home soon."

"I don't think so. *I* might be home soon, but *you're* going to stay."

I took her hand. "I love you."

"Didn't you once tell me that 'I love you' is bad dialogue? Whatever happened to *show*, don't tell?"

We bumped noses as our legs wrapped together, and I slid my hands beneath her t-shirt just as my phone started vibrating. Ignoring it, I stroked Kelly's hair and kissed her neck, but she pushed me away and told me to answer, it might be important—or maybe she just didn't want me touching her.

It was a New York number I didn't recognize. I hated the phone but answered anyway. The voice on the other end was harsh but familiar.

"Donatello Marcino, Jesus…I never thought I'd see *that* name again. Why didn't you tell me you were working on something new?"

It was my agent George—we hadn't spoken in five years, though I did get an occasional royalty check forwarded in the mail.

"I'm not," I said. "I make pizza now, remember?"

"Then what the hell is this script with your name on it doing on my desk?" he said. "*The Revolving Heart* ...don't tell me there's *another* Donatello Marcino out there. White paper, stage directions, dialogue; it's not a pizza, that's for sure. No pepperoni in sight."

"It's on your desk?"

"UPS dropped it off this morning," he said.

I looked over at Kelly. "You're welcome," she whispered.

"I haven't read it yet, but I'm intrigued. What's it about?"

"Well ..."

"Is it about identity? *Male*ness? I'm desperate for a project about toxic masculinity."

"It's about these people ..."

"Hmm," he said, sounding disappointed. "Still, it's good to hear from you. I'll give it a read, definitely. I always suspected you had another one in you."

"It's just a draft."

"Aren't they all?" George said.

I put down the phone and turned toward Kelly, who picked up her guitar and started playing, another REM song, "Shiny Happy People" this time instead of "Everybody Hurts."

I couldn't complain.

. . . . .

When Uncle Dan wanted your attention, he talked about the war, his eighteen months in country like a badge requiring you to listen, since whatever wisdom he needed to impart was hard-earned and battle tested. He talked about his service so much, when I was a little kid I thought Vietnam was somewhere in New Jersey, a rotten neighborhood filled with bullies, giant bugs, and bad pizza. I'd get scared thinking about my uncle getting shot, and the few times we left Holman Beach and went for a ride I'd whisper a secret prayer that we didn't wind up in Vietnam.

I'd stopped at the Jaybird to see if he needed any help in the kitchen. He didn't, but before he let me go, he had something to share. As soon as the word "platoon" came out, I knew it was about me.

"There was a guy in our squad, Tex we called him; I'm not sure why since he wasn't from Texas," he said. "But that's what we called him: Tex, or Crazy Tex, or just 'that crazy S.O.B.' You get the picture."

I had stopped at the Jaybird to pick up a tray of lasagna for dinner at Amy's that night, not expecting much more from him than a head nod, it being so close to the dinner time rush. But Uncle Dan had a story to tell, a *lesson* to impart, no doubt connected to my mother, Nancy, who sat in the booth closest to the register folding napkins with her one, and only, hand. Surprised by her presence, I'd kept to the other side and pretended not to hear when she muttered to the couple in the adjoining booth, "that's him, that's my son."

The lasagna awaited in its tray by the register, and had I been just a regular customer I would have paid and been out the door in thirty seconds. But Uncle Dan had noticed my reaction to Nancy, and at that moment, to him, I was a snot-nosed little brat who needed some *words*. He led me to the back storeroom and put on a fresh apron.

"Crazy Tex was one of those guys who loved the war; man, there was nothing he liked better than killing Charlie, and we just knew that Tex would never go home," he told me. "Had the Army discharged him he might have stayed behind and signed up with the other side just to keep himself in the game. That's what he called it, the game. But that's not important. His hand—*that's* what you need to hear about. So one day Tex is playing around with an M26, that's a grenade..."

"It triggers by accident, right? He loses his hand..."

"No...his hand was fine. Let *me* tell the story, okay? He's playing with the M26 when this giant insect lands on his nose. You've never seen anything like it, Donnie. Picture a mosquito the size of your thumb. Tex hated bugs more than he hated VC. He drops the grenade and..."

"He loses a foot."

"No. The grenade didn't trigger. It just sat there. I *told* you to let me tell it. So...he pulls out his Mark 2, that's a combat knife, and goes after that giant bug while it's still on his nose. Crazy Tex, man, he was fast, probably jacked on bennies; he killed that bug, and took out half his nose doing it. Cut it right off...you could actually see the bone..."

He opened the fridge and pulled out a jar of chopped onions, checking the clock on the back wall.

"What does that story have to do with his hand?" I asked.

"Who said anything about his hand?"

"You did. You said I needed to hear about his *hand*."

"No, you probably misheard."

"Hand and nose sound nothing alike."

"Ah, you've been in California too long," he said, his standard response whenever we disagreed. "You're hearing things."

It wasn't worth arguing. "Okay, I get it. Even without his nose, he was the same old crazy Tex, right? That's the lesson. I shouldn't be weirded out just because she's missing an arm."

"Strike three," he said. "He *wasn't* the same after that. They fixed up his nose and sent him back to the platoon, but he'd lost the edge, and a sniper took him out within a week." He grabbed a red bell pepper and closed the fridge. "The lesson, Donnie, is simple: start treating her *decently* or I'll slice off half your nose."

He handed me the pepper and headed back toward the ovens. I followed, once again his apprentice.

"She *abandoned* me. I don't owe her anything."

"She couldn't take care of you, so she left you with someone who could. What's so terrible about that? The last I checked, you turned out okay. Nobody's asking you to donate a kidney. Just *talk* to her."

A blast of heat smacked us as he opened the middle oven and checked on three mushroom and one pepperoni. He had a point, yet my resentment still felt justified, even righteous.

Uncle Dan closed the oven and headed to the counter, where one of the high school girls was on the phone, writing down an order. He grabbed my arm and pulled me next to him so I had no choice but to see Nancy still folding napkins in her booth. She wore a light, checkered print blouse and grey pants; her face had a pink, healthy glow and her lips were a dark, glossy red, the lipstick, amazingly, neatly applied. Except for the arm, she looked almost normal.

"Go over and talk to her," Uncle Dan whispered.

"I'm just here to pick up the lasagna. I'm due at Amy's..."

"She can wait," he said, nudging me out from behind the counter.

I considered grabbing the lasagna and making a break for it, ten good steps and I'd be out the door, but that was too pathetic even for me, and on some level, I'd never outgrown the instinct to obey Uncle Dan. Since narcolepsy on demand was never an option, I stumbled toward the booth and slid across from Nancy, who looked up at me, blank-faced, then pushed a stack of napkins across the table with her forearm, as if I'd come to help finish the job.

"Hello," I said, and—why not?—I started folding napkins, too. It was better than sitting with a stupid expression on my face; it gave my eyes somewhere to land other than on that missing arm, but after three or four napkins I realized I couldn't keep up. She'd pat each napkin with her open palm, bring one end to the other, pat it again, and then fold the far corners, forming a half-diamond. She worked without stop, as if part-machine, her left sleeve, the *empty* one, hanging limply at her side while the other arm hustled, her eyes on the job except for a few fleeting glances to check on my progress.

From behind the counter Uncle Dan watched anxiously, like the host of a nature special waiting to see if two endangered species could coexist in fragile habitat. Sitting three feet away, I caught her scent, not quite B.O., but still pungent, like vinegar mixed with sour yogurt. I leaned back.

"Do you like working here?" I asked.

"Yes," she nodded. "I come every afternoon when *Ellen* goes off. If *Ellen* isn't on, that means it's the weekend. On Saturday I come here after the second episode of *MASH*. Sunday is my day off."

Her voice was slow, but strong; she looked back toward Uncle Dan, who smiled at her, then picked up a cloth and started wiping the counter. The high school girl, Ashley, played with her smart phone, one arm leaning against the cash register.

Nancy put down the napkins and scratched her nose, her thumb rubbing hard against the crook of her nostril. I studied her face for a resemblance; maybe it was there, maybe not; I wasn't always sure about my own face, which seemed to change depending on my mood. She reached across the table and for a moment I freaked, thinking she might grab my shoulder or grope my face, but she didn't want *me*—she wanted the napkins. My stack now hers, she resumed folding, her gaze focused on the job.

Uncle Dan shot me a thumbs-up.

"I like *MASH*, too," I said.

"Frank Burns eats worms," Nancy giggled, reciting a line from an early episode. When I was a kid, *MASH* re-runs were my religion; I'd stay up till midnight watching old episodes until Uncle Dan came in and killed the TV. So there it was: a bond, a genetic predisposition toward Hawkeye Pierce and Radar O'Reilly.

She turned her head and kept giggling, which was kind of creepy. I tried to distract her.

"I work in a pizzeria, too," I told her. "In California."

"I lived in California once," she said. "Twice, I think. I was an actress, but they didn't like me. So I left."

"It's a rough business."

"I was in a movie once but...they made me do things I didn't like so I never went back." She checked if anyone was listening, then whispered across the table. "I don't like fooling around with other girls."

Another fine fact for the family tree: my mother once did porn.

"Do you live here now?" she asked.

"Just visiting."

"I live here. This is my home." She lifted her shoulders, straightening her posture as she beamed with pride. "I have a job and my own room, two doctors and my own TV. Danny gave it to me for my birthday. I take medicine twice a day. We eat a lot of pizza. I like the garlic bread best."

As she spoke, she seemed childlike and innocent, but that was Hallmark-Movie-of-the-Week crap. Schizophrenics were rarely dangerous, I knew that much, but no matter how much medication, there were always *issues*. How much hell had she been through before she'd found her way back to Uncle Dan? Enough to *lose an arm*, and probably worse. The world could be abundant in its cruelty and neglect, and I felt a sudden urge not to add to it.

"Maybe...before I leave...if you'd like to..."

"Yes," she said, as if anything I might suggest was the best idea ever. "I would like that."

"Okay," I said, and added, "That's great!"

Now *I* was the Hallmark-Movie-of-The-Week. Would we walk together in the park feeding birds from a little brown bag of seeds? Was there a *warm embrace* scheduled right before the last commercial break? Fade out: mother and son, long separated, finally reunited, hand in hand strolling the boardwalk at sunset, a light piano medley tinkling in the background.

"I have a scrapbook," Nancy said. "Danny made it. It has pictures of you, and facts. Before I go to bed, I study the facts." She closed her eyes, like a third grader in a spelling bee trying to spell *kookaburra*. "May 14, 1999—*Confessions of the Mid-Time Chair* debuts off-Broadway." She opened her eyes, nodding. "I study every night. It makes me feel better. I know all about my son."

My son.

I pictured her sitting in bed, flipping the pages of her scrapbook, trying to memorize all the moments of my life she had missed. *It makes me feel better*, she had said, meaning a bond existed between her and the *idea* of a son, whether or not the actual son ever showed up; meaning that I was important and that she *cared* about me; meaning that if I pushed her away it might *hurt,* a responsibility I didn't want but one that had latched onto me anyway. Moral obligations rarely asked permission.

"That's great," I said. "You got the date right."

"I can show you the scrapbook," she said. "Maybe you could sign it. Like an autograph."

At the counter, Uncle Dan slid the pizza wheel across a large plain cheese, dissecting it into the standard eight slices, his head cocked toward our booth, trying to listen.

"Sure," I told her. "That would be nice."

"When?"

"Um, soon." My feet shifted under the table. "But I have to go now."

Her lips, turned upward, dropped to a frown.

"My friends are waiting for dinner."

"Kelly Price," Nancy said. "I met her at the house when you fell asleep. I don't have her picture yet, but we wrote her name in the book. Maybe she'll give me a picture."

"Maybe," I said, and her face bloomed with pride.

"Well, it was nice talking to you," I said, exiting the booth. She adjusted her body and leaned toward me, offering her cheek, and for a moment my instincts drove me toward her. Another milestone for the scrapbook, perhaps—first kiss between mother and son. She sat waiting, cheek turned up, a placid smile etched on her face, just like I'd seen her two mornings ago when Uncle Dan had kissed her goodbye. I leaned toward her and almost did it—I *almost* kissed her cheek—but I couldn't do it. I reached over to pat her shoulder, but my hand landed instead on her empty sleeve, my fingers brushing the hanging fabric and its strange phantom limb before jerking away. Nancy, still waiting for her kiss, sat perfectly still, her big dreamy eyes aimed toward the ceiling as I scooted away.

·　·　·　·　·

During my tenure as an unattached struggling playwright in New York, those what-the-hell-am-I-doing years after Amy married Clyde, I briefly dated an actress who never broke character—whatever her role, Brianna pretended to *be* that character in every aspect of her life. Though sometimes fun, it was mostly exhausting, and we broke up after she landed the lead in *The Sound of Music* at the Bucks County Playhouse and started yodeling "The Lonely Goatherd" at 6:00 AM.

Amy's daughter Jill wasn't *that* bad, not yet, but when I arrived at the house she was already in character, standing on the porch with a sly grin, an empty champagne glass wobbling in her hand.

"Yes, I have tricks in my pocket; I have things up my sleeve," she said, stepping toward me as I exited the car, her voice strong and confident. "But I am the opposite of a stage magician. *She* gives you illusion that has the appearance of truth. *I* give you truth in the pleasant disguise of illusion."

She closed her eyes, pursing her lips before kissing the night air, her bare legs crossed as she leaned back against the porch railing, the hem of her dress climbing her thighs as she cocked her hip, inviting me forward with a graceful sweep of her arm. Her silhouette painted the wooden planks, her shadow stretching from the front door to the edge of the top step, luring me toward her as I walked up the driveway carrying the lasagna. It was impossible to ignore the tight slope of her dress, a short sleeveless pink jersey with an open back and gold beaded trim.

I knew that dress well.

Twenty years earlier in a motel room in Wildwood Crest, free HBO and a continental breakfast for $79 bucks per night, I'd unhooked the back button of that dress and watched Amy shimmy out of it, The Cure's "Just like Heaven" playing over the radio, 106.3 FM, our favorite station; I remembered falling to my knees, like I'd seen someone once do in a bad movie, my hands grabbing Amy's hips as I kissed between her legs, my tongue tracing goose bumps on the inside of her thighs. It was prom night, a prom we happily shunned, the prom too suburban-Molly-Ringwald-flick for the likes of us. We made our own prom—that dress was seared into my memory, the way it accented her hips, the way it opened in back, Amy's tan skin peppered with freckles beneath the arc of her shoulder blades. Somehow that dress had survived, time-traveled twenty years. It fit Jill perfectly; her resemblance to Amy had never seemed stronger, but maybe it was only the dress playing tricks on me. Or maybe it was *Amy* playing tricks. Why else would she give that dress to her sixteen-year-old daughter, knowing that my fingers could recall every stitch of the fabric, every golden bead along the trim of its neckline?

"To begin with, I turn back time," Jill said. "I reverse it to that quaint period..."

"The mid-nineties," I said, interrupting her soliloquy. "Your mother bought that dress for our senior prom, the one we blew off as too bourgeois for a pair of tortured artists like us. I rented a tux, she wore that dress, and that night we wound up at the top of the Empire State Building."

"Really? I had no idea," Jill said, baby-stepping down the porch stairs in stiletto heels. "It's quite beguiling, don't you think? I found it hanging in the closet, all lonely and ignored."

I didn't believe her for a second, but I smiled anyway, running my thumb against the aluminum corner of the lasagna pan, the sharp edge pricking my skin, drawing blood.

"The play is a memory," she said. "Being a memory play, it is dimly lit..."

Suddenly the porch lights shut off; another teenage girl, dressed in black, hid behind the rocking chair, her hand on the light switch. From her iPhone played a rough jazz number with piano and brush stroke drums on a hot Louisiana night. Only they'd gotten it wrong. The next line in the play referenced a fiddle, not a sax.

"I'm the narrator of the play, and I'm also a character." Jill wobbled toward me, putting down the champagne glass and taking the lasagna from my hands. "What do you think? That's the opening from *The Glass Menagerie,* by Tennessee Williams. We're reading it in Drama Class. There's some racist language, but that makes it true, you know, for those characters at that time. So it's okay, right? Ms. Vaughn is giving us a *feminist* reading. It's about ..."

"I've read it once or twice," I told her. Sophomore year at NYU I'd taken a Williams seminar. I'd read everything.

"I know those lines were written for a male, for Tom, but I did okay, didn't I?"

"Five stars."

"I just wanted you to see my *range* as an actress. I haven't read your new play yet, but I can handle any role, I promise. When production starts, all I want is an audience, I mean an audition..."

The other girl rose from behind the chair and hurried down the steps, grabbing the tray from Jill as if even the idea of her carrying something was an insult. Her clothes, black sweatpants and a loose black T-shirt, made it clear who was the stagehand to Jill's shining diva.

"Introductions are in order," Jill said. "This is Ms. Madison Parker-Cattazano. We call her Maddie: we're in love." She draped her arm around Maddie's shoulder and pulled her close for a kiss, her lips smacking wet and loud against the other girl's cheek. "Maddie, this is Obie Award nominee Mr. Donatello Marino, my mother's old boyfriend. He'll be auditioning roles for his *new* play quite soon, I believe...."

"Pleased to meet you," Maddie said, avoiding my eyes.

"Great to meet you as well." The lasagna wobbled in Maddie's unsteady grip. "Why don't I take that tray back?"

"Nonsense!" Jill said. "A gentlemen caller does *not* perform chores. Ms. Parker-Cattazano can handle it."

Maddie shrugged. "Thank you for offering." She turned toward the house, the tray lying flat in her arms, her grip nervous and tight, as if the lasagna might come to life and jump.

"Word of warning," Jill said. "My father and his psycho partner are inside, but they'll be leaving soon. They installed a bunch of security cameras, so we can catch that guy who's stalking Mom. I watched them the whole time so they wouldn't put one in my bedroom, or in the shower, or something sick-o like that. My Dad's partner is pretty rape-y." She checked the house, making sure no one could hear through the window. "I can talk honestly to you, because you're cool. Theater people are the greatest!"

I let her illusions stand. Theater people were the same as everyone else.

"I like guys too, you know, but I *love* Maddie," she said. "My Dad thinks I should be dating football players. Mom *says* she's okay with Maddie and me, but she's not, I don't think. But you're cool! So is Clarissa—Ms. Vaughn, our drama teacher. You two should totally meet!"

So Amy's and Clyde's daughter was gay, or at least experimenting, a curious turn considering how many times I'd heard Clyde use the word "faggot" during high school. I hoped he'd be kind to her.

"Is Kelly inside?"

"You bet," Jill said, and waved for me to follow. "I think the rest of the play will explain itself."

The slow rumble of a thunderstorm bleated in the distance. Jill tapped my arm, pulling open the door and ushering me inside. As we passed the doorway, the overhead light caught the beads in the dress's neckline, just like the moonlight had reflected off it outside a motel at midnight, Amy and I dancing on the boardwalk at Wildwood Crest, the beads glistening like stars stitched across her body, celestial patterns only I could see.

"Attention, everyone: the gentleman caller has arrived!" Jill said, her voice all fake sultry Southern charm. She held open the door, and I followed her into the house.

·   ·   ·   ·   ·

This is a memory play.

I'm outside the Drama Room waiting for Mr. Ronan when Clyde struts down the hallway in his school colors, purple and gold, go Bobcats, number 32 emblazoned below the mountain range of his shoulders. He sees me, the theater geek, fucking Shakespeare junior, Sleeping Beauty standing outside the classroom door, and BAM! Watch the books fall from my hands, watch his arm in motion as he punches me twice in the stomach, his big fist swinging up into my abdomen, not a word exchanged between us as I double-over and vomit a half bowl of Cheerios all over my Chuck Taylors.

In the kitchen Clyde's hand rests on Amy's shoulder as they huddle around a laptop, Clyde demonstrating the new security cameras they've installed along the house's perimeter. My loathing is deep-rooted and instinctual, like a sneeze, impossible to stop.

I walk into The Jaybird, local kid makes good, 'Midnight Chair' in the sixth week of its successful New York run, Frank Rich of The New York Times heralding my arrival as a 'new voice," and maybe my head is a little full of itself but I still take shifts on Sunday afternoon; I still help Uncle Dan whenever I can, and here I am, ready to knead dough and sling pepperoni, but why are Amy and Clyde in the corner booth, our booth, eating calzones and laughing at some private joke, their feet touching beneath the table, his fat football hand stroking her wrist? Haven't they read Frank Rich's review, and doesn't Amy know that saying I love you means past, present, and future? I love you erases even the possibility of Alex Clyde; it strikes him from the world, forever. I love you is for she and I and no one else. I love you means get his fucking hands off your beautiful wrist.

Officer Mike, or whatever the hell his name is, moves toward me with his small-town cop swagger, and even though he's out of uniform, in shorts and a loose, frat-boy-in-Margaritaville Hawaiian shirt, he keeps his hand at his hip, the ghost of his gun and holster in a permanent lock and load. He asks me about his script, *New Jersey Beach Patrol*, have I read it yet? Perfect for the USA Network or maybe HBO; how about Ryan Gosling for the character based on him?

"It's pretty violent," I say, "and you might need a stronger villain...."

"It's a moral story," he tells me. "The crimes are spiritual, transgressions against decency."

No doubt he, and not Clyde, wrote the scene where the teenage girls get shot for kissing on the beach. Jill and Maddie cut through the room and I worry for them as Officer Mike follows with his hard-on eyes. Now I'm far from innocent in the realm of the male gaze, but I've read *The Vagina Monologues* three times, and I get it—it deserved to beat my stupid play and win that year's Obie. So why doesn't Clyde do something about his partner creep-eyeing his sixteen-year-old daughter? Maybe because *his* hard-on eyes have slipped down the opening of his ex-wife's blouse.

That night—you could smell the fire from blocks away, the burning wood, the melting paint; you could still see the smoke in the haze beneath the streetlights, in the black trails twisting over rooftops. Cover your face or you'd choke on it, feel the acid sting in your throat with each labored breath. Touch a windshield and find your fingertips filthy with soot.

The next morning the local paper gloats that it's been forty-seven years since a house burned to the ground in Holman Beach. The Jaybird does mad business that night—order a pizza, watch the fire, point at the smoke-filled sky and drink beer until the last siren fades.

I'm on break outside the front door, pacing the sidewalks, Donnie Pizza in his apron and baseball cap, when Clyde rolls by on his ten-speed and brakes three feet away, tires shrieking against the pavement.

"Wouldn't you know it? It's Ronan's house," he tells me. "Pretty funny, huh?"

He's bare-chested, like Crazy Horse returned from battle, an open bottle of Heineken in his sweaty left-hand. His hair is soaked, as if he'd driven his bike straight from some pirate graveyard in Hell.

"Take a look," he says, shoving the bottle up in my face.

It's too dark. I can't see a thing.

"Lipstick traces," he says, pointing to the bottle's long neck. "Don't you recognize ...the lips?"

He laughs, and kisses the bottle, running his long tongue up from the Heineken label to its dark golden rim.

"You shouldn't have done it."

He's all smirk. "Done what? I didn't do nothing, sir, except kiss the girl!"

The state police and the insurance company will both send investigators, and while the official cause will be deemed arson, no one ever suspects him or Amy.

"Vigilante justice, the way I see it," Clyde says. "Some good citizen with a spare match and an extra can of lighter fluid."

Holman Beach has a single fire truck. Before the fire dies seven towns will send an engine. Black smoke drifts above.

"The fucker deserved it."

"Mr. Ronan had nothing to do with Sarah's disappearance. Amy is confused..."

"You don't know shit about anything. Go back inside and fall asleep. That's about all you're good for anyway, and now she knows it."

He flips the bottle into the air and rides off toward the boardwalk, the empty Heineken shattering around my feet as one more screaming siren joins the fray.

Still a Heineken man, Clyde sips from the bottle as he points toward the laptop. "We set up six cameras," he says. "We've got the entire perimeter covered. If anyone approaches, the motion sensors kick in and we capture every step, every movement. Not even Caspar the Jerk-off Ghost could slip through."

"Thank you," Amy says, at his side, their arms touching. "I owe you."

"You bet your ass you do."

"Nobody's betting any ass," I say, and for the first time I notice Kelly at the far end of the kitchen table, looking bored and forlorn, her chin resting on her fist as she gazes at the ceiling fan spinning noisily above. I walk over and kiss her check; she doesn't return the kiss.

"Let's test it," Officer Mike says, turning to Jill and Maddie. "Girls, go outside and try to sneak up on the house."

Jill checks with her mother, who nods, and the two girls run off, Officer Mike leering as they cut through the dining room and disappear.

We all hover around the laptop, even Kelly, and wait for the cameras to come alive.

"There are six quadrants," Clyde says.

"That's impossible," I say. "A quadrant, by definition, is one of four. The root word quad ..."

"Oh, you're still awake?" Clyde says, cutting me off mid-sentence, and everyone chuckles, even Kelly. "Six cameras, six *quadrants*, and any motion in *any* of the quadrants will trigger all six cameras."

We wait for the girls to appear on the screen.

"Okay, Shakespeare, so what's the right word for six?" Clyde asks.

"In music, it's a sextet," Kelly says.

"*Sex*tet? I like how that sounds." He counts out the adults in the room. "One more and we can do some sextet-ing right here. Or maybe Shakespeare will nod off and we can make it a *quad*."

"A *ménage* a quad," Kelly says, because I deserve it.

"Hey look, the cameras are working."

Amy points to the top left of the screen, where we see Jill and Maddie, on all fours, crawling across the lawn toward the house. The black and white image is sharp enough to capture the goofy grins on their faces, their eyes geared toward the lens as Maddie waves her arms and Jill flips a middle finger.

"I told you: any movement and those babies switch on," Clyde says. Officer Mike clicks the mouse, catching an image of Jill in her slinky prom dress moving toward the camera, Maddie close behind.

"The batteries are charged for at least a week," Clyde says. "If your stalker doesn't show up by then..."

"He will."

Amy reaches for the wine at the center of the table, but Clyde blocks her, grabbing her arm before she can snatch the bottle.

"You're on medication. Don't drink."

"It's a Riesling. It pairs well with anti-depressants."

"Doctor's orders," he says. Officer Mike scoops away the bottle the moment Clyde releases her arm.

"Jesus, Alex, you're not my father. One glass won't..."

"No, it won't, because you're not drinking it."

She throws him a pouty face but opens a Diet Coke instead. Had *I* said anything, she would have chased down the Riesling with a shot of Jack Daniels and a glass of peppermint Schnapps, and perhaps therein lay the inscrutable attraction—Clyde offered *boundaries*. Recast the role of the boyfriend on the day that Sarah Carpenter disappeared, Clyde beside her on the blanket instead of narcoleptic me, and Amy would have been *alert*, not wasted at ten in the morning; she would have kept her eyes on Sarah's every move; she would have kept her *safe*.

Later that night I'm sleeping when Amy crawls in bed beside me, the acrid scent of smoke and gasoline waking me as she rests her arm on my shoulder, her face pressed against my mine as she whispers, "It's over."

I turn, but she pulls her body closer, drapes her leg over my hip; her hands cover my eyes, her breath rum and Listerine.

I manage a single word: "Why?"

She kisses the back of my head.

"You don't understand, but that's how I want it."

"Understand what?"

She kisses my ear and rolls away from me.

"Just go to sleep," Amy says. "It's over."

．　　．　　．　　．　　．

The rain against the roof sounds like microwave popcorn starting to heat, the windows shaking from the thunder, the floorboards rattling while the curtains flutter from Atlantic gusts. In Holman Beach thunderstorms jab and retreat, the black clouds rolling off the ocean in violent flurries before fading, rarely lasting beyond ten minutes but prone to encores, the thunder always weak and distant, teasing before reappearing for sharp, sudden blasts. An immense crack rocks the house, and we all look up, as if the thunder had emerged from the ceiling beams, and the lights flicker twice as a one-two punch of lightning hisses outside.

"My, oh my! That was close!" Jill says, in her mock Southern drawl. "The gods are certainly angry tonight, wouldn't you say, Mr. Marcino, our most esteemed gentleman caller?"

She touches my arm, and I try not to think about that prom dress.

"Knock it off," Amy tells her. "This isn't an audition. Go get the dishes so we can break out this lasagna."

"Oh yes, Mother, of course; the dishes!" She curtsies, and grabs Maddie's hand. "We're just two poor Cockney girls who live to serve the lady of the manor. Lasagna, it shall be!"

Blowing us each a kiss, the girls skip into the kitchen, Jill waving to the imaginary crowd, pausing for a final bow before her grand exit.

"You should have listened to me," Clyde tells Amy. "If we'd sent her to softball camp like I wanted…"

"She hates softball."

"…the coaches might have knocked this acting garbage out of her system."

The lights flicker again as the thunder cracks. I find Kelly's hand and give it a squeeze.

"I'm glad you remembered that I'm in this scene," she says. "I thought I'd be off-stage until the third act."

"I'm sorry," I whisper, though by now my apologies feel worthless, good for, at best, a pitiful smile and a brief grant of clemency.

The thunder bursts again, and this time the lights stay off for ten seconds, maybe longer, the lightning flashing across the lawn as the house rattles and shakes.

"Shit," Amy says. "I've got some extra flashlights in the basement, just in case. Alex, can you get them before you leave?"

"I'll get them," Officer Mike says.

"No, I've got it," Clyde tells him, and for a moment something passes between him and Amy, a sudden communion of eyes before he turns and punches my shoulder. "Give me a hand, okay?"

It seems strange—why does he need my help to grab a few flashlights? But I don't object. The loudest thunder-crack yet explodes over the roof, the windows shaking in their frames as we all gaze up at the ceiling, as if waiting for it to shatter and come crashing down.

I follow Clyde into the basement.

The week after Ronan's house burns down… my narcolepsy goes hyper. Four or five times a day I wake up in some weird, inappropriate spot—under the kitchen table, on the boardwalk outside of Toby's Rock Lobster, against the dumpster in the cramped alley behind the Jaybird. Eventually Uncle Dan brings me to the hospital for tests and observation, but there's nothing wrong with me except perhaps stress, or so they say, and I'm prescribed Adderall for the narcolepsy, which I take once and, after a three-hour bout of vomiting and dizziness, refuse to take again.

During my hospital stay, Amy never visits; only Uncle Dan stops by both afternoons. His eyes on the wall clock, he tells stories about the Army hospital in Saigon where he spent a week after some shrapnel grazed his hip during a night patrol outside of Kom Sun. Before the story ends, I fall asleep, and when I wake up a lone nurse is standing over me with a paper cup of canned peaches and a plastic spoon, Uncle Dan long gone. When they release me, I head back to the Jaybird and manage to stay awake for a six-hour shift; we never discuss it further, and the episode is forgotten. The narcolepsy doesn't stop but reverts to "normal." Three days later I see Amy again, and neither of us mentions Mr. Ronan or the pile of scorched debris that used to be his home.

A bare lightbulb hangs at the bottom of the basement stairs, and Clyde's shadow appears enormous as he ducks his head under a low beam. I follow him down, a dank, damp smell permeating the space; at least twice a year the basement floods—the hazards of living in a beach town. Clyde walks with purpose. It's his house, too, at least on the mortgage; he passes the first shelf, where two propane lanterns and a pair of flashlights sit next to a portable camping grill, and heads toward the long metal filing cabinet pushed flat against the back wall. There's a combination lock on the handle, and Clyde spins the numbers; the lock snaps open.

"She *gave* me the combination," he says. "This is half my house, and we share custody of a daughter. Maybe things change when Jill moves out, but Amy and I, we don't have any secrets."

He pulls open the top drawer and shuffles through the hanging folders. "The lock keeps our daughter out, not that she'd be interested. But just in case. Every house has important papers, right? Insurance policies, wills...divorce agreements ...certain drawings a daughter shouldn't see."

I don't say anything but move closer, the single bulb flickering but keeping its glow.

Clyde pulls the manila folder from the drawer, the loose white pages stacked inside. "I found this in her bedroom, where Jill might have seen it. I put it down here, to keep it private."

He flips open the folder, glancing at the first of the drawings.

"Too bad she dropped out of college and never took herself seriously," Clyde says. "You weren't the only one around here with talent."

"I know."

"Do you? To me, you could have done more to ...whatever, nurture, inspire, encourage. I'm just the dumb jock with a badge...you're the *artiste*. Maybe you should have helped her."

Thunder looms over the house. Clyde rifles through a few drawings, then closes the folder.

"She should have told you. Maybe she wouldn't be such a goddamn mess."

My muscles tense, ready for the blow. "What is it?"

"See for yourself but wait until I'm upstairs. And if you're curious, she *knows* what I'm doing. It's her idea, not mine."

I take the folder, hoping he won't notice the tremor in my hand. Clyde grabs two flashlights as the beams shake, the thunder relentless.

"I think you already know what's in there," Clyde says. "I think you've always known, even if you never realized it, or acknowledged it, or whatever. Finding the right word for things is your job, not mine."

An unexpected softness fills his eyes, sympathy or maybe pity. "She won't get better until this all comes out, and whether I like it or not, this is part of her getting right again. She was my wife. That means something, you know?"

His heavy feet climb the stairs.

"Time to wake up, Donnie Boy."

The morning after the fire I ride my bike to Mr. Ronan's house, now a pile of charred beams, shattered glass, and chemical-soaked fibers, only the mailbox left standing. Yellow police tape rings the property; a pick-up truck is parked in front, and two investigators from the County poke through the wreckage. Neighbors have gathered in pockets on the other side of the street; in hushed speculation and the occasional booming laugh they contemplate the impermanence of just about everything and thank God that the fire didn't spread to their homes.

I'm thirty yards away when I spot Amy on the sidewalk at the far end of the street, walking toward the debris, drinking from her grandfather's flask, tucking it inside her black shoulder bag between furtive sips. Something keeps me in place, locks my feet on the pedals and freezes all motion; all I can do is watch. From the beach a kite has broken loose, its tail fluttering in the soft morning sea breeze, its pink diamond shaped body drifting back and forth above the remains. Amy pauses, watching the kite, standing on her tiptoes and reaching up, as if believing she might touch it. I'm certain she doesn't see me. A wind gust blows the kite toward the ocean, scattering a colony of gulls.

When Amy reaches the house the two investigators, both drinking coffee from silver travel mugs, have their backs to the sidewalk; one of them smokes a cigarette, flicking ashes into the debris. Amy checks to see if anyone is watching, but while the neighborhood onlookers are still at their posts, the gossip hot and fast, no one really pays attention; for the moment she is invisible to everyone but me.

From inside her bag she pulls out an object, too small for me to see, and tosses it over the yellow tape, onto a pile of roof shingles in the center of the lawn. She stares at the object and takes another sip from the flask before turning away, rushing down the street in the opposite direction, away from Ronan's house and whatever might remain. The pink diamond kite lurches toward the ocean.

Once she's gone, I cycle toward the house, lean the bike against a stop sign, and walk toward the site. The investigators, having finished their coffee, are now closer to the front, so I tread carefully, slow and unobtrusive, until I spot the object, face-up atop a stack of black roof tiles.

Immediately I recognize it. Amy and I used to joke that it looked like her; it was a Christmas gift from her grandmother the year Amy turned six, a brunette Barbie™ Hair Play Doll, with a short, purple print dress and wraparound heels, the classic Barbie breasts and hips, the classic Barbie smile. Eventually Amy lost interest in toys, and Hair Play Barbie™ wound up in an old suitcase along with My Pretty Pony and a family of Smurfs. But now there it was, tossed among the wreckage, stripped of its purple dress and plastic high heels, a naked brunette Barbie™ abandoned in the scorched remains. It felt wrong, a betrayal, but there was no way I could claim it, not with the investigators walking toward me, shooting me the evil eye and *ordering me to "move on, kid—get the fuck outta here. This is a crime scene."*

And so I did; I walked back to my bike, and left the naked Barbie™ to its fate among the ash-heaps, knowing that, with its brown eyes and bright, pink-lipped smile, it really did resemble Amy; knowing that it would soon be crushed under a bulldozer's blade; knowing that, the one time it had needed me, I'd done nothing to save it.

In the first drawing the girl is naked, down on all fours, her mouth twisted in a pained grimace, her blank eyes cast bleakly toward an unseen viewer. Dark hair hangs wildly around her face as her bent arms carry her weight, her neck straining as a man prepares to enter her from behind, his erection drawn as an angry snake. I flip the page and see the same drawing again, the same image, on successive pages. Page after page is the same, only *not* the same—each drawing shows incremental change, a slight shifting in the naked girl's position, the snake-cock inching closer to her raised backside, the man's large shaded hands moving toward her hips. Page after page—the naked girl, the naked man, each image another cell in this animated rape scene. Turn the pages fast enough and you see the motion, the snake-cock approaching until finally it penetrates, the girl's eyes inching shut as her face, page by page, slowly disappears. There are ninety-seven sketches in all, and each one depicts the same brutal image—the naked girl, the naked man, a rape rendered in stop-motion, the girl's face slowly disappearing over ninety-seven pages, the pencil lines deep and precise.

The girl's face I have seen in drawings many times before, because it's Amy's face. And the man, too, I recognize, his face a less frequent subject of her drawings yet one I've seen spotted in her sketch pad. Unmistakably, the face belongs to Mr. Ronan.

And finally, one more face, on the last of the pages—the same scene, the man raping the girl from behind, only in this image, the final one, a third face appears, a sleeping face, the body lying motionless in the corner while the man rapes the girl—the sleeping face, of course, none other than my own.

·   ·   ·   ·   ·

Upstairs Clyde and his partner have left, the four women gathered at the table as the last of the thunder fades. The lasagna has already been cut and served; Jill and Maddie sit together on one side, Kelly and an empty chair across from them. Amy stands, topping off her glass of Riesling. From her eyes it's clear that she knows what I've just seen, that through her ex-husband she has orchestrated the reveal.

I'm still in a daze, and maybe my hands are trembling.

"Donnie, are you okay?" Kelly asks.

"It's a very *ugly* basement," Amy says, walking toward me. Jill and Maddie are still in Tennessee Williams' land, smashing dialogue back and forth like old pros.

"Just the narcolepsy," I say, although maybe I've never been more awake. Amy touches my shoulder and guides me toward the table.

"So now you know," she whispers. "Captain Sick was real."

My lips move, words form, but I can't hear them over the screaming beat of my heart. Amy whispers something more, but I am lost, dazed, my knees shaking.

"Donnie, sit down and have something to eat," Kelly says. "You look like you've seen a ghost."

I stumbled toward the table as Jill stands up, Amanda Wingfield in my ex-girlfriend's prom dress, ready to belt out her showstopper line.

"Then go to the moon, you selfish dreamer!" she says as she and Maddie start giggling. I collapse into the chair beside Kelly and start eating my uncle's lasagna, as if the world hadn't just shattered like a glass figurine— like glass always does in a memory play.

-13-

The next day: *The Lion King* on Broadway, a fucking *musical*, just what I didn't need, yet Kelly had bought the tickets and I couldn't blow it off without giving a reason, the only one good enough being the truth trapped deep in my gut, twisting my intestines into harsh, nautical knots. Seeing those drawings of Amy and Ronan had left me raw, as if every inch of me had been covered in Band-Aids, and now, without warning, they'd been ripped off—each tiny hair yanked free, dark dust mites of adhesive clinging to my skin.

Since coming out of Amy's basement, I'd been distracted and morose, almost monk-like in my silence; that obsolete phrase—shell-shocked—seemed to capture it best. Kelly knew my reaction had something to do with Amy but had yet to call me out on what the hell had happened, and by keeping things secret I was pushing her away—again. I could see it in her tight smile, in the tense line of her shoulders as she stared out the window at the B&B calculating how long she should stick around before heading back home to her cats.

The radio filled the silent spaces as we drove to the city, Kelly flipping between stations before settling on sports talk—God knows why; maybe she hoped all that repetitive chatter would annoy me out of my funk.

She dropped her voice and started mimicking the deep-throated bombast of the host. "We still don't know if he can play quarterback in the National Football League!" She killed the volume and poked my shoulder. "As opposed to playing quarterback for the P.T.A. or the New York Stock Exchange?"

I stared through the windshield, the world nothing but asphalt and yellow lines. She switched back to her announcer voice.

"We still don't know if he can play quarterback for the National Association of Calligraphers." Again, she poked my arm. "Hey, not even a smile?"

My lips offered a weak lift. Kelly groaned.

"That's a death mask, not a smile. Okay, I get it. I'll shut up."

"I'm sorry. It's not you—I've still got that headache from yesterday."

"I respect your right to privacy, but please don't lie." She switched off the radio. "It's *not* a headache."

"I'm okay."

"You're not even in the same zip code as 'okay.' That guy said something to you in the basement last night, and obviously it wasn't happy news. I get that you're not going to share, at least not now and certainly not with *me.* But hey, this is my goddamn vacation ...please don't ruin our day in the city because you have hurt feelings."

Hurt feelings! How dare she minimize this as 'hurt feelings? They weren't *hurt*—they were kicked, stabbed, pummeled, and pulverized.

I couldn't stop dwelling on it. Had Amy tried telling me but backed off, afraid I'd blame *her* and not Mr. Ronan, my head so far up my young playwright ass that I couldn't see how someone helping *me* could also be hurting *her.*

He took her—Amy's words the morning that Sarah Carpenter disappeared. *He took her.* I had never believed it, but it *was* the truth, only the "her" wasn't Sarah; it was Amy herself.

And I had done nothing but sleep.

Kelly switched the radio back on and glared out the window, even though, on this stretch of the Parkway, there was nothing much to see. What would she do if I told her the truth? I could already feel her withdrawing, as if her body were dematerializing, becoming translucent. By the time we reached the tunnel would anything remain beside a few red flecks of her nail polish and the feint scent of her conditioner? The exodus had begun, and even as I sat behind the wheel silently pushing her away, I knew how much I'd miss her.

I struggled for something to say, as if the sound of my voice could somehow save us.

"You know that gas station where Phil Leotardo is shot in the last episode of *The Sopranos?* The one where his head gets rolled over by the SUV? I know where that gas station is. It's out of the way, but maybe we could stop there later."

Kelly turned, inventing a new facial expression for the phrase "you're an idiot."

"That's okay. I'm good," she said. "Hey, this is my fault, too. You warned me this trip might get weird, and I insisted on coming. And now things are weird. At least you kept your word."

"I'm sorry. Trust me: it has nothing to do with you."

"I know, and that's a problem, Donnie. If we're a real couple, then this should have something to do with me. Because everything would—that's what it means to be with someone." She picked at her cuticle, pulling the dead skin. "I assume whatever that cop told you last night is connected to her. Are they getting back together?"

"No ..."

"Hey, lucky you; you're still in the game." Her tone was bitter and sharp. "I miss my cats. I think I *hate* New Jersey."

We drove on in silence, the exit signs collecting behind us as we neared the Hudson River. Over the years I'd driven the Parkway so many times I could switch to autopilot, and as I thought about Kelly, and Amy, and the disaster I'd created for both of them, my attention began to drift.

I knew that if I stayed my normal course, keeping Kelly at bay, holding the truth inside, failure loomed; our relationship would fester and decompose, shooting bile through my veins for the next fifty years, or however long it might take for me to die a sad, bitter old man. I called this the Einstein option, from his famous quote defining insanity as doing the same thing over and over and expecting different results.

For the past twenty years, since the day that Sarah Carpenter had disappeared *(since the day she died! You know what happened. Say it!)* I'd been living in a Witness Protection Program of my own creation, always on edge, waiting for the moment when someone I cared about would shake my bones and say, "*It's all your fault.*" My ex-wife Kristin was convinced I was cheating on her. "What are you hiding?" she'd ask, thinking I was sneaking off to bang waitresses in some $79 a night room at the Motel Six. I wasn't— yet she'd nailed me on the "hiding." A few times I came close to telling her, but always held back.

This is how I roll, I told myself. But I knew how that roll always ended.

Yet I still had the chance to subvert Einstein's maxim and try a different course. In three miles we'd hit the next rest stop, the last one before the Tunnel, where we could find a picnic bench and talk openly and *share.* No more hiding, no more Witness Protection—let the mea culpas fly; let Kelly see *exactly* what kind of man I was.

But why did I think this might *help?* She already knew I'd let a four-year-old *drown;* did I really want the profile updated to include my leading role in doing *absolutely nothing* while my first love was raped? It seemed a dreadful option, perhaps worse than Einstein's insanity. Wasn't it better for her to dump me without knowing the full depths of my worthlessness?

Unless:

Was it possible there was a *third* course, in which Kelly, and Amy—yes, it always came back to Amy—might forgive me?

I felt the clock ticking, the rest stop two miles ahead, Kelly scanning her iPhone, probably downloading dating apps and prepping her the-last-guy-I-dated-was-a-disaster story for all who might listen.

I took a deep breath, tapped the brake, and swerved into the right lane, cutting off an SUV, the other driver flipping me the bird, the horn blaring "asshole" in Jersey Morse code.

"Why are you pulling over?" Kelly asked. "Is something wrong with the car?"

"Something is wrong with *everything*," I said.

. . . . .

The white noise from the highway zipped over the rest stop, the whir of the heavy trucks an aural fog as Kelly and I sat in the rental car watching a Sikh couple changing a baby's diaper on the hood of a black Mercedes. Across the parking lot an old man in a Mets T-shirt scattered raisins for the pigeons by his feet; a State Trooper, texting on his smart phone, stood on line by the Rent-a-John, the back of his shirt a Rorschach of sweat. I didn't care about any of them, but they soaked up my attention, which needed someplace to land; they were useful scenery as I waited for Kelly to respond.

I'd told her everything about the drawings, even the last one—my worthless face asleep in the corner while my teacher raped my girlfriend.

The Sikh baby screamed and squirmed as the mother wrestled with the dirty diaper, the father watching sternly, arms folded over his thick chest. The old man with the raisins turned and walked toward us, the pigeons squawking as they followed, begging for more, two of them flying over our car and leaving a black splat across the windshield. I turned on the wipers and pressed the fluid button, the twin blades swooping the windshield clean.

"I don't know what to say," Kelly said, finally. "Anything I say will be trite. I don't want to be a Hallmark card."

The Rent-a-John door creaked open, a young woman in a pretty dress stepping out, her face a corkscrew of disgust. The State Trooper gave her the once-over and disappeared into the john.

Kelly smoothed out her skirt, pushing away the wrinkles.

"I don't know," she said. "All I can think is …maybe you should get out of the car …"

So here it was: *Be gone, you wretched man!*

"...get out of the car, look up at the sky, and scream."

She unhooked her seat belt and opened the passenger door, her legs swinging out.

"Does any other reaction make sense?" she said.

I thought about John Lennon and his primal scream phase, all those haunting shrieks on his first solo album, Lennon's voice haunted and pained, howling out his demons. Uncle Dan said it made more sense than "Imagine," and had I been in the war I might have understood. He played that album every day at the Jaybird until a customer complained that all that goddamn screaming made the pepperoni taste like dirt.

"Yes, definitely," Kelly said. "You need to scream."

She walked in front of the car toward the driver side and reached through the open window, unlocking my door.

I stepped out of the car and glanced at the sky. It was blue, not a cloud in sight—one of those days that the local TV weathermen would always hector you about, badgering you to get outside and enjoy it, as if they had built the day themselves and would be offended if you let it pass without seizing it.

Kelly watched, waiting. The Sikh mother handed the baby to the steely-eyed father and rushed the soiled diaper over to the trash. As I thought about those drawings, I felt something in my gut twitch; my spine grew icicles, my shoulders clenched as the sun painted the back of my neck with a pointed heat. The scene from the last drawing played out before me; you couldn't tell the location, but now I was certain it was the living room of Ronan's house, the coffee table pushed to the side, a blanket spread over the hardwood floor. Sometimes after school I would stop by his house to show him the latest scene I'd written, and sometimes Amy would come along for the ride. Those days, we were inseparable.

From the corner I watch as she takes off her jeans; there's a bottle of Peppermint Schnapps on the coffee table, and Mr. Ronan pours her a shot. He grins as she chugs it down, reaching into his pants to play with himself while Amy slides off her underwear. Another shot of Schnapps and Amy drops on all fours; I hear the keys and the loose change jangling in the pockets of Mr. Ronan's pants as he lowers them. There's a candle burning— a pine scent, but fake and sickening, like aerosol spray on an artificial Christmas tree.

"Tell me you want it," Ronan says, and I hear Amy's voice, because I am there, too. I am there, but asleep. I remember my words from the previous night, the momentary whispers as I passed Amy in the dining room hallway.

My voice is a feather, shedding its barbs. I was there, wasn't I?
"So now you know."

"Scream," Kelly said.

And so I did. My God, did I scream! I screamed so loud, and so long, and with such primal, searing, Please-God-I-don't-believe-in-you-but-please-make-it-stop anger and pain that the State Trooper burst out of the Rent-A-John with his pants unbuckled, service revolver drawn, ready to fire, ready to save someone from a dark and heinous crime.

Me? I just kept screaming, twenty years too late.

. . . . .

Somewhere in the dark of the Lincoln Tunnel, Kelly's voice:

"Just remember, Donnie, Amy is the victim, not you. The trauma is hers. I understand that you're hurt, and you're entitled to those feelings, but when a woman is raped, it's *not* about her boyfriend, okay? Don't make that mistake."

I nodded as she stared out the window. How could she know me so well?

. . . . .

About *The Lion King* I remembered nothing. Just as well—I hated musicals. At least Kelly enjoyed it, if "enjoyment" was possible with me sitting beside her in a black funk. After the show we walked to the Museum of Modern Art, one of the "must-see' locations on Kelly's Manhattan hit list. We grabbed our tickets, dodging a gaggle of noisy private school kids waiting for their docent, and hopped the elevator to the third-floor exhibits. Kelly was eager to check out the Jackson Pollack room, and while museums gave me a headache and left my eyes burning, I tried to be, if not enthusiastic, then at least less blatant in my morose self-loathing. The goal was to be all Buddhist and *in the moment.* Why not? My body felt strong and awake, a loving woman walking beside me in the so-called greatest city in the world. It was all good, and all *now.* Those drawings and what had happened to Amy were twenty years gone. They were *ghosts,* I told myself—step away from the haunted house and appreciate each moment for its sacred and singular essence.

I took Kelly's hand, inhaled, and again thought about Amy being raped by Mr. Ronan. I was a crappy Buddhist.

We found the Pollack exhibit and roamed the open spaces, all those white walls and corner angles, everything so quiet, like a maze inside a cloud. I wasn't much for modern art, but I appreciated the chaos of Pollack's work, the colorful drips and splatters swirling within the frame.

"These paintings remind me of music," Kelly whispered. "Each drip is like a note, and if you catch it the right way, you can almost hear the song."

She stood, nodding her head in some rhythm only she could hear, and I followed her toward a bright open corner by the window, where on the far wall hung a painting even I recognized, one of Pollack's masterpieces: *One, Number 31, 1950*. The canvas was enormous, dominating the wall, and we sat on one of those low benches about twelve feet away so we could take it all in. We were lucky; except for a Japanese guy listening to a guided tour through his ear buds, we were alone with the canvas. The muted black and grey streaks reminded me of the inside of a brain, the looping lines like traffic between the synapses. Being so close to such a massive work, I felt tiny, insignificant, and wondered if I stepped too close, would the colors reach out and snatch me? It wouldn't take much, perhaps a hammer or a brick, for my smashed-up brain matter to splatter over the canvas and fit right in. Future scholars would praise the artist for his skillful placement, never guessing that it was only me, banging my head into oblivion.

We sat on the bench, admiring the genius of it all.

"It puts things in perspective," Kelly whispered. "Imagine having all that chaos inside you."

A security guard entered the room, his eyes bored and grim as he looked at the Pollack, looked at us, and kept walking.

Kelly's hand settled on my knee.

"I'm going home," she said. "I rescheduled my return flight for later this afternoon. I'll catch a cab to JFK. You'll have to ship my luggage back. I hope you don't mind..."

"Wait a minute. You're leaving *now*?"

"Melissa can pick me up at the airport. I already texted her. By tonight I'll be back in my own bed with the cats."

So this was it—I'd told her everything, every ugly little detail, and sure enough, she was leaving. I couldn't blame her, but I felt my pulse quickening, my fingernails ready to dig in.

"It's only a few more days. We can fly back together..."

"Donnie, don't you get it? You're not going back. You're *staying*. This is your home."

"No ..."

"Why would you go back? Everything you love is right here. I know this is sudden, but during the intermission ..."

Fucking musicals!

"...I realized that whatever it is that you need to do ... to work through all of this ...I can't help you. I wish I could, but...I don't belong here. Not now."

We listened to the security guard's footsteps as he made his scheduled rounds. The Japanese guy, a middle-aged tourist in a beige windbreaker and dark khakis, looked out the window, admiring the skyline. I studied the Pollack, hoping my subconscious might find something useful hidden within the dense, interlacing threads, something that might convince Kelly to stay, but all I could see were miniature faces, maybe my own, screaming to escape.

"I shouldn't have told you about those drawings."

"That has nothing to do with my decision," Kelly said. "Or maybe it does, but not in the way that you think. I *want* us to stay together. That's why I'm leaving. Go back to Holman Beach and make things right. Then maybe we have a chance. Or maybe you're meant to be with Amy, or maybe someone else. I don't know, but either way, you need to find out."

"Stay two more days and I'll buy you a first-class ticket home. We won't even go back to Holman Beach. Screw our luggage. We'll buy new clothes and stay at the Ritz-Carlton."

Her hand left my knee as she stood and walked behind me. I tried to follow, but she touched my shoulder and guided me back down, her eyes dark and wet.

"I think your agent will love your play, and a year from now you'll be a great success. I really believe that."

"You can't just leave me here," I said, turning. Her breath was warm against my neck as she leaned closer, her lips brushing the side of my cheek.

"Please don't follow," she whispered. "This is hard for me, too."

She caressed the back of my hair, and then she was gone, the echo of her footsteps diminishing as I closed my eyes and counted each step until all I could hear was the steady white noise of the air conditioning.

I sat there feeling sorry for myself for another ten minutes, then walked around the museum, trying to shake off enough lethargy to make the drive home. As I wandered through the exhibits, too distracted to focus, most of the paintings passed unnoticed, except for one: a Roy Lichtenstein that captured it perfectly, a hand dominating a stark red background, an angry finger pointing straight at the viewer, the accusation clear: it's *your* fault.

-14-

I didn't know what else to do, so I started making pizza.

One good thing about Uncle Dan: he never tried to get inside your head. If you showed up at The Jaybird wearing a vicious scowl, refusing to say a damn thing except "hello" while you tied on your old apron and starting kneading dough, he wouldn't ask you what the hell was wrong; he'd just tell you about the order for twelve large pies due in forty-five minutes and let Jorge, his helper, knock off early. (No worries, Jorge, you'll still get paid for a full day's work.) He didn't ask about Kelly or what I'd been up to since I'd last seen him. It was all "hurry up with that dough" and "pass the minced garlic" and "can you believe this clown wants pepperoni with a white spinach and mushroom?" Maybe it had something to do with Vietnam, or maybe that was just his DNA. Growing up, it had mostly worked. Instead of a helicopter parent, he was more like a field scout observing the terrain of my adolescence through telescopic field glasses. Once a week, usually Sunday, as if he'd written it on a calendar, he'd look me over and ask, "Everything okay?" A simple "yep, I'm fine" would end the discussion, and we'd go back to making pizza or watching TV. Now I wondered if his hands-off approach had doomed Amy to a similar treatment from me. When her drinking became a problem, I never thought to ask why. It had seemed normal; half our high school got drunk or stoned every day. But I should have asked questions.

I was just a kid, I thought, but it didn't fly. If I was smart enough to win all those Young Playwright awards, I should have sensed that something was wrong. I grabbed an onion and chopped the hell out of it, the knife blade mincing the layers down to the pearl of its core.

Suddenly the phone buzzed, a generic ring tone I didn't recognize but hoped was Amy or Kelly calling from a different number. Instead it was Cobb, the lawyer.

"We couldn't find a death certificate," he said, "because your man is still alive."

I made him repeat it.

"He's alive and well and living in Ohio," Cobb said. "There's a name change involved. Your man is now Michael Rooney, but it's definitely him. These things are easy to chase down if you know where to look, and like I said, Sharon is the best. He's a real estate broker, which means licenses in three states, and a very clear paper trail. Doing well financially, from what we can see. If you still want a copy of the death certificate, it'll be a while. Maybe twenty-five years." He chuckled. "Should I set up a retainer?"

So Amy was right—Clyde *had* been lying. *Mr. Ronan was still alive.*

In a fog, I thanked Cobb, who said he'd email me the search results along with the bill. I slipped the phone back into my pocket and started slicing pepperoni and dicing tomatoes, my hands switching to automatic pilot as I strangled clumps of dough into fist-sized knots. *Mr. Ronan was still alive.* I smashed the mozzarella against the grater, grinding it back and forth as ribbons of cheese oozed through the other side. *Still alive.* I thought about that cigarette I'd seen in Amy's driveway the night of the shooting. It had been twenty years, but Mr. Ronan had smoked. My body tingled, as if every cell needed to escape.

The only thing that saved me was a take-out order for a roast beef and capacola sub I needed to assemble. I'd once heard Uncle Dan tell Father Toby there was no better way to work through PTSD than time in the kitchen with a take-out order due in ten minutes. "Everything fades, and your body goes to work."

Mr. Ronan is alive.

Okay, I thought. *I'd only found out he'd died three days ago. This was a reset, nothing more. But what would I tell Amy?*

My mind rushed around, connecting dots. I sliced a pound and a half of roast beef before snapping out of it.

I was wrapping up the sub when I heard some familiar voices out by the counter.

"There's a sign on the boardwalk," Maddie said. "No one's allowed on the beach after sunset. What if we get arrested? It screws up financial aid."

"I don't care. Do I look like some college application zombie? We're artists, Maddie. We're the mad ones."

I popped the sub into a paper sack and walked up front. Jill's Ginsberg reference felt like a pinch; Amy's old copy of "Howl" must have found its way to her daughter, who sounded exactly like her mother during her "I'm with you in Rockland, Carl Solomon!" phase. Jill, Maddie, and a thin, pale girl in a baggy, polka-dot dress stood by the counter checking out the slices.

Uncle Dan, relieved to dodge all that young estrogen, stepped aside so I could help them.

"Well, Mr. Marcino, what a *superb* surprise!" Jill said, blowing me a kiss. She wore a ponytail, which she flipped over her shoulder. The polka-dot girl, looking annoyed, cleared her throat and nudged Jill in the ribs.

"You know Maddie, of course," Jill said, before turning toward the polka-dot girl. "Beth, this is Donatello Marcino, the noted playwright. He's a dear family friend, and an artist, like us. He's casting me in his next play, eventually."

The girl, Beth, sneered as she zeroed in on the garlic knots, her eyes tiny black dots behind her glasses.

"Beth is a theorist," Jill said. "She's going to Brown next fall. Remember what I said about that plan to occupy the beach? We're doing it—Friday night! Some activists are coming down from the city—a few Occupy people, some Black Lives Matter kids —real-life radicals! And ten of us from the Drama Club are doing it too—you and Kelly should totally come."

I didn't tell her that Kelly was thirty thousand feet over Nebraska by now, heading home to her cats.

"It's just the start. Once people see what we're doing, there'll be spontaneous occupations everywhere. It's going to be *beautiful* and *viral.* By the end of the weekend young people—artists, actors, musicians, activists— will occupy every beach in the state. Beth has written a powerful femifesto. Get it? Instead of *mani*festo..."

"I get it," I said. "What are you protesting?"

Beth's eyes cut through me. "You."

"You have my support."

"Beth's femifesto is brilliant. It's about straight white male privilege, rape culture, guns..."

"Climate change," Maddie added. "But I'm a little worried about the signs. We could get arrested."

"We won't get *arrested,*" Jill said. "People hang out on the beach all the time."

"What does your mother think?" I asked.

"I haven't really told her. She's in her own world lately, and this morning she was in this total *mood.*"

"Her Dad warned us not to do it," Maddie told me. "He said the police will take it seriously. People got *hurt* at Occupy Wall Street. They shot pepper spray in their eyes."

"Pigs," Beth said.

"Pepper spray *really* hurts."

"My Dad's creepy partner keeps following us around," Jill said.

"He *stalks* you," Beth corrected her. "The embodiment of straight white male privilege, gun culture, rape culture...you should so MeToo him."

"He's just a jerk," Jill said. "He'll never *do* anything. My Dad would kill him."

"Well, be careful," I said, because I was the adult who was *supposed* to say things like that. "Make sure your mother knows what you're doing."

"I will, but she'll probably forget. And if *you* need me for anything, well, I'm committed to the occupation, but I don't have to *stay* if you need me for an audition."

Beth mumbled something but Jill ignored her as they each ordered two slices and settled into a booth to plot the revolution. Uncle Dan joined me at the counter.

"What are they complaining about?"

"Us."

"Did you charge them for the slices?"

"No."

"So we're part of the underground, supporting the resistance? It's about time." He flashed a half-smile. "Jesus, she looks exactly like her mother at that age. I keep waiting for the sixteen-year-old version of *you* to run through the door and join them." He ran his hand along the back of his neck. "Maybe my hair will turn dark again and my knees will stop screaming."

He grabbed the wheel and dissected a pie into eight perfect slices.

What if our younger selves **could** *reappear?* I thought. Granted the chance of a cosmic do-over, would I spot something in Amy's eyes and recognize what was happening? Or would I sleep through it all over again, narcolepsy as Eternal Recurrence?

Uncle Dan cleaned the counter and checked the order pad. Watching him, I started imagining he was a character on stage, his movements scripted—the old pizza guy carefully tending his kingdom. Enter stage left— me, the protagonist troubled by revelations in the prior scene.

"Did you ever worry about my spending so much time with Mr. Ronan?"

The sound of my voice surprised me. I wasn't imagining it—I had actually spoken. Uncle Dan looked up, wiping his hands on his apron.

"Where's that coming from?" He took a deep breath. "I didn't love the guy, you know that, but he was your teacher."

He opened the oven door and checked two pies, the dry heat smacking his face.

"Why didn't you like him?"

"No special reason." He closed the oven and eyed the clock. "I barely knew him; he just wasn't my type of guy."

"Then why did you let me visit his house all the time? And those drives up to Drew for rehearsals were long, the two of us alone in a car for hours."

"He was your teacher. What did I know about writing plays? *Somebody* had to help you."

He turned away, uncomfortable, and sliced up another pie, my cue to drop the subject.

But something wouldn't let me. When Amy had made those accusations after Sarah Carpenter's disappearance, even after Ronan's house had burned down, Uncle Dan had never really said anything about it or asked me what I thought. *"Everything okay?" "Yep, I'm fine."* Then it was back to the goddamn pizza. He was sixty-five. I was thirty-eight. Had we ever had a conversation that didn't involve *cheese?* I could remember only one: the previous day, when he had called me out for ignoring Nancy.

I felt my anger circling, eager for a place to land.

"You know, all these years, you've never *once* told me what you thought about Amy's accusations against Mr. Ronan."

"We talked about it."

"No, we didn't. You asked if I was okay, and that was it. But I have *no* idea what you thought. Everyone in this town had an opinion—except you."

He checked the oven again—more dry heat—sliding out two pies, sliding them back in for another three minutes. No one could eyeball a pie like Uncle Dan.

"Look, I can handle this place alone for the rest of the night," he said. "Shouldn't you be with your girlfriend or something?"

"Probably, but she's on a plane back to California because I'm a fucked-up bastard."

"Don't say that." He grabbed the pizza wheel and sliced up another pie, the muscles in his arms taut, his earlobes red. I lowered my voice so Jill wouldn't hear.

"Amy burned down Ronan's house," I said. "You know that. Everyone knows it. But you've never said anything. And if she burned it down, and if she and I were always together, wouldn't you think that maybe I had helped her? Isn't that a question you might have asked?"

He shook his head, his eyes drilling holes into a large spinach and mushroom.

"You were here that night, with me," he said. "You couldn't have done it."

"You're right—I didn't. Alex Clyde did. She asked me, but I wouldn't do it. I didn't believe her—I thought Mr. Ronan was innocent. Had I helped her, she never would have married Clyde, I'm sure of that. But like you said, I was here that night, with you, making pizza."

"Look, I knew she was a troubled girl," he said. "But I didn't know she started that fire. I thought it was some wanna-be vigilante, some redneck asshole. This town had no shortage of them. Still doesn't. Hey, if I was supposed to *talk* to you about it, I'm sorry. Nobody ever gave me a field manual. I did the best I could."

A customer, some young corporate type in a shirt and tie, good old Dad on his way home from the office, approached the counter, Uncle Dan rushing forward to help him as if sprung from jail. I followed, waving my hand as I told Shirt-and-Tie we were closed.

"There's a pizzeria three blocks over on Sandpiper and Beach." I pulled a twenty from my wallet and handed it to him. "It's on me."

"Hey, thanks!"

He shoved the twenty into his pocket and hustled out the door.

Uncle Dan grabbed his chest. "You sent him to Tony's? What's wrong with you?"

"Pretty much everything."

"Fuck it," he said, his voice rising.

Hanging over the register was a TV on mute; he grabbed the remote and raised the volume, then pulled me toward the storeroom, his hand cold against my bare skin. Uncle Dan rarely lost his temper, and for a moment his intensity scared me. Back in the storage room he slammed the door and again we were back in our cocoon.

"Look, I know you loved her, and probably still do, so I shouldn't say anything," he said, "but what she did to that man was a *crime*. You don't accuse someone of abducting a child. Even after the cops cleared him, guys would come in here bragging about how they'd cut off his balls if they ever saw him again. I know she was messed up over what happened, and she drank too much, and God knows what else, but what she did to him—that was *wrong*. But I kept my mouth shut because I didn't want to hurt *you*."

"She had a reason," I said.

He threw up his hands. "You said it yourself—that guy had nothing to do with Sarah Carpenter."

"He didn't. But there were other things."

He stepped back, his elbow banging into the steel handle of the fridge. He cupped his funny bone with his palm, his eyes turning toward the floor.

"What do you mean?"

My hands began to shake.

"Ronan did things. Not to Sarah, to Amy."

Uncle Dan froze, as if the stage directions had been erased and he wasn't sure how to act. I felt my heart beating through my ears.

"Why am I talking like a five-year-old? He didn't do 'things.' He raped her. I was there, asleep, like always. I just found out. Amy's avoiding me, won't return my calls." My throat felt like I'd swallowed a thousand pins. "All these years...I never knew."

The muscles in his face grew slack as his shoulders dropped, his hands reaching for the table.

The sound from the television seeped into the room, the YES Network with some nonsense about the Yankees bullpen. I was grateful for the noise as I waited for Uncle Dan to respond. All my life I had never seen him vulnerable, but this was something he couldn't change by strapping on an apron and working.

He turned toward the counter as if he were still in the jungles outside of DaNang and picked up a jar of homemade marinara. I braced myself, waiting for him to smash it, but he just stared into the jar, Hamlet contemplating Yorick's skull, then brought it to his chest and cradled it, a stage direction so unexpected I could never have envisioned it, my uncle holding a jar of marinara sauce like a baby, the jar's oval glass bottom pressed against his heart.

"You didn't know," he said, his voice a whisper. "It's not your fault."

There was a knock at the door, and Jill poked in. "Hey, there's a bunch..." She stopped, seeing our dead faces, Uncle Dan slumped near the counter caressing a jar of marinara. "Is something wrong?" she asked.

"Yep, I'm fine."

Uncle Dan winced.

"Um, sorry." Jill backed away from the door. "There's a bunch of customers waiting outside. I'd thought you'd want to know."

"Tell them we'll be right out," I said.

She turned, shutting the door. Uncle Dan cleared his throat, swallowing hard.

"Go hang the 'Closed' sign and tell them to get lost," he mumbled.

"You want to *close*?" This was heresy. The Jaybird *never* closed early.

"I'm leaving," he told me. He set down the sauce jar, untied his apron, and let it drop to the floor. He reached into his pocket and tossed me the keys. "Lock up. Or don't."

"Where are you going?" I asked, but like a ghost he walked past me, turned the deadbolt, and headed out the door.

I counted the seconds, waiting for him to return, the minute hand on the old clock jerking its way around the numbers. I opened the back door, expecting to see him on the other side, getting himself together so he could help me—at the very least there were pizzas to make—but the alley behind the Jaybird stood empty except for a single crow perched on the dumpster eyeing his next snack. Closing the door, I looked around the kitchen, everything in its place, the supplies, the ingredients, the stacked boxes of soda cups and paper towels, gallon jugs of cola syrup and extra virgin olive oil, everything so familiar, so much a part of me, yet it felt like the floor had dissolved, leaving me hanging over a twenty-foot chasm, waiting for gravity to do its thing.

And yet—for the first time since I'd been back in Holman Beach, I felt like I was exactly where I should be. A strange sense of peace settled over my body.

I was alone, *awake*, and suddenly I knew what I should do. It had nothing to do with pizza or Amy or even Uncle Dan, or maybe it had *everything* to do with them, yet it was the one thing that had always made sense to me. In good times and bad it had been my refuge: when I'd found Kristin fucking the plumber; when Ronan's house had burned down; when Sarah Carpenter had wandered into the ocean and disappeared.

I searched for some paper but couldn't find any, so I grabbed a pizza box and tore off its lid. A pen sat on the counter, and suddenly I was writing, scribbling on the back of the box, the blue ink scratching across the cardboard, the letters merging into words, the words into sentences, paragraphs taking shape—description, dialogue, action.

Act One, Scene One

A man stands alone in a basement holding a drawing showing the worst thing he's ever seen.

. . . . .

When I finally left the storage room the Jaybird was empty, except for Jill, who sat alone in a booth listening to music on her iPhone. While I'd been holed up in back, writing about her mother and wondering what was wrong with Uncle Dan, she'd stepped up and defended the fort. A red "Closed" sign hung over the front door. The tables had been cleared, the ovens shut down and the dishwasher loaded, the spice shakers lined up neatly on the shelf, each spice in its assigned slot. Even the floor appeared freshly swept. It was almost ten o'clock—I'd been writing for nearly three hours, and in my arms were twenty pizza boxes, the inside cardboard filled with the bones of a new play.

"Hey!" Jill said, pulling out her ear buds as she hopped from the booth. "I waited for you. When you didn't come out, I told everyone to go home. I tried cleaning up...you might want to check that I didn't break anything, like the oven or something."

I put down the boxes. "Where are your friends?"

She walked toward me, shoving her phone in the back pocket of her jeans. "They left, but I thought I should stay here...with you."

I put down the pizza boxes, checked the ovens and the stove; everything was perfect.

"Did I do okay?"

I gave her the thumbs up and walked out from behind the counter. She lifted the lid on one of the pizza boxes; her face lit up as if she'd stumbled on a unicorn.

"You were writing? I knew it! That's how it happens, right? You get these flashes of inspiration and you need to get it down, no matter where you are. It's almost like your brain is on fire, right?"

"Not really," I said. "Usually it's a grind, sitting at your desk staring at blank paper. This almost never happens but...I've had a lot on my mind."

She closed the lid and stepped back. "It's brilliant, I bet."

"I'll be surprised if it's coherent."

She undid her ponytail and shook out her hair.

"There's something going on, isn't there? It's not just my mom thinking that someone is stalking her. I know about the girl—Sarah Carpenter. Mom told me about it, and I hear things. But there's something more, isn't there?"

I couldn't lie to her. "Yes."

Jill scratched her cheek. "I'm worried that my mom won't be okay. She and I don't talk about things, not really; I *act* like stuff doesn't bother me...but it's usually just an act. I found her in the tub, and maybe she wasn't *really* trying to kill herself, I get that, but what if I'd stayed at Maddie's that night?" Her voice cracked. "I don't let my mom see it because she's...you know...troubled or something, but most of the time I'm pretty scared. What if something happens to her?"

"Your Mom's a survivor," I told her. "She's been through some...challenging stuff. It's just a bad time right now. She'll be better soon."

Hollow clichés—I wondered if either of us believed it.

She rubbed her eyes, her mascara fading into dark circles, and I noticed she was barefoot, her Nikes under the table, bright pink socks rolled into a ball and jammed into the left sneaker.

"I know you're with Kelly, and she's great, absolutely, but...do you still love my Mom?"

So much for softball questions: Jill was dealing heat, a high hard one aimed straight at my head.

"It's complicated," I said.

"She told me you proposed to her a zillion times. Maybe if you ask again..."

"I doubt that would be a good idea right now."

She jumped toward me and kissed my cheek. "Why not? She might say yes, and I'd make an *excellent* step-daughter."

The warmth of her body as she leaned close left me dizzy.

"I think I should drive you home," I said.

Her hand brushed against my chest, her palm sliding down, fingers fanning out as they covered my heart, the tips of her nails pressing through my T-shirt—and shame on me for not stepping away, for not taking her lovely hand and giving it back.

"Amy must be worried. It's late. Let's get you home."

"Amy is probably passed out on the couch," she said. "But if you and she were *together,* snuggled beneath a blanket, maybe holding hands...I bet she wouldn't drink anymore. If she was in the bathtub with *you*..."

"Jill..."

"I'm just saying, if she was in the bathtub with *you*, she wouldn't have taken those pills."

Guess again, I wanted to say. But the whole conversation was way out of line.

"Let's get you home, okay? Isn't this a school night?"

"I've already been late sixteen times this year. What's one more?" she said but grabbed her socks and slipped them on. "I can walk home. It's not far."

At most it was a ten-minute walk, a trek Amy and I had made hundreds of times, Holman Beach a *safe* community, or so we had thought. A few days earlier I would have let her walk home in the dark by herself, no problem, but now the world seemed akin to one giant threat, the cigarette butt in

Amy's driveway proof enough that one never really knows what might be lurking.

. . . . .

I dropped Jill at the house, resisting her attempts to draw me inside to spend time with her mother, or have a cup of tea, or just say hello; really, all I had to do was stay one minute.

"*Please,*" Jill said, but I could recognize a bad idea, sometimes. I waited until she was safely inside before driving off.

Going back to the B&B, with Kelly gone, seemed eminently grim, so I drove around Holman Beach with no direction in mind, just coasting down the streets, letting coin flips decide if I should turn left or right. For once I was grateful Amy and Clyde had burned down Mr. Ronan's house; seeing the new house built in its place was bad enough. I drove past Sarah Carpenter's house, which looked so much better than it had when she and Laura had lived there. During the real estate bubble, before the big crash, someone spent major bucks on an overhaul, new shingles and windows, a wraparound porch. The renovations looked top-notch, but I preferred it the old way, with Sarah inside.

After Sarah drowned, Laura didn't stick around for long. From what I'd heard, she hadn't moved far, just a few exits down the Parkway, her address changing from year to year. Occasionally Amy or Uncle Dan mentioned seeing her looking pretty haggard at the Ocean County Mall. At one point she did thirty days in the county lock-up for a DWI. I was in Los Angeles, working on a spec script, but she tracked me down and sent a letter asking for 3K for legal fees and fines. Though I was running low on funds, I sent the check anyway, which came back cashed, as always, with *Fuck You* written in the memo line.

My third time around town I started yawning, and pulled over, certain I'd be asleep within minutes. I'd slept in cars plenty of times, knew I'd wake up stiff-necked and cramped, but it seemed a better option than a night at the B&B, where Kelly's things were waiting where she had left them—her suitcase still propped on the ottoman, her new guitar leaning beside it, her nightgown folded on the left side of the bed, Kelly's side, her calico slippers waiting on the floor by the nightstand. I was certain those slippers would break my heart.

-15-

I was packing up Kelly's things, my hands lingering over all that soft cotton, when the phone rang—Kurt Cobain and good old "Lithium," a ringtone I really needed to change.

"Hey, I'm thinking of buying a dog," Amy said. No "hello" or "how's it going?" I could hear the pot of coffee racing through her voice. "Some mean big-ass pooch who'll scare the hell out of everyone except Jill and me, like a Pitbull or my grandfather before the Alzheimer's. What do you think?"

"If you're getting a dog, you should adopt,' I told her. "But I think you're more of a cat person."

"You mean pampered and lazy?"

She wanted to play, but my heart wasn't in it.

"We should talk," I said.

"We should talk," she mimicked, her voice deep and gloomy. "Let's be serious and *talk*."

"We need to..."

"Jesus, when did you become a Lifetime movie?" she said. "We can talk, but we're *not* turning this into a 'very special episode,' okay? I kept my mouth shut all these years for a reason. Come to the house tonight. We'll watch a movie and *maybe* we can talk. Bring Chinese—no pizza, okay? I assume the California Girl likes Chinese."

"She does, but...she won't be joining us."

"Trouble in paradise?"

"She flew home yesterday."

"Interesting."

"No big deal," I said, trying to sound casual, which Amy saw right through.

"I'm sorry, Duck. But what the hell were you thinking bringing her here?"

"I'm not sure. She said she wanted to see New Jersey."

"And you believed her? No one *wants* to see New Jersey. Couldn't you have bought her a Bonjovi album and watched *The Sopranos*?"

"She didn't *leave* me," I said. "She just went home."

"The eternal optimist; that's why I love you, Donnie. How about seven o'clock? Bring Chinese, and remember, spring rolls, not egg roll, and extra duck sauce. Jill loves the stuff."

· · · · ·

"Okay, gang," Amy said. "Showtime."

We sat in the living room, Amy and I on the couch, Jill and Maddie cross-legged on the floor on opposite sides of the coffee table, the girls trading open white cartons of lo mein and fried rice while they struggled with their chopsticks, stray dumplings rolling off plates and tumbling into their laps. I speared a stalk of broccoli with a cheap plastic fork and dipped it into the soy sauce.

Amy pointed the remote, and the TV snapped to life.

"What are we watching?" Maddie asked.

"Probably something boring," Jill said.

"Not at all," Amy told them. "It's an indie film from twenty years ago—very low budget, but you'll recognize one of the stars."

I wracked my brain. Micro-budget—maybe "Dazed and Confused" or that lodestar for every film geek from New Jersey, Kevin Smith's "Clerks." Back in high school if we weren't at the Jaybird we'd hang out at the Film Shack, a video store on Ocean Avenue that offered dollar rentals off-season and had a decent inventory of the eclectic stuff we preferred: French New Wave, David Lynch, British TV like *The Prisoner* and all those great Nineties films like *Slacker* and *Sex, Lies, and Videotape*. Though our peers considered us pretentious, at least the few who knew what the word meant, that didn't stop us from binge-watching Godard films before anyone even knew what binge-watching meant. A clerk at the Film Shack, Ricky B., was a year ahead of us but considered himself our personal Siskel and Ebert. He had a major crush on Amy, yet still turned me on to some excellent films like "The Brothers McMullen." At NYU I ran into him a few times at the Student Center—he was a film studies major—but the last I'd heard he was back clerking at the Film Shack until it shut down sometime around 2010.

Amy hit the remote a second time and the DVD started playing, lines of static twitching along the edge of the screen before the image stabilized and focused: a close-up of a white horse with a red bridle and a dark brown saddle trimmed in gold.

The horse, impaled on a yellow pole, slowly began to rise as a calliope played jaunty carnival music over low-grade speakers. Zooming out, the camera showed a second horse, and then a third, before suddenly the horses began moving, rising up and down as the merry-go-round commenced its revolution, the painted ponies spinning in succession as the camera panned right, revealing Amy, age sixteen, standing in the frame like a TV reporter, an empty Diet Coke bottle serving as the mike.

AMY: *We're here at the annual carnival for St. Theresa's Church in beautiful downtown Manahawkin, New Jersey, where tonight, local three-year-old Sarah Carpenter will attempt to ride the notorious wooden pony Zeus for three whole minutes.*

The camera tilted, and Sarah Carpenter entered the frame, her blonde curls flopping as she ran toward Amy with an ecstatic smile, a Smurfs T-shirt tucked into her blue jeans, the laces of her left sneaker precariously untied. Dropping to her knees, Amy held the Coke bottle up to Sarah's mouth.

AMY: *Tell us, Sarah, are you ready for the challenge of the mighty Zeus?*

Sarah looked straight into the camera, meaning she looked straight at *me,* and I zoomed in for a close-up.

SARAH: *You ride with me, Duck. Please.*

The close-up held as Sarah, still smiling, her big green eyes eager for fun, waited for my "Yes"—of course I would ride the merry-go-round with her.

SARAH: *Please!*

Amy hit the Pause button, and the image froze across the screen: Sarah in close-up, her eyes imploring me to join her.

"Oh my god!" Maddie said, rolling up a napkin and tossing it at Jill. "Your Mom back then could have been your *twin.*"

Jill ignored her, checking over her shoulder to make sure Amy was okay. Seeing Sarah in such an extreme close-up gave me a chill, but Amy seemed amused, even peaceful, as she watched a piece of our lives play out on screen, Sarah Carpenter's face projected in fifty-four inches of High Def. I'd had no idea this footage still existed. I remembered, right away, what it had sounded like hearing Sarah laugh.

"Last year I had those old Sony tapes transferred to DVD," she said, then turned toward the girls. "His uncle gave him a camcorder for his sixteenth birthday, and for a while he video-taped *everything.* Those camcorders were expensive back then. It was a big deal. Everyone didn't walk around with a mini-film studio on her phone."

"That camcorder's still in my room, I bet," I said, for a moment forgetting that it was Nancy's room now. "Uncle Dan keeps everything."

On screen Amy picked up Sarah, carrying her toward the ticket line as Sarah waved, my camera hand unsteady as I hustled to keep up, the image jumpy but holding focus as the girls joined the line. The camera panned right, showing the queue of kids ahead of them, families loaded down with popcorn and cotton candy, a big stuffed animal against every other dad's hip as they all waited in line for the merry-go-round's next turn. The camera again held focus in a close-up of Amy and Sarah, their faces cheek to cheek, their eyes reaching out, inviting me in.

Amy paused the disc again, sipping from her mug of Chinese tea.

"Fair warning, girls; there's another two hours of this. If you're not in the mood for home movies, I won't be pissed."

Maddie looked over at her friend. "We're not going anywhere," Jill said, staring at her mother's face, so young and happy on the screen. Maddie grabbed an almond cookie and settled back against the coffee table.

"This is a surprise," I said.

Amy smiled. "I promised you a movie night, didn't I?"

She reached across the couch and held my hand, and for a moment it felt like our lives had been recalibrated—welcome to one more night at home with my wife, my daughter, and her BFF, the family Marcino watching silly home movies and reminiscing. Later we would upload the videos to the Internet so Sarah Carpenter, out of college now, making her way in the world, could enjoy the old movies, too; she could see her former babysitters goofing around with her and recall how much she was loved.

Amy squeezed my hand as the disc resumed. There were so many images: Sarah and I sharing a wooden pony on the merry-go-round; she and Amy on the Ferris wheel while I shoot from level ground, the camera catching their feet dangling in the tilting carriage as the wheel climbed higher into the dark sky, a canvas of stars at the back of the frame. We see Sarah and Amy at the beach, building sandcastles; making cookies in the kitchen of Sarah's house; Sarah tucked under the blankets in her bedroom as I orchestrate a puppet show with her menagerie of stuffed toys. At one point the camera is hitched to a tripod, and three of us appear together in frame: Amy cross-legged on the bed, Sarah on her lap, and me—so *young*, not a crease or a whisker anywhere, thick hair spilling over my forehead, a skinny kid with an eager smile, the puppeteer holding Sarah's favorite, a white teddy bear with a red hat and scarf, who sang silly lullabies in a sing-song rhyme. (Scarf-Hat, we called him.) I hear my voice in a goofy, low register, trying to sound like the kind of teddy bear who'd wear a red scarf and a hat.

Bedtime, bedtime, it's time for bed
Say goodnight to the little thoughts in your head
Let's pull up the blankets and turn out the light
It's time for Sarah to say goodnight.

At the end of the song Scarf-Hat bows, and I bring him up to Sarah for a big teddy bear kiss.

I remembered that night, Sarah's mother Laura coming home drunk and crying from another disastrous hook-up with her latest local loser. Amy and I were ready to leave when Laura threw up in the kitchen right in front of Sarah, hurling a gross mélange of tacos and vodka straight into the sink; five minutes later she was passed out on the couch and Sarah was crying. That night Amy and I slept over in Sarah's room, my little song-and-dance with Scarf-Hat an impromptu distraction from her mother's dissolution. Somehow back then it had seemed possible to keep Sarah safe. I watched Amy on the screen, sloe-eyed and beautiful, hugging Sarah as they both drifted toward sleep. On screen I disappear from the frame, the last thing visible before the camera goes dark: my thumb crossing in front of the lens.

Toward the end of the DVD we watch a short film I had made with a few friends from the theater department—a ten-minute absurdist detective story about Sherlock Holmes' pot-smoking younger sister, Amy in the lead role, and wasn't that Ricky B. from the Film Shack playing the dead body? It was both stupider and funnier than it should have been, and the girls got the mad giggles from watching Amy act.

Eventually Maddie fell asleep in the corner rocking chair and Jill went upstairs to finish some homework, leaving Amy and I to savor the final moments of the video: the boardwalk at sunset, Amy and Sarah walking slowly away from the camera, waving goodbye.

．　．　．　．　．

Later, we sat in the kitchen sipping green tea, a single white candle burning between us. On the counter the laptop showed the camera-eye perimeter of the house, Clyde's security system keeping watch.

"It started junior year," Amy said. "We were at his house on a Saturday afternoon. You wanted to show him a scene you had written the night before, and I came along because that's what we did back then, right? Duck and Amy, the Siamese twins."

She dropped a second sugar pack into the tea.

"At first it was like any other visit. I sat there flipping through the *TV Guide* while Ronan read your pages, and then all of a sudden you were asleep on the floor. We just sat there for a minute, watching you sleep, and then he asked me to go into the kitchen to get a Dr. Pepper for when you woke up. I did, and when I came back, he was holding a baggie with three joints in it. They were sticking out of my purse, he said, but that was bullshit. The second I left he must have gone through my bag, hoping to find something, and I was dumb enough to let it happen. And that's how it started. I should have let him call the cops or tell my parents or whatever. Christ, it was only pot. But I'd already been busted once, and I was scared. He said he'd forget all about it if he could see me in my underwear."

My heart tensed, pounding hard.

"At first it was total creep city, and I kept praying you'd wake up, but I knew you wouldn't, at least not anytime soon, and I figured, well, what's the difference between underwear and a bathing suit? And it was flattering, too, in some sick way, and maybe a little exciting, like a game, like I was a Beat chick in some older guy's apartment breaking my parents' rules. I knew at least ten girls at school who had a major crush on him, and there he was, wanting to look at *me*. It happened so fast ...there was a lot going on in my head. You need to understand that, Duck. It was complicated. He let me smoke one of the joints, and so what the hell ... I did it. I took off my jeans and pulled off my T-shirt. I didn't see the camera until he'd already taken the picture."

She stirred the tea, clanging the spoon against the rim.

"*That* I didn't like. I didn't want any photographs. But he was very polite that first time, and though I knew it was 'wrong', it didn't seem like a big deal. I was already dressed when you finally woke up; by then I was stoned out of my mind. And that's how it started."

The ceiling fan circled above us as Amy sipped her tea. I didn't say a word—she'd asked me not to interrupt so I sat like a mute while she sipped from her mug, the candle flame painting the ceiling with its flickering shadows, each jagged silhouette slashed by the fan blades spinning on High.

"A few days later he called me down to his class during homeroom. He'd made about fifty copies of that photograph and said he'd leave them in the cafeteria one day before first period if I didn't stop by his house that night. He said it like a joke, but I knew he meant it. He said he just wanted to see me in my underwear again; he swore he wouldn't touch me, and he didn't— but he sure as hell touched himself. That's when it got scary. The fucker— sitting in a rocking chair with his pants around his knees jerking off while I stood there smoking another joint in my bra and panties. I told myself that I should just go with it, act like an artist, *all experiences are useful,* that kind of crap, but I knew if I didn't stop it, it would get worse. But I was scared, and confused, and I didn't want anyone to see those pictures of me in my underwear. When I think about it now, I should have gone to the principal and gotten him fired. Maybe *some* people wouldn't have believed me, but enough people would have. I thought about telling Ms. Donavan ..." The art teacher, Amy's favorite. "...but I never did. And somehow things kept escalating. He talked a good game, was always polite. 'We're just experimenting,' he'd say. And each time it went a little further. He never threatened me physically. I just smoked a joint and did whatever he said."

She drank her tea, staring into the dark brew.

"That's about all I'm going to tell you, Duck. It lasted a year, until Sarah disappeared. Each time he pushed it further until finally, well...you've seen the drawings. Sometimes you were there, sleeping, sometimes I went alone. He said if I ever told anyone, he'd testify to that Young Playwrights Foundation, or whatever the hell it was, that you'd plagiarized your script. They'd take away your award and your career would be shit before it even started. I didn't know if it would matter or not, but I couldn't let him do that to you. Maybe he was bluffing, but how was I supposed to know? I was too scared to confront him. And then ... when Sarah drowned..."

It was the first time she'd ever said it: *Sarah drowned.*

"...I thought the police might put him away—get him out of my life forever. It was wrong—I knew that almost immediately. So was burning down his house. I was so pissed at you that I went straight to Clyde, but you did the right thing, refusing to help. I was out of control. If Ronan hadn't left...but he did, and then it was over. Except in my head."

She grabbed her prescription bottle of Xanax from the counter and shook out a half-pill, popping it into her mouth and swallowing it with the last of the tea. I looked up at the fan; if you stared long enough, the individual blades became invisible—all you could see was the blur of circular motion.

"I know it's weird that we never slept together, Donnie, but ...every time I have sex I still think of that bastard, and I never wanted that to be part of you and me. Maybe that's why I'm usually with guys I kind of hate. I know I messed up—we should have been together all these years. Sometimes I slept with guys just to see if those feelings would stop. It's sick, right? I thought if you and I were ever together like that it would ruin the one good thing I've had in my life, except for Jill, which is you and me. And that's it..." She tapped her hands on the table in a drum roll. "That's all, folks."

There was so much more I needed to know, so many questions, but I didn't want to push her, not then. She placed the cap back on the pill bottle, her bare feet crossed at the ankles, her pink toes touching the floor. There'd be plenty of time to filter those years through a new, darker lens, to create revisionist histories and myriad interpretations, but now all that mattered was this specific moment.

I reached across the table and touched her hand.

"I'm sorry."

Her eyes began to tear. "You'd better be."

"I should have known. I trusted him. I thought ... I don't know ...everyone loved us and we were indestructible. We were the *mad* ones."

"You were asleep," she said. Our fingers intertwined. "You were asleep and in love."

"If you had told me..."

She looked away. "I can forgive you for almost anything, Donatello, except the word 'if'."

I nodded, my hand sliding over hers, my thumb pressing circles around her slight, tender wrist, my palm warm to the touch of her skin. Her other hand wrapped with mine, and we sat without words, the refrigerator humming, the clock above the sink ticking steadily.

"And now we don't talk about it," Amy said, "which should be easy, since we've been practicing for twenty years."

"What can I do?"

"I don't know," she said.

Upstairs the toilet flushed, and we heard Jill's footsteps as she padded back to her room.

"Watching those videos of you and Sarah ...I miss her," I said.

"God, so do I."

We walked back into the living room, where Maddie was asleep on the couch, but you could play a DVD on Amy's old laptop. I crept over to the TV and ejected the disc. Amy adjusted the blanket over Maddie's legs before shutting the lamp, and I followed her upstairs to her bedroom, the DVD held carefully between my fingers, all those moments that we'd once considered infinite reduced to the time travel of pixels and scratchy megabytes of sound. But thank God for time travel.

Amy's bed was an explosion of blankets and sheets, a wall of fat pillows stacked against the headboard. There were empty cookie boxes and yogurt cups on the floor, a brown, withered banana peel next to the lamp. The air conditioner hummed softly in the corner window.

Her laptop was on the nightstand, a peace symbol sticker plastered on its front, and I handed her the disc.

"We miss you Sarah, wherever you are!" Amy said.

We climbed into bed, and Amy hit Play.

．　．　．　．　．

Though she invited me to stay, spending the night seemed like a mistake, and once she dosed off, her pretty head slumped against the pillow, I pecked her cheek, then scooted out the door.

It was past midnight, the streets dark and still, and it reminded me of the times I would leave the Carpenter house late at night, Amy asleep on the couch, Sarah nestled in her room, Scarf-Hat standing guard at the foot of the bed. Sometimes Laura would call from Ray's Tavern, where the locals drank, and tell us she was going home with some guy she just met, *a great guy, really,* she'd say, slurring her words, the great guy's hand no doubt clamped to her ass while Laura shouted into the phone over the Guns N' Roses song playing on the jukebox. She'd promise to pay Amy another twenty if she'd hang out until morning, and though the twenty never came, Amy always stayed. I might have stayed, too, but late nights were a time of heightened creative energy for me, at least back then, and I needed to be at my desk, in my room, at home, writing for at least an hour before I went to sleep. No matter how enticing a night on the couch with Amy might seem, I kept to that routine like a budding monk, yet whenever I left Laura's house, I always felt like the neighbors were watching me. What exactly is he *doing* there so late at night?

Were people checking their windows and thinking the same as I left Amy's house? *Just nerves,* I thought, but the moment I hit the driveway, a car across the street turned its engine, popped its lights, and drove away, the car's interior too dark for me to spot the driver.

Something about it felt personal, the timing too synched with my departure for it to be coincidental. The car had been parked beyond the range of Clyde's camera set-up, though if the driver had gotten out for a closer look, perhaps it had caught him.

I stopped myself. Mr. Ronan was alive, but why would he be stalking Amy *now* when, according to Cobb's report, his life was a success. *Just nerves,* I thought, but before I unlocked the rental car, I checked the backseat to make certain it was empty.

For a while I drove around with no purpose except avoiding the B&B. In Holman Beach, when you have no place else to go, you head for the water.

In a few days Ocean Avenue would be buzzing with tourists, the scent of fried funnel cakes and cotton candy seizing the ocean breeze, but for now things were dark, except for Ray's Tavern. I parked the car and climbed the wooden ramp to the boardwalk.

I checked for a message from Kelly but so far nothing, so I slid the phone into my pocket and started walking. The ocean, as always, reminded me of Sarah. The spot on the beach where she'd disappeared wasn't far, but I kept to the opposite direction. I found a bench and tried to get my head straight, a hopeless task, as all I could think about was *everything.*

Why hadn't Amy told me after that first time, before he'd ever touched her? Was she afraid I wouldn't believe her? And was it possible that she was right?

Suddenly I yawned, my fingers tingling.

Twenty minutes later, I woke up with my head under the bench, my legs curled around a metal garbage can. Every muscle ached as I sat up and rubbed my eyes, my head still foggy as I reached for my wallet and keys. While I rarely dreamt during my blackouts, this time I dreamed that I was at the Jaybird with those pizza boxes from the other night, revising dialogue and adding a scene in the middle of the first act. I couldn't remember what I wrote in the dream, only the feeling that it was *good,* the best thing I'd ever done. Unlike Kelly, I didn't believe in dreams, but maybe my subconscious was nudging me. I needed to re-read those boxes.

I stood up and looked around, didn't spot a soul, and checked my phone. It was almost 2:00 AM.

At the far end of the boardwalk, fifty yards ahead, I saw a light outside of Toby's Rock Lobster, the music shop surprisingly still bright. I pulled myself up and started walking in that direction, the light useful in waking me; if I hadn't started moving, I might have lay there forever, my bones melting to a paste, my hair like strands of old cotton candy hardened in the sun.

When I reached the front window, I saw Toby standing beside the CD racks tuning an acoustic guitar.

Next to him, his back to the door, was Uncle Dan.

I must have lingered too long because Toby looked up and saw me in the window, waving me inside as if he'd been expecting me. The bell over the door chimed twice as I entered.

Uncle Dan turned, startled to see me. An open bottle of Sam Adams stood on the counter, a second one by the register.

"Donatello, welcome: there's always room for one more penitent at midnight mass," Toby said, "which tonight, at least, started well past the witching hour."

His priest collar was missing, but a gold crucifix hung low around his neck, Jesus's pointed feet dangling between the two Z's in "OZZY" printed across his T-shirt.

"What are you doing here?" Uncle Dan asked.

"Just walking." We hadn't spoken since he'd stormed out of the Jaybird.

Toby smiled. "I'm always surprised how many pilgrims wind up at my door." He tightened one of the guitar strings and plucked it, a single flat note ringing out, his fingers turning the knob until each note sounded right. "Guitars are wonderful instruments, aren't they? Each string holds equal potential for beauty and pain. It's all in how you tune it, and even then, play it long enough and the sound will slip." He paused, making sure we were paying attention. "Consider life a perpetual exercise in re-tuning. The pitch-pipe, the tuning fork...I call them God."

He plucked another string and tweaked the knob.

"Thanks for closing up the other night," Uncle Dan said.

"Jill did most of the work."

"Tell her stop by tomorrow. I'll pay her for the hours."

He grabbed the Sam Adams bottle and took a long swig.

"But that's not all, is it, Dan?" Toby said. "Isn't there something *more* you need to say?"

He finished the bottle, holding it tall as he tilted his head, draining the last drop.

"Look, I'm sorry I ran out on you. Back in 'Nam they shot guys for that."

He put down the bottle and stared at the floor. Toby plucked another string, the note ringing sharp.

"Donatello, your uncle and I have been talking about the past."

"The war," I nodded.

"Yes, but not Vietnam. There are other wars, equally destructive. You understand that, of course. You've been in one yourself."

Uncle Dan leaned against the counter, staring at the empty beer bottle as if he could re-fill it with his eyes.

"I have no patience for religion, you know that, but when Toby talks about God, it makes sense," Uncle Dan said. "Maybe I'm just getting old. The hell with 'getting,' I *am* old. But after what you said the other night, ...I'm having a rough time with it. Toby's helping me, I don't know, work through it."

"*God* is helping you, along with the fine craftsmen at Fender." The ex-Priest strummed all six strings, the guitar finally in tune. He closed his eyes, savoring the sound. "Our Father, who rocks in Heaven..."

"I'm not blaming you for anything," I said. "You didn't know. *I* didn't know."

"I should have," he said. "Because I know about those things." His voice cracked. "I've seen it before."

Toby opened his eyes, reaching across the counter and resting his hand on my uncle's shoulder. "Go on," he whispered. Uncle Dan let out a breath.

"Your mother...Kathy ...I mean Nancy; after I was drafted, she wrote me letters about what was happening, but I couldn't do anything. I was halfway around the world, and she would write these letters about how much she needed me."

He swallowed, looking toward Toby, hoping for permission to stop, but Toby kept nodding, urging him on.

"I showed the letters to my C.O., hoping for a hardship, but he thought it was a scam. They didn't care—they just wanted their grunts in the field. I'd always suspected something was wrong at home...the way he looked at her ...touched her just a little too often in places a father doesn't touch his daughter once she reaches a certain age. She was so beautiful back then. She wanted to be a model. He took away the locks on the bathroom door, the locks on our bedrooms." He grabbed a Sam Adams and guzzled it down. "He waited until I was out of the house before he did it."

My gut tightened. "What are you saying?"

"You know exactly what he means," Toby said.

"There's a reason you never met your grandparents," Uncle Dan said. "When you told me that Amy had been molested, that you were there, asleep...I was right back in 'Nam reading those letters from my sister. I shouldn't have run out on you the other night. I get that. But what was it you said earlier, Toby?"

"We can't always be our better selves."

He nodded. "After my discharge I came back home...I pulled a knife and told him I would kill him if he ever touched her again. Hardest thing I ever did. There are four dead bodies on my soul, maybe more, one a civilian I'm pretty sure, but that doesn't touch what it feels like holding a knife against your own father's throat."

Toby set down the guitar and patted my uncle's shoulder.

"After that he stopped, I think, but she'd already started running away, using heroin. And then you came along," he said. "Toby and I, we argue about it all the time. You know what he calls you? My redemption."

Uncle Dan took another swig of the beer, his eyes shifting between Toby and me. "This goddamn world …" he mumbled. "I never thought it would happen to *you*."

I struggled to take it all in. "It happened to Amy, not me. I just slept, like I always do."

"This goddamn world …"

Toby picked up the guitar again and started strumming.

"Let's not talk anymore," he said. "We're such crazy word-grabbers, aren't we? Something happens, and we rush to twist it into language, but often words are the last thing we need. Let's give this experience a color instead. How about blue? Whatever you're thinking, gentlemen, stop, and imagine the color blue instead. And let's pray."

My uncle and I looked at each other, shifting our feet. We weren't praying men, yet we'd both wound up at a music shop run by a defrocked priest, and maybe, at that moment, with Toby playing the jumpy chords of the apostle Springsteen's "It's Hard to Be A Saint in the City," the only thing left to do was to let the music do the praying—as we thought about all that had happened to the people that we loved, and about all the different shades and textures found in the color blue.

-16-

When I arrived at the house the next morning Uncle Dan's truck was gone, but I stopped in anyway, thinking I should ...well, I wasn't sure *what* I was thinking except that my mother was somewhere inside that house—my obese, one-armed, incest-victim mother—and that any reasonable definition of common decency required an adult son to look after his mother, there being no exclusionary clause for pizza boxes or concrete stoops.

I walked up the driveway and let myself in, my key from twenty years back still turning the lock. I expected quiet, but as I entered, the noise was immediate and unavoidable, the television blaring from my old room, "The Price is Right" at full obnoxious volume: the fake applause, the chanting crowds; the irritating comic patter of the host—everything I hated about game shows maxed out to its high-decibel glory.

Like a five-year-old, I covered my ears and stepped toward the kitchen. On the stove a greasy frying pan sat on the burner, the lingering spirits of bacon and eggs permeating the air, the soiled plates, streaked with yolk, stacked in the sink. I grabbed a sponge and started cleaning.

From the bedroom Nancy shouted at the TV. "Higher!" she cried. "It's higher!"

I put away the dishes, checked my phone—still nothing from Kelly—and then headed for the door. Despite Uncle Dan's message to the contrary, my presence in Nancy's life seemed an unnecessary complication, as if her severed arm had returned for a short visit. She might be curious about what the arm had been up to all these years, but without the possibility of re-attachment, the arm seemed superfluous, just like me. What did she need a son for when she had Uncle Dan and "The Price is Right" to keep her company with reliable, vicarious thrills?

"Lower!" Nancy shouted. "Guess lower!" The stage announcer's voice boomed, "...brand *NEW* barbecue grill!"

I reached for the door, my hand on the knob, ready to bolt, but something held me. The truth was—I had nowhere else to go. Kelly was gone; Uncle Dan was at the Jaybird; Amy was at work, selling underwear to the stay-at-home Moms killing time at the Mall with their strollers and sippy cups. I had no desire to make pizza or hang around the boardwalk or lie on the beach. Back at the B&B there were twenty inside-out pizza boxes covered in manic script, the new scenes I'd written the other night at the Jaybird, but I lacked the energy to deal with those, either. A movie seemed the best idea, but first there was Nancy, only a few feet away in my childhood bedroom. There'd been times in my life when I'd wanted nothing more than my mother's reappearance, yet wasn't it too late for her presence to have meaning?

From the bedroom the TV volume dropped, the game show clamor yielding to music, guitars and a flute, piano chords in a simple rhythm.

I walked down the hallway. "Nancy? It's me, Donatello ..." I peered through the bedroom door.

"Hush!" she said.

In the center of my room, *her* room, Nancy stood facing the television, her one arm close against her side, her posture straight; her gaze intense. She wore the same floral housecoat she'd worn the other day and, strangely, a pair of black high heels at least one size too small for her feet, her massive ankles spilling over the tight leather straps. The bed was pushed against the wall, and I leaned forward to catch a glimpse of the screen.

"My favorite show," Nancy whispered. *Dancing with the Stars.* "You can watch, too."

"That's okay. I'll..."

"Hush!"

She wobbled toward me, knees shaking, and I waited for her to go down, contemplating the hopeless comedy of my trying to lift her without pulleys and a rope. But her legs steadied, and she found her equilibrium, her hand clamping onto my wrist, pulling me toward her.

"Look, there's Valentin!"

On screen a sleek, sinewy dancer bowed toward the audience, his black shirt open to mid-chest, black pants fitted closely to his waist before flaring out below the knees. He had a black beard and mustache, his teeth electric-white, and Nancy smiled as he gracefully spun in a double-circle, his arm extended at his shoulder as a blonde woman in a short silk dress glided across the stage. They clasped hands, and the orchestra began playing.

"I watch at night, too," Nancy said. "I'm learning. Look—the foxtrot."

On screen the two dancers began sweeping across the stage in continuously flowing movements, Nancy shaking her head in rhythm to their elegant steps.

"Slow, slow, quick-quick," she said, and her feet started moving, two steps forward, two toward the side, and then back again, only to repeat the steps—slow, slow, quick-quick—as she lumbered back to her starting point.

"I was a dancer once," she said. "Not like this. Naked stuff, but I was pretty good. I know the tango, the meringue. Danny won't dance with me. I always ask, but he doesn't watch this show."

On screen Black Pants lowered Silk Dress into a dip and the crowd roared. Nancy, too-she patted her hand against her shoulder, the nearest she could come to clapping, and I thought about that Zen koan: what is the sound of one-hand clapping? Apparently, this was it: Nancy tapped her shoulder-stump with her open palm, her ghost sleeve dangling. *Why doesn't she just cut off the extra sleeve and sew up the opening?* It made me sad that no one had bothered to do this, but she seemed not to care. She moved her big body around the room in a one-woman foxtrot—her feet moving in shaky rhythm, forward, forward, side-side, slow, slow, quick-quick—spinning around and even dipping herself once, timing it with the dip on the screen, as if Black Pants were dipping *her* instead of Silk Dress, her knees buckling in tremors but holding steady, her sloped neck angled toward the ceiling with a child-like grin.

"Do you want me to teach you?" she asked.

"That's okay. I'm not much of a dancer."

"Sure you are," she said. "You take after me."

No, I don't, I thought, instinctively, ready to flip, ready to testify on a stack of Bibles that I was *nothing at all* like her—but I stopped myself, because what did I really know about her that mattered?

In the corner, on the bureau, was her photograph, a high-school yearbook shot of her pretty, eighteen-year-old face, her blonde wavy hair corralled around her shoulders, pink lips posed in a smile, her eyes bright and intelligent, ready to take on the world. Beside it, in a second frame, was a six-by-eight of a newborn swaddled in a hospital blanket, a shock of brown hair sticking up at the crown of his head, his eyes open, wide awake.

"Is that me?" I asked, but I already knew the answer. I walked to the bureau and lifted the frame. It was the first time I'd ever seen my baby picture.

"They give it to you at the hospital," she said, and belched. "You don't even have to pay for it. I kept telling the nurse 'are you sure it's mine?' and she said, 'He looks just like you'."

I compared the two photographs, the resemblances hard to spot. Maybe there was something in the shape of the face, but I couldn't be certain. *This is me.* Unlike most parents, Uncle Dan had never taken all those standard baby pictures people took for granted. There was no visual record of me before I started school, and even though we always bought the class photos they'd send home each year, the photographs themselves never ventured from the envelope, all those wallet-sized shots meant for relatives remaining on the contact sheet, upside down and untouched. I looked at my new-born self, a froggy-faced baby in a navy-blue onesie, and felt my throat grow hard.

Nancy held her yearbook photo so it stood side-by-side with her face, the frame resting on her shoulder as if her younger, prettier head had sprouted from her flesh to form time-warp Siamese twins, identical faces separated by forty years and a pair of double chins.

"That man at the agency told me I'd be famous," she said, turning her head so she could see her younger self. "He was a liar."

She put down the frame and moved back toward the television, picking up the remote and rewinding back to the start of the dance, the foxtrot, Black Pants and Silk Dress once again set in each other's arms, the orchestra playing in 4/4 time. I held my baby photo, touching my baby nose with the tip of my pinkie.

"Slow, slow, quick-quick," Nancy whispered, two steps forward, two to the side. Her breath soon grew heavy from the stress of her weight, dark sweat patches spotting her housecoat, but she kept at it, her steps surprisingly graceful, her concentration unwavering as she counted out the rhythm, slow, slow, quick-quick.

Slow, slow, quick-quick.

"I've never done this with a partner," she said.

And there it was, my exit-cue, hit the road, Jack—the only dance I knew by heart, a two-step out the door. *No way; no way,* I thought, even as my body did exactly the opposite, putting down my baby photo and moving toward her so that we stood face to face, inches apart.

"Like this," she said, her arm reaching out, her open hand waiting for me to take it. Her hip nudged my side, bumping me in place as I took her hand. The loose empty sleeve hung awkwardly until I threw it over my shoulder, as if her arm had never left, my own arm wrapped around her back, at least as far as it could reach, and we held the position, our frames upright and lifted, her arm folded over mine—not exactly Black Pants and Silk Dress, yet still, momentary partners.

Nancy's foot began tapping. Her breath was bacon-sour and I could feel the dampness beneath her housecoat, a rank scent wafting from her body, yet I didn't back away. My feet started moving—forward, forward, side-side, slow, slow, quick-quick—and suddenly my mother and I were dancing the foxtrot.

My mother and I.

We bounded across the room, collided with the dresser, backed into the closet door and stubbed our shins against the nightstand, Nancy huffing, out of breath but unwilling to let go. Slow, slow, quick-quick—we pivoted, turned, completed a box step; my god, I even dipped her, and even when the music ended, when Black Pants and Silk Dress slipped apart blowing kisses to the loving crowd, a Toyota commercial grabbing the screen, we continued moving through our bumbling waltz; forward, forward, side-side; slow, slow, quick, quick, her one good arm folded over mine, my childhood bedroom as worthy a locale as the dance-floor as the Ritz, both of us grateful for the music, the movement; the surprising comfort of 4/4 time.

Forward, forward, side-side; slow, slow, quick-quick.

-17-

Imaginary Interview – Donatello Marcino, September 22, 20XX – NPR Morning Edition

Q: Was it always your intention to confront him?

A: No. But I began thinking about those Truth and Reconciliation commissions they held in Rwanda after the genocide, how it was healing to look your abuser in the eye and talk about what had happened. Kelly gave me a book about it once; she liked to read about the "resilient human spirit." So I thought maybe if Amy confronted him, it might help. And maybe I'd seen too many movies over the years with "revenge" as the motivating factor.

Q: You wanted to avenge what he did to her?

A: On some level, yes. Everyone's seen those films where Liam Neeson or The Rock hunts down the bad guys who hurt his wife or daughter, and then goes on an utter ass-kicking barrage. I always hated those movies, but there's a reason they're so popular, right?

Q: So you wanted to kick Ronan's ass.

A: Well, I'm not Liam Neeson or the Rock, but...yes, I wanted to kick his ass.

. . . . .

I had no clue what to do but *action* seemed required. In my head the scene played out in dark, twisted scenarios, from the sour recriminations of a Swedish art film to the full-on bloodbath of a Tarantino flick. I didn't think I could actually hurt Mr. Ronan, but if I confronted him and forced a confession, an acknowledgement of guilt and a gesture of penance, perhaps it would help Amy release all that sticky trauma. Was it possible that I could make things, if not right, then at least better?

Yes, find him, confront him, truth and reconciliation.

If nothing else, I could at least find out *why*. He knew how much I loved Amy, yet he had still raped her. Was it possible that he'd raped her *because* of me, or was that just my hard-to-shake tendency to wander down the rabbit hole of making everything about me?

After three hours of madman brooding, driving around in the rental car, Nine Inch Nails and the air conditioner blasting, drinking Diet Dr. Pepper and ruminating over Ronan and Amy, I'd worked myself into a froth, ready to burst into his house bare-chested, ammo clips strung across my chest as I flung newly-sharpened Ninja stars at his ugly rapist face. Outwardly I might have seemed even keeled, but the inside of my brain was pure Grand Guignol. To calm myself I broke out some techniques I'd learned at the meditation center with Kelly (the annoying but useful "*Breathe!*")

I'd agreed to drive Amy to her outpatient appointment that afternoon, so I picked her up at the Mall and headed for the hospital. As expected, the ride was a bumper to bumper Jersey classic, every other light turning red the moment we approached; the cars in front of us slamming on brakes, the cars behind us pounding irate horns, the unofficial flag of New Jersey—the raised middle finger—jutting out from rolled-down windows, *drive, you fuckin' moron, yeah, I'm talkin' to you!*

The familiar comfort of Amy's presence steadied my mood. I turned toward her as we waited for the light.

"What are you doing?" she asked.

"Just looking at you."

"It's free, I suppose."

She unzipped her purse and started digging for her hairbrush.

"God, you're pretty," I blurted, not meaning to say it aloud, still upside down from those madman thoughts. Amy faced me, smiling, brushing the bangs from her forehead.

"Thanks, I think."

"After all these years, it's still you and me, isn't it?"

"Is that some country song you're writing?" She looked at her brush and plucked out a wayward grey strand. "I don't like it, Donnie—stick with pizza. We sound like a couple in a commercial for reverse mortgages."

Instinctively, as if in that moment no other action were possible, I leaned over the driveshaft and kissed her neck, the locks of her hair soft against my cheek, the avocado-lime scent of her shampoo giving me a jolt, a desire for more.

"What are you doing?" she said, not pulling back. She patted my shoulder, her hand staying long enough for it to mean something. The light turned green and we rolled forward, the traffic finally easing as we hit a four-lane stretch and picked up speed. Amy looked out the window, the big "H" sign looming at the intersection, pointing toward the hospital.

"I can't afford it, but I'm thinking of taking Jill to Europe this summer," she said. "Don't tell her please, because God knows where I'm finding the cash, but I think we need a break from this town. I'm sick of the ocean, and the tourists, and that stupid goddamn boardwalk. I don't want to be here anymore. I'm sure I'll come back, at least until Jill graduates, but a change of scenery...I really need it." She examined her nails, and bit off a cuticle. "What do you know about Estonia?"

"Nothing at all."

"Sounds perfect."

I pulled into the hospital lot and found a spot in the second row, squeezing the Honda between two oversized pick-ups. Amy zipped up her purse and opened the door.

"Thanks for the ride. It should be around forty-five minutes. Are you waiting?"

"I'll walk in with you. There's a cafeteria, right?"

I killed the engine and locked the doors. We stepped across the asphalt lot, side by side, a man in a wheelchair being pushed by his wife a few steps ahead.

"If you need money, for that trip to Estonia, or wherever, maybe I can help."

"I can't take your cash," she said. "When did I become a GoFundMe page? Of course, if you came with us, to Estonia, I might let you treat now and then."

"I'll get my passport and start packing."

She stopped, grabbing my arm and pulling me back, moving us from the walkway as a pregnant woman passed.

"Okay, what are we doing here?" Amy said. "Is this our normal B.S., or is this something different? I can't tell anymore—you're dealing with a mental patient, remember? I know we're not going to Estonia, but... where *are* we going?"

The wheelchair couple disappeared through the door as Amy's hand dropped from my arm.

"I might be staying," I told her. "I don't really know. Kelly sent my play to George. I doubt anything will come of it, but I might be around for a while."

"Kelly, too?"

I didn't know what to say. Insert the moment into a film and you'd have a two-shot of Amy and me facing each other in a hospital parking lot, the script directions clear.

His love for her is obvious and deep, part of his bones. The weight of the moment isn't lost on her, either—she is hesitant, perhaps anxious, but eager, too. Something they've both wanted for a long time may finally be happening.

But when the camera pulls back in a wide-shot, panning left, we see Kelly seated on a wooden bench petting one of her cats, and he's shocked by how glad he is to see her again, the urge to scoop her into his arms nearly as strong as his desire to hold onto Amy and never let go.

"It's complicated," I said.

"Let's hope your new play has better dialogue than *that*." She headed for the entrance. "Of course it's complicated. It's called being an adult."

. . . . .

After her appointment we met by the elevator, Amy looking calm and upbeat as she reapplied her lip gloss, sliding the tube over her lips and then smacking them together in a plucky air kiss.

"Marvelous Moxie," she said, showing me the tube. "What do you think?"

"Sei molto bella," I said, laying on the accent.

"Is that some new dish at the Jaybird?"

"You're the new dish."

"Jesus," she groaned. "If people could hear you, they'd club us to death."

We walked side by side, just like our years at West Ocean High, but Amy's comment about my not being "adult" had hit a nerve.

"So what do you talk about during these appointments?" I asked. "I know it's confidential..."

"But you want to know anyway."

"Just curious. I've been to some counseling myself over the years."

"I remember." She dropped the lipstick into her bag. "I expected to hate this whole therapy deal, but it's worth the co-pay. Among other topics, we talk about *you*. Don't worry—*most* of it's positive. Let's just say you never would have found those drawings if Sheri hadn't encouraged me to tell you. I've been meaning to 'discuss this' for years."

"If I'd known ..."

She stopped, then punched my arm, *hard*.

"What did I tell you about the word 'if'? I'm serious, Donnie. It's poison."

"Right," I said. We were almost at the exit when I decided to tell her about Mr. Ronan. What could be more "adult" than that? I couldn't think of a better place—if the conversation went seriously shit's creek, I could always wrestle her upstairs to find the counselor before the inevitable blow-up. "There's something you should know," I said. "About Ronan. I know where he lives."

Her forehead tightened. "Where he *lives*? I thought he was dead."

"No. I thought you knew ...you said Clyde was lying..."

"I *thought* he was lying, but I didn't know. I *hoped* it was true."

"But you said he was stalking you...that you saw him. Remember, you shot out your front window!"

"Don't make this about me," she said, looking toward the corner, where a large red sign pointed toward the Burn Unit. She paced down the corridor, shook her head and turned back. "Okay, he's alive," she nodded, her eyes turning hard. "Whatever. Where is he?"

"He lives in Ohio. He's changed his name. He's Michael ..."

"I don't care what his name is. Whatever." She looked at the ceiling, at the wall, anywhere but at me. "Jesus. I was almost ready to believe that he *wasn't* stalking me. Thanks a lot, Donnie."

"I thought ..." Yet suddenly I didn't know *what* I thought. Truth and reconciliation, and all that crap. My pulse jumped into my throat, and I wondered if a massive coronary would be less painful for me than the troubled look on Amy's face. "I thought maybe we should confront him," I said, my voice unsteady. "In Rwanda, they had these truth and reconciliation councils, where people met with their attackers. The U.N. ..."

"Rwanda?" she said. "They hacked people with machetes in Rwanda."

"I know."

"What exactly are you suggesting, Donnie?"

"I don't know ..."

"Sometimes you really are a stupid shit," she said, which hurt, *a lot*, yet seemed like a fair assessment of sixty percent of my life.

"Forget I said anything."

"Too late," she said. "You wouldn't have said anything if you didn't have some kind of dumb-ass plan. So how exactly does this play out?"

At least I was smart enough not to mention any films starring Liam Neeson or The Rock.

"I don't know," I said. "I thought maybe if we confronted him, made him apologize, you'd realize that he couldn't hurt you anymore, and maybe you'd feel better. Forget it. It was a bad idea."

"You want to beat him up, don't you?"

"No."

"Why not?"

"Okay, yes. I do want to kick the shit out of him. But I'm not going to ..."

"Why not?"

"Do you want me to?"

"Maybe," she said. "Although if that's really what I need, I'd bring Clyde instead of you. The only thing *you've* ever punched is pizza dough."

"I thought maybe if we talked to him..."

"... we could create this great dramatic scene, right?" she said. "Act II is starting to drag, so let's get these three characters in a room and make something happen. That's what you're thinking, isn't it? Add a little tension and some cathartic dialogue and maybe she'll have an epiphany. Voila—the happy ending. You can even work a stupid *chair* into the scene."

It was a dig at my first play. "Forget it. Just pretend ..."

"We've been pretending for twenty years," she said. "Isn't the whole point that we need to *stop*?"

"I love you," I said—admittedly bad dialogue, but hopefully a useful truth.

"And I love you," Amy said, "but that really hasn't helped us much over the years, has it?"

She paced in a circle, nodding her head, her brain spinning, and I looked away as some poor guy in a hospital gown with an IV drip attached to his arm followed a nurse down the long blank hall toward Radiation.

"How did you find his address?"

"I hired a lawyer. I wanted a copy of the death certificate so you wouldn't think he was stalking you anymore. But—"

"Stop talking," she said. "Let's think about this. You said he lives in Ohio? I'm not driving to Ohio in a Honda Civic from Budget Rental. I'm thinking a Porsche or a Jaguar, whichever has more leg room." She nodded, the idea taking hold.

"Let's take a few days to think it over ..."

"This was *your* idea, Donnie. You opened a door. What did you expect...I'd polish the knob and walk away?"

"No, but ..."

"Truth and reconciliation ...I like how that sounds."

INTERLUDE

We're an hour past the Pennsylvania State Line when Amy mentions the monkey.

"Suppose you needed a life-saving operation, like brain surgery," she says. "You have two choices to perform the procedure. The first surgeon is a middle-aged white guy with a degree from Harvard and salt and pepper hair. A classic afternoon-soaps jawline, anchorman good-looks. His success rate with this type of operation is about 85%—he's the top surgeon in his field, and everyone says that if you need this operation, you're lucky to have him." She turns, making sure I'm paying attention. "Now your second choice has done just as many surgeries, and his success rate is actually better: 100%— he's never lost a patient. The only thing is, he's a monkey."

She gives me a few seconds to imagine it: strapped to the gurney, moments before the anesthesia kicks in, I look up and see a chimpanzee in green surgical scrubs holding a scalpel, ready to slice into my brain.

"Your life is on the line," she says. "Who do you choose?"

"Is the monkey in-network?"

"Excellent question. Yes, they're both in-network, and all other factors are equal. Who would you pick?"

"Is there a catch? Do you make it through the surgery, but die of an infection because the monkey threw feces at the head nurse?"

"The monkey is a professional. Any feces throwing occurs *outside* the hospital."

"Who would *you* pick?"

"Irrelevant. I don't need the surgery," she says. "Hurry up, the tumor's growing. Is it the monkey or the man?"

This is what you talk about when you're stuck in a car for ten hours and what you *really* need to discuss feels like a man-made virus in a lab—let it out of its box and God knows where it might spread. But at least she's talking. For the first hour she barely said a word, her silence like an accusation; I'd sneak glances at her face and wonder how much she hated me, the urge to find the nearest U-turn and head back to Holman Beach like a nagging friend camped in the backseat, tapping my shoulder whispering, *bad idea.*

"The monkey," I say.

"Good choice. But too bad, that perfect record was due for a hit." Amy grabs my thigh and squeezes. "Sorry, Donnie, you didn't make it."

. . . . .

Twenty miles from Pittsburgh we stop at a diner, our legs creaky-stiff, our backs wracked in knots, the rented Porsche a terrible choice for the long, broken-down highways dragging us into the Rust Belt. Forget the cool factor and the zero to sixty in five seconds flat; the leg room sucks, and the seats take every bump and pothole and shove them straight up your spine. Even the Civic would have been a smoother ride, but we can't abandon the damn thing, so we make the best of it, pretending to appreciate how smoothly the tires hug the lanes and how the trio of teenage boys outside the diner get excited the second we pull into the lot.

We both order the chickpea salad and a plate of french fries, a reasonable compromise between health and grease. While we wait for the server to bring the food, Amy flips over the paper placemat and starts drawing, an impromptu sketch capturing our trip. I do some quick mental math, subtracting miles and calculating average speeds, the anticipated number of bathroom stops. At our current pace, in less than five hours we'll be outside Ronan's door, leaving the magic question: then what? By now I am nothing but doubt.

"Maybe we should turn around, head home," I suggest.

She doesn't look up, her pencil gliding over the placemat. "What about truth and reconciliation?"

"It's usually done with a professional facilitator, someone trained in ...I don't know..."

"Reconciling?"

"Something like that."

"This was *your* idea. I thought you were going to kick his ass."

"I know..."

"You opened a door, Donnie. You can't close it until we walk through. We keep going."

End of debate. She turns over the placemat so I can see it—a drawing of the two of us standing on a porch, my face twisted in comic anguish, cartoon flop sweat flying from my brow; Amy with a smile, and in her hand, a pistol. Thankfully Captain Sick is nowhere in sight.

"Please tell me you're not armed."

"Okay, I'm not armed," she says. "But don't worry. It's unregistered; my grandfather bought it fifty years ago during the Newark riots. There's no way to trace it. If we have to, we wipe the prints and leave it."

"Wipe the prints? What are you saying?"

The waitress arrives with our salads and fries; Amy flips the placemat and smiles.

"Ground pepper?" the waitress asks. We decline, and she drops two straws and ambles away.

"It's never seemed right that the only person I ever shot was *you*," Amy says.

I'm pretty sure she's playing with me, testing my limits. "If you brought a gun with you, we're going home right now."

"Jesus, Donnie, relax ..." She spears a French fry and dips it in ketchup. "I'm not armed. Pat me down if you don't believe me."

The fries look crisp, the salad fresh, but my appetite is dead. I sip ice water and wish for sleep.

"I get that you don't want me to shoot him," Amy says, "but what exactly *are* we going to do? Ring the doorbell and say, 'trick or treat?'" She claps her hands and goes girl-group, swaying her shoulders in a Sixties shimmy. "*My boyfriend's back and you're gonna be in trouble. Come on, Donnie, sing ...*"

Two tables over, a truck driver gives us a *look*. I stab my salad with a dingy fork.

"Chickpeas? If you're really planning to kick his ass, you need some red meat. Should we order a few burgers to go?"

It occurs to me that I've never punched anyone in my life. Even when I found the plumber penis-deep in my ex-wife's ass, the most I did was pelt him with a bad slice of pizza, and when he finally hiked up his pants, it was *me* who moved back, not him. Was it possible that Mr. Ronan would kick *my* ass? He'd be in his mid-fifties now, hardly decrepit. Uncle Dan was sixty-five but one glance at his arms made it clear he could clobber me and barely break a sweat. Or what if Amy and I knocked on Ronan's front door, and suddenly I fell asleep. Who was I kidding? I was nobody's hero.

I stop myself. *Just remember what he did—adrenaline and anger will take care of the rest.*

As if reading my mind, Amy reaches across the table and touches my wrist.

"Don't stress it. I'm not expecting you to be anyone but yourself."

Why does that feel like an insult?

"I'm a big girl now," she says. "Whatever's going to happen, I'm writing the scene—not you, not him. And I lied. I do have my grandfather's .22 with me, just in case, and his silver flask, too, liquid courage, thirty proof peppermint."

Unzipping her purse, she pulls out the flask and takes a swig. "I'm with you in Rockland, Carl Solomon!" she says, that old line from Ginsburg's "Howl." I never paid much attention to that poem until an Intro to Lit class freshman year. It turned out that Rockland was a mental institution where Ginsburg had spent time ducking a robbery charge.

Amy leans over and pecks my lips, her mouth salty-sweet, French fries and peppermint Schnapps.

"Finish your chickpeas," she tells me. "Rockland awaits!"

. . . . .

The alcohol opens a door, unleashes her memories, her voice low but steady, the Porsche gobbling up the miles as we head West, the Ohio border minutes away.

"After the first time it happened, he sent me flowers. A dozen red roses," she says. "My parents assumed they were from you. They probably thought I'd lost my virginity, which, in a sick way, I guess I had. There wasn't any note, but I knew they were from him. My mother put them in a crystal vase by the front door. A dozen beautiful red roses."

The traffic is thin, the highway clear in a flat straight-away, and the Porsche breaks one hundred with a tap of my foot.

"My mother loved those roses." We pass a dead deer on the shoulder, its legs elevated in rigor mortis. "Why didn't I throw them away?"

. . . . .

"The first few times, I knew it was wrong, but he never hurt me physically. He said he was in love with me, and that a girl's first time should be with an older man, who can teach her the right way to do it. I knew that it was crap, but he was a good actor, you know? He gave me vodka, let me smoke a joint. I knew it was wrong, but it was just so weird and confusing."

. . . . .

"He said that if I told you what happened, he would say that I seduced *him*, and that you'd believe him instead of me. And the way he said it, it made sense. Why *wouldn't* you believe him, you know? And he had those photos of me ... he said he'd show the whole school, my parents, *you*."

The last fifteen miles have been nothing but farmland, giant corn stalks lined along a two-lane county blacktop, crows pecking another road-kill deer near the shoulder.

"How many times?" I ask her.

"Nineteen," she says. "Not counting when he only made me undress."

"Nineteen," I whisper, eyes on the road, all those corn stalks closing in.

· · · · ·

"I almost told you once," she says. "We were at Laura's house, with Sarah, and there was this terrible Lifetime movie on television. Sarah was asleep, and we were on the couch, snuggling together like we always did. In the movie there was a rape scene, an older man and a teenage girl. The man was her swim coach, or maybe her father's business partner—I forget. It was Lifetime so of course the film was bad, and you kept going on and on about how fake the scene was, how unrealistic and contrived. That was the word you kept using, contrived. And you had a point—it was a crappy film—but the scene itself...it kind of got it right. How the girl felt, how the man kept manipulating her. Sometimes *life* is contrived, you know? And I almost told you...the words were in my head, but you kept talking about how lame the film was, and I just couldn't say it; I couldn't tell you to shut the fuck up, that the scene was real and that it was happening to me, too."

· · · · ·

"I pointed a gun at him once. He laughed and told me to take off my skirt. And I did it. I put down the gun and undressed. Jesus."

· · · · ·

"While it was happening, I went to the doctor once and she asked me if I was sexually active. I didn't know what to say. I still don't. I mean, how do you respond to that? My boyfriend and I haven't done it yet but the Drama Teacher rapes me twice a month? How exactly do you categorize that in a patient file?"

.　.　.　.　.

"Are we *there* yet? How many more miles, Donnie? I have to pee soon."

.　.　.　.　.

"Three times it happened while you were in the room. God, you could sleep through anything. And I was glad, too; I was afraid you'd wake up and see me with him, and I didn't want that. I never wanted you to find out. That's one reason why I never said anything. I don't say that to make you feel guilty, it's just the truth, although maybe I do want you to feel guilty sometimes, because *I* still feel guilty sometimes, which is crap, because *he's* the one who's guilty, right? Not us. We were just kids."

.　.　.　.　.

"Sometimes I'd get so mad at you I'd want to …I don't know, smash your head in with a toaster. Because half the time I was worrying about you— what *you'd* think if you found out. And I resented the hell out of that. I should have been worrying about *me*."

.　.　.　.　.

"He gave me invitations; can you believe that? Party invitations like you'd buy at Party City, with a date and time for me to visit his house. He *scheduled* the rapes. And I went. Sometimes I'd be late, but I was too afraid not to show up. He had those photographs, and each time he'd take another picture of me naked."

She holds the flask up straight, draining the last drop.

"The invitations had red and blue balloons on the front, with 'Party Time' written inside one of the balloons. When Jill was about six, she got invited to a party, one of her kindergarten friends, and when I opened the invitation it was the same one—those red and blue balloons with 'Party Time' on the front. I almost died. Seriously, that 'my heart stopped' crap that always seems ridiculous when you read it in a book—sometimes it's true. The same *exact* invitation. Even if it *was* a coincidence, no way was Jill going to that party."

. . . . .

"I'm out of Schnapps. Stop at the next town and find a liquor store, okay? It's not a question, either. And I still need to pee."

. . . . .

"Maybe I do want some kind of revenge. To make him sit there and feel that sense of powerlessness. A gun can be useful even if you never fire it."

"No guns," I tell her. "You know Chekhov's rule."

That old theater maxim: if a gun appears on stage in Act I, it must go off in Act III.

"Don't worry, I'm not here with Chekhov. I'm here with *you.*"

. . . . .

"We never found those photographs," she says. "Clyde and I tossed his house but couldn't find a damn thing. That's why we burned it down, you know. We wanted to scare him, sure, and I wanted to hurt him, but what we really wanted were those damn photographs. After the police let him go, I was terrified they might surface, that he'd mail them to my parents, or to you, or that he'd spread them all over school like he'd threatened. God knows what he did with them. We couldn't find them, that's for sure. So we burned down the house. Those flames were fucking beautiful."

. . . . .

"I *did* tell you what was happening, once. You were asleep. It was a few weeks before everything...before Sarah ..."

Drowned. Amy still avoided it.

"We were at your house, getting ready to watch a movie, and you went into the kitchen to microwave the popcorn. I was on your bed, listening to the corn pop, and suddenly I smelled it burning. I ran into the kitchen and you were face down in the sink, totally sleeping. It was funny—your head was in a pasta bowl, and I started talking, telling you everything. Somehow it felt good—I thought on some level you might hear me, even if you'd never realize it. I told you everything, then ate all the popcorn, even the burnt ones."

．　．　．　．　．

I wait in the car while Amy hits the liquor store and finds a restroom. It's one of those times when I wished that I smoked; how great it might feel to strike that match and light up, inhale a little death and blow white dragon-trails out through my nose. Instead I play with my phone and text Kelly a simple message: *Miss you.* The moment I send it, it feels like a betrayal of Amy. And of Kelly, too.

Amy pops back in the Porsche with a fresh bottle of Schnapps and a bag of Tostitos. "Never underestimate the pleasure of an empty bladder," she says, and tosses me a Slim Jim.

"You expect me to eat this?"

"Protein," she says. "Slim Jim's are *manly*. What—you don't like petrified beef?"

"Maybe later."

"We're in the Midwest, Donnie. The last good slice of pizza was two hundred miles back."

I'm pretty sure she's busting me, but with Amy you never know. She refills the flask as I restart the engine.

"I've figured it out," she says, checking her face in the mirror as I pull back onto the road. The GPS tells us we're ten minutes from Ronan's street. "I know how we should play it."

I stay in the right lane, thirty miles per hour being fast enough when you're headed toward a reckoning. Amy stares out the front windshield, her hand unconsciously tugging at the seatbelt.

"I want him to feel exposed, humiliated," she says. "Scared, too. Exactly how I felt when he took those photographs. He should know that feeling. Donnie. Even if it's only for a second. So here's what we're going to do."

The way she explains it, everything sounds simple. "And then we drive back home," she says.

I have my doubts; it's a terrible idea, certain to backfire, but it's Amy's truth, not mine. It's *her* reconciliation. All I can do is be there.

"Will that make it better?"

She takes a final swig from the flask before we pull onto Ronan's block.

"It won't make it worse."

. . . . .

Davenport Drive—Michael Rooney has done well for himself, better than a certain Mr. Ronan could have done teaching high school Drama in Ocean County, New Jersey. Manicured lawns and stately two-story homes, a maple tree on every lot, the driveways filled with BMWs and Lexus SUVs—a block where no one cuts his own grass, let the Mexicans do it on Tuesday morning while Mom and Dad are away at the office, while the nannies take the children to the park and the retirees wait at the club for their scheduled tee times. Each lot is at least an acre, a far cry from the cereal box yards of Holman Beach. *This is what America looks like, to people who don't know what America really is,* I think. Not the 1%, perhaps, but somewhere between percentages four and five. Maybe I'd be living somewhere like this if I'd taken that job writing *Diapers 4.* I can see it in Amy's face as we inch down the road toward Ronan's house, number fourteen. She's been stuck in her grandmother's run-down Cape Cod for sixteen years, probably another sixteen or more to go, working at the Mall for a crap salary, while this rapist bastard rolls around in some tony McMansion. When she points the gun, will she make him drop his Tag Heuer before he drops his pants?

"I wonder what he does," she whispers.

"Real estate, I think."

"I hate real estate."

It's Saturday, late afternoon, the neighborhood quiet except for two kids kicking a soccer ball on a side lawn. A dog barks, somewhere, and the house numbers diminish as we drive: 22, 20, 18. Amy reaches into her bag, the handle of her grandfather's gun protruding like a snake. One more house and we are there, 14 Davenport Drive, chez Michael Rooney, so unlike the rented bungalow where he'd lived in Holman Beach, where he'd once seen a loose joint in a sixteen-year-old girl's purse and pounced.

"Are we really going to do this?" Amy asks, her way of passing responsibility. *You could have stopped us.* But it's too late for that.

"The gun isn't loaded, right?"

"I'm not going to kill him," she says. "Humiliation—that's all I want."

And then, voila, we are there, number 14, if not the finest house on the block, then in the top three. And even though it's been twenty years, I recognize him immediately, the angle of his shoulders, the shape of his head, his fast, rhythmic gait. We pull in front of the house as Mr. Ronan walks up the driveway, eyes down as he flips through the day's mail, and damned if I don't feel a trace of excitement, even affection, forever the theater geek rushing to the Drama Room in search of praise. *Mr. Ronan, guess what? I wrote twenty pizza boxes worth of dialogue the other night!*

"Rapist," Amy whispers, breaking my daydream. We watch Mr. Ronan walking his beautiful driveway, a bluebird on the branch of a Japanese maple singing on his American Dream front lawn.

"Do we wait until he's inside?"

"No. Park the car and let's go."

And just like that, we're commandos, we're the Justice League of America, we're Bonnie and Clyde, Mr. Ronan turning as he hears the engine stop, the doors of the Porsche slamming shut. We're twenty yards away, and he smiles...we must be looking for the Coopers next door, he thinks, though maybe he recognizes us in some layer of his reptile brain because the smile seems to freeze, Amy like a panther as she heads for the driveway. Maybe in that moment when he sees her, twenty years older but still the same girl, he knows that there's always a time to answer for one's sins. He turns toward me, his eyes shifting between us, and he must know, the realization must click, his star pupil back from the past, and Michael Rooney is once again Michael Ronan, and Amy's hand is in her purse, her fingers curled around the hidden handle of a .22.

"Can I help you?" he says, his voice apprehensive. We cross the border of his property, and I can feel it—*he knows, he knows it's us*—and what do we do if he breaks into a run? Will Amy turn vigilante and pull the trigger, his blood splattering in raindrops over his perfectly manicured lawn?

And then—a little blonde girl in maroon pants and a yellow-flowered T-shirt comes running from the backyard.

Amy and I freeze, only one thought possible. *Sarah Carpenter.* If the girl turns around, will she be holding a vanilla ice cream cone with rainbow sprinkles and a maraschino cherry?

"Daddy, will you push me on the swing?" she says, and then she sees us, two strangers standing at the lip of her driveway.

Ronan looks at the little girl, looks at us. *He knows.*

"Daddy," the little girl says, moving toward him, taking his hand. Except for the blonde hair she looks nothing at all like Sarah, but it is enough. Amy's hand, empty, slides out of her bag.

"You have the wrong house," Ronan tells us. "The wrong person."

His four-year-old daughter looks up at him. "Daddy, who are those people?"

Amy grabs my arm, pulls me close. Turns.

We're back in the Porsche, twenty miles down the highway, when we both fall apart.

-18-

At the pizzeria Uncle Dan was all business, sorting through documents and cursing at a paper cut as we sat in the booth near the counter. Since nobody ate pizza at 10:30 AM in Holman Beach, not off-season, the place was empty except for the two of us, and Nancy, too, seated at her table in the back, folding napkins with her one hand and humming what sounded like The Blue Danube Waltz.

"Okay, it's this one," Uncle Dan said, scanning a page as he pulled it from the stack. "I set it up a few years ago when I was having some chest pains. It's a basic trust agreement."

"You never told me you had chest pains."

"It's no big deal."

"Maybe, but I should know about it."

"Yeah? Last month I had a case of the runs. You want the details?" He handed me the papers, leaning back.

"Fine. But next time, please tell me."

"I'm not planning on a next time. My heart is fine. But if it's not ...things are in order."

Legal documents gave me a headache. I leafed through them, catching the highlights, avoiding any paragraph over six lines. The trust had been established for the "well-being and maintenance" of Kathleen Marcino, to provide for her comfort and care for the rest of her life. Its total value shocked me.

"I never realized you had this much money."

He shrugged. "Some of it are the proceeds from the sale of our parents' house after they died. Taking anything from *those people,* for myself, would never happen, but she might need it someday. That's when I set up the trust. Over the years, I've contributed some. It builds up, but if she ever needs extended care, it'll dry up fast, believe me. There's also this place..." The Jaybird, of course. "...but that goes to you. I'm hoping you keep it, but if you do sell out, you'll do okay."

All this talk about his dying left me nervous. "You'll be making pizza for another twenty years."

"Probably," he nodded. "But I'm tired, you know. And there's really no reason for you *not* to stay and be part of this. I'd be happy cutting back my hours. Jorge could step up and run the place, probably, but I'd want you around, too, keeping the Marcino blood in the game. We can arrange the finances anyway you want it. And you'd look after the trust, and Nancy ...your mother...once I'm not around anymore to do it myself."

Neither a question nor a statement, it sounded more like a prayer, something you kept repeating, hoping that with enough recitations it would somehow come true.

"The way I see it, you'll be sticking around anyway...for her," he said, meaning Amy.

"I'm not so sure about that."

Since our encounter with Ronan, Amy and I had barely spoken. On the drive home she had curled in her seat and slept or pretended to. So far she had ignored about thirty texts, and I still had no idea where I stood with Kelly. "I really care about them both. It's complicated, you know?"

"Then un-complicate it," he said. "Pick one and stick with her."

"It's not like I'm choosing between regular and pepperoni. There are conflicting emotions here: attachments, desires ..."

"Now that's where you're wrong," he said. "Every day people walk in here and have to choose between some excellent options. Attachments, desires...it's all right here. I've seen it for forty years. The pepperoni looks good, but hey, you can't beat a slice of plain cheese, not *my* plain cheese, that's for damn sure. But that pepperoni smells great, you can almost taste that salty tang just by looking at those little red circles of meat on a hot bed of sauce and cheese."

"Women aren't pizza."

"Everything is pizza. You pick one, you eat it, and it's great. That's life. If you think about it later, you might wish you'd had the pepperoni instead of the plain, or maybe the pepperoni gives you a little heartburn and you wish you'd gone regular cheese. That's life, too. But either way you had a damn good lunch, so be happy about it. Because what are you going to do, stare at the slices all day and eat nothing? Walk out and go eat Chinese? Hell no, you'll be hungry again in an hour, all worked up about the MSG and wondering 'why didn't I get a slice of that plain?' So you make a choice and love what you have."

He nodded, pleased with the advice.

"I doubt it matters, anyway. Kelly is probably done with me, and Amy and I never get it right."

"Then write another play," he said. I wondered if he'd noticed all those missing pizza boxes I'd used the other night. "Stop thinking, make pizza, and things will work out. As for your family, I need your signature to make you co-executor of the trust. Here you go."

He offered the pen but still held on, his thumb and forefinger squeezing the cap.

"Before you sign, let's be clear: this isn't about cutting checks or looking after a bank balance. It means you take care of her the best that you can. Hire a nurse if you need to, and some of those assisted living facilities are okay—I'm not asking you to change bedpans or anything like that—but you'll need to spend time with her, be her family; maybe not her son, if it's too late for that, but a nephew or a damn good cousin or even just a friend. Don't stick her in a home somewhere and let her spend Christmas alone. If that's what you're thinking, tell me now. I can make other arrangements."

He let go of the pen, pointing at the dotted line awaiting my signature.

"So I can't leave her in a pizza box on a stoop somewhere?"

"I never should have told you that."

The dotted line waited before me, three inches on a sheet of white paper, but it seemed so much bigger, the pen like a knife pointed at my wrist, eager for a vein; forget the ink, this signature needed Grade A whole Marcino blood.

I looked over at Nancy, who was folding her napkins, humming her song, her fat body jammed between the table and the back of the booth, her feet on the floor tapping to some imaginary rhythm, slow, slow, quick-quick. Uncle Dan might easily outlive her, my signature on the trust nothing more than an I.O.U. no one would ever cash, but I couldn't accept being *that* kind of weasel. If I was going to sign, it had to mean something. I handed back the pen.

"I need to think," I told him.

He slipped the pen into his pocket, his mouth turned in a grimace.

"Just a day or two. I'm not sure about anything right now."

"Sure, sure. I'm disappointed, but I get it." He scooped the papers into a messy pile, corralling them with a rubber band. "Whenever you're ready, let me know. But talk to her, okay? Can you do that for me? It means a lot to her, and to you too, I'm guessing, even if you won't admit it."

Papers in hand, he rose from the booth and ducked behind the counter, where soon he'd be pounding dough and spreading cheese. I turned around so I could watch Nancy, who, every few seconds, turned her head and looked at *me*, glancing over her shoulder then shifting back the moment we made eye contact, giggling each time, as if I were a clown or a dog with a funny face. *That woman is your mother*, I thought—it still seemed foreign and trippy, like a bad practical joke. As I kid, I'd sit in class and daydream, imagining her outside the classroom window on a two-seater bicycle, balloons tied to each handlebar, my mother young and pretty, the girl from the Sears circular decked out in a bright floral dress. One time they called my name over the loudspeaker and I thought *this was it*—my mother would be waiting in the principal's office ready to squire me away to some amazing new life. Instead it turned out to be a head check in the nurse's office—the kid seated next to me had reported a case of lice.

Go over and talk to her.

But she left me in a pizza box!

For once even I was sick of hearing it. I'd been in Holman Beach for a week and most of what I'd known had been flipped upside down and tossed on the ash-heap. Maybe it was time to add that pizza box to the pile.

I was nearly out of the booth, ready to talk to her, my mother, (*mother*—it sounded so strange!) when Jill and Maddie burst through the entrance, both in cut-off shorts and white T-shirts with *Occupy the Beach* hand-scrawled in tie-dye across the front of their chests, Jill bouncing like she'd just won a Tony, Maddie walking behind her as if the cops might jump out from behind the soda case with handcuffs and pepper spray.

"The revolution has arrived!" Jill said, rushing over and pecking my cheek. Maddie hung back, hesitant.

"Tell the revolution we won't be ready for another half hour, unless you want leftovers," Uncle Dan shouted from behind the counter.

With her usual flourish, Jill pulled off her Greek fisherman's cap and swung into the booth, Maddie close behind.

"Isn't this a school day?" I asked.

"Yes, but we're blowing off school to prepare for the occupation. Tonight, the beach is ours!"

"Your mother is okay with that?"

"Well …" Jill said. "I think so. I didn't really ask. Ever since you guys got back from that road trip, she's been a mess. Did you have a fight or something? She drank too much wine last night and fell asleep on the couch. She was still in her PJ's and her hair was a wreck when I left so I'm guessing she called in sick. You really should marry her, you know—she'd be happier, I think."

"You're going to scare him away," Maddie whispered.

"No, we're like family. She's *my* mother, and I'm the star of *his* new play." She took the fisherman's cap and set it on my head. "Maybe you and Kelly can both move in, and it'll be like this giant free love experiment. I think my Mom's done some freaky stuff."

"He doesn't want to hear that," Maddie said.

"Not *sick* freaky, good freaky. I found this Tumblr once with photos of couples who—"

"Let's talk about something else, okay?" I said, handing back the hat. The news that Amy was a mess seemed predictable, but still had me worried.

"The whole idea is to perform an act of civil disobedience, to show that we won't always follow their rules," Maddie said. "Beth says that we need to develop ourselves through communal action so we're ready—psychologically, socially—when the revolution is for real."

"You know, like a dress rehearsal," Jill said. Beneath the table the girls held hands.

"Most of the time we're like machines," Maddie said. "Go to school, go to college, get all this debt so you can get a job with some evil corporation to pay off the debt, and then buy more stuff and just go along with everything and never think. We don't even know that another world is possible because we're programmed to live in this one. Like the SAT...we study and stress over it but there's nothing on the test about how the world *really* works. Beth says occupying the beach, and *not* doing what we're supposed to do, will help us develop a new consciousness. She says you can't *grow* when you're stuck in your same old role."

"Where is Ms. Manifesto?" I asked.

"She's trying to get some African-American kids to join us. We're too white and privileged."

"We need some old people, too, if you want to join us," Jill said.

"It's good to know we geezers are still in demand."

"I didn't mean *old* old."

Uncle Dan must have heard them. He wiped his hands, pulled off his apron, and rushed over to the table. Through the door I saw a cop car parked by the entrance, Clyde's creepy partner Mike idling in his cruiser, staring through the window as if searching for perps. What should have seemed harmless felt sinister instead, the black steel battering ram on the cruiser's front bumper a reminder of how easily something can be crushed. Jill and Maddie slouched in the booth holding hands, expecting the worst; Uncle

Dan saw their fear and leaned out the front, one hand on the door as he caught Mike's eye and waved. "Have a good day, Officer!"

Mike rolled down the window, flashed a salute, and said, "Thank you for your service!"

The window raised shut, and the cruiser resumed its crawl down the block, Uncle Dan turning his back and flipping his middle finger.

"Twerp. You only salute officers. I'm an enlisted man."

He joined us at the booth. Jill and Maddie sat up, relieved.

"He's such a perv," Jill said. Maddie, shoulders still hunched, patted Jill's wrist.

Uncle Dan glared out the window, his jaw clenched. "You need to be protesting these goddamn wars," he said, turning to the girls. "All this 'thank you for your service' crap is a scam to make everyone shut up and cheer. When I came back, nobody thanked me for my service, and I'm glad. Making pizza, wiping off a table and bringing a diet Snapple to somebody, that's *service*. We weren't doing *service*. We were killing people, like we're still doing." His face blanched. "When I started taking care of this little guy here…" Meaning *me*. "…people joked about staying up all night with a crying baby. With me it didn't matter—I was up anyway, thinking about what I'd seen, what I'd done. I still know every inch of that goddamn ceiling. I didn't sleep through the night until 1982."

The girls looked up at him, surprised, the old guy behind the pizza counter suddenly off on a tear. From her booth Nancy watched closely, no longer humming, her face caught in a long frown over her brother's agitation.

"You know why this place is called The Jaybird?" he asked.

They shook their heads. Nobody knew.

"I've been waiting forty years for people to wake up in this goddamn town. Maybe you girls are finally doing it." He rubbed his neck, as if soothing an old wound. "The best person I ever knew, PFC Jason Bird, from Brattleboro, Vermont. The Jaybird. Killed in action, November 4, 1972, in a firefight outside of some piss-poor peasant village. Friendly fire. You know what that means?"

We sat there like stones.

"One of *us* shot him. Maybe me. It was dark, and something moved, and the whole damn war was like that—you never knew what the hell you were shooting at. I pulled the trigger just like the other guys. It could have been me who killed him. I'll never know." His eyes grew dark. "He died over a piece of land the size of two football fields. An old buddy told me there's a

McDonald's there now, so I guess the Jaybird's life was worth it." He looked away, toward the wall, maybe through the wall, all the way to Southeast Asia. "I loved him. I still fucking do."

His shoulders quivered as he choked back the emotion, the girls awkwardly avoiding his eyes.

"We're sorry," Jill said, because what *could* you say?

Suddenly Nancy rose from the booth and waddled over, heading for her brother.

"Danny," she mumbled, her one and only arm laying across his shoulder as she pulled him close, rubbing her chin against his cheek and cooing in his ear.

"Hush, baby, it's okay...hush..." she whispered, embracing him, and an icepick chill shot through my body. I was two months old again wrapped in my mother's arms, a police siren wailing outside the window of a third-story rat-hole. Maybe I was imagining it—I didn't give much credence to repressed memories—yet suddenly I felt like a child again, a baby cradled against his mother's breast—and now, in a booth at the Jaybird, I *was* that child. I burst out crying, bawling like an infant even as I told myself *you can't cry over this, not here, not now.* A professor at NYU once told me that characters should *never* cry. It was melodramatic, weak and lazy, but maybe if she'd ever watched her uncle and her mother hugging in the middle of a pizzeria, she might have amended that rule. Or maybe I was just melodramatic, weak, and lazy, because I stopped fighting and let go—I cried like a man who'd spent thirty-eight years waiting for his mother, like a man who suddenly realizes that maybe he's found her.

Uncle Dan saw me wailing and broke away from Nancy, who stared at me, blank-faced and confused.

"What the hell's wrong with *him?*" Uncle Dan asked.

"We just came here to order twenty pizzas, for tonight," Jill said.

"He needs a tissue," Maddie added.

"I'm okay," I said, a middle-aged infant looking up at his Mommy. I grabbed a paper napkin and blew my nose. "I'm okay."

"Hush," Nancy whispered, her palm now on my shoulder, heavy and warm. Uncle Dan wiped his face with his sleeve and stepped back.

"Too much," he mumbled. "Who wants a slice of pizza?"

Jill and Maddie raised their hands, and Uncle Dan, his game-face reapplied, gave them each a high-five. "Two slices, coming right up. And tonight, go occupy that beach and tell anyone who tries to stop you to go fuck himself."

He stormed behind the counter and went to work, pans clanging, dough flying, oven doors slamming shut, the Jaybird as it should be, the imperative to make pizza its strong, steady heart. While the girls grabbed for the comfort of their phones, grateful for a screen to stare at instead of blubbering old me, I looked up at Nancy, her eyes distant now, even glazed, yet her hand still on my shoulder as I touched her one arm and whispered, "Thanks, Mom."

-19-

The music grabbed me the moment I hit the driveway, waves of sound blaring through the open windows—Amy's house like a giant Marshall Amp jacked past ten. The song was an old favorite of hers: "Fake Plastic Trees" by Radiohead, the melody gloomy and ethereal, the ghost keyboards and Thom Yorke's desperate, high-pitched vocals leaving you numb, like you were floating blindfolded inside a cloud the moment before it rained.

And it wears you out, Yorke sings, the chords quiet and resigned, the guitars strumming sadly. *And it wears you out.*

In the days after Sarah Carpenter's disappearance, Amy had listened to that song endlessly, the surreal, abstract lyrics all about death and reincarnation. And now she was playing it again, blasting it call-the-cops full volume, the vocals and the haunting chorus a chrysalis of heartbreak and surrender. It wasn't a good sign.

Jill's comments had me worried, so after I left the Jaybird I decided to drive over. Even if she told me to screw off and slammed the door in my face, at least I'd know she was okay.

The front door was locked, so I knocked, loudly, hitting the doorbell three times. That .22 still lurked somewhere in the house, and I didn't want her opening the door with it pointed at my face. After a minute, I punched the bell twice more and she shouted, "Hold on," her voice finding the quiet pocket before the song's final lyrics.

And it wears you out.

The door pulled back and Amy waved me inside, the music still ear-bleeding loud as the song started playing again. Her stereo, an old Bose I'd given her for Christmas one year, sat on a wine table in the front hallway. I found the dial and lowered the volume.

"Hey, I'm listening to that," she said.

"So was half of New Jersey. Your ears must be screaming."

"They're entitled to their opinion."

Like Jill had warned, she was still in her pajamas, the top at least, red and white stripes, a candy cane of cotton-polyester; the discarded bottoms hung over the sofa arm, the legs dangling toward the floor. She wore a single white sock, the toes of her bare foot an iridescent pink, her hair matted in bed-headed tufts, yet her lips were marvelous moxie, and with the top two buttons of her pink-striped PJ's teasingly undone, she was as desirable to me as ever, and I kept my eyes floating as I followed her into the kitchen, the smooth cream of her thighs endearingly close—too much the trigger for questions I wasn't sure how to answer.

"Are you okay?"

"You bet,' she said, scooping up a half-filled goblet of red wine and chugging it empty. "But I shouldn't operate heavy machinery anytime soon. You didn't bring your crane, did you?" She refilled the goblet and offered me the bottle. "Drink up, Donnie. Today it's just you and me. Jill is ...I don't know, somewhere."

"The occupation?"

"Is that what they're calling it? Whatever ...it won't last long. I love my daughter, but mass struggle isn't her thing. Three mosquito bites and she'll call it quits."

I recorked the bottle and set it on the table. Blue paint speckled her shins and several loose strands of her hair, and I caught a quick whiff of turpentine as she adjusted her top, straightening the hem at mid-thigh.

"I've been thinking," she said, "which is a stupid thing to say since we're *always* thinking. But specifically, I've been thinking about you and me. Remember that guy, Mark? I re-did the math. It turns out you're six times better than him. In fact, when you really crunch the numbers ..." She opened the fridge and pulled out a Greek yogurt. "... You top every guy I've ever met by a factor of three, minimum."

"I'm flattered, but you might want to check the math."

"Nope. I used Excel ... it's all true, Duck. Math—I always hated it, but you can't fight it. Addition, multiplication; even long division...no matter how I work the numbers, you and I are the answer to one long-ass word problem. It's all you, Donnie. *No one* could be more loyal, not even a golden retriever. We don't have to *do* anything about it, but I thought you should know." She peeled back the yogurt lid and grabbed a spoon. "Hungry?"

She stirred the cup, mixing the creamy top layer with its black cherry bottom, skimming the spoon along the rim and holding it up to my lips, the yogurt cool and sweet as the spoon slid against my tongue, Amy's finger brushing my chin as she plucked away the traces of dribbling black cherry. I swallowed, and Amy licked the spoon before handing it back along with the cup. Now it was her turn—closing her eyes, she waited as I topped off the spoon and brought it to her mouth, her lips parting, her tongue rolling for a quick taste as she licked around the edges, my hand steady, my heart thumping as she nibbled at the cream, her bare knees pressing against my legs. With eyes shut, she leaned closer, licking clean the spoon save for a single white dollop, which, eyes open, she dabbed with her pinkie and brought to my lips. Our noses touched.

"There's something upstairs," she said. "I want you to see it."

Moving through the house, past the wine table and "Fake Plastic Trees," we climbed the stairs, my eyes pulled toward the shifting tease of her pajama top, our arms extended as she led me to the landing. Down the hall her bedroom waited, the door ajar, the scent of fresh paint suddenly ubiquitous, dizzying and thick.

"I've been a busy girl," she said, guiding me into her room, and I stopped, stunned by what she'd done.

Inside her bedroom she had pushed the furniture to one side; the mattress and box spring, both upright, were propped against the closet door, the bed frame disassembled, the pieces shoved together like a bone pile, leaving the far wall open and clear, the frames pulled from their hooks. A cloth tarp, splattered in swirls, covered half the floor, cans of paint resting on old magazines and the torn-off tops of pizza boxes; a stepladder stood in the center.

A moment passed before I realized what she'd done, but once it clicked, my spine shook.

The far wall had been painted blue, like the ocean on a morning in mid-May, the color pulling you in as if her room had become a diorama. She had captured the look and texture of the water: small, rolling waves in the background; a grainy, sandy beige by the floorboard; white cirrus puffs and the haze of the sun where the wall met the ceiling; and at the bottom, in the dark patch between the sand and the ocean, a set of tiny footprints leading into the blue.

"I started last night with some paint I had in the basement, not really thinking anything, just throwing paint like some bad Abstract Expressionist, you know? But then I saw what it wanted to be, what it *needed* to be, and then I put on Radiohead, opened some Riesling, and everything just flowed."

She stared into the blue, saw something missing, then grabbed a brush from the coffee can on the stepladder, adding a blue-green mix in broad arching strokes at center eye-level. The image was uncanny, as if she'd cut through a dimension, the ocean beckoning, Amy's bedroom wall morphed into Holman Beach itself.

"It's still not finished ... I think ...but I wanted you to see it."

She grabbed a second brush, tinting the blue near the shoreline.

"It's...overwhelming. I didn't know you were painting again."

"I wasn't, until today. Now I might never stop."

She kneeled, adding dots to the shoreline near those tiny footprints, her eyes burning with a deep focus, seeing things that weren't there yet. I knew the look; sometimes, when a scene started working in my head, the edges of the world would fade, and I'd step into the wormhole. She was there, I could feel it—as if the blues and yellows and greens were emanating from her body, coloring the wall like stigmata.

The brush dotted the surface with pinprick black, and she backed away, edging toward the ladder.

"I've always been pissed at myself for giving up. You should have encouraged me more, Duck. It didn't always have to be about you and your plays."

"I bought you those oil paints for Christmas one year," I said, the king of lame. But she was right: in high school she'd won prizes too, but they could never compete with the glory of Donatello.

"It's not your fault. I ignored me, too. It was easier being in your shadow, or being drunk and stoned, or C: all of the above. It's not like I'm Frida Kahlo or anything. And then when Sarah ..." It was still so hard to say. "...when Sarah died, all the good parts shut down. I couldn't see anything... except that I'd let it happen."

She set the brush back in the can.

"*We* let it happen."

"You couldn't help it; it's a medical condition. Remember when we were eight and you fell asleep at the playground on top of that slide? All these kids were on the ladder behind me, waiting their turns, yelling at us, calling us these terrible names, and you just sat there sleeping like you were tucked into bed. Even when I shoved you and you headed down the slide, you were still asleep. You just laid there in the dirt until somebody's mother came and carried you off. The other kids thought it was hilarious, and I did, too, but it scared me, because you were my best friend, and I knew that sometimes you wouldn't be there, even if it was only for a few minutes. The world can fall apart in that little time."

I reached for her hand, our fingers locking.

"On the beach, with Sarah...I was happy that day, you know?" she said. "The school year was nearly over. We were graduating and finally getting out of this stupid town. You'd be in the city and I'd be at Montclair, just a train ride away. The museums and the theaters and all those people who had never even heard of Holman Beach—the world was changing, and I couldn't wait. I could walk away and never see that bastard again. I wasn't even stoned that morning. I had maybe two hits, just to take the edge off. I was reading ..."

"... *Rolling Stone*. Drew Barrymore on the cover..."

"... The sun was so bright over the water; I was face down, and I put on that floppy hat and started reading. God, it should have been just another day. We'd been bringing Sarah to the beach since she was two. She was so smart, and careful ...she knew to keep away from the waves. She wouldn't even let the water touch her ankles without one of us standing next to her. It was *safe*, Duck. She should have been *safe*."

I'd told myself the same a thousand times.

"She never screamed or called out. It was so *quiet* ...you could hear the cars on Ocean Avenue and the sandpipers doing that weird thing they do with their wings. If she had called out, I would have heard it. I swear, Duck ...I would have heard. How could something that ruins your life be so *quiet?*"

On the wall the streaks of blue seemed in motion, like waves, the footprints near the floor edging toward the surf. We stepped forward and dropped to our knees, our hands reaching out, touching those small, beautiful footprints.

On my palm I saw traces of damp paint, the impression of a four-year-old's foot, the half-circle of her heel, the sole, even the tips of each tiny toe. Again I touched the wall, Amy's hand covering mine as we knelt on all fours, side by side, sensing those footprints as if they were alive and beating, the vast blue expanse looming above us, the water, the ocean ...if only we could follow those footprints and bring them back to us whole—we would dive into the blue and keep searching until we found her. We would carry her; we would float above the crest until we reached the shore and replaced those fading footprints with the soles of her feet. We'd lead Sarah away from the water, across the sand and back to our blankets, our footsteps leaving new impressions, deep and strong; we would carry her back toward the rest of her life.

We both sensed it, the need to be part of it, the need to be *closer*, and so we stood, hands linked, and fell back against the wall, extending our arms as if we were floating on the water, closing our eyes and feeling the wall against our backs, and perhaps Amy imagined it too, Sarah Carpenter between us, our bodies like a raft, carrying her.

"She's here," Amy said, and I squeezed her hand, those tiny footprints all over me now, the wall behind us seemingly in motion, like waves against flesh, lulling the three of us deeper into the blue, and somehow it was okay; whatever might happen was good and right because we were together again, Amy, Sarah, and I. Bringing her back was only a dream but maybe we could carry her forward, toward the light or the spirit or whatever, if anything, might lie beyond this broken life. Those footprints didn't have to drift away alone, and it was crazy but I felt the pressure of those feet up and down my body as we swayed against the wall, *I feel it, too,* Amy said, and maybe ghosts were just memories and wishes and everything you ever dreamed coming together in your mind for a single moment.

Amy pressed her forehead against the wall, her arms spread like angel wings as her lips touched the blue, and I swear I heard the softest breath, neither Amy's nor mine, and two simple fading words: *you're forgiven.*

· · · · ·

Downstairs I pulled together a snack tray: diced cheddar, apple slices, baby pretzels, and some fresh chunks of avocado. After all that time in my head with Sarah, I was grateful to be moving again, my hands chopping and slicing, separating the avocado from its skin in one long, perfect peel.

I'd turned off the music, so I heard Amy coming down the stairs, the bottom steps announcing her arrival with that familiar wooden creak common to an older house, each step, even the lightest, like the crack of a withered bone. She was still in her pajama shirt, the sleeves rolled to her elbows, but she'd added a second white sock and combed her hair, the flecks of blue paint scrubbed from her knees.

She stood in the doorway while I poured two glasses of iced tea.

"You're quite the host," she said, looking around her kitchen. "Thanks for having me over."

"I thought you might want a snack."

I handed her a glass and set the tray on the table. She checked the clock on the stove.

"My outpatient appointment is in twenty-seven minutes. I'm thinking of blowing it off."

"Is that allowed?"

"I'll call and reschedule. They won't send the rubber suits after me—too expensive." She dug into the snacks, grabbing an apple slice and spearing the avocado with a toothpick. "Actually …I have a better idea, something more therapeutic. More fun, at least."

She smiled, leaning back against the counter and popping the avocado into her mouth. She seemed lighter now, almost playful, rubbing her feet against each other as she sipped the iced tea. Maybe the sadness had been left upstairs, absorbed into the vast blue of her bedroom wall.

"Great. What are you thinking?"

"Well …"

The front door banged open and Jill's voice filled the house. "It's me! I forgot sunscreen!"

Amy speared another avocado chunk. "My daughter, the revolutionary. Didn't Che Guevara have the same problem? Not enough SPF?"

Jill swung into the kitchen. "We've already got twenty people. Beth says if we …"

She saw her mother half-dressed, eating an avocado; saw me standing by the fridge with a handful of baby pretzels and suddenly started applauding.

"Oh my god! This is great!" She ran to Amy and pecked her cheek. "Your daughter totally approves!"

"It's not what it looks like," I said.

"Actually, it is, or will be in another twenty minutes," Amy said, grabbing her daughter and returning the kiss. "Assuming you get the hell out of here and give us some privacy."

Jill plucked some stray avocado from the bottom of Amy's lips, then turned to me and bowed.

"She exits the scene with dignity and grace, like a true professional." She grabbed an apple slice and touched my hand. "See? I know how to read a scene. You *really* need to cast me in your play."

"Bye, Jill," Amy said.

Like some 1940s Hollywood icon, Ava Gardner in a white hat and gloves, Jill backed out of the kitchen, blowing kisses, then calling from the hallway, "Radiohead? Jeez, don't be so emo, Mom. Put on some Bruno Mars!"

We listened to her footsteps scurrying up and down the stairs, and then she was gone, her key turning the deadbolt, the screen door falling shut.

Amy finished her iced tea as I wiped off the counter.

"You have no reaction?"

"She's a charming girl," I told her. "You should be proud."

"Not about Jill, you big doofus. I basically said I was going to sleep with you. Did you miss that little nugget?"

"I thought we were just doing our thing—you know, bantering back and forth…"

She looked out the window, where some birds were buzzing a small oak.

"If we're too late, I get it," she said. "You've got the California Girl waiting back in Paradise. And who knows? Maybe you'll be Mister Off-Broadway Big Shot again, all those hot young actresses lined up backstage. I get it."

"No, you don't," I said, knowing that, if we stopped to *think*, or *talk*, or do *anything,* the moment might collapse. "The only thing you get is *this*."

And I rushed across the room and kissed her beautiful mouth.

.   .   .   .   .

"This is the worst sex scene I've ever read," a producer once told me. "It's too long. Nobody fucks for four pages—half a page, at most. And the characters never shut up…"

"They're expressing their love," I said.

"That's what the sex is for! And all this description…look, Marcino, there *are* no good words for certain body parts, and as soon as you write the word 'panties' you're a creep. And there's too much direction. Does it really matter that his *left* hand touches her right *breast?* And what are you, some kind of foot man? You can't write that a male lead kisses each of her toes. Ninety percent of the bankable male actors in this town will see that and stop reading. Leading men *do not* suck toes."

"I think this character might …"

"…might never make it to the screen if you don't fix this rotten scene."

"What do you suggest?"

"Get them in a room and get them naked," he said, "and let the rest take care of itself."

.   .   .   .   .

Perhaps we should have left the house and gone back to the B&B—after waiting our whole lives, an extra ten minutes seemed hardly an impediment—but the moment demanded spontaneity; we could feel it in our fingertips, in our pores, in every nerve ending firing beneath our skin. Amy bolted the front lock and joined me on the couch.

"This feels right, doesn't it?" she said. "We've done everything but …"

"You and me," I said.

"I'm not drunk. I know what I want."

"What about that warning against operating heavy machinery?"

"Isn't it more like a hand tool?"

She wasn't wearing a bra. We undid the buttons of her pajamas, slowly, as I kissed the tiny freckles between her breasts.

"We love each other," she said.

"Always have."

"Everything else...all the shit..."

"Doesn't exist," I whispered. "You and me."

She tugged on my belt as I touched her hips, our hands grabbing and stroking. Suddenly we were naked, in a room ...and the rest took care of itself.

.   .   .   .   .

Another great thing about making pizza: after you finished, you didn't have to think or reflect; there were no questions or discussions about what the mushrooms or the green peppers *really* meant; you didn't have to talk about whether pizza *changed* everything between you and the person who ate it. For sex and pizza, the time commitments were about the same, yet you didn't have to stress on whether the pizza really *satisfied.* You wanted it to be good, but if the sauce was too bland, or God forbid, the crust too soft, it wasn't an indictment of your worth as a man. You could blame the oven or the dough or even the tomatoes and go make another pie. With sex, it wasn't that easy. Unsatisfied customers rarely waited while you readied a second serving.

Maybe it was crazy that after finally making love with Amy I was thinking about pizza, but it seemed a safe harbor from all those rampaging emotions I felt hanging between us. Over the years, we'd done almost everything except that all-important "it," and now that the final ingredient had been added to the recipe, did it change the dish, or were we still, as always, a big hot loving mess?

We cuddled on the couch under a soft blue blanket, Amy's head resting on my shoulder, her legs wrapped around mine as her fingers kneaded my chest.

"Maybe I'll get pregnant," she said.

"You're not ...?"

"On the pill? Not for years. It messes with your ecosystem. Probably invented by a misogynist."

She pressed her hand over my chest.

"I could have...used protection."

"Please tell me you're not one of those guys who carries a condom in his wallet."

"No ..."

"Well, I don't have any either. It's not like I keep a box around just in case. 'Just in case' hasn't happened for months. After all these years, did you really want to stop and run out to Quick-Check for a three-pack of rubbers?" She pecked my cheek. "Don't worry. My cycle's been off. Attempted suicide will do that sometimes ..."

"If you *do* get pregnant—"

"Of course you would. If I asked, you'd probably carry it."

The sole of her foot slid up and down my calf as her palm covered my cock, which lay exhausted and useless.

"We might need some time. I'm not eighteen."

"The Viagra years, already?" she giggled. "Okay, I can wait."

Yet I worried that the names "Ronan" or "Sarah Carpenter" might fill any open spaces the way flood water will seep into the cracks, building up until suddenly you're waist-deep and wading through the muck. I wanted to believe that Amy and I could exist without ghosts, but what if, instead of keeping us apart, those ghosts were the essential link?

I sensed my thoughts slipping down a long dark well, the walls too mossy and slick for me to climb out, and somewhere in that dark space Kelly's name might be written on the wall. Though our relationship had no binding agreements (*she abandoned me in a room full of Jackson Pollocks!*) I still felt like I'd cheated, something I had never done. And damned if I didn't miss her.

And yet—at that moment; with Amy and I nestled together, our bare skin touching, her breath warm against my neck, everything seemed, if not perfect, at least perfectly earned.

·   ·   ·   ·   ·

When I woke up Amy was gone, the room dim except for the glow of the porch light through the living room window. I grabbed my pants and checked my phone; I'd been asleep for four hours.

In the dark I threw on my clothes and switched on the light.

Amy padded down the stairs in a sleeveless summer dress, her feet still bare but her hair washed and pretty, her contacts replaced by funky red frames.

"Don't worry, I just woke up, too," she said. "Maybe a half hour ago. I shook you a few times, but you were dead."

I rubbed my eyes. "Now I have risen."

"Great. Walk on water and I'll post it on Facebook."

"Sorry. I didn't mean to sleep ..."

She smiled. "Hey, it's what you do best."

Her voice held no sarcasm, yet the words stung. *It's what you do best.*

"Since there's no need to wait up for Jill, I thought we could spend the night at your place," Amy said. "A suite at the Beach House Inn—that's always been a dream, you know? It's silly, but as a little girl I fantasized about getting married there someday. Growing up in this stupid town, it's hard not to."

"You never told me that."

"There's plenty I haven't told you." She sensed my hesitation. "Hey, it's okay if you'd rather not ..."

"No, it's a great idea," I said, thinking about Kelly's things—her suitcase, her guitar, her fuzzy, calico slippers—still waiting back at the room.

"I'll need a few minutes to pack a bag and then we can go," she said, and headed back upstairs.

She was gone only a second when the doorbell rang. I pulled back the curtains to see who was there.

"Fuck! Who is it?" Amy shouted.

Through the glass, I saw the police car double-parked in front of the driveway. "It's Clyde."

"Get rid of him, please," she shouted from her room. "Tell him I have cramps. He'll vanish like a bad magic trick."

I opened the door. "Well, if it isn't the friendly neighborhood man in blue ..."

Clyde smirked, his "Serve and Protect" partner standing two steps behind; they were both in uniform, yellow safety vests strapped over the blue. The porch light caught the yellow and made them both shimmer.

"Why am I not surprised you're here?" Clyde said.

"Deductive reasoning: impressive. Binge-watching all those *CSI* repeats must be paying off."

He scratched his nose, ignoring me.

"I need to talk to Amy. It's about our daughter," he said, pushing through the door. Officer Mike followed, casing me with his eyes as he barked "step aside" like I was a character in his fascist TV script.

"You need to go down to the beach and get Jill out of there," Clyde said. "We just got word from the State Police. There are six other beaches being 'occupied' and the Governor's office wants it squashed immediately. Some anarchists from New York and Philly have come down to stir up trouble, and it won't be tolerated, not this close to tourist season. There's a sweep scheduled in ninety minutes."

"They're in violation of a local ordinance," Officer Mike said.

"I don't want Jill there when things go down. If they don't disperse, we have to arrest..."

"They won't get special treatment," Officer Mike added. "We can hold them for forty-eight hours without processing. Everyone we bring in gets strip-searched."

Even Clyde noticed the glee in his voice. He shot him a look, and Mike backed off.

"Isn't this an over-reaction?" I said. "They're hanging out on the beach at night. Kids have been doing that for years. Christ, *you* did that for years. Who cares? Is it really necessary to bring out the long knives?"

"I'm not calling the shots," he said. "The State Police are coming down to coordinate. I just want my daughter safe. I don't care what happens to that lesbo friend of hers ..."

"She has a name—Maddie."

"...but Jilly needs to be out of there before we arrive. I've texted her but she won't respond, and I can't go down there and warn her in person. She'll listen to her mother. Or tell her you need her for an audition ...anything. I don't care, just get her home."

Amy came down the stairs, an overnight bag slung over her shoulder.

"What's up?" she said, reading their faces, sensing it wasn't just Clyde with his usual crap. He told her the deal, Amy nodding, taking it in.

"Okay, we'll go get her," Amy said. "Thanks for the warning."

"You've got eighty-five minutes," Clyde said. "We're going in sharp."

"She won't be happy about it," I said.

"I don't really care. I'm not letting my daughter get arrested," Amy said, dropping her bag on the couch. I imagined the local cops, all that pent-up Dirty Harry machismo, and texted Uncle Dan, hoping the cops might check their brutality if a local businessman was on scene to observe. He responded with three words: *To the barricades!*

"If anyone ever asks, I was never here," Clyde said.

"Can we take it a step further and say you were never born?"

He shot me a raised middle finger. "Oh yeah, you'll need to take the Santa Fe," he said, meaning Amy's SUV. "Your rental car has two flats. Looks like somebody slashed your back tires."

"Are you serious?"

"Sorry, buck-o. Hope you paid extra for the insurance."

I rushed past him and checked out the tires, the back two deflated, dead rubber sinking into the pavement. A cigarette butt lay nearby, just like the one I'd found the night Amy shot out the window. Obviously it wasn't Ronan, who was ten hours away in Ohio and wanted nothing to do with us. So who was it? Scrawled on the rear bumper, in black magic marker, was *Fuck You.* Maybe it was random, but it felt personal. Yet if not Ronan, then who?

It's just some teenagers looking for trouble, I thought. *Stop being paranoid.*

Clyde stepped over and chuckled. "We'll check the video later. If you're lucky, the cameras picked up something and we can nail the jerk. But do it later—get over to the beach and get Jill home."

Inside, Amy waited by the door with her keys and purse.

"There goes my night at the Beach House," she said. "Maybe Jill can stay at Maddie's tonight and we'll still have time, but you heard Clyde, we need to get her out of there. *You* need to get her. She'll give *me* all kinds of crap, but she'll do anything you say. Tell her an arrest will keep her out of Actor's Equity."

She pulled on her sweater and gave me a look. "Just don't fall asleep on me, okay?"

-20-

The guy with the beard had me and wouldn't let go.

"This spot, this *exact* fucking spot ..." he said, jabbing his finger toward the sand in case it wasn't clear. "In twenty years it'll be under water. I *dare* you to find a legitimate climate scientist who disagrees. Go ahead, I dare you." He paused, as if there might indeed be a scientist hidden in my pocket, ready for debate. "Submerged, flooded, completely sunk—if we stood here, we'd *drown.*"

Welcome to the occupation. Tall, thin, and heavily inked, he walked one step ahead of me, the true believer; even under the cloud-filtered moonlight his eyes blazed, frustrated and indignant because *shit, you just don't get it, dude.*

As soon as we'd arrived, he'd latched onto us like some radical maître d', making sure we understood the menu before offering us a seat. He wasn't there for a *party* or to have *a good time.* This was serious shit. Amy spotted him immediately, his long, looping strides angling toward us, and being three steps quicker than me, or maybe just more willing to blow people off, she dodged his approach and went to find Jill while I made the dual mistakes of eye contact and an affable head-nod. Snagged—the fish on the hook squirms but never escapes. A simple "Hi, how's it going?" was all it took for him to launch into his shopping list of inconvenient truths. The guy knew his stuff, citing sources and data like they were song lyrics, and his points were powerful and depressing, but what did he want me to *do* about it? Shove the polar ice caps into the freezer at the Jaybird?

"The goddamn mainstream media ...They never report the truth. The Koch Brothers!"

"Look, I *agree* with you," I said, which should have appeased him, but no, my agreement was problematic because of my privilege.

"Aren't you a white guy, too?"

"For now," he said. "But I'm developing an app to correct for it."

"Good luck," I told him, knowing that Clyde's psycho partner and his itchy nightstick were less than an hour away. Hopefully they wouldn't beat his ass *too* badly. "Peace."

He sneered as if I'd just told him to fuck off—peace, apparently, being too white Gen-X male middle class. "Justice?" I offered. "Fight the power?"

He shrugged and checked his phone. "Hey man, it's your world."

"Has anyone told the world that?"

As I headed off to find Amy, a barefoot college girl in a white peasant skirt ran up to me, her left arm ringed with dozens of orange glow sticks.

"You're with us, right?" she asked, and when I nodded, she grabbed one of the glow sticks and snapped it around my neck.

"With enough people we can light up the world," she said, which was hokey and beautiful, and she grabbed the glow stick around her own neck and started spinning it like a hula hoop, the orange neon reflecting across her long slender shoulders. Around the beach the glow sticks were ubiquitous, the only lights except for the moon and the light pollution from Ocean Avenue. Clusters of people gathered in scattered pockets, most in the vicinity of the ten-foot lifeguard chair—on which someone had stuck a homemade white flag reading "Occupy the Beach – Now and Forever!" the letters stitched carefully in red and blue thread. To its left were folding tables with coolers beneath them as two people struggled to raise a canopy, the poles unsteady against the night breeze. A hand-painted sign, *Dining Station,* lay in the sand, and I grabbed one of the poles and held tight while some kid fastened the tie line and drove a tent spike into the sand.

"Thanks," he said, shaking my hand, and I realized that what I'd expected to be random and chaotic was well-organized instead. It wasn't just about hanging out—they were working, building a makeshift community—with a first aid station, a child-care station, even a library: two senior citizens stacking books and magazines on a picnic table across from the Port-o-John. Tents were propped in circles, sleeping bags spread out over tarps, and as I moved closer to the shoreline two more college girls approached, both wearing yellow armbands with "Security" printed on them, a lanyard and a whistle hanging on each of their necks.

I felt tempted to warn them that the cops were on the way, all their work soon to be dismantled and smashed, but doubted it would change their actions. The beach was charged with cooperation and visions for a better world—who was I to be the town crier, shouting out their doom?

I stopped the two Security women and asked about a designated spot for Entertainment. I couldn't imagine Jill being anywhere else.

"That's theater and media," one woman said, pointing fifty yards down the shore, where a group was building a platform, their glow sticks bobbing. A second woman, the taller of the two, eyed me skeptically, her gaze jumping from curiosity to concern.

"I don't know you. I didn't see you at any of the affinity meetings."

"A friend's daughter told me to come. Do you know Jill Clyde?"

They exchanged glances, the shorter one whispering to Ms. Suspicious.

"There's a Jill here, but we don't know her last name. Is she one of the high school kids?" Suspicious asked.

"She's a drama queen, right?" the other one said.

"That's her!"

"Yeah, she's here," Suspicious said, as if it were bad news. "But she's not *serious*. This isn't a game, you know."

"Right. In twenty years we'll be underwater."

They both smiled. "That's so Jeremy!" Suspicious said. "Look, we need to be careful. There are narcs here looking to start trouble. They do that, you know. They incite violence and then arrest you when you respond."

"Most of the high school kids are building the stage. Maybe you can find her over there," the other one said, and off they walked, their glow sticks bouncing with their strides.

"Hey, Donnie, over here!" a voice called, and I saw Uncle Dan trudging through the sand, a tall stack of pizza boxes balanced in his arms. I rushed over to help.

"The girls ordered twenty pies this morning," he said, looking around and counting people in his head. "They'll need a hell of lot more than that."

I grabbed half the boxes and followed him toward the Food tent as people began splintering off from their groups, gravitating toward the scent of warm food. Anyone in need of a smile should arrive somewhere with a pizza—wherever, whoever, they'll be happy to see you. I couldn't recall a single delivery I'd done over the years in which someone wasn't grateful to find me at their door with a large cheese pie, and this time was no different. "Jaybird Pizza has arrived!" Uncle Dan announced, and even the bearded climate change guy ambled over for a slice.

We set up the food and stepped aside, my uncle watching with pride. I once asked him why he'd opened a pizzeria and, not surprisingly, he tied it back to the war.

"Before I was drafted, I wanted to be an engineer," he'd told me. "Bridges, dams, roads—I was going to be that guy in the white shirt and tie wearing a hard hat managing all these great, heavy projects, but over there—seeing all those bridges bombed to shit, the bulldozers demolishing these sad little huts to build roads for our trucks—I knew I couldn't do it. I wasn't that guy anymore. Then one day a buddy and I brought a pizza from the mess hall to this local family we'd befriended, and you should have seen the smiles on those kids' faces. Unbelievable—and this was *Army* pizza. My buddy and I— Jason Bird, the guy I told you about—we both felt it right there—we were pizza guys."

I spotted Jill's friend Beth in the queue waiting for her slice, but Jill herself wasn't in sight. Uncle Dan nudged my side and handed me a roll of tens and twenties wadded together with a rubber band.

"When you see Amy's kid, give her the money back. I can't charge them for this," he said.

He looked up at the clear night sky, admiring the shining darts of light illuminating the dark. A sea plane flew over the beach with a banner: *Another World is Possible* flapping in the night air.

"We've been lucky, you and I," he said.

"Maybe we have," I said, an admission that felt strange and counter-intuitive, like a devout Muslim agreeing that Muhammed was just "okay." But I could see how fortunate I was. I turned and hugged Uncle Dan, whose body tightened even as his arms welcomed the embrace. We weren't hugging men, far from it, but I patted his back, kissed his cheek, and told him how thankful I was that he'd saved me.

"Maybe we saved each other," he whispered, his hand grasping the back of my neck. "Who the hell knows?"

His breath was hot on my face, redolent with the slightest hint of garlic, and I felt like a kid again, pretending to be asleep while he checked my room, making sure I was okay before turning out the lights and heading to bed himself. I patted those broad, strong shoulders which, years back, had discovered a pizza box on his front stoop and had carried the box—and me— into his home. Suddenly I knew it: I'd take over the Jaybird and look after Nancy if or when Uncle Dan couldn't do it anymore. Hand me a Tony and an Oscar both in one night and I'd still be tied to the Jaybird. Maybe you couldn't go back in time and save a four-year-old from drowning, but you *could* go back home and make pizza. You could try to make a life with the people you loved in the place that you belonged.

I took off my glow stick and placed it around his neck, his forehead leaning into mine as a firecracker burst over the ocean, the red, green, and blue dancing and sizzling against the black.

"Now *that* is a beautiful sight!" a voice said.

We pulled apart as Father Toby approached, a pizza slice in one hand, his guitar case in the other, his priest's collar *and* a glow stick hanging loose above a Springsteen concert Tee and a pair of orange board shorts.

"The radical priest is here to get you released," he said, smiling. "Where are the cops, anyway? You promised me cops, Marcino."

"Don't worry, they'll be here," Uncle Dan said. "I'm sure there's a night stick with your fat skull's name on it."

"Power to the People," he said, looking at all the millennials scrambling around the beach. "Good Lord—do any of these kids even know that song?"

"They will once you play it for them," I said, and Toby finished his slice and snapped open his guitar case. Out came a Martin acoustic, and as he slipped the strap over his shoulder and began to strum, I started thinking about Kelly, who should have been there with me even if her presence would have complicated, well...just about everything.

I thought about calling her, but suddenly my phone buzzed—good old "Lithium." I fumbled with the phone, dropped it in the sand, answering just in time to hear Amy's harried voice, hammers pounding in the background.

"Where *are* you?" she said. "One second we're walking together and then you're gone."

"Sorry. I stopped to talk. I shouldn't have, but then Uncle Dan showed up..."

"Whatever. Get your ass over here. Jill's giving me all kinds of crap, but she'll listen to you. Tell her you'll cast her in your stupid play if she comes home now," she said, the line going dead.

I started hurrying down the beach toward the makeshift stage near the shoreline, my feet dodging the rhythmic surges of the late-night tide. But suddenly my fingers began to tingle, and when I looked back at the lifeguard chair, the realization hit: twenty years earlier I'd fallen asleep at the exact spot where I now stood. I'd fallen asleep when I shouldn't have, and Sarah Carpenter had drowned.

I shook my hands, hoping for a false alarm, but my eyelids began twitching, became lead-plated shades, and I felt my legs growing heavy, as if the sand had risen to my waist, every step becoming harder than the last. Still—*I'm okay*, I thought, taking a deep breath.

I tried to recall what I'd been thinking when I'd gone down that terrible morning: the warm sun; Sara's vanilla ice cream cone with rainbow sprinkles and a maraschino cherry; the taste of Amy's lips.

I won't fall asleep, I thought.

But it couldn't hurt to sit for a minute, could it? Again, the phone rang, good old dead Cobain. *I'm so happy because today I found my friends, they're in my head,* and I closed my eyes, just for a moment ...

.　.　.　.　.

"I said, disperse!"

A boot smashes into my shin, and I wake up to a blazing Klieg light shining into my eyes. Voices through bullhorns...*disperse, disperse.*

"Vacate the beach immediately. Failure to comply..."

My eyes burn under the light, still half-asleep, but I awaken fast, the adrenaline dump flooding my veins; my heart is a nervous fist against my chest as the boot kicks me again, harder this time, and I look up into the mouth end of a pepper spray can pointed at my face.

More voices through bullhorns ...*disperse, disperse*...and wait, is that a *horse* moving along the shoreline, a cop in a helmet waving his nightstick as the horse gallops through the sand?

The Klieg light doesn't blink; my pupils collapse into pinholes.

"Local ordinance 57:29 prohibits sleeping on the beach after 10:00 PM," the cop says.

I shield my face with my forearm. "I'm not *sleeping* on the beach. I *fell* asleep—I can't control it. I'm narcoleptic."

He pulls back the pepper spray, clipping it to his belt, but kicks me again just for the hell of it. "You need to disperse, or we'll charge you..."

"Terry, I've got this one. They need you up on the boardwalk," a voice says, and suddenly Clyde looms above me. The other cop, Terry, heads up the beach without a word as Clyde offers his hand, pulling me up.

"I should have known," he says. "How the hell can anyone *sleep* through this?"

"What's happening?" I ask, but then it all snaps clear: the beach, the occupation, the cops, *Jill.*

"You were supposed to be out of here before we arrived. What the hell happened?"

"You know what happened," I say, brushing sand from my face. "Maybe Amy got her out..."

"Wrong. She flipped off one of the troopers and they're holding her on the boardwalk."

Two cops rush past us, dragging a dreadlocked kid by his shirt, the front cop pulling, the second one whacking the kid's legs with a nightstick to keep him from resisting.

"Jesus. When did this become a police state?"

"It's always been one. You just never paid attention," Clyde says. "Look, just find Jill and get her home, okay? Some of these assholes are too loose with the pepper spray. My daughter *cannot* be here, understand?"

He runs off, shouting toward his partner as he raises his nightstick and chases three kids toward the dunes.

At the center of the beach there's a scrum of orange glow sticks, twenty or thirty people, and though it's dark and hard to see, I spot Jill in the middle of the pack, holding hands with Maddie and some dude with a shaved head, the bearded climate-change guy, Jeremy, three places down from them.

Suddenly the scrum breaks into a long, continuous line, and someone shouts a countdown to three before they all start running—heading for the water with exuberant howls, an unwavering band of orange light darting toward the ocean, a phalanx of blue uniforms chasing after them but hesitant to break the shoreline, unsure if their marching orders include getting wet.

The line splits as the protesters hit the shore and plunge into the water, Jill among them, Maddie at her side, people shouting and laughing, legs kicking wildly in the spray, the collective mind no doubt believing that they've won—no way will these uniformed bastards with their helmets and guns ever follow them into the ocean.

And maybe they're right—the cops halt at the edge of the water and start ordering the protestors back in amplified bullhorn war shouts—*Failure to comply will result in arrest*—but no one listens, no one gives a damn; they've found sanctuary in the water, which belongs to all of us, doesn't it? They keep swimming further out, the waves building; orange glow-lights bobbing in and out of the sea.

Suddenly I remember Amy's words: *I never taught Jill to swim.*

I run closer toward the water, toward the night-black of the ocean, and see Jill moving away from the shoreline, clutching onto Maddie as a wave breaks over them. Who in her right mind would rush into the ocean if she couldn't swim—unless she was sixteen and caught up in the moment, moving with the crowd, believing she was immortal like every sixteen-year-old does in her young crazy heart?

And if your simple, naïve faith has been dead for twenty years, do you stand helplessly on the beach while another girl drowns, or do you rush into the ocean to save her?

The hell with my shoes—I dive into the water, my body descending into the harsh Atlantic soup.

Damn it's cold, the shock of the water slapping me further awake, and the truth is I've never been a good swimmer myself, Uncle Dan too busy making pizza to teach me properly. I see Jill with her arm around Maddie at the end of the orange line, the glow sticks shining even when wet, and I swim toward her, calling her name but of course she can't hear me, salt water splashing into my mouth, my lungs wheezing as my head strains to stay above surface.

The band of orange light, no longer unbroken but still cohesive, moves further out, and I keep swimming after them even as a wave pushes me away, dunking me under. The tide drags me back toward the shore, but I push further, Amy's daughter is somewhere in that fucking ocean and I won't let her drown. My arms flail, I've hated the ocean since the day Sarah drowned, my head dunking under a wave, my legs weary and dense, the adrenaline draining, my arms pushing against the heavy water, Jill no longer in sight.

The undertow nips at my feet, and I keep thinking, *I need to save her, I need to save her*, as another wave dunks me, turning me around—is that a horse galloping across the shore? *Sarah would have loved that, a horse trotting across Holman Beach*, and another wave, and another.

I should have *told* Clyde that I was a bad swimmer, but who wants to admit that in a beach town, and I see the orange lights coming nearer; I see Jill and she's holding Sarah Carpenter's hand as they descend into darkness and Kelly is an excellent California swimmer and here comes another wave and damn, I'm going under.

My lungs choke with salt water and god knows what else, this is Jersey, syringes and tire dirt and the follicles of dead wise guys; I can't help but gag and swallow more water, my head surfacing one last time and shit, *I'm going to drown*, which is maybe the first thing that's made sense to me since that morning twenty years ago.

Another wave, the undertow at my waist.

Hello, water, I think. *Hello, death.*

-21-

My death by drowning lasted twelve seconds before Jeremy spotted me floundering and pulled me back up, my lungs burning but my brain cells intact.

Perhaps it was climate change that saved my life. As Jeremy dragged me back to the shoreline, he said that soon people would be drowning on Wall Street and on the Mall in D.C., massive floods as common as the full moon; you'll go to bed in a dry room and wake up in ten feet of water, your mattress repurposed as a raft.

"Underwater rescue, that's the future," he said. "I'm ready for it. Are you?"

Considering that I was wrapped in his arms, shivering and coughing out sea scum, the answer seemed obvious: I had work to do.

When we hit the beach, the cops acknowledged his heroics and offered to let him go, but he insisted they arrest him, refusing to move until the plastic cuffs snapped around his wrists.

"It's only my third arrest," he smiled. "My cousin's been busted fourteen times. I need to catch her by the end of the year."

"Again, thank you," I told him. "If there's anything I can do ..."

"Organize," he said. "And hey, the polar caps are melting fast. Take some swim lessons, dude!"

. . . . .

Jill and Maddie made it out safely, swimming back to shore and avoiding the cops by sneaking into the dunes. Though Amy had never taught Jill to swim, Clyde *had*—a secret kept from Amy, who would have freaked at the thought of her daughter practicing her strokes in the murderous Atlantic. Amy, too, escaped arrest, the charge of flipping off a cop apparently not worth the requisite paperwork, the troopers letting her go with that old standby, the stern warning. Maddie's mother had texted her that the girls were safe, so when the trooper told Amy to get lost, for once she didn't argue. The next morning the local paper reported twenty-seven arrests, including Father Toby, who, inexplicably, had stripped off his clothes and began singing The Sermon on the Mount to the tune of U2's "Sunday, Bloody Sunday," the placement of his guitar negating a public lewdness charge yet still earning a summons for a visible ass crack.

"Who even knew there *was* such a law?" Uncle Dan said the next day. "There's a two-inch exception but show more than that and you're hit with community service and fined five hundred bucks."

"Two inches? Did they measure?"

"They didn't have to," he said. "You could fit a truck through that crack."

"Good thing there's no parking on the beach."

. . . . .

As a precaution they brought me to the Emergency Room, where I spent six hours before a doctor told me I was lucky and sent me home. While I waited, Nancy sat in the hard-backed chair beside my hospital bed humming what sounded like a tango. It was a double room, and the patient on the other side moaned behind the paper curtain while a woman comforted him with a string of Hail Mary's in a dirty mix of English and Russian.

Nancy stared at the TV hanging over the bed, which was tuned to an infomercial for hair products, or maybe it was a George Foreman grill. There was nothing wrong with me, but my attention was scattered; I felt shot, beat, ready for ten hours of uninterrupted slumber, and I must have nodded in and out as I lay there on crisp white hospital sheets trying to remember what it had felt like to be dead.

I dreamt of Amy, one of those goofy erotic dreams in which no actual lovemaking occurs but everything is charged with sex. When I woke up the nurse told me that my wife had stopped by, seen me sleeping, and left. Amy, of course.

"Did the woman *say* she was my wife, or are you just assuming?" I asked.

"There are seventy-five patients on this wing," she said. "I really don't remember."

"We made love last night, for the first time," I said, because I had to tell *someone.*

The nurse smiled, then double-checked my chart for any notes on head injury.

I continued to drift in and out, the only constant being Nancy, parked beside the bed as if never planning to leave.

"This is a nice hospital," she said, to herself, I think. When an orderly brought me a cup of canned peaches and a pair of dinner rolls, Nancy stared at them longingly until I muttered, "Help yourself."

The peaches disappeared in two spoonfuls; she dunked the roll into the fruit syrup and bit off a chunk.

"That hospital in Kansas City, that was a bad place," she said. "I did not like it, but Carl said they would help me. They didn't help at all. Doctor Langhorne is a monster man. I sure hope he doesn't work here."

"Who's Carl?" I asked, not expecting an answer.

"My husband," she said. "Carl Adanaro, 14 Regency Court, Fairway, Missouri."

The next day Uncle Dan confirmed that in her early thirties she'd been married for four years to a certified public accountant. "I met him a few times. Carl Adanaro. Not a bad guy, just in over his head. Every year for her birthday he sends her a VISA gift card and a box of chocolates. He's remarried now. They met while she was working at Macy's."

"I didn't realize she ever worked."

"She's had a life, Donnie. Did you think she's been in a storage crate all these years?"

"No ..." But maybe I did. I needed to start paying attention.

Suddenly freezing, I pulled the sheets up to my shoulders. The admitting nurse had warned that I'd probably get the chills. "Press this button if you need soup or hot tea," she said. "And there's an extra blanket on that shelf over there."

Nancy grabbed the remote and aimed it at the television, surfing the channels until settling on the Food Network, a Chinese guy with a knife dissecting a stalk of bok choy. "When's Danny coming back?" she asked.

I didn't know. After they loaded me onto the ambulance and drove me from the beach, he'd gone home to pick up Nancy and then disappeared. I couldn't call him—my phone was somewhere in the Atlantic, shark food by now.

"He'll be back soon," I told her. "But for now it's just you and me."

She nodded, and surfed some more channels, leaving the Chinese guy and his knives for the local weather, sunny skies and mid-seventies for the remainder of the week.

As my strength returned, the thoughts of Amy grew stronger. We had finally made love, but what did it mean? Was it the long-delayed consummation of our forever back and forth, the official seal deeming us a normal couple, or something that we'd look back and consider a mistake? Or was the significance only in my head?

I'd make a great thirteen-year-old, I thought. I needed to find Amy and get answers.

As if sensing my agitation, Nancy patted my thigh.

"I'm warm, but I think you're cold," she said, and she walked from her chair to the shelf against the wall, pulling down the spare blanket with her one good hand, spreading it over my legs and smoothing out the wrinkles.

"Thank you."

"A mother's work is never done; they say that on TV."

She grabbed the second dinner roll and shoved it in her mouth. I needed to distract myself from Amy, so I started talking.

"Tell me about Carl," I asked.

"He was Donna's friend. He wore black sneakers, and sometimes a hat."

Next to us the Russian woman switched from Hail Mary to the Lord's Prayer as a second nurse arrived to check vitals. When it was my turn, Nancy didn't miss a beat, telling me about a picnic in 1986—potato salad, watermelon, Carl stung by a bee!—while the nurse strapped on the blood pressure cuff and started pumping.

"Everything looks normal," the nurse said. "The doctor should be here soon. In the meantime, we'll get the discharge papers ready."

Nancy belched twice, then patted my head.

"He didn't know I had a son, that's you. And then it rained and my umbrella was in the car, but that's life, Carl said."

She sipped my apple juice as the nurse left the room, then told me about her wisdom teeth and the chocolate cake on her thirtieth birthday.

It wasn't everything, but it was a start.

·　·　·　·　·

Oddly it was Clyde who drove me home.

Someone (Uncle Dan? Amy?) had dropped off dry clothes while I'd slept, and after I signed the discharge sheet and headed for the exit, I saw him waiting by the door in his policeman blues.

"Come on, I'll give you a lift," he said.

"You're working for Uber now?"

He ignored me as I followed him into the parking lot, his cop cruiser double-parked in a handicapped spot. I waited for his big hand to clamp on my head and shove me in back behind the safety glass, but he spared me the indignity and opened the passenger door.

"Wow, shotgun. Who's Starsky and who's Hutch?"

He flipped me the bird and sat behind the wheel.

"While you were lying in the ER thinking up stupid shit to say, I was doing police work. Real work that makes a difference." He started the engine but didn't pull away. Instead he reached across the console, grabbed a tablet, and started swiping. "I know who slit your tires."

In the fog of almost drowning, I'd forgotten about it, but it came back fast and hard, a nervous flutter circling my gut.

"So now we know who the stalker is," he said. "You thought those cameras were a dumb idea, and honestly, I thought it was all in Amy's head, but she was right. Take a look."

He showed me the screen, grainy night footage of Amy's house, a ground-level point of view of a dark figure moving up the driveway, the rental car's tires about to meet their fate. For a moment all I thought was, *Captain Sick! He's real!*

"Recognize her?"

"Her?"

He tapped the screen until a different angle appeared, the dark figure kneeling by the back fender, screwdriver in hand. The scraggly blonde hair seemed familiar, but the image was too blurred until Clyde zoomed in, and I spotted the tattoo on the back of her neck: a black crow with an arrow through its heart.

"Jesus."

"She's about as far from Jesus as you can get," Clyde said.

I stared at the screen, watching Laura Carpenter puncture the back tires, the screwdriver jabbing into the rubber like a prison-yard shank.

"I tracked her down, scared the living crap out of her," Clyde said. "She lives in Long Branch now, shares a house with three other women. She wasn't drunk, but I could see it in her eyes. Opioids. It's a lot worse down here than people think. Do you want to press charges?"

The idea seemed ludicrous, considering my narcolepsy had cost her daughter her life.

"Of course not."

"Good answer," Clyde said. "Here's what we'll do. You'll write her a check for a thousand bucks and give it to me. I'll dummy up a restraining order and drop it off along with the check. That'll keep her away. And this is something we never tell Amy."

I could have fought him on the thousand bucks but was grateful that he'd taken charge. She'd probably endorse it with her standard *fuck you*, but wasn't it deserved?

"Did she say anything about why? Or at least why *now?*"

"She said she was doing okay until she saw Amy at the mall, and everything came back, hit her hard. If she bought her goddamn panties at Wal-Mart instead of going to Victoria's Secret the whole damn thing could have been avoided. But she saw Amy behind the register and flipped; she said it felt like twenty years ago, like her baby had just drowned. She gave some jumbled explanation about the stalking, but it didn't make sense. And then she saw *you* show up. Too many ghosts, that's my guess. Sometimes people snap ...it happens more than you think. If *New Jersey Beach Patrol* ever gets on the air, we'll never run out of story ideas, that's for goddamn sure."

He shut down the tablet, Laura's image disappearing as the screen turned black. For a moment it felt like I was underwater again, the tide pulling me down.

"The sooner I get her that check, the faster this thing ends. Let's get you back to the hotel."

He put the car in drive and rolled toward the exit. "Remember, we never tell Amy about this. Right?"

I nodded. "Thanks for taking care of this, Clyde."

"Serve and protect," he said, and shook his head. "This whole thing ...what a goddamn shame."

Though I'd once written a play about it that had earned Frank Rich's raves in *The New York Times*, Clyde had captured it best in his four simple words: what a goddamn shame.

There was nothing else to say. We drove back to town in silence.

-22-

Two days later, I was alone at the Jaybird making a few pies before opening when I heard a knock on the front glass.

My instincts said ignore it, but after two more knocks I heard my name, a familiar voice calling from the sidewalk, and when I left the kitchen to check it out, I saw Kelly standing by the entrance, a small backpack slung over her shoulder as she peered through the glass.

I blinked, made sure I wasn't imagining it, then unlocked the door.

"Really, Donnie? You leave me a message that you lost your phone, but you don't mention that you almost *drowned?*"

Even under the stark lighting of the Jaybird she looked beautiful, her hair tied back, her skin glowing, her lips curled in that playful Kelly smile. She put down her bag and pecked my cheek.

"It was only twelve seconds," I said. "You need to hit thirty to earn your drowning badge." My fingers were sticky with mozzarella, and I grabbed a towel and rubbed them clean. "Who told you?"

"Your uncle called. He made it sound *really* bad."

"He'll do that when he wants you to visit." *Or when he's hoping to distract me from Amy,* I thought. "No worries, I'm still here," I added, sounding flip and nonchalant, although sometimes when I thought about it (*I almost freakin' died!*) my knees started shaking and I'd fight back vomit.

I asked about her flight, and she caught me up on her last few days back home. Her cats were fine; there were still no bites on the job front; she'd stopped by my place and picked up the mail, watered the three plants that I'd forgotten I even had.

She leaned back against the counter and folded her arms.

"I know this is awkward," she said, "and maybe a terrible idea, but I missed you, and when I found out that you were in the ER ..."

"Only for a few hours."

"...I felt so *bad* about the way I left. I'm not someone who just walks away, Donnie, but that's exactly what I did."

"I don't blame you," I said. "This whole trip...even before...you've put up with a lot."

"I was jealous and confused...it was immature. And so I went online, found a cheap flight, and here I am; I have no idea what's going to happen with us, but I'm not running away." She dropped her arms and offered a smile. "So until you say *fuhgeddaboudit* I'm still here."

She looked away, as if bracing for rejection, as if Amy might be lurking behind the counter in a wedding dress ready to squeeze off a few rounds from her .22.

"That's not the correct usage of fuhgeddaboudit," I said.

"Shut up and hug me."

So I did, and God it felt good to hold her again, to feel her body pressing against mine, to breathe the warm-honey scent of her skin, and I kissed her pink lips until I felt dizzy, her breath vanilla and peppermint, my hands sliding from her shoulders to the perfect slope of her waist.

"I know we have things to talk about," she said, her arms resting on my shoulders as we bumped noses. "But it can wait, right? I'm not here to get all heavy on you—or on me, either. Whatever might have happened while I was gone ..." In this case, w*hatever* had one definition: *did you sleep with her?* "...I don't need to know about it, meaning I don't *want* to know, okay? I've made questionable relationship choices, too."

"Understood," I said, thinking: *what questionable choices? Me?*

"I'm kind of exhausted," she said. "The flight landed at 8:00 AM, and then I rented a car and drove to the hotel, and then drove to your Uncle's house. Nancy, your mother—she said you might be here."

"I'm just making a few pies before we open."

"No need to stop." She brushed my cheek before pulling away. "You know, all this time we've been together you've never once showed me how to make the famous Marcino pizza. Can I help? Or is it some treasured family secret?"

"Well, I said, "we don't share it with just anyone...."

We headed for the kitchen, where three rolls of dough waited on the counter. Reaching back, I untied the strings and pulled off my apron, then slipped it over her neck.

"Wow—the official Donnie Pizza apron! I'm honored."

"I can't believe you're back," I said. "All the way from San Diego ..."

"It's not like I *walked.* I had an aisle seat and watched a movie. They gave us peanuts and cranberry juice—I even got points for the miles."

"Still ..."

She turned around so I could tie the back, then spun like a runway model, flipping her hair in mock-chic. It was all so wonderfully Kelly, the lightness of it, so *baggage*-free. I hated that word—*baggage*—and felt like a dick for even thinking it because Amy's baggage was *my* baggage, too—we'd acquired it together, we'd built it side by side. But it made me want Kelly to occupy my life.

I'd already chopped the onions and garlic and the kitchen was redolent with their sharp aromas. Kelly put on a hairnet and we washed our hands before stepping up to the counter. With pizza most of the work is done during prep, and all the ingredients were lined up and waiting. I sprinkled some semolina and rolled the dough, coating both sides, covering every crevice.

"Try it."

Kelly picked up the dough, her hands hesitant.

"You can't break pizza dough," I told her. "It's virtually indestructible. If it tears, we just roll it out again and start over. Like this."

I poked my thumb through the edge, creating a hole, then smooshed the dough back with my palm until the hole disappeared.

"See? It's back the way it was. Too bad that doesn't work for the rest of our lives."

Pizza philosophy—Jesus, I sounded like Uncle Dan!

I pressed the dough out flat and created the crust, Kelly watching from my left, adorable in her apron, studying me intently as if expecting a quiz.

"It's all in the thumb and forefinger," I said. "You pinch the edge so it rises, and then press it together, making your way around the circumference, like this."

I pinched out half the crust, then took her hand and guided her around the dough, her thumb sliding along the rim, her hand inside the circle as she pinched and pressed, pinched and pressed, my hand letting go as she picked up the rhythm, her hands switching to automatic pilot, which always makes the best pies.

"Am I doing it right?"

"Perfect. Are you sure you not an Italian from New Jersey?"

I checked the oven, adjusting the temperature to 500 degrees, then showed her how to pound out the dough. I leaned closer, our hips touching, beads of sweat forming on the back of Kelly's neck. She pressed out the dough as she leaned against me, her upper arm brushing my chest, and for the next hour I turned off my brain and made pizza with Kelly, doing everything I could not to think about the diamond ring wrapped in a tissue in my front left pocket.

. . . . .

I'd bought it with the cash from my first royalty check, and even though Amy had rejected me, I had kept it anyway. Over the years, whenever I proposed to her, I'd pull out that same ring and slide it down her finger before her hand could retract into a fist, few things saying *this is not a joke* better than a diamond, one full carat, marquise cut; I'd been broke a few times and tempted to sell it, but I sensed how much Amy admired that ring—even if she never accepted it—and I always suspected, even while married to Kristin, that life had curious ways of turning, and there might be a time and place for that ring to assume its long-delayed destiny on Amy's left hand. No way could I have ever sold it for *money*, and so for the past few years it had lived in the safe at the Jaybird, tucked behind Uncle Dan's first jar of homemade pizza sauce and five thousand bucks in cash.

. . . . .

Three pizzas later I walked Kelly back to the B&B, enjoying the sun and the warm almost-summer air, the familiar comfort of her hand wrapped with mine.

Ocean Avenue was still quiet, the calm before the Memorial Day storm. Live in a shore town long enough and you can feel the change in the air—not the temperature or the humidity but the charge of the soon-to-arrive crowds, almost as if Holman Beach were taking a deep breath, one last peaceful inhalation before three months of 24/7 wild.

It had been a long time since I'd experienced a Jersey summer. According to Uncle Dan, the last few years had been crazy. With the economy stagnant people stayed closer to home, and so instead of Disney or Hawaii it was load-up-the-car-and-head-to-the shore, which was good news, at least for the Jaybird and the other businesses in town. Half of them had "Help Wanted" signs hanging in their windows.

"Maybe I could get a waitress job," Kelly said as we passed the Oceanside Bistro, the nearest Holman Beach came to fine dining. "During college, I worked at Appleby's. I've told you that, right? It was hard work, but we had fun. Who knows? With tips, waitressing might beat my old salary at the school."

I smiled, not sure if she was serious or feeling me out about her staying. I told her about the email from George I'd received earlier that morning: *I read your script. Interesting. Let's talk...Friday lunch?*

"Donnie, that's huge!' Kelly said. "If he didn't like it, he wouldn't want to meet. Didn't I tell you it was great? I should be a producer ... specializing in scripts rescued from major appliances."

"We'll see what happens," I said, feigning nonchalance even as my adrenaline spiked just thinking about it. Even if George didn't like it, my back-up plan was ready—twenty pizza boxes with my next play written on them waiting in the trunk of the Honda. I needed to re-read them with a careful eye, but my gut told me they were *good,* maybe even special. I thought about calling George and telling him to scrap what he'd just read— there were twenty pizza boxes on the way, the best damn takeout order he'd ever get.

Back in our room, Kelly kicked off her sneakers and collapsed onto the bed, peeling off her socks as she stretched out across the comforter. "This feels *so* good," she said, hugging the pillow, and I wanted so much to join her, to crawl across the bed and land inside her arms. Everything I wanted seemed clear and right in front of me.

I could have remained with her forever, but there was someplace I needed to be.

"Um, I wish I could stay, but ..."

Kelly turned on her side, the pillow squeezed between her legs. "Is it her?"

I nodded, but it wasn't what she thought. Yes, I was due to meet Amy in fifteen minutes, but Amy wasn't the "her" I was thinking about.

"It was twenty years ago today ..." I said—twenty years since Sarah Carpenter was caught by the ocean and never came back.

.   .   .   .   .

Voices from the Town: Derek L., Holman Beach Maintenance Department, June 20XX:

I'm sure they didn't notice me—nobody pays attention to the guy who picks up the trash—but I recognized them immediately. Her I see all the time at the mall, but I hadn't seen him since high school. I went to see his play in New York once and tried to get backstage, but they told me he wasn't at the theater that night. I assumed the security guy was lying and I was kind of pissed. Just because you write a play that runs in New York, you're too important to say "Hi" to an old high school friend? Hey, it's not like I'm still mad about it. During high school, I always liked them. Senior year I was in the play that he wrote for Spring Drama. I played the Assistant, and I really nailed my three lines. Good times. After the show I thought maybe I'd go to New York and become an actor or something. That was a really bad summer around here. Well, I never became an actor, obviously, and here I am picking up the trash in the town where I grew up, but hey, I get benefits and four weeks of vacation, and my wife has a decent job at an insurance agency, so who's complaining? When I saw them walking down the beach, I wanted to say, "Hey guys, remember me? It's Derek!" but they looked like they weren't in the mood for talking, you know?

. . . . .

I had no idea what to expect when I met Amy at the beach.

Would she be calm, pissed at the world, pissed at *me*? I tried reading her mood, but her face was inscrutable as we approached the water in our bare feet, heading toward the spot where the three of us had spread our towels on that terrible morning. The late afternoon surf was choppy and strong, the waves cresting thirty yards from the shore, as if the water too remembered that day and felt ashamed to approach us. *A wave is a wave*, a Buddhist teacher once told me, trying to explain life and death. We don't consider the wave separate from the water; it need not die for it to be water again. *Each life is a wave*, the Buddhist said. When the wave ends, the water still *is*. We are never born. We never die. There is no difference between the water and the wave.

Comforting words, particularly when spoken in the high-pitched cadence of a shaven-headed monk, but hours later it had seemed like nonsense. Sarah wasn't a wave. The water had killed her.

We stood ten feet from the shoreline, Amy and I each holding a vanilla ice cream cone with rainbow sprinkles and a maraschino cherry. Sunlight skimmed the top of the water as the gulls flew low, squawking and trolling for fish. We had hoped to be alone, but it was close to eighty degrees and the bright almost-summer sun was like a sign on the dunes reading "Hey, we're open. Welcome back!" There were mothers with kids playing in the sand, seniors in baseball caps counting off their daily steps, a familiar-looking guy in a town uniform picking up beer cans, another guy scraping bird shit off the lifeguard chair. Just another day at the beach.

I wanted to say something touching or wise, but every thought that strived for the elegiac crash-landed in the boneyards of the trite and the tedious. Maybe, after all this time, there was nothing left to say.

"This might be the last time I do this," Amy said. "At the hospital Sheri keeps talking about closure. No matter what I say, the answer is closure. Closure *this*, closure *that* ...sometimes I want to scream, 'how about some closure on the goddamn *closure?*' But I think she's on to something. No more secrets, Donnie. No more being stuck. From now on, we move forward, right?"

"Right," I said, but did I mean it? Had anyone asked, I would have sworn on a Bible signed by God Himself that I wanted Amy to "let go" of the past, but now that the possibility seemed real, I felt apprehensive. I've been playing the role of Donatello-Who-Loves-Amy-Who-Fell-Asleep-And-Let-Sarah-Die for my entire adult life—I had all the lines memorized; I inhabited the character with such intensity even Stanislavsky might have raved. But who exactly was this Donatello character without that?

Time to find out, I thought. Suddenly the diamond ring in my pocket felt juvenile and stupid.

A trio of sandpipers popped in front of us, poking around chirping *poo-tee-weet*. I'm sure Amy thought it, too—Sarah had loved running after them, flapping her arms and making bird-sounds, running in crazy circles across the sand.

We finished our cones, and I took Amy's hand.

"I feel like I should say something."

"No, you don't," Amy said. "Let's just walk for a while, okay?"

The damp sand felt cool beneath our feet as we headed north, the sun behind us as we followed the shoreline. I thought about Sarah—what else *could* I think about? The first time I met her, she was only two. Amy was babysitting at Laura's house, and she told me to meet her there during my break. I was only fifteen but already working at the Jaybird; I told Uncle Dan I needed to do homework and ran the six blocks to meet up with Amy, thinking we'd make out on the couch while the kid—I didn't even know yet if "the kid" was a boy or a girl—slept upstairs, out of sight. Yet when I arrived I found a curly-haired blonde girl in red pajamas sitting wide awake on the sofa holding a teddy bear and snacking from a Dixie cup filled with Cap'n Crunch; it was *Amy* who was napping, her head propped against the cushions, her mouth half-open, snoring lightly.

"Hi," I said, bracing for the two-year-old to pitch a fit over some strange dude standing in her living room, but instead she waved and said, "Hi," right back, like she'd been waiting for me, as if I came through the front door to see her every night. She offered me some cereal and shook Amy awake, and for the next hour the three of us played teddy bears and stuffed kangaroos; we played Hide and Go Seek, and Tag, and Sarah climbed on my back for a Magic Unicorn Ride, Amy finding an empty toilet paper roll and taping it to my forehead for the full unicorn effect. When it was time for me to leave, Sarah looked up with those two-year-old eyes and called me Duck for the first time.

"Duck, don't go," she said, and suddenly I felt *wanted.* Had I been anyone but the boy who'd been left on the stoop in a pizza box, the moment might have carried little weight. But I *was* that boy. I don't remember when I realized that I loved her, but I knew it with more certainty than I knew almost anything. My family was Uncle Dan; that was it—until Amy, Sarah, and I formed a family of our own.

As we walked along the shoreline, the crowd began to thin until suddenly it was just the two of us. Beach towns are like that sometimes—everyone clusters within these invisible boundaries, as if worried they might turn a corner and find the Statue of Liberty sticking out of the ocean like at the end of *Planet of the Apes.* I was grateful for the solitude, not that I was thinking "great thoughts." I tried to focus on Sarah, but my mind was like a box of unedited film loops, all these jumbled brain waves about Amy and Kelly and Sarah, Uncle Dan and Nancy, even my meeting with George about *The Revolving Heart.* All I knew was that over the next few weeks I had some high stakes improv work waiting for me. I hoped I was ready.

We walked another quarter mile before Amy stopped and pointed toward a disruption in the otherwise smooth beach twenty feet ahead of us.

"Oh god, you didn't plan this, did you?"

I squinted for a better look—there were divots and piles of sand ten feet from the shore.

"You do see it, right? It's not a mirage?"

"Not a mirage," I said—it was just the beginning of a sandcastle someone had started and abandoned.

I checked our surroundings. We were still alone, as if we'd wandered into a ghost town. Exactly how long had we been walking?

"I've got goosebumps," Amy said. "There are probably a dozen unfinished sandcastles on this beach—it's not like we stumbled on a unicorn—but doesn't it feel like someone wanted us to find it? Like it's a sign?"

There were two plastic buckets between the mounds of sand, along with a pink plastic shovel mounted like a flag atop one of the sandpiles. A red Igloo cooler waited by the dunes. It was possible we'd strayed onto a patch of private beach, but I hadn't noticed any warnings.

"Tell me it's a sign, Donnie."

We stepped closer as the waves grew stronger, the high tide coming soon. I picked up the plastic shovel as Amy dropped to her knees, her fingers digging into the sand. Up close, the design was impressive. There were parapets connecting the towers, a carefully dug moat, another building taking shape within the courtyard. I'm sure Amy was thinking the same thing: on that terrible morning twenty years earlier, Sarah never got the chance to finish her sandcastle.

"Okay, it's a sign," I said, and Amy and I went to work.

Who knows how long we stayed there building that sandcastle? We passed the buckets back and forth, scooped sand, drew water from the ocean, shaped the mounds into two-foot-tall towers; I even made a steeple. We weren't very skilled, but that didn't matter—what mattered was that Amy and I were together, with Sarah in our hearts, moving all those grains of sand to create something beautiful. Even the sandpipers joined in, three of them poo-tee-weet-ing around the edges of a broken conch shell.

Our proximity to the shoreline meant that the tide would eventually wash it all away, but we still had time to finish it, to turn those abandoned piles of sand into something whole.

"One more bucket and I'll be done with the East Tower," Amy said. "How are you doing on your end, Donnie?"

I looked out at the ocean, unsure of almost everything, but for once, completely awake.

"Still needs work," I said, "but I'm getting closer."

Acknowledgements

The initial idea for *The Revolving Heart* came to me while walking in the dark through an old Quaker cemetery with my dog, Azul. The last sentence arrived during a different walk, with a different dog, Bella. Nearly every word in between was written, revised, and rewritten again with a dog or a cat either at my feet, or in the case of my departed cat Homer, draped over my shoulders or standing on the keyboard. Thank you, Homer, Chloe, Miles, Bella, and Azul. Readers are encouraged to visit their local shelter and provide a loving forever home to an animal in need.

The opening chapters were drafted during my time in the MFA Program at Queens University in Charlotte. Anne Cummins provided much-needed encouragement for a version of the early chapters. David Payne saved me from some wrong turns and pushed me toward a higher standard. Jonathan Dee and Fred Leebron offered valuable insights about the art of fiction that helped make *The Revolving Heart* a stronger work. My fellow students in the program gave their time and attention to my fledgling efforts and are among the best readers I'll ever have.

A special thanks to H.L. Nelson, whose comments were critical during the early revisions. Marcy Dermansky and Emily Bell both provided input integral to the finished novel.

Thanks to Reagan Rothe and the team at Black Rose Writing for taking a chance and bringing *The Revolving Heart* into the world. Your efforts are much appreciated.

Finally, thanks to my wife Sheri Burkat and her warm loving spirit. Her presence in my life is ongoing proof that love makes a difference. In my life, I love you more.

Note from the Author

Word-of-mouth is crucial for any author to succeed. If you enjoyed *The Revolving Heart*, please leave a review online—anywhere you are able. Even if it's just a sentence or two. It would make all the difference and would be very much appreciated.

Thanks!
Chuck

Thank you so much for reading one of our **Literary Fiction** novels.
If you enjoyed our book, please check out our recommendation
for your next great read!

The Five Wishes of Mr. Murray McBride by Joe Siple

2018 Maxy Award "Book of the Year"
"A sweet...tale of human connection...
will feel familiar to fans of Hallmark movies."
–KIRKUS REVIEWS

"An emotional story that will leave readers meditating on the
life-saving magic of kindness."
–Indie Reader

View other Black Rose Writing titles at
<u>www.blackrosewriting.com/books</u> and use promo code
PRINT to receive a **20% discount** when purchasing.